Eighteenth-Century British Erotica II

General Editors: Alexander Pettit and Patrick Spedding

Volume 5

Sodomites, Mollies, Sapphists and Tommies

EIGHTEENTH-CENTURY BRITISH EROTICA II

GENERAL EDITORS

Alexander Pettit
Patrick Spedding

VOLUME EDITORS

Deborah Needleman Armintor
Janine Barchas
Kevin L. Cope
Rictor Norton
Lena Olsson

EDITORIAL ASSISTANT

Laura Thomason Wood

Eighteenth-Century British Erotica II

Volume 5

Edited by
Rictor Norton

LONDON
PICKERING & CHATTO
2004

Published by Pickering & Chatto (Publishers) Limited
21 Bloomsbury Way, London, WC1A 2TH

2252 Ridge Road, Brookfield, Vermont 05036, USA

www.pickeringchatto.com

BRITISH LIBRARY CATALOGUING IN PUBLICATION DATA

Eighteenth-century British Erotica II
   1. Erotic literature, English   2. Erotica – Great Britain – History – 18th century
   I. Pettit, Alexander, 1958–   II. Spedding, Patrick
   828.5'080803538

ISBN 1851967702

LIBRARY OF CONGRESS CATALOGING-IN-PUBLICATION DATA

Eighteenth-century British Erotica II / general editors Alexander Pettit and Patrick
Spedding.
    p. cm.
  ISBN 1-85196-770-2 (alk. paper)
  1. Erotic literature, English.   2. English literature – 18th century.
  I. Title: Eighteenth-century British erotica 2.   II. Title: Eighteenth-century British
erotica two.
  PR1111.E74 E36 2003
  820.8'03538'09033--dc22

                                                              2003016763

New material typeset by
P&C

Printed and bound in Great Britain by
Cromwell Press Ltd., Trowbridge

Contents

Acknowledgements

I am grateful to members of C18-L, the Eighteenth-Century Interdisciplinary Discussion List on the Internet, who have helpfully responded to my queries during the past year: Theodore E. D. Braun, Jim Chevallier, Maurice Goldsmith, Robin Hamilton, Ruth A. Herman, Catherine Labio, Christopher Mayo, William McCarthy, Ellen Moody, John H. O'Neill, Tedra Osell, Irwin Primer, Betty Rizzo, Linda V. Troost and Gregory M. Weight.

Introduction

The eighteenth-century homosexual man is a cocktail containing greater or lesser proportions of four or five major ingredients. According to how these are mixed, the result may be called a 'sodomite', a 'fop', a 'molly', a 'woman-hater', a 'he-whore' or an 'unnaturalist'. And, like dry or sweet martinis, there are two kinds of sodomite, the one a sinner in the biblical tradition, the other a sexual predator or debauchee; and two kinds of fop, the one a sexless eunuch, the other a secret catamite. The one constant ingredient – the ever-present gin in most cocktails – is what we today call homosexual orientation. Nearly all pertinent satires and plays written during the eighteenth century portray the sodomite or molly as being exclusively attracted to men (or youths) and as having no sexual interest in women. The female homosexual, on the other hand, is usually constructed as a bisexual woman (I will discuss the lesbian material towards the end of this introduction).

Since all of the works in this volume were published in the 1700s, we cannot directly address one of the major issues in the historiography of homosexuality, the claim that there was a 'shift' around the year 1700, before which the model was that of the sodomitical bisexual libertine whose relationships were age-structured, and after which the model was the effeminate molly who was exclusively homosexual and whose relationships were mostly with adults. The mainstream historian who has most consistently developed this argument is Randolph Trumbach, in half a dozen articles published in the late 1970s through the early 1990s (and restated in more recent work).[1] Most historians of this subject have followed Alan Bray's elegant formulation of this 'revolution' in his influential book *Homosexuality in Renaissance England* (1982). A major criticism of the 'watershed' theory is that the data from the 1600s are insufficient to support claims about sexual experience in the 1600s. In addition to John Wilmot, Earl of Rochester, there are really only three or four exam-

---

1 See especially 'London's Sodomites: Homosexual Behavior and Western Culture in the 18th Century', *Journal of Social History* 11 (1977): 1–33; 'The Birth of the Queen: Sodomy and the Emergence of Gender Equality in Modern Culture, 1660–1750', reprinted in *Hidden from History*, ed. Martin Duberman, Martha Vicinus and George Chauncey (New York, 1989): 129–40; and 'London's Sapphists: From Three Sexes to Four Genders in the Making of Modern Culture', reprinted in *Third Sex, Third Gender*, ed. Gilbert Herdt (New York, 1994): 111–36.

ples of 'the bisexual libertine' in England – 'Anyone who reads widely in the history of homosexuality finds these few examples repeated incestuously from one work to another.'[1] A less theoretically committed survey of the historical evidence should show that no models 'superseded' other models, but that all models were available more or less concurrently. Unfortunately, as Michael B. Young points out, 'the hypotheses of a few early scholars have tended to become doctrinaire viewpoints'.[2] The dominant view uses the Foucaultian model of social construction, which sees various homosexual 'roles' as being constructed by society to support its ideologies, and as having no inherent link to the person performing these roles. The minority view, sometimes called 'essentialist',[3] sees a consistency in homosexual behaviour and perception across cultures and across periods, which suggests that something besides culture (e.g. biology) is the key determinant of sexual behaviour. The constructionist privileges change, the essentialist privileges continuity. Both camps, however, are looking at the same glass of water: the constructionist sees it to be half empty, the essentialist sees it to be half full.

The material in this volume undermines the more radical constructionist claim, that the homosexual was invented in 1869 when the term was coined, and brought into being by the medicalization of homosexuality in the late nineteenth century. In most eighteenth-century texts, the homosexual man is perceived as belonging to a distinct class of men, significantly different from other men, having a set of interrelated personality traits, rather than as a man whose only difference from other men is his favourite carnal sin. That is, the sodomite or homosexual or molly is conceived of as a whole person rather than simply as the performer of a sexual act. The men who frequented molly houses, where they socialized with other mollies, adopted female nicknames, exhibited camp mannerisms and deliberately mimicked women, formed a subcultural self-identity before the end of the first decade of the eighteenth century.[4]

Regardless of one's position in this debate, we can at least agree that literary products, most of which are satires, will reflect to a large degree the public perception – or 'construction' – of the homosexual. The major typologies are represented in this collection.

1 Michael B. Young, *King James and the History of Homosexuality* (New York, 2000), p. 146.

2 Young, *King James*, p. 141.

3 The 'essentialist' is usually a straw-man set up by constructionists; but see Rictor Norton, *The Myth of the Modern Homosexual* (London, 1997).

4 Rictor Norton, *Mother Clap's Molly House: The Gay Subculture in England, 1700–1830* (London, 1992).

The first selection, Thomas Baker's *Tunbridge-Walks: or, The Yeoman of Kent* (1703), illustrates the transition from the fop of seventeenth-century drama to what appears to be a full-fledged molly, or effeminate homosexual. A major point of the play is to set up the opposing categories of masculinity and effeminacy, of which the major exemplars are respectively the heterosexual man and the molly. Mr Maiden, whom the women call 'Miss Betty', was once apprenticed to a milliner, where 'a Gentleman took a fancy to me, and left me an Estate'. Maiden is not just a dandified fop, he is a transvestite: 'I love mightily to go abroad in Women's Clothes'. He has a circle of like-minded friends who meet in his chambers in the Temple and 'play with Fans, and mimick the Women, *Skream, hold up your Tails, make Cur[t]sies, and call one another, Madam*'. Though these men acknowledge 'We're Women, meer Women i' th' end', their mimicry has an object: 'Ye Nymphs, have a care, / Be more Nice, and more Fair, / Or your Lovers in time we may gain.' In sum, Maiden is neither fop nor eunuch: he is a molly.

The Women-Hater's Lamentation (1707) illustrates how the ideology of the 'natural' love of men for women is so strong that it is impossible to comprehend the unusual subject of the 'unnatural' love of men for men except as men's hatred of women. Hence the characteristic identification of the homosexual during the eighteenth century as a woman-hater rather than a man-lover. The woman-hater has the following characteristics: his lust (conceived as both behaviour and desire) is 'unnatural', more specifically, 'brutal', i.e. that of an animal rather than a human. It is also 'criminal' and sinful, specifically the sin of Sodom – i.e. outside the laws of both man and God. He hates or 'despises' women and is 'vow'd a Batchelor', and he associates with other men of his sort in a 'club'. Although the city of Sodom is mentioned, the woman-hater is not actually called a 'sodomite' – that is, the representation or construction derives not so much from Scripture as from apparent observation of actual men – in fact, men in contemporary dress, as shown in the illustration at the top of the broadside. At least twenty-eight sodomites entrapped by members of the Societies for the Reformation of Manners were tried in October 1707 (see headnote). This prompted the publication of many newspaper reports, several broadsheets summarizing the trial of seven of the men, and *The Women-Hater's Lamentation* – a 'pillory broadside' meant to be distributed while the sodomites stood in the pillory.

James Morphew, who published *The Tryal and Conviction of Several Reputed Sodomites…at Guild-Hall, the 20th Day of October, 1707*, in order to exploit public interest, also published *The Case of Sodomy: In the Trial [in*

1631] of Mervin Lord Audley, Earl of Castlehaven, for Committing a Rape, and Sodomy with Two of His Servants (1707) which was advertised in the *Daily Courant* beginning on 19 November 1707. On 27 November, in *A Review of the State of the British Nation*, Daniel Defoe was prompted to speak of 'the foul Cases that have lately sullied our News-Papers'. It was his opinion that the English should follow the Dutch practice of conducting trials of sodomites with all possible secrecy: 'smother the Crime and the Criminals too in the dark, and let the World hear no more of it'. Defoe argued that the virtuous were offended by the open discussion of such indecencies, and that foreigners would form the view that the English were more wicked than other nations in this matter. He complained that a consequence of public trials and punishments and satires prompted by trials was that 'the vicious, debauch'd Youth made Sport at it, and glutted their vile Inclinations with a double Pleasure; 1*st*. That of reading it, and 2*dly*. seeing it'.

John Dunton's *The He-Strumpets: A Satyr on the Sodomite-Club* (1707; 'fourth edition', 1710) was also prompted by the arrests of sodomites in 1707. The 'he-strumpet' type of homosexual has the following characteristics: his lust is 'unnatural' and 'unclean'; he is a 'Brute' or 'Beast' (despite a section showing that animals do not have homosexual relations); his lust is a 'vile Crime', specifically the sin of Sodom, and the biblical construction is more in evidence here. Further, 'Girls they hate', and they form a 'Club of Sodomites'. Dunton equates homosexual men with female prostitutes. Much of the satire develops the parallels between whoring and 'he-whoring', to the extent that the homosexual is identified as a 'tail' (i.e. the active man's 'pussy') in direct competition with women. Although Dunton recognizes that 'buggery' can include bestiality, i.e. sex between humans and animals, and that sodomy, i.e. anal intercourse, can also be performed between men and women, he nevertheless posits two types of opposing sexual orientations: normal lechery (i.e. heterosexuality) and 'he-lechery' (i.e. male homosexuality). His negative stereotyping does not differ substantially from the representation of the faggot in the late twentieth century. Dunton also introduces the subject of lesbianism, or 'unnat'ral Venery' between women, not involving penetration but nevertheless 'chang[ing] the nat'ral Use', i.e. having sex contrary to nature. Women are alleged to have taken up this fashion in imitation of sodomites.

The Play of Sodom, A Tragedy (1707) specifically enacts the biblical story of Sodom. The type of homosexual it portrays is the 'sodomite', a 'Base filthy Leacher' whose 'unnatural Lusts' are 'filthy Crimes' and 'sins', an 'abominable' 'Beastliness'. However, this sodomite is not literally a homosexual. For one thing, he is married, and for another, the specific act consists of the ambiguous biblical description, 'That in Conjunction they did strive to joyn / With Substances Ætherial and Divine' (which, insofar as this would 'get a Race', is heterosexual). In other words, the medieval 'discourse of sodomy' is still current, though it became increasingly marginal outside of sermons. Despite the biblical discourse, the play was prompted by the arrests and convictions of homosexual men in 1707, to which it refers in the Prologue. This topicality supports what would seem to be fairly obvious, that 'unnatural lusts' and 'filthy crimes' draw a good part of their force from the secular perception of sexual behaviour between men.

Edward (Ned) Ward's *The Second Part, Of the London Clubs* (1709), containing 'The Sodomites, or Mollies Club', represents the homosexual as the 'molly', whose characteristics are largely the same as in *Tunbridge-Walks*. The mollies are effeminate men who associate with others in a 'club' or 'gang', where they 'rather fancy themselves Women', calling one another 'sister' and mimicking women to the extent of engaging in highly developed mock-birth pantomimes. Ward concentrates on their social intercourse, while alluding darkly to their 'preternatural Polotions' and 'Beastly Obscenities'. Although they are called 'sodomites' and may be 'sunk into a State of Devilism', the biblical story is not mentioned, and their behaviour is perceived to be 'scandalous' rather than 'sinful'.

Ward's sketch of the Mollies Club is perhaps the main source for our modern understanding of eighteenth-century homosexuals. It was quoted in Ivan Bloch's *Sexual Life in England Past and Present* (1934)[1] and since the 1960s it has often been cited in popular histories of sexuality. It has not been noticed that Ward's description of the Sodomites or Mollies Club in *The Secret History of Clubs* (1709) is a very much enlarged and embellished version of the original sketch which had appeared earlier in the same year in *The Second Part, Of the London Clubs*. In the enlarged version, Ward inserted a brief reference to 'a Christian Abhorrence of all such Heathenish Brutalities' and expanded the section on the tattle from six gossips complaining about or praising their husbands and unprepossessing children. In addition to these obviously fictional details, Ward concluded with a long poem, thereby making his sketch much more obviously a literary product than the original version. Cameron McFarlane in *The Sodomite in Fiction and Satire* (1997) quotes from the verse

---

1 The book is a partial translation of Bloch's *Das Geschlechtsleben in England, mit besonderer Beziehung auf London*, 3 vols (Berlin, 1901–3), published under the pseudonym Eugen Duehren; it was often reprinted through 1996.

additions made to the second version to support his theory that the work is simply a literary construct. All students of the subject quote from the second version, as the first version has not been available. I think that a useful distinction can be made: I see Ward's 'first thoughts' (in *The Second Part, Of the London Clubs*) as the more realistic product of the news reporter's observation, and his 'second thoughts' (in *The Secret History of Clubs*) as the more fanciful product of the writer's imagination. Although some of the clubs described by Ward are obviously fictional, and although Ward sensationalized his stories as all journalists do, he was also a close observer, and his detailed attention to low-class life in London is much valued by historians for its accuracy as well as its 'local colour'.

That men engaged in camp, effeminate behaviour in the molly houses and used female nicknames is documented in trial records and newspaper reports, though these date mainly from the 1720s, and in pamphlets written by persons familiar with the underworld. In October 1728 Julius Cesar Taylor was convicted of keeping a disorderly house for the entertainment of sodomites, where 'When any Member enter'd into their Society, he was christned by a female Name, and had a Quartern of Geneva thrown in his Face; one was call'd Orange Deb, another Nel Guin, and a third Flying Horse Moll'. In other words, these 'maiden names' were assigned during initiation ceremonies in the molly subculture. Jonathan Wild, the famous 'thief-taker' and head of organized crime in London, exposed Charles Hitchen, London's Deputy City Marshall, as a sodomite, and claimed that Hitchen had once introduced Wild 'to a Company of *He-Whores*....they had no sooner enter'd, but the *Marshal* was complimented by the Company with the Titles of *Madam* and *Ladyship*....The men calling one another *my Dear*, and hugging, kissing, and tickling each other, as if they were a Mixture of wanton Males and Females, and assuming effeminate Voices and Airs.'[1] Wild also said that Hitchen had spitefully arrested a gang of mollies in the midst of their festivities: 'Next Morning they were carried before the Lord-Mayor in the same Dress they were taken in. Some were compleatly rigg'd in Gowns, Petticoats, Head-cloths, fine lac'd Shoes, furbelow'd Scarves and Marks;...and others had their Faces patch'd and painted, and wore very extensive Hoop-petticoats, which had been very lately introduced.' Arrests of mollies at their private masquerade parties are occasionally reported in the newspapers. For example on 28 December 1724 about twenty-five mollies were arrested at a house in Hart Street, Covent Gar-

1 *An Answer To A Late Insolent Libel…With a Diverting Scene of a Sodomitish Academy* (1718), quoted in *Select Trials at the Sessions-House in the Old-Bailey* (Dublin, 1742), vol. ii, pp. 223, 231–4, 247–9.

den: 'many of the Men were taken in Womens Cloaths, and generally go amongst themselves by Female Names or rather by the Names of the Racers at New-Market, such as *Cochineal Sue*; *Flying Horse Moll*, *Green-pea Moll*, *Plump Nelly*, *&c.* and that one of them was convicted last Sessions for an Attempt to commit Sodomy, which Crime the Assembly in general lies under the Imputation of.'[1]

A series of raids on molly houses in 1726 prompted newspaper reports describing molly behaviour, for example:

> how they assume the Air, and affect the Title of *Madam*, or *Miss Betty* or *Molly*, &c. with a Chuck under the Chin, and, *Oh you bold Pullet, I'll break all your Eggs*, and then frisk and walk away to make Room for another, who thus accosts the affected Lady, with, *Where have you been you saucy Quean? If I catch you strouling and caterwauling I'll beat the Milk out of your Breast, I will so*, with a great many other Expressions of Buffoonery and ridiculous Affectation.[2]

We are reminded of Maiden's camp distress in *Tunbridge-Walks*: 'O Lard I shall be Ravish'd; Captain you are the rudest Man, as I hope to be Sav'd I'le call out....Oh! She's a Bold Pullet.' Did the news reporter see one of the revivals of *Tunbridge-Walks* and use it to help him construct his vision of the mollies? However, Constable Samuel Stevens, a dour undercover agent for the Societies for the Reformation of Manners who probably was not a play-goer, witnessed a similar scene in Mother Clap's molly house which he described at her trial in July 1726:

> Sometimes they would sit in one anothers Laps, kissing in a leud Manner, and using their Hand[s] indecently. Then they would get up, Dance and make Curtsies, and mimick the Voices of Women. *O, Fie, Sir!* — *Pray Sir.* — *Dear Sir.* — *Lord, how can you serve me so?* — *I swear I'll cry out.* — *You're a wicked Devil,* — *and you're a bold Face.* — *Eh ye little dear Toad! Come, buss!* — Then they'd hug, and play, and toy, and go out by Couples into another Room on the same Floor, to be marry'd, as they call'd it.

Although the mock birth ceremony described in Ward's account is the earliest known reference to this behaviour – and might therefore be attributed to his fancy – such pantomimes are referred to sporadically throughout the century. James Dalton in *A Genuine Narrative* in 1728 said

> they sometimes have a Lying-inn, when one of them is plac'd in a Chair, and the others attending with Napkins, a Bason of Water, &c. *Susan Guzzle*, a Gentleman's Servant, is the Midwife, and with a great Deal of

---

1 *Weekly Journal; or, British Gazetteer* (2 Jan. 1725); the incident was widely reported in other newspapers. None seems to have been convicted on this occasion, though Plump Nelly, whose real name was Samuel Roper, kept a molly house himself and died in the Poultry Compter in December 1726 while awaiting trial as a sodomite.

2 *Weekly Journal: or, The British Gazetteer* (7 May 1726).

Ceremony, a jointed Baby is brought from under the Chair he sits on. Mrs. *May* was sometimes since brought to Bed of a Pair of Bellows, and *Aunt Grear* was brought to Bed of a *Cheshire* Cheese, *Madam Blackwell* and *Aunt England*, standing Gossips.[1]

The Ten Plagues of England (1757) describes this sort of '*Sham Lying-in*' as a feature of the 'plague of effeminacy' and a homosexual subcultural ritual (p. 12). Indeed other instances are recorded. In 1716 in a village in Gloucester, a tenant farmer named George Andrews seduced and sodomized his labourer Walter Lingsey, and was ridiculed by the village men in a mock groaning. Lingsey, as the lying-in woman dressed in a petticoat, was delivered of a wad of straw dressed in baby's clothes by another man dressed as a midwife, and a mock parson christened the 'baby' with the name of George, its 'father'. At a subsequent trial for sodomy, Andrews was acquitted.[2] Mock groaning survived into the early nineteenth century: according to the lawyer Robert Holloway, sometime between 1810 and 1813 several people in Clements Lane 'near the new Church in the Strand were seized in the very act of giving caudle to *their lying-in women*, and the new-born infants personated by large dolls!'[3]

Love-Letters between a Certain Late Nobleman and the Famous Beau Wilson (1723) is complicated by the possibility that the twenty-nine letters this work contains may be genuine homosexual love-letters dating from 1693–4. In the headnote I present the evidence that the correspondents are intended to be understood as Captain Edward Wilson (who was killed in 1694) and Charles Spencer, 3rd Earl of Sunderland. That *intended* identification, however, does not prove that the letters really were written by Wilson and Sunderland.

Most students of this work call it 'an epistolary novel'. Examples of this genre range from the *Lettres portugaises* (1669), a novella consisting of five letters, to *L'Espion turc* (1684–5), whose English translation contains hundreds of letters in eight volumes, to Samuel Richardson's novels *Pamela* (1740) and *Clarissa* (1747–8). The title probably tries to exploit the popularity of Aphra Behn's best-selling epistolary novel *Love-Letters between a Nobleman and His Sister* (1684). Behn's novel, however, consists of three volumes totalling more than 500 closely typed pages, consisting entirely of letters without any explanatory framework, which convey a continuous narrative story. In contrast, *Love-Letters between a Certain Late*

---

1 See set I of *Eighteenth-Century British Erotica* (London, 2002), vol. v, p. 334, and my accompanying notes about the real-life mollies mentioned by Dalton.

2 D. Rollison, 'Property, Ideology and Popular Culture in a Gloucestershire Village 1660–1740', *Past and Present* 93 (1981): 70–97.

3 *The Phoenix of Sodom, or The Vere Street Coterie* (1813), p. 28.

Nobleman consists of only fifty-three pages in large type, containing only twenty-nine short letters, framed by twenty-four pages of editorial comments or 'Observations' – without which the 'story' of the letters alone would be incomprehensible. *Love-Letters between a Certain Late Nobleman* lacks the narrative continuity which is the distinguishing feature of the epistolary novel, and it is better considered as an example of exactly what it claims to be, a 'Discovery', i.e. an exposé. The letters may well be false fabrications, but that is the most useful sense in which they can be classed as 'fiction'.

In terms of internal evidence, the letters do not seem to be written by the person who edited and commented upon them. The 'Observations' are moral and earnest, while the letters from the Nobleman are amoral and arrogant, which one might associate with an aristocratic libertine, and the letters from Wilson have an insinuating sycophancy one might associate with a commoner. If the author/editor had the skill necessary to create the realism of the letters, with their discontinuity and loose ends, then he has not demonstrated that skill in the bathetic moral fable of Cloris which closes the book.

No-one has demonstrated that the letters contain any anachronisms revealing that they were written in 1723 rather than 1693–4 (which also would require more historical expertise than most pamphleteers possess), though they contain one mistake: Wilson's first name was Edward and therefore he would never have signed himself 'W. Wilson'. However, we know that the editor interfered with the signatures – e.g. the noble Lord's signature is never given – so perhaps he supplied the signature, or perhaps he mistakenly expanded a signature of just 'W.' The Nobleman's use of 'my dear *Willy*', which occurs within the body of the letters, is arguably an abbreviation for 'Wilson' rather than 'William'.

There is also nothing in the letters that could not have been written in 1723 rather than in 1693–4. However, their depiction of the bisexual sodomite libertine uses a model which seems old-fashioned for the 1720s. The mollies of 'The Sodomites or Mollies Club' (1709) and *Plain Reasons for the Growth of Sodomy, in England* (1730?) occupy a different world from the figures in *Love-Letters between a Certain Late Nobleman*. George S. Rousseau's central argument, that the 'development of a sodomitical subculture…is crucial for understanding the genesis of the work',[1] fails to explain why the letters do not contain any references to such a subculture. If *Love-Letters between a Certain Late Nobleman* is 'a

1 George S. Rousseau, 'An Introduction to the *Love-Letters*: Circumstances of Publication, Context, and Cultural Commentary', in *Love Letters between a Certain Late Nobleman and the Famous Mr. Wilson*, ed. Michael S. Kimmel (New York, 1990), p. 55.

homosexual, or sodomitical, bourgeois fantasy primarily intended for the newly broadened heterosexual and homosexual reading public' in 1723,[1] then why didn't the author exploit the image of the molly that his reading public would expect in 1723? Wilson's cross-dressing is part of the old seventeenth-century model of disguise for the sake of intrigue, not an example of mollies mimicking women and calling one another 'bold pullets'.

Plain Reasons for the Growth of Sodomy could be characterized as expressing the doctrine that homosexuality is a social construct. That is, the sodomite is not born that way but is brought up as a spoilt sissy by his close-binding mother or, alternatively, he chooses to become a sodomite by aping the customs of foreign cultures, particularly those of Italy, and by reinforcing behaviour such as men kissing one another in public. It does, however, also offer the alternative, essentialist, view, *viz.* that Nature has not blessed such men with 'a Call equivalent to other *Men*' (i.e. the power and desire to please women), and therefore 'they take the *contrary Road*'. Homosexuality/sodomy is in effect nature nurtured. Effeminate milksops, 'unable to please the Women, chuse rather to run into unnatural Vices one with another, than to attempt what they are but too sensible they cannot perform'. *Plain Reasons for the Growth of Sodomy* also characterizes the sodomite as a predator in search of '*Proselytes*' who 'intice unwary Youth'.

The author insists that 'each Sex should maintain it's peculiar Character', and the key justification for sex is procreation. *Plain Reasons for the Growth of Sodomy* contrasts the hard manly man with the weak effeminate man, using images similar to those in *Tunbridge-Walks*: the boy who will become a proper man plays rough games with other boys and is athletic and 'a little Dirty [though] his Understanding was clean'. The modish young man, who will grow up a sodomite, plays with girls, takes dancing lessons, is spoilt by his mama. The manly boy sticks to his studies whereas the effeminate boy ignores them (which is the reverse of modern stereotypes). Italy is of course 'the *Mother* and *Nurse* of *Sodomy*; where the *Master* is oftner *Intriguing* with his *Page*, than a *fair Lady*'. He adds that France has expanded upon Italy: 'the *Contagion* is diversify'd, and the Ladies (in the *Nunneries*) are criminally *amorous* of each other, in a *Method* too gross for Expression' (presumably with a dildo).

Plain Reasons for the Growth of Sodomy has often been discussed by historians of homosexuality, not through the original published in 1730 or a year or two earlier, but through a plagiarized appendix to *Satan's Harvest*

---

1 Rousseau, 'An Introduction', pp. 57–8.

Home, published in 1749. One consequence of the failure to recognize
that the 1749 work plagiarized the 1730 work has been that periodiza-
tions about attitudes towards homosexuals have gone askew by nearly a
generation.[1] For example, Crompton wrongly concludes that
'homophobia reached its zenith...in 1749',[2] not realizing that his evidence comes from 1730, not 1749. Similarly, Senelick cites *Satan's
Harvest Home* to support his argument that 'by midcentury, moralists
were complaining that the Italian opera was a major contributing factor
in the breeding of sodomites'.[3] And Rousseau concludes that *Satan's Harvest Home* in 1749 'capped the decade' in which Smollett's *Roderick
Random* (1748) and Cleland's *Memoirs of a Woman of Pleasure* (1748–9)
appeared (both of which contain important homosexual passages), making the 1740s an 'all-important decade', 'a decade I suggest is crucial in
England for the perception that sodomy was spreading rapidly'.[4] But the
arguments which have employed *Satan's Harvest Home* to demonstrate
change by 1749, on the contrary demonstrate continuity since 1730.

College-Wit Sharpen'd; or, The Head of a House, with, A Sting in the Tail
(1739) specifically focuses on a 1739 incident involving the Warden of
Wadham College, Oxford. In terms of the typology of the homosexual,
it makes no use of the effeminate stereotype beyond reference to 'the
Epicene Gender' on the titlepage. The sodomite is said to be a practitioner of devilish arts, but references to the biblical sinners of Sodom
don't seem to be meant very seriously. The sodomite is, more seriously,
a deceiver and an underminer of truth and good order. He is also shown
as having an exclusive sexual orientation, as when the Warden laughs
when the two students he is trying to seduce offer him a whore in their
stead: 'Your Inference, can never follow; / My ART may seem most
strange to you, / Your Ign'rance, that's the Cause; 'tis true.'

Nathaniel Lancaster's *The Pretty Gentleman: or, Softness of Manners Vin-
dicated* (1747) is an ironic faux defence of effeminacy. The pamphlet was
written in response to Garrick's ridicule of 'mollifying Elegance' in his
two-act 'afterpiece' *Miss in Her Teens*, which was first performed at Covent Garden in January 1747, in which Garrick played the character of

---

1 Historians and critics drawing upon publications in the 1970s and 1980s by Vern L.
Bullough, David Greenberg, George Rousseau, Alan Bray, Randolph Trumbach and others have compounded this error in chronological perception, so that the year 1749 has
wrongly become a fixed watershed in rigid linear models.

2 Louis Crompton, *Byron and Greek Love* (Berkeley, 1985), p. 55.

3 Laurence Senelick, 'Mollies or Men of Mode? Sodomy and the Eighteenth-Century
London Stage', *Journal of the History of Sexuality* 1 (1990), p. 56; see also p. 54.

4 G. S. Rousseau, 'The Pursuit of Homosexuality in the Eighteenth Century: "Utterly
Confused Category" and/or Rich Repository', *Eighteenth-Century Life* 9.3 (1985): 132–68,
see esp. pp. 147–51; the quotation is from p. 151.

William Fribble, a mincing macaroni. Mrs Delaney in a letter to a friend observed 'It is said he mimicks *eleven* men of fashion.'[1] Arthur Murphy in *The Life of David Garrick* (1801) wrote that Captain Flash and Fribble in Garrick's play were 'copied from life': 'The coffee-houses were infested by a set of young officers, who entered with a martial air, fierce Kavenhuller hats, and long swords. They paraded the room with ferocity, ready to draw without provocation. In direct contrast to this race of braggarts, stood the pretty gentlemen, who chose to unsex themselves, and make a display of delicacy that exceeded female softness.'[2] The ethos illustrated in both *The Pretty Gentleman* and *Miss in Her Teens* is nearly the same as that portrayed in *Tunbridge-Walks* half a century earlier. The influence may have been direct, if Garrick had seen the 1738 revival of *Tunbridge-Walks*. And *Tunbridge-Walks* was revived again in 1748 as a direct consequence of the popularity of the effeminate character in *Miss in Her Teens*.

Lancaster's defence of the 'pretty gentleman' echoes Maiden's defence of the molly type of man versus the hearty manly man in *Tunbridge-Walks*. In terms of the nature–nurture debate – or to use eighteenth-century terms, 'nature' and 'affectation' – the pretty gentleman has an 'Infantine Constitution' which is inherently soft, but he cultivates refined manners – that is, many features of his inborn temperament are consolidated by conscious cultural choices. Overall, the pamphlet could be seen as emphasizing homosexuality as a social construct, though that interpretation would be anachronistic. Many satires do, indeed, portray foreigners, notably Frenchmen and Italians and Turks, as being more likely to be homosexual than the English, and do indeed suggest this is because of the cultural values of these foreign countries, but this is more a matter of xenophobia than sociological theory.

Here it is worth mentioning some works that we have not reproduced, as they are easily available. Garrick in *The Fribbleriad* (1761) attacked the Irishman Thaddeus Fitzpatrick as a member of the 'fribbling race': 'A *Man* it seems – 'tis hard to say – / A *Woman* then? – a moment pray – / … / Nor male? nor female? then on oath / We safely may pronounce it *Both*' (ll. 11–12, 75–6). This is the same trope Alexander Pope had used to attack John, Lord Hervey as Nero's catamite Sporus in *An Epistle from Mr Pope to Dr Arbuthnot* (1735): 'Amphibious Thing! that acting either Part, / … / Now trips a Lady, and now struts a Lord' (ll. 326–9). To this Garrick has added the tell-tale signs of 'stretch'd out fingers, and a thumb / Stuck to his hips, and jutting bum / … [and] mincing feet' (ll. 211–12, 216).

---

1 Quoted in Ian McIntyre, *Garrick* (London, 2000), p. 129.
2 Quoted in McIntyre, *Garrick*, p. 130.

Charles Churchill in the 1763 edition of *The Rosciad* (1761) added lines portraying Fitzpatrick as an hermaphroditic neuter, an 'it' (a usage that occurs in *Love-Letters between a Certain Late Nobleman*): 'A motley figure, of the Fribble tribe, / ... / Nor male, nor female; neither, and yet both; / Of Neuter gender, though of Irish growth; / A six-foot suckling, mincing in Its gait, / Affected, peevish, prim and delicate' (ll. 141–8). Although Churchill here portrays Fitzpatrick as what Garrick had called a 'lady fellow', we cannot conclude that by mid-century the model of the molly has superseded the model of the sodomite, because Churchill himself returns to the model of sodomite as he-whore for his very long diatribe against homosexuals in his long poem *The Times* (1764) : 'Go where We will, at ev'ry time and place, / SODOM confronts, and stares us in the face; / They ply in public at our very doors, / And take the bread from much more honest Whores' (ll. 293–6).

Garrick would eventually find himself placed among the fribblers/sodomites. William Kenrick in *A Letter to David Garrick, Esq.* and the appended *Love in the Suds; A Town Eclogue* (1772) accused Garrick of having a homosexual relationship with the dramatist Isaac Bickerstaffe (see headnote). Kenrick places this scandal within the classical traditions of male-male love, specifically the mythological tradition of paired lovers such as Hercules and Hylas, Nisus and Euryalus; the philosophical tradition of 'Platonic love…that burns with undistinguish'd rage, / And spares in fondness neither sex nor age'; and the homoerotic pastoral tradition of Virgil's *Eclogues*, especially the second eclogue describing the love of Corydon for the beautiful boy Alexis. Although the Corydon–Alexis relationship is the classic age-asymmetric love of a man for a boy, Kenrick actually applies it to the equal-age love of a man for a man: 'In common-council Corydon may burn, / And Corydons for Corydon in turn, / Till every alderman about the chair / Find his Alexis in a new lord-mayor.' Homophobia and xenophobia, as we have seen before, go together: Kenrick rejoices in being 'A Briton blunt, bred to plain mathematics, / Who hates French b[ou]gres, and Italian pathics.'

Sodom and Onan: A Satire (1776) is a scandalous attack on the dramatist Samuel Foote, portraying him as the archetypal sodomite, at the head of a crew of contemporary sodomites. Aside from the interest of its biographical details (see headnote and notes), it is probably the clearest construction in the eighteenth century of the homosexual as a sexual being rather than a sexless eunuch, and, for the most part, as a non-effeminate sexual agent rather than a 'molly' or pathic. The Preface is full of italicized *double entendres* suggesting the active role in anal intercourse: '*Man-œuvre*', '*enterd into*', '*prick'd* on to Action', '*extensive* Abilities…calculated for the *Deepest Penetration*', '*practical Essays on Man*' (i.e. sexual assaults), '*dark* and *difficult Recesses*', '*Fundamental* Knowledge'. Much of the poem is obscene. Its eighteenth-century discourse of homophobia differs little from the late twentieth-century discourse of homophobia. The author, William Jackson, was a minister, and fully familiar with the story of Sodom and Gomorrah (and the story of Onan), yet he constructs the homosexual not as a Christian sinner but as a practitioner of a filthy sexual vice, a degenerate. This is not so much the old discourse of sodomy, but the new discourse of perversion. Jackson even uses the term 'inverted' to characterize the sodomite ('his inverted Eye disdains / Objects of Female softness').

The construction of lesbians follows a somewhat different path from the construction of homosexual men. Lesbianism is only very briefly mentioned in the Bible,[1] and the Christian tradition developed no clearly focused image of the female homosexual. Western society has tended to treat lesbian relations as a secular vice rather than a religious sin, and no monstrous figure equivalent to 'the Sodomite' has arisen, except in some quasi-medical texts, which have constructed the 'tribade' as a hermaphrodite with an enlarged clitoris. Literary depictions of 'the lesbian' are more likely to draw upon the classical tradition of the excessively lascivious woman, and her lust is more likely to be part of a wide range of vices in which same-sex love plays only a part. The ancient poet Sappho, for example, was often viewed as a figure of lust in general rather than 'sapphism' in particular. But by the eighteenth century Sappho was represented as a modern sapphist, as in *The Sappho-An. An Heroic Poem, of Three Cantos, in the Ovidian Stile, Describing the Pleasures Which the Fair Sex Enjoy with Each Other, According to the Modern and Most Polite Taste* (1749).[2]

A Sapphick Epistle, from Jack Cavendish to the Honourable and Most Beautiful Mrs. D**** (1778?) draws on the story of Sappho of Lesbos, who is the origin of most constructions of the lesbian and whose birthplace became a byword for female homosexuality, in the same way that the destroyed city of Sodom is the origin of constructions of the 'sodomite'. (Gomorrah is sometimes treated as being inhabited by lesbians, but there is no biblical justification for this view.) Unlike the construction of 'the homosexual', which has varied between the sodomite, the molly, the homosexual, the faggot, the construction of 'the lesbian' has been fairly consistent and uni-

---

1 'Even their women did change the natural use into that which is against nature' (Romans 1: 26–7).

2 Reproduced in set I of *Eighteenth-Century British Erotica* (London, 2002), vol. ii, pp.403–46.

form since classical times, mainly because it is rooted in the story of one person who, as the author of *A Sapphick Epistle* says, 'was the first young classic maid that bestowed her affections on her own sex'.

Although the *Oxford English Dictionary* traces the first use of 'lesbian' (in a homosexual sense) and 'sapphism' only back to the late nineteenth century, Emma Donoghue has established that throughout the seventeenth and eighteenth centuries the word 'lesbian' was used in the same sense as it is today, and that lesbians were viewed as a distinct sexual and social group.[1] For example 'Lesbian Loves' and 'Tribades or Lesbians' are described by William King in *The Toast* (1732; rev. edn 1736): 'she loved Women in the same Manner as Men love them; she was a Tribad'. A 1762 translation of Plato's *Symposium* used the phrase 'Sapphic Lovers' to describe women-lovers. In 1773 a London magazine described sex between women as 'Sapphic passion'. From the late eighteenth century, lesbians were called 'Tommies' (as in *A Sapphic Epistle*). The first usage of this term may have been in *The Adulteress* (1773): 'Woman with Woman act the Manly Part, / And kiss and press each other to the heart. / Unnat'ral Crimes like these my Satire vex; / I know a thousand Tommies 'mongst the Sex: / And if they don't relinquish such a Crime, / I'll give their Names to be the scoff of Time.'[2] The other common slang term, 'the game of flats', is mentioned in *Pretty Doings in a Protestant Nation* (1734), reproduced in the first volume of this set (see volume i, pp. 349–410). Its meaning is illustrated in 'Venus's Answer' (1698–9): 'a New Game / Call'd Flats with a Swinging Clitoris'.[3]

Especially in French-influenced works, lesbians are called 'tribades' and 'fricatrices'. But in many English works, throughout the century, lesbian desires are regularly called 'predilections', 'propensities', 'unnatural appetites' and 'inclinations'. Sarah Churchill in 1708 said that Queen Anne had 'noe inclination for any but one's own sex', which is the background to the selection *A New Ballad. To the Tune of Fair Rosamond* (1708). A footnote in a 1798 English translation of the works of Sappho refers to the rumours of her 'unhappy deviation from the natural inclinations'.[4]

---

1 Emma Donoghue, *Passions between Women: British Lesbian Culture, 1668–1801* (London, 1993).

2 Cited in Donoghue, *Passions between Women*, p. 5.

3 'Venus's Answer', Bodleian MS. Rawl. poet. 159. The slang term can be traced back to 1663: 'Strangely pleasant were their chatts, / When Mayne, & Steward play'd at flatts: / Their marriage night so taught them, / Till Charles came there, / And with his ware / Taught how their father got them' (from an untitled libel published in John Harold Wilson, *Court Satires of the Restoration* (Columbus, Ohio, 1976), p. 3). I am grateful to John O'Neill for these references.

4 These and many others are documented in Donoghue, *Passions between Women*.

Similar to the many satires on homosexual men, *A Sapphic Epistle* draws upon real-life scandal and rumour, and is not simply a literary construct. It is a verse equivalent of a *roman à cléf*, containing references to actresses and courtesans, mainly those in the friendship network surrounding the lesbian sculptor Anne Damer (see headnote and notes). *An Epistle from Signora F—a to a Lady* (1727), on the other hand, though it is a product of the feud between the two opera divas Signora Cuzzoni and Signora Faustina, probably does not reflect Faustina's actual sex-life. The satiric mockery usually attendant on portrayals of lesbians is handled very lightly in this piece, which comes across as a positive celebration of lesbian love.

Grand theories about the construction of homosexuals tend to overlook the specific historical contexts behind these constructions. Of the texts reproduced in this volume, only *Plain Reasons for the Growth of Sodomy* is plainly ideological. Most of the other works arose from personal histories. The effeminate man in *Tunbridge-Walks* is a self-portrait of the effeminate author; *The Women-Hater's Lamentation*, *The He-Strumpets*, and *The Play of Sodom* resulted from the arrest of sodomites in 1707; *A New Ballad* is a direct result the Duchess of Marlborough's resentment at being rejected by Queen Anne in favour of her distant cousin Abigail Masham; Ned Ward's depiction of 'The Mollies Club' was prompted by the arrest of sodomites by agents for the Societies for the Reformation of Manners; the publication of *Love-Letters between a Certain Late Nobleman* was politically motivated, but the letters themselves may genuinely reflect the erotic experience of two men; *An Epistle from Signora F—a to a Lady* arose from a personal feud between two opera divas; *College-Wit Sharpen'd* arose from a homosexual scandal at Oxford University; *The Pretty Gentleman* is among a number of works arising from a personal feud between Garrick and Fitzpatrick; *A Sapphick Epistle* is a product of rumours about the personal life of Anne Damer; *A Letter to David Garrick* was due to William Kenrick's personal hatred of Garrick and Bickerstaffe and to Bickerstaffe's failed seduction of a guardsman; *Sodom and Onan* was a duchess's revenge upon a playwright who had insulted her. Theories which foreground 'the investment that satire as a genre has in social surveillance and regulation',[1] and which argue that anti-homosexual satires, like anti-Communist witch-hunts in the 1950s, construct a 'discursive presence' (rather than describe an actuality) whose function is to 'exert a social power and control through an incitement to vigilance', vigilance not just over deviants but over everyone,[2] need to be tempered

---

1 Cameron McFarlane, *The Sodomite in Fiction and Satire, 1660–1750* (New York, 1997), p. 61.

2 McFarlane, *The Sodomite in Fiction and Satire*, pp. 61–2.

by close attention to contingent circumstances. Reverend William Jackson was not operating on behalf of society in general when he attacked Samuel Foote; he was operating on behalf of the Duchess of Kingston, and she herself had little interest in supporting a hegemony of social control – quite the contrary, as she continued to wear see-through blouses even into her old age.

Tunbridge-Walks: or, The Yeoman of Kent (1703)

Thomas Baker matriculated at Brasenose College, Oxford, in 1697 and graduated with a BA from Christ Church in 1700. His first play, *The Humours of the Age*, performed at the Theatre Royal, Drury Lane in 1701, 'was written in two Months, and that when the Author was but barely of Age' (David Erskine Baker, *The Companion to the Play-House* (1764), vol. i, p. K1r). *Tunbridge-Walks*, his second play, was first performed on 27 January 1703 by Christopher Rich's United Company at Drury Lane. It was revived in 1738 and 1764 (Drury Lane), 1748 (Covent Garden) and 1782 (Haymarket). Published editions appeared in 1703, 1714, 1725, 1726, 1736, 1751, 1758 and 1764. His third play, *An Act at Oxford* (1704), was banned by the University authorities, prompting a satire of Baker as 'the Finnikin Yeoman of *Kent*...an Attorney turn'd Fool' in *The Tryal of Skill* (1704). Rewritten with a new setting as *Hampstead Heath*, it was performed at Drury Lane on 30 October 1705. His next and last play, *The Fine Ladies Airs; or, An Equipage of Lovers*, was performed at Drury Lane on 14–17 December 1708 – the shortest run of any play during the 1708–9 season. It was 'hiss'd off the Stage for its Scurrility' (*British Apollo*, 26 Oct. 1709), but revived in 1747. Several actors including William Bullock were tried (and acquitted) in June 1701 for producing an obscene play, *The Fox*, possibly by Baker. Thomas Durfey in *Modern Prophets, or New Wit for a Husband* (1709) criticized Baker's plays as plotless and said the audience had hissed them. Durfey accused Baker of 'barbarous assassination attempts' upon him.

Baker was 'the Son of an eminent Attorney in *King-street*, near *Guildhall*, in the City of *London*', but 'being under Disgrace with his Father, who allow'd him but a very scanty Income, [he] retired into *Worcestershire*, where it is said he died the Death of the great *Sylla*, the *Roman* Dictator, of that loathsome Distemper the *Morbus Pediculosus*' (Thomas Whincop, *Scanderbeg* (1747), pp. 166–7). (According to Plutarch, Sylla's bowels festered and his corrupt flesh swarmed with lice, which multiplied faster than they could be cleansed away.)

David Erskine Baker suggested that in *Tunbridge-Walks* 'the Character of *Maiden*, which is perhaps the Original of almost all the *Fribbles*, Beau *Mizens*, &c. that have been drawn since, and in which Effeminacy is carried to an Height, beyond what any one could conceive to exist in any

Man in real Life, was absolutely, and without Exaggeration, a Portrait of the Author's own former Character, whose Understanding having at length pointed out to him the Folly he had so long been guilty of, he reformed it altogether in his subsequent Behaviour, and wrote this Character, in order to set it forth in the most ridiculous Light, and warn others from that Rock of Contempt, which he had himself for some time been wrecked upon' (vol. i, p. Z1v). D. E. Baker hints that Thomas Baker's 'effeminate Turn of Disposition' may have caused the bad relations between him and his father (vol. i, p. A4v).

It is virtually certain that Baker, using the pseudonym Phoebe Crackenthorpe, was the author of the *Female Tatler* number 1 (8 July 1709) through number 51 (31 Oct.–2 Nov. 1709). Mrs Crackenthorpe's effeminate manservant 'Mr Francis' – 'if his mistress goes to Tunbridge without a maid-servant, Francis pins up a gown beyond e'er a mantua-woman in Christendom' (no. 4 (13–15 July 1709)) – is surely a continuation of the character of Francis Maiden from *Tunbridge-Walks*. Baker was beaten up by thugs after 'Mrs Crackenthorpe' satirized a police constable in October, and on 15 October the Middlesex Grand Jury declared the paper to be 'a great nuisance'. In number 51, 'Mrs Crackenthorpe', 'resenting the affront, offered to her by some rude citizens' gives notice that she has resigned the paper to 'a society of modest ladies'. These would include Bernard Mandeville and others never identified (M. M. Goldsmith, *By a Society of Ladies* (Bristol, 1999)). Baker is clearly revealed to be Mrs Crackenthorpe in a series of poems and letters that appeared in nearly every issue of the *British Apollo* from 31 August through 26 October 1709: 'this wise Undertaker / By Trade's an *At—ney*, by Name is a *B—r*, / Who rambles about with a Female Disguise on' (14 Sept.); 'the Title of *Monsieur Crackfart* had been better than *Mrs. Crackenthorpe*…when [readers] come to discover *It*, A Coarse *He Thing* in Petticoats' (5 Oct.). His cover blown and his reputation destroyed, Baker was not heard of after 1709.

The text is reproduced from the copy held by the Cambridge University Library (shelfmark Brett-Smith 20).

Tunbridge-Walks:

OR, THE

Yeoman of Kent.

Tunbridge-Walks:

OR, THE

Yeoman of Kent;

A

COMEDY.

As it is Acted at the

THEATRE ROYAL

By Her Majesty's Servants.

By the Authour of the *Humour o' the Age.*

————*Ridentem dicere verum*
Quid vetat? Horat.

LONDON:
Printed for **Bernard Lintott**, at the *Middle Temple-Gate,*
Fleetstreet. MDCCIII.

To the Right Honourable

John How, Efq; &c.

S I R,

I Muſt own, that 'tis more the Reſult of Affection than Opinion, makes me ſo Solicitous to continue the Reputation of this Comedy, by putting it under the Protection of a Patron, whoſe Character can alone be both it's Honour, and Defence.

I was ſoon determin'd there to Offer it, where I cou'd at once Satisfie my Ambition, Secure my Hopes, and Pay the Gratitude which I Owe as an *Engliſhman ;*

A 3

The Dedication.

lifhman; for 'tis from the happy Scene of our Affairs, that any can think, or be Diverted with that Eafe the Town was pleafed to fhew at the Reprefentation of this Play ; the Succefs of which I truly Afcribe more to the Juftnefs of the Action, and Favour of the Audience, than either Turn of Plot, or Correctnefs of Style. I am fenfible it may want Support, therefore I prefume to Infcribe your Great Name in the Front, which will not only Defend, but Perpetuate it; for no Age will ever forget, how Brave an Affertor of *England*'s Intereft and Liberty you have been ; Neglected your own Eafe by a conftant Attendance in Parliament, Oppos'd all the Grievances that often Incroach'd upon the People, and rather Chofe to be Diftinguifh'd than Dignify'd.

'Twas you, *S I R*, That kept alive the Warlike Genius of the Nation, and

was

The Dedication.

was the chiefest Advocate of her Bra-
vest Sons, against Starving and Oppref-
fion: 'Twas from your Care and Humanity in Procuring the Support of
Half-Pay, that those Gentlemen, who
are now not only Defending *England*,
but Saving *Europe*, Sunk not under the Mifery of Want, and the
Envy of those who hated such Inimi-
table Courage; but how agreeable a
Theme must it be to Contemplate the
Happy Change; Such a Soveraign, So
Glorious a Caufe, and our Rewards fo
Honourably and Juftly Secur'd, What
may we not Hope from *Englifh* Valour
fo Encourag'd, when we have feen fuch
Inftances of it's Force in fpight of all
Depreffions?

From the Succeffes of the laft Campaign may we not juftly Expect, That
in After-Times, the Annals of this Seventeenth Century will begin with the Fame
the

The Dedication.

the Fifteenth Concluded; and when Parallels shall be Drawn of the Two Glorious Female Reigns, tho' *Eliza* was Numerous in her Councils, *Anna* is Greater in her Few. That I Live under the Easie Happy Influences of this present Ministry, of which You are a Principal Part, is my Satisfaction; but that you will Accept this Proof of my Esteem, will be my Lasting Honour, in giving me Opportunity to tell Ages to come, that I am,

SIR,

Your most Humble,

most Devoted,

and most Obedient Servant.

TO THE

AUTHOR

OF

TUNBRIGDE-WALKS.

By C. W. Esq;

'TIS hard to pleafe, in fuch a Carping Age,
When Criticks with fuch Spleen, Inveft the Stage ;
But fuddain Death's the Fate of Modern Plays,
For few we fee, are Born to Length of Days ;
And yet the *Searchers* fay, 'Tis rarely feen
Amongft the Dead, that any fell by Spleen ;
Many they find, were by the Poets flain,
The dull Pretenders, in a Scribling Vein,
Set up for Comedy, with little Wit,
Borrow a Plot, and when the Play is Writ,
They leave it Starveing in an empty Pit.
Your better Care, has caus'd a better Fate,
Your *Teoman*'s Life, is of a longer Date.
It fhews us Humour, and an eafie Plot,
(Which in the Plays deceas'd, was oft forgot)
No Smutty Jefts, but Wit without Offence,
(For with Ill-Manners, Wit grows Impudence.)
You're not to Blame, if Envious Fools will find
Scandal, and Lewdnefs, which were n'er defign'd :
Your Play Inftructs us too ; That we beware,
That Riches are not made, our only Care,
Since Wit and Breeding, ferve to gain the Fair.

TO THE
AUTHOR
OF THE
Yeoman of *KENT*.

PErmit my Friendfhip, my Defects I know,
  Nor can my Senfe give your's the Praifes due ;
Yet when both Tongues and Pens advance your Name,
Can a Friend Offer nothing to your Fame?
The Stage her Skill and Gratitude has fhown ;
But from the Clofet Springs the True Renown.
Applaufe is Vain, which Action only gives,
'Tis by the Reading Part a good Play lives :
Grimace, or *Comick Tone*, may flafh the Ear,
Solid Wit only will Infpection bear————
The Prefs Eftablifhes the Poet's Character.
With how much Spirit, Strength and Skill you Write,
Such eafie Language, fuch Command of Wit ;
With fo much Sweetnefs every Speech abounds,
The Humour Heals, where e're the Satyr Wounds.
From whence can all this Wit and Fancy flow ?
From Nature—— What cou'd your green Studies know,
Some Toil whole Ages for what's Born with you.
No Time, Records, fince Poetry began,
So Ripe a *Genius* in fo Young a Man.
Apollo, both Surpriz'd and Pleafed, looks down ;
Go on, fays he, The Bays thy Temples Crown,
My Youngeft, my Renown'd, my Fav'rite Son.

CHARLES VAUGHAN.

TO THE
AUTHOR
OF THE
Humour of the A G E;
On his Play Call'd,
TUNBRIDGE-WALKS.

By an unknown Hand.

THen we may hope there will agen appear,
 Humour and Wit on th' *English* Theatre,
Unborrow'd from the *French:* For to our Shame,
Our Comedy of late from *Gallia* came :
Our Heroes learnt from theirs the Art of fighting,
Our Poets too have mimick'd theirs in writing ;
And by Tranflation ftrove to build their Fame,
Barren of Mother-Wit, and of Invention Lame.
But you, Aufpicious Youth, have now begun
To make old *English* Wit in *English* Channels run.
You think it needlefs over Sea to roam,
In fearch of Knaves and Fools, with whom we're
 ftock'd at home.
 Let fuch alone feel your Poetick-Rage,
And as you fcourge the Vices of the Age,
Retrieve the drooping Honour of the Stage.

PROLOGUE.

Spoken by Mr. *Pinkethman.*

YOU *dreadful Sons of War, who hither come,*
    To fright fair Maids in Masks, and Storm their Boom;
You foft Sirs, who at home Indulge your Eafe,
And hate French *Bullets worfe than* French *Difeafe*;
You Courtiers, who in Wit, and Judgment grow,
For where the Money Ebbs, the Wit fhou'd Flow ;
And you Citts, who fo brisk, and plump appear,
Fatn'd with good Queft-*Ale, and* Chriftmas *Cheer* ;
The Poet by me, Envoy, *here to Day,*
Welcomes you to a pleafant, airy Play :
The Comick Writer ftill Supports our Stage,
We live by the Good-Nature of the Age.
Let others be with Tragick Lawrel's Crown'd,
Where undifturb'd the Heroe ftruts around,
And Empty Boxes Eccho to the Sound.

Plays.

Plays are design'd for Mirth, to make us glad,

Damn'd Fortune's Plagues too often prove us sad ;

Debts, Judgments, and a Bayliff at the Door,

Or cruel Sempstresses, when Love boils o're :

But tho' to teaze us, more such Plagues combine,

All are dispers'd with Humour, Wit, and Wine.

This Night our Author to divert your Spleen,

'Mongst Crowds o' Fools at Tunbridge *lays his Scene ;*

Where Beaus, and City Wives in Medly come,

The Brisk Gallant supplies the Husband's room,

Whilst he, Dear, harmless Cuckold, packs up Goods at home.

Some Plot he has, some Conversation too,

Some Characters found out, he thinks are new,

But with what Skill they're Drawn, he leaves to you.

A Nice built Play, he begs you'l not expect,

Young Poets have the Fire, Old Authors are Correct.

To Humour chiefly, he'd his Genius bend,

On your Judicious Smiles his hopes depend,

And as he still Writes on, he'll strive to mend.

E P I-

EPILOGUE.

By a Friend.

Defign'd for the Captain.

AT Tunbridge *I have made my firſt Campaign,*
    Nor have I wore theſe borrow'd Plumes in vain,
Since my Red-Coat has helpt me to a Spouſe,
Who has, (I thank her) brought me, ---ne're a Souſe.
The World's a Cheat, moſt Men Diſguis'd appear,
And fain wou'd ſeem to be, what leaſt they are.
The Out-ſide's all, Virtue's an empty Name,
That Cloaks the ſubtle Knave, and willing Dame.
Each Proſtitute, worn out with frequent Sinning,
Wou'd ſtill perſuade you, 'tis her firſt Beginning.
Amongſt you well-dreſs'd powder'd Sparks that Sit,
The Awful Judges of the Poet's Wit,
Here's ſome perhaps my Character wou'd Hit;
Who think it Safer, here at home to fall
By Ladies Eyes, than by a Cannon Ball:
But as the Painter, ſo the Poet too,
What ſhou'd be hid, Screens from too Nice a view;
And when ſome Stroaks have the Deſign expreſt,
Chuſes to draw a Shadow o're the reſt.

Dramatis

Dramatis Perſonæ.

MEN.

Loveworth,	{ A Man of an Eſtate, in Love with *Hillaria*, }	Mr. *Mills*.
Reynard,	{ A Gentleman that lives by his Wits, }	Mr. *Wilks*.
Woodcock,	A Yeoman of *Kent*,	Mr. *Johnſon*.
Squib,	{ A Fluttering, Fop-Militia Captain, }	Mr. *Pinkethman*.
Maiden,	{ A Nice-Fellow, that values himſelf upon all Effeminacies, }	Mr. *Bullock*.

WOMEN.

Belinda,	Daughter to *Woodcock*,	Mrs. *Rogers*.
Hillaria,	{ Siſter to *Reynard*, a Railing, Mimicking Lady, }	Mrs. *Verbruggen*.
Mrs. Goodfellow,	{ A Lady that loves her Bottle, }	Mrs. *Powell*.
Penelope,	{ Her Neice, an Heroick Trapes, }	Mrs. *Moor*.
Lucy,	Maid to *Hillaria*.	Mrs. *Lucas*.

Singers, Dancers, and other Attendants.

The SCENE, *TUNBRIDGE*.

Time, Twelve Hours.

(I)

Tunbridge-Walks:

OR, THE

Yeoman of Kent.

ACT I. SCENE I.

A Common Room in a Lodging-Houſe.

Reynard *and* Loveworth *meeting.*

Lov. **F**Rank Reynard !·

Rey. Ned Loveworth ! Slave to *London,* and Darling of the fair Sex, left his Miſtreſs, his Bottle, and his Friend, to viſit the Country.

Lov. To the Pleaſures of the Town I own my ſelf devoted, but *London* now is a perfect Solitude, Buſineſs and Diverſion have diſpers'd every Body—— Lawyers are gone their Circuits to plague the poor Country People——— Tradeſmen to Cheat at Fairs---Courtiers to avoid their Creditors, and Younger Brothers to Spunge a Month with their Relations ; no Plays, no Park, no Intreagues, not a Cully left to keep Wenching in Countenance ; ſo that the poor Women o' the Town are forc'd to live virtuoufly. in fpight of Nature.; But *Tunbridge* I fuppofe is the Seat of Pleafure; Prithee, what Company does the Place afford?.

Rey. Like moft publick Affemblies, a Medly of all forts, Fops majeftick and diminutive, from the long flaxen Wig with a fplendid Equipage, to the Merchant's Spruce Prentice that's always mighty neat about the Legs; Squires come to Court fome fine Town-Lady, and Town-Sparks to pick up a Ruffet-Gown; for the Women here are wild Country-Ladies, with ruddy Cheeks like a *Sevil*-Orange, that gape, ftare, fcamper, and are brought hither to. be Difciplin'd; Fat City-Ladies. with tawdry Atlaffes, in Defiance of the Act of Parliament; and-flender Court-Ladies, with *French* Scarffs, *French* Aprons,, *French* Night-Cloaths, and *French* Complexions.

Lov. But what are the chief Diverfions here?

Rey. Each to his Inclination—— Beaus Raffle and Dance-—— Citts play at Nine-Pins, Bowls, and Backgammon—— Rakes. fcoure the Walks, Bully the Shop-keepers, and beat the Fidlers—Men of Wit rally over Claret, and Fools get to the *Royal-Oak* Lottery, where you may lofe Fifty Guinea's in a Moment, have a Crown return'd you for Coach-hire, a Glafs of Wine, and a hearty wellcome—— In fhort, 'tis a Place wholly dedicated to Freedom, no Diftinction, either of Quality or Eftate, but ev'ry Man that appears well Converfes with the beft.

Lov. But who is the top Beauty of the *Wells*, the grand Toft of the Men, and Envy of the Women?

Rey. Ev'ry one wou'd be fo: But your old Miftrefs *Hillaria* ftill bears the Crowd; her Wit and Beauty fupport each other,, and her Drefs and Converfation are ev'ry Day fo prettily vary'd, fhe always appears new: The Women love her Company, but hate her Pow'r, and the Beaus flutter about her in all the aiery Poftures of *French* Gallantry, whom fhe ftill keeps off with, her eafie Raillery, and not one dares engage her.

Lov. If fhe has fo many new Sparks, fhe'll look but coldly on an old Pretender; but if fhe's fo fevere upon the Beaus, I wonder they don't appear Dafh'd, and retire.

Rey. Not at all.; becaufe their Vanity conftrues every thing
to

The Yeoman of Kent. 3

to their own Advantage; and they take Raillery from a Lady to be as great a mark of Efteem, as they think a Lampoon is of being confiderable enough to be taken notice of——I always obferve, That Men of the greateft Senfe are moft doubtful of their own Merit; but a Fool, that has Affurance enough to fupport his Folly, thinks he has Wit enough to carry him thro' the World—But here comes old *Woodcock*, the Yeoman o'*Kent*, that's half Farmer, and half Gentleman; his Horfes go to Plow all the Week, and are put into the Coach o'*Sunday*; he has brought his Daughter hither, a Lady ev'ry way agreeable; but her Father is fo great a Humorift, that notwithftanding he allows her all the Gaiety of Body, he obliges her to the Ancient Cuftom of wearing a High-Crown-Hat; to her I intend my Addreffes, but would firft Sound his Inclinations; for when an old Fellow knows he has a handfome Daughter, and can give her a good Fortune, he is generally very capricious in the dif-pofing of her.

Enter Woodcock.

Good morrow, Mr. *Woodcock*; you are exercifing your felf after the Waters, I fee.

Woodc. You are miftaken Mr. *Reynard*; we Country Gentle-men live honeftly, and have no occafion to fcoure our Veffels.

Lov. But *Tunbridge*-Waters, Sir, have another Virtue; they help the Underftanding, and quicken the Wit, and that, you Country Gentlemen, may have occafion for.

Woodc. When I find, Sir, they have had a better effect upon you *Londiners*, perhaps I may try 'em——Look you, Gentle-men, we in the Country don't pretend to Raillery; If we have Wit enough to keep our Chickens from the Kites, and our Wives, and Daughters, from you ravenous Town-Sparks, we neither Envy your flafhy Air, nor defire to be thought Wea-thercocks.

Rey. But they fay, Sir, you are bleft in a Daughter, that's Beauteous to Admiration, your only Child, and Heirefs to

B 2 your

4   Tunbridge-Walks : *Or,*

your Eftate ; and notwithftanding your Averfion to the Town, I fuppofe you defign her for fome very fine Gentleman.

Woodc. No, no, Mr. *Reynard* ; Your Modern fine Gentleman is too much a *Narciffus*-to value a Wife; he Marries only to repair his Eftate, never appears abroad with her after the firft Month, nor Lies with her but in *Lent*, for Mortification— the Prodigal Citt too takes a Wife only for Conveniency to look after his Shop, while he goes a Stock Jobbing ; grows Jea- lous from his own Imperfections, Swears fhe keeps Company with my Lord fuch a one, Sues out a Divorce right or wrong, and turns her out of Doors; then Spends her Fortune upon fome *Covent-Garden* Mifs, and like the reft of your Whoring Citizens, pretends he's Ptyfichy, and is forc'd to lie out of Town ev'ry Night——No *Londiner* fhall either ruin my Daughter, or waft my Eftate——If he be a Gamefter 'tis rat- tl'd away in two Nights—If a lewd Fellow, 'tis divided into Settlements—If a Nice Fop, then my Cherry-Trees are cut down to make Terras-Walks, my Ancient Mannor-Houfe, that's noted for good Eating, demolifh'd to Build up a Modern Kickfhaw, like my Lord *Courtair's* Seat about a Mile off, with Safhes, Pictures, and *China*; but never any Victuals dreft in the Houfe, for fear the Smoak of the Chimny fhould Sully the Nice Furniture---Look ye, Mr. *Reynard*, The *Wood- cocks* of *Kent* are an Ancient Family, and were the firft that oppos'd *William* the Conquerour ; therefore I'le have my Name kept up ; and to Marry my Daughter to a Beau, with Spindle Shanks, a fmall Shape, and a long meagre Face, I'm fure is'nt the way to encreafe her Family.

Rey. So that inftead of providing her a Gentleman, you'd Sacrifice her to a Brute ; who has neither Manners enough to be thought Rational, Education enough for a Juftice of Peace, nor Wit enough to diftinguifh fine Converfation from the yelp- ing of Dogs ; Hunts all the Morning, Topes all the Afternoon, and then goes lovingly Drunk to Bed to this Wife.

Woodc. And pray, what are your Town Diverfions ?—— To hear a parcel of *Italian* Eunuchs, like fo many Cats, fquawlr

out

The Yeoman of Kent. 5

cut fomewhat you don't underftand——The Song of my Lady's
Birth-Day, by an honeft Farmer, and a merry Jig by a Coun-
try-Wench that has Humour in her Buttocks, is worth Forty
on't; Your Plays, your Park, and all your Town Diverfions
together, don't afford half fo fubftantial a Joy as going home
throughly wet and dirty after a fatiguing Fox Chace, and
Shifting one's felf by a good Fire—— Neither are we Coun-
try-Gentlemen fuch Ninnies as you make us; we have good E-
ftates, therefore want not the Knavery, and Cunning of the
Town; but we are Loyal Subjects, true Friends, and never fcru-
ple to take our Bottle, becaufe we are guilty of nothing which
we are afraid of difeovering in our Cups—— To fuch a Man
I'de marry my Daughter; One who has Humanity enough to
know how to ufe a Woman well, and loves the Country well
enough to live in't, and manage his Eftate himfelf, without
trufting it to a rafcally Steward, who will ruin my Family to
raife his own.

Lov. But, who have we here?

Enter Squib.

Rey. Captain *Squib?*

Squ. Gentlemen, I kifs your Footfteps.

Lov. But how now, *Squib?* How long haft thou been entitled to Scarlet? Prithee, what Regiment has the Honour of
thy Protection?

Squ. Why truly, Gentlemen, Finding how irrefiftable a Red
Coat is among the Ladies, I have lately made Intereft to be
an Officer in *the City Train-Bands*——When I march through
Cheapfide on a Training-Day, How the Citizens Wives ftare
after me—— There's an Air, fays one; There's a Face, fays
another; There are Legs, fays a Third; Sigh, then go to Bed,
and Cuckold their Husbands by the Force of Imagination.

Rey. But wou'dn't it gain you more Reputation, Captain,
to make a Campaigne? There you might ferve your Country,
and juftly merit the Title of an Officer.

Squ

6　　　Tunbridge-Walks : *Or,*

Squ. No, no, Mr. *Reynard,* 'tis only for your fwarthy ill look'd Rogues to go to the War ; we Spruce Officers ftay at home to guard the Ladies, Fight Mock-Sieges upon *Bunhill,* and Storm the Outworks of a Ven'fon Pafty : Befides, Sir, I have an Eftate, therefore need not put the fair Sex into Doubts, and Fears, by hazarding my Perfon.

Lov. But if you don't ferve one Compaign, How will it appear to the World you are a Man of Courage ?

Squ. That Mr. *Loveworth* is evident enough at home ; For there's feldom a day, but I have occafion to draw my Sword either in the Pit, the Side-box, or fome publick *Coffee*-Houfe.

Lov. If you are fo defperate, Captain, People will be afraid of keeping you Company.

Squ. You are miftaken, Sir ; I'me one of the well-bred Officers that Challenge no Man ; and if any Man challenges me, [*afide.*] I fend my Lieutenant to meet him——But to fhow you I have Generofity as well as Courage, I quarrell'd yefterday with a Gentleman for treading on my Toe, which you know is an unpardonable Affront in this honourable Age ; but at the Interceffion of fome particular Friends, Pardon begg'd, and a Supper given, I was prevail'd upon to put it up—— Ha ! My Yeoman o' *Kent,* Honeft Hop-Sack and Cherry-Tree, How does thy handfome Daughter, what think you of me for a Son-in-Law ?

Woodc. Thee— Doft think I'll marry her to a Pot-Gun, a Fop Militia Captain ; who, inftead of having Courage to ftand an Enemy, flies at a Show'r of Rain : She fhould fooner have a common Trooper, that's a Man of Mettle, and follow the Camp.

Squ. Very blunt, and ill-bred ; like a true Country Put, that was Conceiv'd under a Hedge, Litter'd in a Barn, and brought up in a Hog-Stye——Look you, old Gentleman, If your Daughter falls in Love with me, as 'tis ten to one but ev'ry Woman does , tell her, fhe may Sigh her felf into the Green-Sicknefs, Eat Oatmeal, Chalk, Coals, Candles, and die o' the Pip.

Enter

The Yeoman of Kent. 7

Enter Maiden.

Mai. Are you for the Walks, Gentlemen ?

Rey. Ay, But Mr. *Maiden,* You are very late to Day, the Ladies will be all there before you.

Mai. Why really, Sir, I us'd to be dress'd sooner ; but I have been mightily out of Order this Morning with the Vapours, and the Chollick, and was forc'd to stay to Eat a little Chicken Broth—Pray, Gentlemen, What new Company have we here ? They say, There's a world of Quality come down this Week.

Woodc. Quality !' What then ! They'll neither furnish the *Wells* with more Wit, nor more Money.

Mai. But the Ladies, Sir, always respect People of Rank— They say, Mr. *Woodcock,* You have a fine Daughter to dispose of here ; I design to make her some Overtures.

Woodc. You—Thou Effeminate Coxcomb, Dost think she'll like one of her own Sex—[*Aside.*] D'slife, all the Fops in this Place have got a Notion of my Daughter ; I shall have 'em Bait her, as a parcel of Hounds do a young Leveret. I'll go find her out, make her pack up her Auls, and we'll be gone to morrow Morning. [*Exit.*

Lov. Prithee, *Frank,* Let's to the *Coffee*-House, and leave these Fools together.

Rey. I'll step but to my Chamber, and follow you instantly. [Exeunt *differently*

Squ. Well, Friend, And what Accomplishments d'you pretend to, with the Ladies ?

Mai. Why, I can Sing, and Dance, and play upon the Guittar ; make Wax-work, and Fillagree, and Paint upon Glass. Besides, I can dress a Lady up a Head upon Occasion, for I was put Prentice to a Millener once, only a Gentleman took a fancy to me, and left me an Estate ; but that's no Novelty, for abundance of People now-a-days, take a fancy to a handsome young Fellow.

Squ. And

8   Tunbridge-Walks : *Or,*

Squ. And wou'd Sooth the Women with thefe Fooleries?
they hate a Nice Fop, that's fo much an Image of themfelves;
and love a robuft Mafculine Fellow, that will kifs 'em, tumble
'em, and towze 'em about.

Mai. [*Afide.*] Poor filly Creature; Lard; Does he think fine
Ladies will fuffer themfelves to be us'd like Oyfter Women——
Sir, I hope, I hav'n't ftudy'd the Ladies fo long, not to know
how to Addrefs 'em; neither have I taken fo much pains to
polifh my felf to be rejected for you: Therefore you may
give your felf what rough Airs you pleafe, and yet not fucceed
half fo well as thofe that have a little more Modefty.

Squ. Modefty——Here's a Fellow now——Prithee, What does
Modefty fignifie? Did it ever get a Lover a Maidenhead, a
Lawyer a Caufe, or a Courtier a Place——But to pretend to
Modefty in this Age; Why the Women have laid it afide now,
and are refolv'd, *A-la-mode en France,* to appear bare-neck'd,
gallop without Stays, drink their Bottle, keep Fellows, and
be out of Countenance at nothing;——Thank Heav'n, Modefty's an Infamy my Family can ne're be branded with; for
all my Relations from the beginning, have been either Pimps,
Poets, Attornies, Projectors, Stock-Jobbers, or Cuftom-Houfe
Officers——But you may e'en quit your Modefty, your Airs,
and your Graces; for I refolve to ingrofs all the Ladies to my
felf; and if you dare meddle with one——

Mai. D' you think I won't talk to 'em, and give 'em Sweet-
Meats?

Squ. That I grant you; But if you offer Love to any thing
that's under Fifty, above the degree of a Chamber-Maid, and
has a Nofe on her Face, I'le cut your Throat——[*Afide.*] I may
Hector this Fellow without danger.

Mat. As to that matter, Captain, we fhall never quarrel;
For if I can Raffle with the Ladies, Dance with them, and
Walk with 'em in publick, I never defire any private Love-
favours from 'em.

Squ. Nay, Then gi' me thy Hand, thus we agree the Point,
and will affift each other. I'll recommend you for a Partner

in

The Yeoman *of* Kent.   9

in Dancing; you fhall commend me for a Lover to wait on
'em home.

Mai. With all my Heart.

Squ. Come along, Frigid.   [*Exit.*

Mai. Lard, What rude Monfter is this? Sure fomething
that come out of the *Bear-Garden !* But I'me glad we are
Friends; for if he had drawn his Sword, I fhou'd ha' fwoun-
ded away.   [*Exit.*

Enter Hillaria, *and* Lucy.

Hill. Lucy, See if the Ladies are ready for the Walks, and
order a Coach to the Door——Well, This *Tunbridge* is the Joy
of my Life; fuch Treating, Dancing, Serenading, Raffling,
and Scandal, I cou'd die here——But let me fee, what new Acquaintance have I made here——There's Mrs. *Goodfellow* that
makes fo many great Suppers, I cou'd like her, but fhe Drinks
fo prodigioufly hard, I can never hold out with her—Lady
Bubble that's perpetually at Cards, and always Lofes, lends one
Money, and has never Affurance to ask for't again, I'll be intimate there——Mrs. *Smallware,* the Tradefman's Wife in the
City; there I can have things upon Credit; and then *Belinda,*
the Lady that lives in *Kent,* I'll be very great with her, fhe'll
Invite me down for a whole Summer——I find every now and
then I'me forc'd to pack together fome new Intimates; for by
that time I have liv'd a Year upon one Set, I run 'em out fo
much Money in treating my Vifiters, keep fuch late Hours,
and breed fo many Differences in their Families, they are
quite tir'd of me.

Enter Reynard.

Rey. So, Sifter; you are in your Airs, I fee, ready for the
Company, mighty gay and fplendid; Prithee, how doft maintain thy felf fo well without a Fortune?

C   *Hil,* Tho'

10　Tunbridge-Walks : *Or,*

Hill. Tho' I want a Fortune, Brother; Yet while there are Fools that have Money, and I have Wit and Affurance to manage 'em, I'll wear the beft Cloaths, Vifit the greateft Quality, enjoy every Diverfion, and Defpife all that pretend to be better than my felf.

Rey. But how d'you infinuate your felf to the World?

Hill. As moft Women that live by their Wits do; I praife ev'ry Body to their Face, and Mimick evry Body behind their Back; fo that all Court my Favour, becaufe they are afraid of being abus'd——By keeping a World of Company, appearing in all publick Places, and giving my felf a Liberty of Railing, I have acquir'd the Character of a Judge——No Body dares buy a Suit of Cloaths without my Advice, for whatever I condemn is thought ungenteel; and half the Tradefmen in Town make me Prefents to promote 'em Cuftomers—— I make Intereft for the Players o'Benefit Nights, fo have the Liberty of the Box——Now and then introduce a poor Poet with a Dedication, to go Snacks in the Reward——I live one Month with this Lady, a Month with that, Cheat at Cards for Pocket-Money; fo make fhift to rub through the World——But, how d'you manage your felf, Brother? 'Tis more difficult for a Man to Spunge a Maintenance than a Woman; to be treated, prefented, and addrefs'd, you know is the Prerogative of our Sex.

Rey. Like a true Town-Spark; One day at Court, and the next in Jayl: I have generally fome Money at command, but feldom any more at a time than what I have in my Pocket.

Hill. Why truly, Brother, I believe moft of you Wits do carry your whole Stock about you.

Rey. I always keep Company with thofe of the higheft Rank, whom I find moft eafie to be bubbl'd: Now and then perhaps I get to the Groom-Porters, and lend a Nobleman Twenty Guinea's upon a Pufh, to pay me Five advance the next Morning; and Courtiers punctually difcharge what they lofe at Gaming, tho' they run in ev'ry Body's Debt for Neceffaries—— But this Courfe of Life, Sifter, is but for a Spurt; we muft

now

The Yeoman of Kent. 11

now think of fettling our Condition; Our Family you know bears no common Fame, and our Education was the beſt; but our Parents, by ſupporting the Ancient *Engliſh* Hoſpitality, liv'd beyond their Eſtate, and left us to Traverſe the World, therefore, whatever Offers you have, accept nothing below your ſelf.

Hill. No, Brother, I have a Soul too great to harbour any thing that's mean; and if my Circumſtances wou'd not Countenance my Character, before I'de condeſcend, like a decay'd Gentlewoman, to dreſs Heads, make Mantoes, teaze People with my Birth and Education, and my willingneſs to get a Livelihood in an honeſt way, I'de ſcorn the World, and with an undaunted Spirit, repeating ſome Heroick Strain, plunge a Dagger, and fancy my ſelf an Actreſs in a Tragedy.

Rey. My own Siſter to a Hair——But let this Maxim joyn your noble Spirit——Still preſerve your Virtue; For if you part with that, you ſtain our Blood, and render your ſelf below every Circumſtance.

Hill. You know, Brother, we are all Frail, and ſometimes there's no reſiſting the Charms of a well-dreſs'd Side-Box Beau; But if I ſhou'd make a Slip, this I'll promiſe you, to keep a good Reputation, and that's the moſt faſhionable Virtue.

Rey. But of all your Lovers, whom are you moſt inclin'd to Marry?—— There's my Friend *Loveworth*, a Man of Senſe and a tolerable Eſtate.

Hill. Good.

Rey. Then, Captain *Squib*, with a larger Eſtate, but a Fool.

Hill. Better.

Rey. And then, the fine Mr. *Maiden*, who has a very great Eſtate, and is a prodigious Fool.

Hill. Beſt of all.

Rey. But cou'd you love a Fool, Siſter?

Hill. Love is a ſtupid Paſſion, that betrays the weakneſs of our Minds; who that has Reaſon wou'd ſacrifice the Pride of Life to a momentary Joy? which ev'n in the Name of Marriages extinguiſhes; but a Man that wou'd maintain me in all

C 2 the

12　Tunbridge-Walks: *Or,*

the Pomp of Quality, to out-fhine the Court, and be the Envy of the vying World, I fwear, were he Old, Difeas'd, Perverfe, were he any thing, I cou'd Love him, Carefs him, and dote on him to Death.

Rey. My own Sifter agen— For my part, I'me fix'd on *Belinda,* the Yeoman of *Kent's* Daughter, and have luckily found out what fort of Man he's refolv'd to Marry her to: I'll firft folicite the Lady; then, contrive how to win or deceive the Father: The Cuftom of this Place allows our Familiarity without being fufpected for Relations, fo that we may Subtily commend each other—— To day we ftrike our Fortunes, for in fo great a Crowd of Fools, 'tis hard, if we don't find fome Opportunity to Profit by our Wits.

　　Thus runs the World, one half the other Rules,
　　The Wife are Workmen, and the weak are Tools,
Hill. But yet the Greateft Wits are Women's Fools.

The End of the Firft Act.

ACT. II.

The Yeoman of Kent. 13

ACT II.

SCENE, *The Walks.*

Enter Hillaria *and* Belinda.

Hil. **I** Wonder, *Belinda*, How a reasonable Soul, and a Genius for the World like you, can brook a Country-Life ?

Bel. Custom, *Hillaria*, makes ev'ry thing familiar ; and tho' I hate the Country, I endeavour so much Philosophy to be easie in it : Indeed, my Father's Intentions of settling me there wou'd try the utmost of my Temper.

Hil. But I suppose you have too much of a modern Spirit to let his Will sway your Inclinations : Shou'd any old Father pretend to Associate me where I don't like, I shou'd plainly desire him to leave Doting, or march into the other World ; But sure my Parents were the civilest People ; for after they had liv'd sparingly to encrease my Fortune, found they grew Old, and I began to grumble, they made their Will, left all to me, except Fifty Gninea's to the Noncon-Preacher, and a few charitable Legacies I ne're paid, and went off so sweetly, without so much as a Fit of Sickness to put one to Charges, and keep one in Doubts and Fears.

Bel. But what wou'd you Advise me to do, *Hillaria* ? For my Father resolves to move home to morrow ; where I shall be Coup'd up like a Turtle-Dove, that's Melancholy without a Mate ; and have not the least Prospect of any other Match than what's first propos'd to him.

Hill. Why, faith, e'en take the Advantage of this publick Place ; Select one that looks most like a Man of Honour, strike

up

up the Bargain while you ftand ftill in a Country-Dance, and
be tackt to him out o' hand——— What think you of Mr.
Reynard? If I who have feen fo many Men, and obferv'd
fuch Variety of Shapes, from Beau *May-Pole* to Beau *Dapper,*
may judge of the Sex, I fay *Reynard's* a pretty Fellow.

Bell. Since you draw me into a Confeffion, *Hillaria,* I muft
own the fame Opinion; Mr. *Reynard* was my Partner at the
Bath laft Year, and mention'd a Love there, which he has not
fince had an Opportunity to renew——— But then, my Father;
to be hated, turn'd out of Doors, and Difinherited !

Hill. Never fear it——Indeed, when a Woman Difgraces
her Family by a mean Paffion, and runs away with a Fidler,
a Barber, or a Taylor, 'tis fit fhe fhou'd be Difcarded, and
joyn in her Husband's Drudgery all day for a little Love at
Night : But if you Marry a Gentleman, and can look the
World i' the Face; perhaps the old Man's tefty for a Month;
but then you put on a little Hypocritical Sorrow, down o'
your Knees, tell him you are forry you fhou'd Carnalize
without his Confent, but 'tis what can't be undone now——
Nature Pleads, the old Fool Bleffes you ; then come Treats,
Balls, fine Cloaths, all mighty well, and not a word o' the
Balcony.

Bell. Dear *Hillaria !* Let me intreat your Friendfhip ; but
you engage ev'ry Body, all Court you, and are uneafie without you ; Prithee, What is it fo bewitches 'em ?

Hill. Upon thefe Love-Occafions, I am mightily follow'd :
For after I have perfuaded a young Lady to run away with a
handfome Fellow, I interceed with the Old Folks, and reconcile 'em, fo that I oblige both fides ; *(Afide.)* And often get
a good Prefent by the Bargain——Then People are fond of a
pretty fleering Air I have got ; for you muft know, this Age
is mightily addicted to Self-Love; and the higher Efteem
People have of their own Perfections, the more they Defpife
others : Therefore I pleafe this Lady, by railing at that; and
my felf, by making a Jeft of the whole World alternately,——
When I'me at Court, I ridicule the City-Wives, thofe over-
                                                    dref's'd

The Yeoman *of* Kent. 15

dress'd Creatures, that stand gapeing six Hours at a Shop-Door, and the Aldermen's Ladies, who by their Bulk, and manly Voice are taken for Hermaphrodites —— When I'me in the City, I laugh at the Court-Ladies, their Gameing-Clubs, and Intreagues with Players, wearing *D'Oyley* Stuff-Suits for want of Money or Credit to buy better, and borrowing Jewels o' Birth-Nights; and when I'me among People of true Merit, I make a Jest of both—To particular Families, I recommend my self by being throughly good Humour'd, and always conforma- ble to what's propos'd——One Lady loves hot Tea, another cold Tea; I drink both——My Lady *Jiegu's* for a Fidddle, and a Country-Dance, so am I——Mrs. *Townly* loves a Hackney- Coach, sending for Fellows out o' *Chocolate*-Houses, Coquet- ting half an Hour in a Mask, and make the Fools treat us without so much as the Favour of seeing our Faces; Then from *India*-House to *India*-House leaving Letters, tumbling Goods, Buying one *China*-Cup, and Stealing half a Dozen; And at my Lady *Rampant's* in *Essex*, they are for clambering over Hedges, Riding in Hay-Carts, Hot-cockles, and Blind- Man's Buff——I can Romp as well as the best of them—— Then I am mighty happy in keeping a Secret; so that if a Merchant's Wife has a mind to make merry when her Hus- band's out of Town, to be sure I'me sent for—— But here comes the He-things.

Enter Reynard *and* Loveworth.

Rey. Your Servant, Ladies; how goes Scandal at the *Wells* to day? What fine Lady had an Intreague last Night, which the rest out of Envy have reported?

Hill. Rather, Sir; What Intreagues have your Vanities boasted of, which neither your Persons, nor Accomplishments, had force to gain you?

Lov. Real Intreagues, Madam, we never discover; and on- ly talk of Favours in opposition to those Ladies, who pretend to a Crowd of Lovers, and yet value themselves in having Pow'r to resist 'em all.

Bell

16   Tunbridge-Walks : *Or,*

Bel. A Woman, Sir, need not affume much Power to refift any thing fhe fees in your Sex ; but we can't blame the good Opinion you have of your felves, when we confider the weaknefs of your Judgments.

Rey. But if you Ladies did not defire a Conqueft, Why d' you take fuch Pains to adorn your felves ? What are your high full Rumps, but to make you follow'd ?——Your Fans in Winter, but to give Airs, and the various Difpofition of your Curls, but Baits for fo many Men ?——Then there's more Policy and Confultation us'd in placing your Patches to Advantage, than at a Council of War, in the difpofing a whole · Army·

Hill. Pray, Mr. *Reynard,* Let not your Sex pretend to Satyrize the Women, 'till you are lefs Foppifh, and affected your felves——What are your light Wigs, curl'd behind, but to hide your round-Shoulders, and fet off your Wallnut Complexions ; and your fine Sword-knots, but to tie the Hilt and the Scabbard together—— But the furprizing Joy when two Fops meet in the Side-Box, tho' they parted but two Minutes before, at a *Chocolate-Houfe* ; The Side-Bow, the Embrace ; and the fulfome Trick you Men have got of Kiffing one another. Then down you fit, and obferve the Women—— She's well enough—— fays one, but they fay fhe has been had—— Mind how fhe Ogles us, fays t'other, when they are a couple of wretched hatchet Fac'd things, that are Phyfical to look at 'em—— Then, the Tofs o' the Head, the Airs o' the Snuff-Box, and the Leer at an Actrefs on the Stage ; and all the ridiculous Actions of a Monkey, or a Madman ; but I think, they fay moft of you Beaus are craz'd ; for taking fuch a prodigious deal o' Snuff, it open'd your Heads fo much, the Wind got in, and quite turn'd your Brains—. And when any Expreffions on the Stage are fmart upon the Side-Boxes, how you force a Grin, and wou'd fain Laugh 'em off.

Rey. I find, Madam, we may Truce the Debate, and Unite our Forces ; for I fee Mr. *Woodcock* coming down the Hill, that's Satyrical upon both Sexes.

Bel. My

The Yeoman of Kent. 17

Bel. My Father, Dear *Hillaria*; Lets avoid him.

Rey. We'll ftep into a Raffling-fhop, Madam.

[Exeunt Rey. and Bell.

Lov. I fuppofe, Madam, by this time you are pretty well tir'd with Fops, and Fiddles; and like a Ship tofs'd by Winds and Waves, may be glad to fteer into the Harbour of Matrimony.

Hill. Good Mr. *Loveworth,* don't mention Marriage at *Tunbridge*; 'tis as much Laugh'd at as Honefty in the City: This is a Place of general Addrefs, all Pleafure, and Liberty; and when we happen to fee a Marry'd Couple dangle together like a Knife and a Fork, they are a Jeft to the whole Walks.

Lov. But *Tunbridge*, Madam, ought to diftinguifh Lovers, my Services bear a longer date, and therefore Merit more particular Notice.

Hill. For which reafon you might expect 'em flighted: Is there any thing more fcandalous than an old Lover to our Sex, who are fo fond of Novelties? But if after all your Solicitations, I were inclin'd to Article the Matter, you'd find me fomewhat odd in my Propofals. For in the firft place, When ever I Marry, I defign to have it a mighty Secret, People feldom care to let theWorld know they have play'd the Fool; neither wou'd my Vanity lofe the Serenades, the Treats, and Addreffes a fingle State affords me—— Then I'me for a Man in fome Bufinefs, that I may have his Company at night, and yet not be troubl'd with his Impertinence all day; for fure nothing is fo infipid as a Fop Husband, that ftays at home with his Wife, takes the Air with his Wife, and fhows his Fondnefs in ev'ry thing but what he fhou'd—— Then I refolve to have an abfolute Sway; for, I find by Experience, no State, either publick or private, profpers fo well as under the Government of a Woman; therefore I forbid all Toafting Clubs, where you drink Profperity to your Miftreffes, and Confufion to your Wives, quarrel about the Conftancy of fome common Trull, and break one anothers Heads to prove

D

the

₁8   Tunbridge-Walks: *Or*,

the Emptineſs of your Argument——— No Converſation with Wits, where you muſt treat half the Company ; nor Aſſociating with Men of Quality, where you are ſure neither to improve your Underſtanding nor gain a Friend——— Then I'le always be Conſulted in State-Affairs ; for 'tis a mighty Credit to our Sex to have an Aſcendant over them that Biaſs the whole Nation——— And cou'd you, Sir, perform all this for me ?

Lov. All, Ten times more ; You ſhall do what you pleaſe, govern how you pleaſe, be ſole Miſtreſs of me, your ſelf, and my Eſtate.

Hill. Then let me tell you, I diſſembl'd all this while only to try your Temper, and now find you a down-right Aſs— What ! Be ſubject to your Wife ; let a Woman rule you : Why, the meereſt Coward in Nature has Courage enough to Domineer over his Wife— I ſee, Sir, you are not for my purpoſe, yet I'le give you this Advice, The next Lady you Addreſs, neither Fawn, nor Flatter, but uſe a generous Courtſhip, and Aſſert the Prerogative of your Sex ; for 'tis the worſt Air you can have with us to be found any ways deficient in a true Man-like Character——— But here come the *Canterbury* Ladies, Mrs. *Goodfellow*, that's as big as the Cathedral, and enough to ſcorch a Body with her fiery Complexion ; and her lean, ſcragged Neice *Penelope*, that fancies her ſelf a mighty fine Creature, and has more Fantaſtick Airs than the Pewterer's Wife in *Bedlam*.

Enter Mrs. Goodfellow, *and* Penelope.

Goodf. Dear *Hillaria*, I am glad we ha' met you, theſe Men are ſo troubleſome and dull, we have wanted your Company mightily to divert us.

Pen. (*Aſide.*) Theſe old Women affect ſo much Wiſdom in deſpiſing Lovers, becauſe they are Conſcious what's ſaid to 'em can't be in earneſt——— Methinks, Madam, 'tis very pleaſant

The Yeoman of Kent: 19

fant to have the Beaus Buz about one, Talk to one, and give one Things; it fhows one's pretty.

Goodf. You are young, Neice, and love to be flatter'd; when you come to my years, and have a true Senfe of things, your Vanity will wear off, and you'll find more fubftantial Joys in a Bottle, and a She-Friend; For my part, I never mind the Men; I have Three hundred a Year, and am refolv'd to live fingle, and enjoy it : Therefore I wou'd 'nt have Lovers pretend to Conquer me, for I come out of *Kent*, and the *Kentifh* People were never Conquer'd.

Hill. Truly, Madam, I agree with you; I hate the Company of Fellows, where Cuftom forces on a Modefty Nature never meant us; There's nothing like a Club of our own Sex, where we can be Frank and Free, Play our own Pranks, and Talk our own Talk.

Pen. (Afide.) Wou'd the reft of our Sex were of their Opinion, that I might have all the Men to my felf.

Goodf. But pray tell us, *Hillaria*, Who have you feen this morning?

Hill. The ufual Crowd —— Sir *Tirefome Crumpling*, that old affected Fop, that has been the Jeft of the place thefe fifty years; and the reft o' the Fools that take pains to be Laugh'd at, cringing after a parcel of ftrange Trollops in Callicoe Gowns—— Well, Thefe late Mournings have been very happy for Women of no Fortunes, that have made a good figure in an old Sheet printed black and white—— Then comes a knot of *Jew* Ladies, that have lately Bubbl'd their Parents out of a Sum of Money by turning *Chriftians*, according to Act of Parliament; and have juft as much Religion as fome of our *Chriftian* Ladies, that fpend half their Church-time in quarreling for Haffocks, and the upper-end of a Pew—— But then to fee a fwarm of Mercers and Drapers Wives, move down the Walks, like a Sail of Ships, that are known to be the worft of the Company by being the fineft drefs'd, with Diamond Ear-Rings, Diamond Necklaces, and a great Gold Watch as big as a Warming-Pan; and yet thefe City

Things

20   # Tunbridge-Walks : *Or,*

Things are fo confounded proud, they never think themfelves
confiderable enough till they are Ladies too ; a mighty piece
of Honour indeed to have ones Husband a Knight, and no
Gentleman ; tho' really fome of our Modern Gentry are as
ridiculous on the other fide, by valuing themfelves upon
their Births, when they have no Eftates to fupport 'em ;
keep a Coach when they can't afford a Livery, and Starve
themfelves to Feed their Horfes——— What if we fit down
here——— Mr. *Loveworth*, give us fome Coffee.

Lov. With all my heart, Madam.

Hill. Oh ! Herc's Mr. *Maiden*, and the Mufick ; now we
fhall have a Performance.   [*They Sit,* Coffee *brought in.*

Enter Mr. Maiden *with Mufick.*

Maid. Ladies, I have brought a fine Singer, that came
down laft night to Entertain you with a new Compofure ;
one that's mightily admir'd *at the Small-Coal Mufick Meeting.*

S O N G.

[*While the Song's Performing,* Maiden *ufes a Fan, a Pocket Lookinglafs,* &c.]

IF moving foftnefs can fubdue,
    See, Nymphs, a Swain more foft than you :
        We Patch, and we Paint,
        We 're Sick, and we Faint,
    To the Vapours, and Spleen we pretend ;
        We play with a Fan,
        We Squeak, and we Skream,
    We 're Women, meer Women i' th' end.

        Your Airs we defie,
        Your Beauty deny,
    Be as Gay, and as Fine as you can ;
        Ye Nymphs, have a care,
        Be more Nice, and more Fair,
    Or your Lovers in time we may gain.

Goodf. Mr

The Yeoman of Kent. 21

Goodf. Mr. *Maiden* is the moſt uſeful Perſon in ſuch a pub-lick Place, and diſtinguiſhes himſelf ſo obligingly by pro-moting ev'ry Diverſion.

Mai. Oh, Madam, I am Maſter of the Ceremonies here; appoint all the Dancing, Summon the Ladies, and Manage the Muſick; tho' really, theſe Fidlers are ſuch a parcel of idle, ſcoundrel Fellows, one has more trouble in keeping 'em together, than Mr. *Rich* has in governing the *Drury-lane* Players.

Hill. But pray, Mr. *Maiden,* How d' you employ your ſelf for want of an Office in *London?*

Mai. Why, Madam, I never keep Company with lewd Rakes that go to the naſty Taverns, talk Smuttily, and get Fuddl'd, but Viſit the Ladies, and Drink Tea, and Choco-late; They think me the beſt Creature; for they Conſult me mightily about their Dreſs; I tell 'em when the Sleeve's rowl'd too high, and the Gown Pinn'd too flat; fancy their Knots, and help 'em make their Patchwork; and they call me Mrs. *Betty*—— Then, I have Chambers at the *Temple,* and keep a Levee, and a Viſiting-Day; for ſince the Lawyers are all turn'd Poets, and have taken the Garrets in *Drury-lane,* none but Beaus live at the *Temple* now, who have Sold all their Books, Burnt all their Writings, and furniſh'd the Rooms with Lookinglaſs and *China.*

Lov. But if you neither Read, Study, nor Converſe with Men, How d' you employ your ſuperfluous hours?

Mai. Why, Sir, I can Pickle and Preſerve, raiſe Paſte, and make all my own Linnen; Then I love mightily to go abroad in Women's Clothes: I was dreſs'd up laſt Winter in my Lady *Fuſſock*'s Cherry-colour Damaſk, ſat a whole Play in the Front-Seat of the Box, and was taken for a *Dutch* Woman of Quality.

Enter Woodcock.

Woodc. Sure my Country is the Seat of Plagues—— At *Canterbury* we are more peſter'd with *French* Folks, and *Pres-byterians*

22   Tunbridge-Walks : *Or*,

byterians, than the *Egyptians* were with the Frogs and Lice—
At *Maidstone*, twice a year, we have the Devourers o' the
Law, that breed a Famine where-ever they come; and if two
or three Dozen of my best Poultry are not presented to my
Lord Judge, I am put into Commission, and Plagu'd with
all the Scolding Controversies in the Parish; and *Tunbridge*
here is the Rendezvous of Coxcombs, I have walk'd this hour
and hav'nt met one sociable Creature— So, here's a blessed
Cabal; when the Fops, and the Women get together, there's
generally more Noise, Nonsence, and Impertinence, than a-
mongst a knot of Lawyers Clerks, and drunken Whores in
the Middle-Box of the Eighteen Peny Gallery.

Hill. But I wonder Mr. *Maiden*, How you Nice Beaus, that
frequent all Assemblies, avoid mixing with the ruder sort?

Mai. Oh, Madam; We that are acquainted with the Town,
distinguish People by their Airs; there's as much difference
between Men of Breeding, and Rakes, as between a Lady's
fine Shock, and an ugly Dutch Mastiff— One knows a Gentleman by a great deal of good Manners, and a chast, modest
look that may be trusted in a Lady's Bed-Chamber; and a
Rake by a dirty double Button-Coat, a cursed long Sword,
and a damn'd *Irish* Face, with more Impudence than the Box-
Keepers that are always teazing Quality for Money.

Wood. [*Approaching.*] And pray, Friend, By what token
d' you know a Fool, when you see him?

Lov. There Mr. *Maiden* can never be at a loss, who is so
well acquainted with a Lookingglass.

Woodc. But where have you dispos'd my Daughter, good
People.

Hill. To her own Satisfaction, I guess, amidst a Crowd of
Beaus, Raffling, Toying, and receiving Presents.

Woodc. Very good; And pray what Favours d' you Ladies
allow these Beaus in return of their fine Presents?

Hill. Why, The liberty of Talking, Dancing, or a Game
at Cards; and if we happen to meet Men of true Wit, perhaps
we may be Charm'd into Marriage.

Wood. But

The Yeoman of Kent. 23

Wood. But fhou'd my Daughter fuffer her felf to be Corrupted by any of your *London* Wits, fhe fhou'd e'en live by the Air of *Covent-Garden*, before I'de have a Wit inherit my Eftate, I'de Stockjobb it away at *Jonathans*, lay it out in Cloathing a Regiment where I fhou'd never fee a Groat on't' agen, or fell it for a Place at Court, to be turn'd out upon the next Revolution.

Hill. What, I warrant you'd match her to a Country Juftice, that like fome of our modern Commiffioners, has no more Senfe than to Commit old Women for Witchcraft, or fome blockheadly Mayor of a Corporation, with a Country Mace carry'd before him like a Chocolate Mill —— Well, You old Men, have the moft unaccountable reafons for difpofing your Daughters; One marries her to a Fool, becaufe he's a-Kin to Quality; Another to a Knave, becaufe he's a Man in Vogue, and expects Preferment; a third Superftitious Old Rogue gives her to a Sot, becaufe he's a Sober Perfon, takes Short-hand, and belongs to the fame Congregation. I wonder what Religion there is in Love; and your Worfhip for fear the Sow fhou'd baulk her litter, wou'd marry your Daughter to a Swine,—Oh the! joys of a Country life, to mind one's Poultry, and one's Dairy, and the pretty bufinefs of milking a Cow, then, the foft diverfions of riding on Horfeback, or going to a Bull-baiting, and the Charming Converfation of high-Crown Hats; who can talk of nothing but their Hogs, and their Husbands; for fhame Mr. *Woodcock*, fince you have an Eftate, you fhou'd have polifh'd your Family, and given your Daughter a Town Education.

Wood. And have you, Madam, no more reverence for the memory of your Anceftors than to prophane a high-Crown-Hat, that token of Modefty, and Humility, for fince your fantaftical Geers came in with Wires, Ribbons, and Laces, and your Furbulo's, with 300 Yards in a Gown and Petticoat, there has not been a good Houfwife in the Nation—Then you'd give my Daughter a Town Educa-

tion

24   Tunbridge-Walks : *Or,*

tion; I'le tell you what the Education of a Town Lady is—Firſt ſhe's ſent to a Dancing School, where ſhe's led about the Room by a Smooth-fac'd Fellow, Squeez'd by the Hand, and debauch'd before ſhe comes into her Teens : I'le be Sworn Dancing Maſters, Singing Maſters, and ſuch followers o' the Women, make greater Havock among Maidenheads in *London*, than the *Germans* did among the fine Fiddles at the Battle of *Cremona*—As you grow up you learn to be very Coquette, and are taught the Languages that you may Intreague with the whole World, and inſtead of riſing early to inſpeɕt your Families, you ſtew abed till Noon, dreſs all the Afternoon, go to Dinner at Night, and play at Cards till the next Morning : When you have gam'd away all your Mony, you take your Cloaths upon Tick, and when you have run up a hundred pounds in ſeveral Tradeſmen's books, you pretend you have Husbands at the *Eaſt-Indies*, and no body can Arreſt you.

Hill. Why, Mr. *Woodcock*, you are perfeɕt Scurrulous, I find, the Steely Soil of *Kent* has an Effeɕt upon your Natures, as well as the Waters ; but I don't wonder you ſhou'd abuſe the poor Women, when with that Petitioning Face you think you have Wit enough to correɕt Parliaments.

Mai. Indeed, Madam you ſay right, Spleen, and Ill-nature are as common in *Kent*, as Apple-dumplins; I wonder Sir, you Satyrs like the reſt of your Brother Monſters, hav'nt a pair of Horns.

Wood. And I wonder you Beaus, like the reſt of your Brother Aſſes hav'nt a Tail.

Enter Squib *and another fighting*, People interpoſing, *Maiden and the Women Shriek, and run to a corner of the Stage.*

All. Nay, Good Captain, you fright the Ladies.

Lov. What's the matter, Captain !

Squ. An Impudent Dog that belongs to the Laſt Will and Teſtament-Office, had the aſſurance to boaſt of favours from my Sempſtreſs.   *Woodc.* A

The Yeoman of Kent. 25

Wood. A mighty piece of Vanity truly.

Hill. But Mr. *Maiden,* What makes you fo terrified ?

Mai. Why really, Madam, I am naturally Apprehenfive of a naked Sword : They fay, my Mother was frighted at a Quarrel, when fhe was with Child o' me.

Woodc. (*Afide.*) So, now the Walks begin to Swarm—— What are thefe Fops good for? They are too Lazy to Work, and too Cowardly to Fight—— I'de fain have Beaus, Fidlers, Dancing-Mafters, Poets, and Players, knockt o' the Head as they do ufelefs Puppies, that they might 'nt over-run the Nation.   [*Exit.*

Hill. Come, Ladies, the Bell-Rings to Chapel, Mr. *Loveworth,* I muft not force you thither contrary to your Inclinations ; but Mr. *Maiden*'s always difpos'd for the Ladies.

Lov. You, Madam, May Command me any where.
                                        [*Pufhing* Maiden *afide.*

Maid. Breeding.   [*Leads Mrs.* Goodf.

Goodf. Sweet Mr. *Maiden.*   [Exeunt, *all but* Squib *and* Pen.
          Reynard *and* Belinda *appear at the upper-end of the Walks.*

Pen. I wonder, Captain, You'll expofe your valuable Life upon fuch frivolous Occafions : You great Commanders fhou'd be referv'd for more worthy Enterprizes.

Squ. Oh ! Madam, I am always a Champion for the Ladies ; yet I endeavour to fecure my own Safety : For tho' Valour be neceffary in a Soldier, moft of our modern Heroes prefer good Conduct, and feldom enter upon an Engagement that Surmifes Danger : And really, Madam, When I confider the prefent Scarcity of good Officers, I'me forc'd to curb the unrulinefs of my Paffion out of a National regard.

Pen. Sure nothing is fo Moving as an Heroick Spirit, nor any thing fo Becoming as Scarlet, it looks fo graceful, and darts fo noble a Luftre on the Face.

Squ. And yet ev'ry pert Prig with a Patch, and a Cropt-Head o' Hair, pretends to a Red-Coat forfooth ; Scarlet's grown fo common now-a-days, one hardly knows a Colonel from a *Coftermonger.*

                              B   *Pen.* Wel

26   Tunbridge-Walks : *Or,*

Pen. Well, When ever I Marry, I'me refolved to have an Officer ; for next to being a Woman of Quality, in my mind, nothing Sounds fo great as the Captain's Lady.

Squ. Divine Lady, your Hand.

Pen. Noble Sir, you have it.   [*Exeunt.*

Reynard *and* Belinda *come forward.*

Bel. I own your Merit, Sir, and wou'd not Slight your Love; but you know my Father's Temper, and I am fix'd, never to Marry without his Confent : When you have found a means to Court his Favour, you may then hope for mine.

Rey. Conduct, and Courage, ev'ry way. I'le prove,
     First try by Pray'rs, and Arguments to move,
     Then Summon ev'ry Art, and Shape of *Jove* ;
     Tho' oft repuls'd, Love still the Fight maintains,
     And for each Thought we gladly beat our Brains,
     When the Reward fo nobly pays the Pains.

The End of the Second Act.

ACT III.

The Yeomen of Kent. 27

ACT III. SCENE I.

Woodcock *and* Reynard.

Woodc. IN love with my Daughter, Ha, ha, ha, Av ery good Jeſt indeed.

Rey. Why ſhou'd you doubt my Paſſion, Mr. *Woodcock*, have I not ſhown my ſelf a zealous Lover; follow'd her to the *Bath*, thence to *Tunbridge*, watch'd for her, Courted her, and Reſpeĉted you.

Wood. 'Tis true, Mr. *Reynard*, I believe you have a very great Affeĉtiou for my Daughter, I muſt applaud your Judgment, and tell you, ſhe deſerves your Love. As to her Perſon, I can't ſay much; but ſhe's Heireſs to near Six thouſand Acres of Arrable and Paſture; beſides, a good Manſion-Houſe, with Hop-Grounds, Cherry-Gardens, and other Appurtenances, ſituate, lying, and being in the Pariſh of *Maidſtone* in the County of *Kent*; and if a Woman with ſuch Charms can want Followers in this Fortune-Hunting Age, I am deceiv'd.

Rey. I grant you, Sir, an Eſtate is a comfortable Convenience; but you ought not to prefer a few dirty Acres to a Woman of Beauty.

Wood. What ſignifies Beauty without Money? 'Tis Money makes the Beauty— Tho' a Woman be ſurpriſingly Witty, fair to a Miracle, eaſie, and unaffeĉted; She's thought Diſagreeable without Money; but tho' ſhe's Crooked, Squints, Ill-Natur'd, and a meer Changling, ſhe muſt be an Angel, when ſhe's an Alderman's Daughter, and has Ten thouſand Pounds—We plainly ſee how Beauty's valu'd at *London* by the Women o' the Town, who are forc'd to live by their Faces. In Term-time, indeed, they'll ſqueeze Half-a-Crown; after *Term* they are glad of Seven-Groats; in the long Vacation,

E 2 you

28   Tunbridge-Walks: *Or,*

you may have a Furbulo for a Tefter ; and your poor Whores
that ply the *Rofe*-Paffage, have fo bad a Trade, they can fcarce
afford you an Anniverfary clean Smock— Beauty, Mr. *Rey-
rnad's* a Jeft, I never Marry'd for't my felf—— Indeed, I
thought the Woman well enough, but if her Fortune had'nt
equall'd my Eftate, we had ne're Pig'd together—— [*Afide.*]
Tho' cou'd I have lik'd her better, a Son might have Inherited my Eftate; for I think they fay, Girls are but the Product of half Inclination.

Rey. Come, come, Mr. *Woodcock*, ne're Difpute the matter, I like your Daughter, and your Daughter likes me ; 'tis
true, Fortune allotted her the largeft Share, but had it been
my Chance; we generous Hearts Marry for Love, and ne're
value Money.

Woodc. Not value Money—— Very like, If it were not for
fuch extravagant Sparks as you, that want a true Senfe of
Money, we fhou'd'nt have fo much Subfcription-Mufick, nor
fo many *French* Buffoons skipping over to run away with it——
Mr. *Reynard*, You have unluckily difcover'd your felf, and I
hope now you'll not pretend to my Daughter, I fhall hardly
give my Eftate to one that don't know the worth of it——
But I miftake, noble, Sir, I fhou'd Admire your Philofophy,
the Contempt of Money fhows fo great a Soul—— 'Twou'd
be happy for the Nation, if every Country cou'd furnifh fuch
worthy Perfons for Affeffors, Collectors, and Receiver's General.   [*Exit.*

Rey. That a plain, rough-hewn Fellow fhou'd have fuch
profound Knowledge— I own her Fortune is the chiefeft Bait—
Yet I Love her too, but how fhall I convince him that I Love
her— What if I feign my felf Diftracted—— It fhall be fo—
That may not only move Belief, but Pity—It muft be Love,
when the Mind feems Difeas'd.

Enter Loveworth.

Lov. Frank Reynard Contemplative ! What mighty Bufinefs
can there be depending that fhou'd make thee thoughtful——

Yonder

The Yeoman of Kent. 29

Yonder come the two Fools, *Squib* and *Maiden*, you know the Oppofition of their Tempers— Lets fet 'em together by the Ears, 'twill make Sport.

Rey. Prithee, *Ned*, Enjoy the whole Diverfion thy felf, I have greater Matters to mind. [*Exit.*

Lov. Go thy ways for a Brainfick Fellow, Pox o' the Women, I fay, this damn'd Love fpoils all manner of Society.

Enter Squib.

Squ. Mr. *Loveworth*, I beg a multitude of Pardons, I fhou'd Rob you of my felf fo long; but I have been earneftly engag'd in Mediating a prodigious Quarrel between two Members of the Kit-Cat Club that challeng'd about a Pun.

Lov. I find, Captain, You are the Grand Umpire o'the Nation—— But, I wonder, how you Ambitious Officers can reft fatisfy'd with Trifling away your time at *Tunbridge*, when your Affiftance is fo much wanted in *Italy*.

Squ. Indeed, Mr. *Loveworth*, when I reflect how much my Prefence wou'd Encourage the whole Army, on the Confideration of a good Preferment, next Campaigne I may oblige the Allies; but you muft know, Sir, we Military Gentlemen have a mighty tendernefs for one another's Fame, and I fhou'd be very cautious of performing any thing to Eclipfe my very good Friend Prince *Eugene*——But Mr. *Loveworth*, here comes *Maiden*, prithee lets teaze him a little——What if we get him to the Tavern, and make him Drunk?

Lov. With all my heart.

Enter Maiden.

They fay, Mr. *Maiden*, You are in the Lampoon that came out this Morning, for having an Affair with Mrs. *Motion* your Lanlady's Chambermaid.

Mai. That's an Impudent Report, Mr. *Loveworth*, only to Spoil one's Reputation among the Ladies, for 'tis well

known

30   Tunbridge-Walks: *Or,*

known I have more Madefty, and never lay with a Woman in my life.

Squ. And will your Virtue gain you any Credit with the Ladies, you filly Toad ; If you wou'd Settle an Intereft there, you muft Swear you ha' worry'd half the Sex; but thou haft'nt Wit enough to fubdue any thing above a Sempftrefs.

Mai. Lard! What fignifies Wit? How particular a Wit wou'd look at Court now-a-days; Your poor fcoundrel Wits are forc'd to Cringe to us Men of Figure——I'me to have a Dedication next Winter: Well, a Dedication is the prettieft thing— To fee one's own Name in the Front of a Book— To the Honourable *Francis Maiden* Efq;—— Then to have the World told of one's Airs, and Equipage, and the Valour of one's Anceftors— You may talk what you will of your Wit and Senfe, but you'd part with all your Qualifications to have my Complexion.

Squ. O Lord, Complexion! Who the Devil minds that? And haft thou the Affurance to defpife Men of Wit, and value thy felf upon thy white Gloves, thy Honey-Water Bottle, and thy painted Face?

Mai. Well, Where it not for a little Art, one fhou'd look like other people, But what then, 'tis only a Wafh from the *Dove* in *Salisbury-Bury* Court, which all the Quality ufe, and tho' I fay it, when my Face is fet out to the beft Advantage, it has given many a Lady a Palpitation at the Heart— But you know, Captain, We have agreed not to quarrel: I hate tefty Folks, when I was at School, I cou'd never abide the Boys ; they were always Rangling, and Fighting, but I lov'd mightily to play with the Girls, and drefs Babies, and all my Acquaintance now never quarrel'd in their lives.

Lov. No, what fort of people are they good now?

Mai. Oh! The beft Creatures in the World; we have fuch Diverfion, when we meet together at my Chambers, ere's Beau *Simper*, Beau *Rabbitsface*, Beau *Eitherfex*, Colonel *Coachpole*, and Count *Drivel*, that fits with his Mouth the prettieft Company at a Bowl of Virgin-Punch;

we

The Yeoman of Kent. 31

we never make it with Rum nor Brandy—like your Sea Captains, but two Quarts of Mead to half a pint of White Wine, Lemon-Juice, Burridge, and a little Perfume; Then we never read Gazets, nor talk of *Venlo* and *Vigo*, like your Coffee-Houfe Fellows; but play with Fans, and mimick the Women, *Skream, hold up your Tails, make Curfies, and call one another, Madam*—— But Mr. *Loveworth*, Are you for the Dancing at *Southborrough* to Night? I'me going to be all new drefs'd.

Lov. Ay, But we are too Soon yet; lets take a Flask firft at the *Rummer*.

Mai. O Lard I never to go the Tavern.

Squ. But faith you fhall, Mr. *Loveworth*, lets force him along.

Mai. O Lard I fhall be Ravifh'd; Captain you are the rudeft Man, as I hope to be Sav'd I'le call out : Well, don't tumble a body then, and I will go, but I never drink any thing but *Rhenifh* and Sugar.

Squ. Dam Rotgut *Rhenifh*, we'll have Mrs. *Motion*'s health in a Bumper of *Barcelona*.

Mai. Oh! She's a Bold Pullet.   [*Exeunt.*

Enter Woodcock, *and* Belinda. *A Chair,* Woodcock *Sits.*

Woodc. Belinda, Come hither.

Bel. (*Afide*) Now fhall I be ask'd, a thoufand more Whimfical Crofs Queftions, than a Bafhful Witnefs, by an Impudent Yelper at the *Old-Bayley*.

Woodc. What Notion ha' you of Mankind?

Bel. Notion, Sir, I think of 'em as the reft o' my Sex do.

Wood. As the reft of her Sex do——I never knew a Woman give a direct Anfwer in my Life; but if I muft explain your Meaning, that's as much as to fay, You think of nothing elfe——But Pray, Madam—If I may be fo bold—What mighty Acquaintance, and Intimacy——is there between Mr. *Reynard* and you?

Bel. Mr.

32   Tunbridge-Walks: *Or,*

Bel. Mr. *Reynard*, Sir, No more than what's General, I have no farther Knowledge of him, than the Freedom of the Place allows.

Woodc. The Freedom o' the Place—— Why if you know as much of him as the Freedom of the Place allows; you have known him in every Sense : And *Item,* For what Lewdness is there this Damn'd Place don't Countenance? —Look you Daughter, I smell your Affections, and resolve to Spoil the Intreague; therefore be pleas'd to Bundle up your Night-Cloths, your Patches, Pomatum, and the rest of your Trumpery ; for positively I'le be gone to Morrow——When I think it Seasonable for you to Marry, I'le take care to provide you a Husband my self.

Bel. But I hope Sir, you'll not enjoyn me any Man contrary to my Inclinations.

Woodc. Your Inclinations——Perhaps your Inclinations are to half the Sex ; I know very well you are for a Beau; a Flattering Coxcomb, that wou'd make you believe your Eyes are a pair of Flamboys, and Cringe to you with Bits of Love-Songs, in a Damn'd Couuter-Tenor Voice——(*Singing*) *Then prithee, prithee give me gentle Boy*——But I shan't leave my Estate to a Periwig-Block ; And since that must descend with you, I shall consult my own Judgment, and not your Inclinations; therefore if your Ladyship don't think fit to Marry whom I shall Assign, you may e'en Fast 'till your Stomach comes to you : I leave you to think of that, and prepare for your Journey.   [*Exit.*

Bel. What Noise and Discord sordid Interest breeds !
Oh ! That I had shar'd a levell'd State of Life,
With quiet humble Maids, exempt from Pride,
And Thoughts of Worldly Dross that marr their Joys,
In any Sphere, but a Distinguish'd Heiress,
To raise me Envy, and Oppose my Love.
Fortune, Fortune, Why did you give me Wealth to make me wretched ?   [*Weeps.*

Enter

The *Yeoman of* Kent. 33

Enter Hillaria.

Hill. Belinda in Tears—— Now has that old Rogue been Plaguing her— Poor Soul! She weeps more heartily than ever I did, when I was Whipt for Romping: I find People have two great Satisfactions in Children; first to get 'em, and then to cross 'em: But were he my Father, I'de sooner break his Heart than he shou'd force a Tear from my Eyes—— Come, Child, Let's retire, and take a Chiriping Dram, Sorrow's dry; I'le divert you with the New Lampoon, 'tis a little Smutty; but what then; we Women love to read those things in private.   [*Exeunt.*

Enter Lucy.

Luc. How many Resolutions have I made to be **V**irtuous? And cou'd never keep 'em above two hours: Therefore I design never to make any more—— This *Tunbridge* is the Devil; For here are so many handsome Fellows proffering Love, that let a Body protest never so much against it, there always comes some rub i' the way.

Rey. (Without Singing.)

Luc. Bless me, Here's Mr. *Reynard*, that's just run Distracted, they say, for Mrs. *Belinda*, the Yeoman of *Kent's* Daughter; I'le Swear a good clean Limb'd sort of a Man—— What pity 'tis he wants his Understanding.

Enter Reynard *Singing.*

Rey. Then Mad, very Mad let us be, &c.

Luc. Poor Gentleman! How active he seems to be: Well, Of all things, I love a brisk Man—— Pray, Sir, How long have you been Mad?

Rey. Ever since, I first saw a Woman: Woman fir'd my Breast, rackt my Soul, and confounded all my Senses.

Luc. Good lack, Was there ever any thing so strange, I hope he's Mad for me too—— Sure, Sir, That was some cruel Crea-

F   ture,

34   Tunbridge-Walks : *Or,*

ture, that did'nt return you love for love; I fancy a kind
Nymph wou'd recover your Wits agen.

Rey. The whole Sex are kind, I meet no Oppofition; for
now Honourable Love is out of Date, and Maidenheads are
Drugs that lie upon their Hands; you may have 'em like Eggs,
Ten a Groat.

Luc. Indeed, I'me glad then I Sold mine before they came
fo cheap.

Rey. But if they refift me; then I grow outragious, ftorm,
ftare, rave, and force all I meet.

Luc. My Stars! The Man talks ftrangely terrible, if a body was afraid on't; I believe, Sir, you, like other Knight Er-
rants o' the Age, boaft a great deal more than you perform.

Rey. No, I am all Action, my Life, my Soul; thou Varni-
fher of thy Miftreffes Imperfections, Cabinet of her Intreagues,
Heirefs of old Cloaths, and Mender of fufty foul Linnen.

[*Tumbles her, throws her down, and goes out Singing,*
Then mad, very mad let us be, &c.

Luc. Was there ever fuch a Whelp, to throw a body down,--
and then run away, but I'le go tell my Lady; for if he fhou'd
meet her in this wild Fit, fhe'd be quite Scar'd.   [*Exit.*

Enter Hillaria.

Hill. I have put all the Mifchief imaginable into *Belinda's*
Head, and have left her to Mufe on't—— Now for my own
Matters—— This Mufick, Rambling, Tea, and Scandal, are
very pleafant, but all don't fecure the main-Chance; and that
muft be done before I leave *Tunbridge*; for Faith, I'me fo damnably in Debt, I dare'nt fhow my head in Town, 'till I have
got fome body to clear Scores—— Here comes *Woodcock,* if I
cou'd trap the old Fellow now for a Husband; what variety
of young Lover's wou'd his Eftate Purchafe——Sure no Body
in this World had ever greater occafion for a Fool than I have
at prefent.

Enter

The Yeoman of Kent. 35

Enter Woodcock.

Wood. Who wou'd be troubl'd with Daughters ? thofe Puff-Paft Things, that like Race-Horfes coft one more in keeping than they 're worth ; for my Daughter, fhe's made up of nothing but Pride, and Difobedience ; and if her Vanity's but the leaft oppos'd, then fhe's Sick, and nothing but *Tunbridge* will Cure her —— That People fhou'd come hither for Air, a damn'd Hole amidft a parcel of counfounded Hills more ftifling than a Bagnio, and Stinks worfe than the Upper-Gallery in hot Weather—— I am plagu'd to that degree, that cou'd I meet a Woman in any meafure, abating the Impertinence of her, I wou'd yet hope a Son, only to difappoint my Daughter's Expectations.

Hill. (*Afide.*) Then e'en take me, and try what you can do. I'le employ the hint; this may be the lucky Minute for ought I know —— I begin, Mr. *Woodcock*, to be tir'd of this noify Town-life, and wou'd fain Settle in the Country : D'you know never an old Shepherd that's in mighty diftrefs for a Wife ?

Woodc. He muft be in a damnable Diftrefs indeed that wou'd Marry a *London* Lady.

Hill. Oh! Mr. *Woodcock*! A Woman bred in *London* makes the beft Country-Wife ; for being Surfeited with Hurry and Confufion, Solitude is a perfect Elizium ; 'tis like repofing one's felf after a fatiguing Journey ; and of all Parts, I fhou'd chufe *Kent :* They fay you *Kentifh* Men are the beft natur'd People, and make the kindeft Husbands in the World, I know feveral Ladies extreamly fond of *Kent*.

Wood. Very like; moft of you Town-Ladies are naturally Fond of ftrong *Kentifh*-men— But pray, Madam, What has made you fuch a Friend to the Country, who but now took fo much Pains to ridicule it ; tho' few regard what your Sex fay, fince 'tis agreed, Woman ne're fpoke her Meaning yet ; for your Minds are fo very mutable, that whatever you think

F 2 at

39 　Tunbridge-Walks: *Or,*

at prefent, you're of a quite different Opinion before you can utter it.

Hill. But the Thoughts of Marriage, Sir, are more Solid, and tho' a flafhy Fop may divert one for a quarter of an hour; were I to chufe a Companion for Life; nothing's fo agreeable as your Humour.

Woodc. My Humour— Why you hav'nt a defign upon me, Madam? D'fdeath, She has almoft given me a *Kentifh* Ague-- Marry thee, no Faith, I'de fooner breed out o' my Wall-Ey'd Mare, for whatever fhe may be for Beauty, I fhou'd have one at leaft that wou'd'nt talk me to Death.

Hill. Thou art a rude Beaft, and 'tis pity any thing that's Humane fhou'd Couple with thee.

Enter Lucy.

Luc. Oh! Madam, The faddeft Accident, poor Mr. *Reynard's* quite raving Mad; he met me juft now in this Place, and threw me down after that robuft manner, I thought he wou'd have Ravifh'd me.

Woodc. Mad, ha, ha, ha, very diverting truly, a rattle-headed *London* Rake, to give out he's Mad; Why who the Devil e're thought him otherwife, ev'ry Body's Mad there—— Lawyers are Mad in finding out new Querks to make their Clients more Mad—— Poets, after new Whimfies---- Phyficians after new Poyfons---- Muficians, whofe Brains are fcatter'd into Semi-quavers, and Women have been Mad from the Creation.

Enter Reynard.

Rey. I have been talking to the Weather-Cock on yonder Church-Steeple, and 'tis the prettieft tatling Company, I fancied my felf at the Drawing-Room amongft all the Ladies-- (*To* Woodcock.)--- Ha! Who art thou with that blustering Face, like the North-Wind at the corner of an old Map, Ha,

The Yeoman of Kent. 37

Ha, ha, ha— Nay, be'nt Angry, good *Boreas* ; thou look'ft like a Wife Politician, we'll talk of State-Affairs ; Prithee call for Pipes, and let's Smoke the Nation ; bring me fome Gunpowder.

Woodc. Gunpowder !

Rey. Ay, Gunpowder ; Thou art one of thofe heavy, thinking Animals, that funk Tobacco ; I'me a Courtier, and Courtiers Smoke Gunpowder, for they are all Flafh— I'le tell you News— There's a Civil War broke out among the Cards, the Four Knaves are to be no longer Court-Cards— Pam, is a fly, cringing Parafite, flatters ev'ry Body, buys of ev'ry Body, and pays no Body— The Knave of Diamonds, borrows other People's Wit, and begs other People's Eftates— The Knave of Spades, is a Court-Rake, Scoures the Streets, breaks Windows, and beats the Watch—- And the Knave of Hearts, is a fine Dreffing Courtier, that Debauches the Citizens Wives ; befides, the whole Pack are up in Arms ; The Four Queen's are to be Banifh'd, and the Four Kings Depos'd.

Woodc. Why fo ?

Rey. Becaufe each petty Card is like a grumbling Common-Wealth's Man, that hates Monarchy, and will allow no Body to be above himfelf—- But I have made Peace.

Woodc. How ?

Rey. Why henceforward there's to be no Hereditary Honour, Mony's to be made Protector ; and ev'ry paultry Cit that has but Ten thoufand Pounds to Purchafe a Title, is to be made a Peer.

Hill. Why, That fancy now wou'd be very pleafant, to have fome of our Citizens Ennobl'd ; I warrant we fhou'd have my Lord *Leadenhall*, Count *Cheapfide*, and the Earl of *Stocks-Market*.

Rey. But hang Politicks ; Pleafure's my Bufinefs : Let dull, ftudious Mortals poife the tottering Globe, I am light as Air ; and make a Tennis-Ball of the World, Tafte ev'ry Diverfion without Care, that's always new becaufe it leaves no Impreffion

preffion? and feed on the Sweets of a ravifhing Miftrefs;
without the Puny Senfe of Love---- But where's *Belinda?*
Where's my lovely Charmer? We'll fteal together to fome
fecret Wood, and there we'll reft our felves from all Mankind; carelefly on fome rifing Bank we'l lie, fhaded by
Myrtles, fann'd with gentle Gales, and lull'd by purling Ri-
vers into Sleep.   [*Stands fix'd.*

Hill. Now are not you an old Brute to occafion a poor Gentleman's Diftraction, and have no more Charity?

Woodc. Charity--- Why, Madam, Shou'd half the Town
run Mad for my Daughter, muft I Ruine my Family to
recover their Wits? Wou'd your Ladifhip's Charity Marry
a Man under the Gallows to fave him from being Hang'd----
Look you, Sir, I underftand the World, and can fee thro'
thefe Stage-Devices; therefore, if your Worfhip thinks you
have lefs Wit than you brought down with you, and fufpect you have been Robb'd here, you'de'en Sue the County.
                                              [*Exit.*

Rey. Curfe on his Ruftick Senfe, 'twill never take: What's
to be done, *Hillaria?*

Hill. Ne're be difcourag'd, Man; When you engage an
obftinate old Mifer, fortify'd with Experience, you attack
a ftrong built Town; ev'ry Stratagem muft be thought of,
and ev'ry Faculty employ'd--- I Swear, were it not for her
Eftate, one wou'd'nt take fo much Pains about the Creature;
indeed, her Face is well enough, but fhe has a Shape like a
Candle; then fhe's horrid Silly; for when one tells her of a
likely Fellow, fhe crys, My Father--- If the reft o' the World
were but half as 'fraid of the Devil as fhe is of that Old Tott,
he'd hardly have fo much Pow'r over us--- I hate any thing fo
mealy-mouth'd.

Rey. Prithee, *Hillaria,* Leave this Woman's Railing, and
fay, what Courfe fhall I take.

Hill. Well, You Men are the faddeft Souls at an Intreague
without the Affiftance of our Sex--- Come, I'le tell you what's
to be done--- You know, he's mightily averfe to any thing of

a

The Yeoman of Kent. 39

a Gentleman, and refolves to Marry her to fome Country Grazier like himfelf: D'you affume that Habit, Forge a Commendatory Letter from fome Neighbour of his, whofe Name you may eafily learn, and carry it with all the Impudence of *Fuller*; and if that don't Cozen the old Fellow, I'le be doom'd to Die a Virgin, and that's a damnable hard Sentence.

Rey. By Heav'n, I like the Project, and will about it inftantly.

Hill. For my part, I'le e'en go make Love to Mr. *Maiden*, 'tis a fign our Sex are in fad want of Husbands, when we are forc'd to Court the Men;. but my Pride muft be fupported; [and faith I know the Town too well to lofe any thing for want of Affurance.

Rey. Come, *Hillaria.*

> Tho' Fortune, like the wav'ring Sun-fhine, Dance,
> With conftant Eyes, I'le Humour ev'ry Glance;
> No Jars, no Croffes, fhall my Hopes deftroy,
> New Ways, I'le Study, and new Arts employ,
> And in all Shapes, purfue th' Amorous Boy.

The End of the Third Act.

ACT

ACT IV.

SCENE, *Continues.*

Enter Maiden.

Mai. I 'ME glad I ha' got away from 'em, I hate the
Stinking Taverns, and they made one drink Bum-
pers o' four Claret; without so much as Nutmeg
and Sugar----Here comes Mrs. *Hillaria*, if she
wou'd but make Love to me now; for tho' we Beaus seldom
care for Marriage, 'tis pretty to have the Ladies Fond of us.

Enter Hillaria.

Hill. Mr. *Maiden*, we have wanted you extreamly at the
Tea Table, I heard you were'nt well.

Mai. Indeed, Madam, I was forc'd to lie down a little;
I'me but a weakly body, this Hot weather overcomes one
strangely.

Hill. Nay really I have often accus'd, the Tyranny of the
Mode, in obliging you to wear those Great Wigs, 'tis well you
Beaus are not Inclin'd to be Hot-Headed——But Summer
time is tedious to ev'ry body; I wonder, how so many Fat
Gentlemen, can endure the Green all Day, tho' 'tis pleasant e-
nough to Look out o' the Window and observe 'em----To see
a Tun o' Grease, with a broad fiery Face, and a little black
Cap, waddle after a Bowl rub, rub, rub, rub, rub, and lose more
Fat in getting a Shilling---Than wou'd yield him a Crown at
the Tallow-Chandlers.

Mai. Why truly, Madam, we have a World o' Greasy Beaus
about Town, I fancy half the Gentlemen o' the last Age, Marry'd their Cookmaids: But I never appear upon the Green a-
mongst 'em, for in two Minutes one's tann'd abominably, besides I hate those fatiguing Diversions.　　　　*Hill.* Then

The Yeoman of Kent. 41

Hill. Then your *Kentish* Men here are for leaping; and throwing a great Iron-Bar, as if the Slavish Exercises of a Porter, cou'd heighten the Character of a Gentleman.

Mai. These *Kentish*-Folks, value themselves so much upon their Strength, and because they carry'd a few Boughs against *William* the Conquerour; they talk of bearing Oak-Trees. I warrant in time, they'll pretend to remove the City of *London* into their own Country—— Some People too are fond of a Horse, I wonder what pleasure there is in Jumbling one's Bones to a Jelly, I'me sure, I was as weak once with Riding a Mile and a half, as if I had Lain-in: But I Love a Spring-Chariot mightily, and there's nothing we Beaus take more Pride in, than a Sett of Genteel Footmen, I never have any but what wear their own Hair, and I allow 'em a Crown a Week for Gloves and Powder; if one shoudn't, they'd Steal horridly to set themselves out, for now not one in ten is without a Watch, and a nice Snuff-Box with the best Orangerie, and the Liberty of the Upper-Gallery, has made 'em so confounded pert, that as they wait behind one at Table, they'll either put in their Word, or Mimick a body, and People must bear with 'em, or else pay 'em their Wages.

Hill. Nay, a Shining Equipage, sooths my Vanity to the last degree, we shall make the most Suitable Couple.

Mai. (Aside) Couple—I knew she wanted a body.

Hill. And really, Mr. *Maiden*, to conceal the matter no longer, I am in Love with you to Death.

Mai. Truly, Madam, Marriage is a thing I hav'n't thought on yet.

Hill. That Meen, Air, Face, Wit, Shape, that moving Softness, and those Speaking Eyes, at once have rais'd me to the height of Joy, and thrown me to the bottom of Despair.

Mai. (Aside) She's mighty fond methinks, She may be a Cheat for ought I know; for so many Rakish Women come down to *Tunbridge*, to make their Fortunes among us Men of Estates, that if a body han't great care one may be Stole—— How shall I get away from her—Madam, Il'e but Step into

G   the

42 Tunbridge-Walks : *Or,*

Back-Yard, and wait on you prefently. [*Exit.*

Hill. I find nothing can be made of this Fellow, there's fomewhat in his Nature contrary to Love——Oh ! here comes my Spruce Militia-Captain, as remarkable for Impudence, as the other for Modefty——With what variety of Fools. is this place Supply'd.

Enter Squib.

Squ. (Afide) A flinching Son of a *Sucubus* to pretend calling for a Lookinglafs ; and Sneak away——My Miftrefs —— Hem—— Now for my Rhetorick——Madam, I am Ravifh'd with your Air, the Luftre of your Eyes, the Acutenefs of your Wit, and the Symmetry of your Perfon ; there is not a Lady, whofe Prefence I admire more, throughout the Cofmical Syftem.

Hill. I find, Captain, you have Eloquence to engage the Women, as well as Valour to fubdue the Men, but 'tis my Mis- fortune, not to be touch'd with thofe extraordinary Faculties, that bait fo many of my Sex.

Squ. Some Ladies, indeed, are of a Cold Conftitution ; but can you Madam object, to one particular, throughout the finifh- ed Catalogue of my Perfections ? but 'tis the general Fate of us Men o' the Fafhion, to captivate the Crowd o' Ladies, and yet be flighted by a fingle She we Love. (*Sings*)

> *Take me, take me, while you may,*
> *Venus comes not ev'ry Day.*

Hill. (Afide) Was there ever fuch a Coxcomb——I muft own, Captain, your Graces are very infinuating, but fo many reafons perfwade me againft a Martial Love—A Woman that values her Husband, is always apprehenfive of the Chance o' War; then, fhou'd you be kill'd in a Battle, one muft Sneak to the Government, for a Penfion of twenty Shillings a Week to Subfift half a Score Children, and hammer out the reft with Wafhing, and Starching ; befides, a Soldier's Wife has- fo very little Credit abroad, that fhou'd one happen to be out o' Cafh, one may want fo much as a Paper o' Pins.

Squ. Want.

The Yeoman of Kent. 43

Squ. Want Pins— Madam, you fhall eat Pins—Thofe are your poor Starving Officers that live by Bullying, and their Wives by Cullies; I have three Hundred a Year in poffeffion, and two more in Reverfion, when my Grand-mother *Ptyfick* Dies; fo that you may have ready Mony, you may go to the Tripe-Woman's with ready Money, to the Strong-Water-fhop with ready Money, and to the Mercers with ready Money; and that's what half the Women o' Quality can't pretend to——Then for Pedigree, the *Squils*, Madam, are as Ancient and Numerous a Race, as the *Hittites*, the *Jebufites*, or the *Girgifhites* ; I have Relations confiderable in all parts o' the World; Don *Greazywhiskers*, Renegado *de Vigo*, Seignior *Furiofo Flammofo de Mount Ætna*, Lord *Hounfditch*, Mounfieur *Ne're a Shirt*, and in *Holland* my Dear Uncle, *Myn Heer Belch Van Butter-Box*, will not all this prevail? Ye Stars, is there no way to make her mine?

Hill. One way, Captain, there is, and but one; I have fworn never to yield my felf without a Duel; a Woman's hardly fpoke of 'till fhe has occafion'd Blood-fhed : All Ladies o' Figure, when they defign to Marry, contrive fome way to be fought for, then receive the Conquerour, to fhow they approve the Deed——Mr. *Loveworth*, Captain, is your Rival ; d' you Engage him, if you Succeed, my Perfon is the Reward: You'll not find it difficult, he's a Coward, and will fcarce ftand the Brunt.

Squ- (*Afide*) A Coward, Nay then I may venture to Challenge him——If that be all, Madam, 'tis done already—I'le mince the Dog——Rival me, an Audacious Rafcal—Madam I'le Anatomize him for your Ladyfhip's Curiofity—(*Afide*) I'le to the Tavern and get a little flufh'd, few have Courage enough to fight in Cool Blood. Now Fortune; for my Miftrefs, and my Fame.

> *'Tis my laft Refuge, and if that don't win her,*
> *O all You Gods above.---The Devils in her.* [*Exit.*

Hill. Now have I a mighty Pleafure in fetting two Fellows a tilting; fhou'd one of 'em be run thro', what an Air 'twill

44　　Tunbridge-Walks: *Or,*

be upon the Walks, for People to obferve a Body, and cry, fhe had a Man kill'd about her; if they both prove Cowards, 'twifl afford Mirth, to fee two Fools parry at a Diftance, they are fure not to hurt one another, and that's not unlikely in this Periwig Age.　Pfha! my old Suitor, Mr. *Loveworth*, how infipid is a Fellow's Company one has been acquainted with a Month; I begin now to hate him fo very heartily, that the Devil take me, if I don't---- marry him---- but what Humour fhall I affect, in the Morning I rally'd him, now I'll ha' the Spleen, that will give him an Opinion of my Underftanding, for the moft fafhionable Sign of a modern great Wit, is a great deal of ill-Nature.

Enter Loveworth.

Lov. Save you, fave you, Madam! what, melancholy!

Hill. One's apt to be fo, Sir, at the Approach of dull Company.

Lov. Oh, fhe has got the Spleen, I'll fetch her out of that prefently.　　　　　　　　　　[*Sings and dances a Minuet.*

Hill. Now were I really out of Humour, Splenetick, and Sick ev'n to Death, that Minuet wou'd fet me a dancing. [*Sings the fame Tune and dances.*] I find Mr. *Loveworth*, 'tis in vain for us Women to affume ill Nature with you Men that know our blind Side.

Lov. We know, Madam, your Natures are not rough, but you Ladies fo damnably diffemble Cruelty, where you find you are belov'd, we don't know what to make on't.

Hill. Good Sir, don't mention Love, that will give me the Vapour's indeed; but where's *Belinda*, Mrs. *Goodfellow*, *Penelope*, and the reft o'the Company?

Lov. Oh! Madam, they are all got to Cards in the Summer-Houfe at the lower end o'the Garden.

Hill. At Cards, and I here! Heav'n forgive me, I don't ufe to flip an Opportunity of getting Money; I'll be with 'em this Moment, but dear Mr. *Loveworth* that Minuet agen.

[*Both fing and go out in the Minuet Step.*　*Exeunt.*
　　　　　　　　　　　　　　　　　　　　　　Enter

The Yeoman of Kent. 45

Enter Woodcock *with a Letter, and* Reynard *in a Country Habit.*

Wood. [*Reading.*] Numerous Tenements—Great Store of Cattel—And Lands very extenſive in *Romney Marſh*—(*Aſide.*) A moſt convenient Place for my Owling Trade, exporting Wool, and running French Goods—I find, Sir, you are commended to me for a Son-in-Law.

Rey. Yes.

Wood. Pray, what Eſtate may you have about *Romney Marſh?*

Rey. Eſtate, Why I have Eſtate enough to ſet up who I pleaſe for Parliament Man, and when I ha' done, think I ha' Wit enough to gi'n Inſtructions how he ſhall behave himſelf.

Wood. A notable Fellow this ; no great Orator I ſee, but his Meaning's good.

Rey. Now, pray, what has your Daughter, for if her Vortune don't anſwer my Eſtate, I'ſe not have her, be ſhe a Cherubim, ſouſe me.

Wood. (*Aſide.*) My own Humour——He knows the Market, I find, and I warrant has bought many a Horſe—— And I'd have a Man inſpect a Wife as he does a Horſe, ſee if ſhe has all her Teeth, and her Quarters tight, and ſound. I'm ſure, he that marries a *London* Dame has Reaſon enough to do't, for the better ſort, what with drinking hot Liquors, and eating Sugar-Plumbs at Church, not one in ten has a Tooth left ; and for the middle ſort, I don't believe there's an Orange Woman at the Play-houſe, or a Sempſtreſs on the *Exchange,* that's Pepper-proof---- Well, Friend, I'll ſhow you my Daughter, if you like her Perſon, you may find her worth more than you imagine. [*Exit.*

Rey. An honeſt old Fellow——So, thus far the Plot ſucceeds ; but how ſhall I blind him in Relation to the Eſtate—— That's eaſy----- 'Tis but getting a few falſe Deeds, and the matter's done----- We can't want Forgery, or Perjury while the Nation affords Lawyers.

Re-enter

46 Tunbridge-Walks: *Or,*

Re-enter Woodcock *with* Belinda.

Wood. Daughter, ufe him courteoufly, and endeavour to like him ; his Eftate join'd to yours will make you the grea-teft Woman in the Country.

Rey. A Strapper i' faith---- a Well built Lafs ; tho' White, and Red like a Stockgilliflower, and a choice pair of Ud-ders---- I muft taft her.-- b'your Leave Forfooth--- (*Kiffes her*) As tender as a Pullet,and I warrant as juicy as a Burgamy Payre.

Bel. 'Pleafe to fit, Sir.   [*They Sit.*

Rey. They fay, we fhall have a good Crop t' Year.

Bel. As the Weather proves, Sir.

Rey. Ay----'T zeems, forfooth, I and you are to be Zweet-hearts, and lig together for the good of our Kind---- Nay pray you now be'nt fo fhy ; look a little fmirking upon a Body--do--If I don't love you with all my Soul, Heartsblood, Liver, and Lights, I'fe gi' you leave to make a Harcelet of me.

Wood. Very well, but I'll leave 'em together, 'tis 'nt fair to obferve Lovers.   [*Exit.*

Bel. (Rifing) Ha, ha, ha, methinks Sir, the Clown's very natural, and the Gentleman but affected ; I'd advife you to wear this Habit always, turn perfect Farmer, and go to Plow.

Rey. In the Field of Love, Madam, I agree with you; you fee what Forms and Shapes you have Power to turn us into ; I'm glad you kept your Countenance, for tho' a Defign be carry'd on to the very finifhing Point, your gig-ling Sex are apt to burft out, and fpoil all----but dear Crea-ture, let's contrive fome Way to be marry'd inftantly, for fear of a Difcovery.

Bel. The only way I can think of is to follicite him in *Propria Perfona,* which you know he'll ne're confent to ; and the more you prefs him for Mr. *Reynard,* the Gentleman, the more you haften the Match with Mr. *Reynard* the Clown.

Rey. My Life, my Angel, let me hug thee for thy Inven-tion---'Sdeath the Old Man, let's be a little familiar. [*They fit.*
              (Sings.)

The Yeoman of Kent. 47

(Sings.) *I'll tell you a Story, a Story so merry,* [Woodcock
    Concerning the Abbot *of* Canterbury,   *Enters.*
    And of his House-keeping, and high Renown,
    Which made him repair to fair London *Town,*
    Derry down, down, hey derry down,
Wood. So, so, I'm glad to see 'em so Great already.
Rey. *How now quoth King* John, *'tis told unto me,*
    That thou keepest a far better House than I,
    If thou dost not answer me Questions Three,
    Thy Head shall be taken from thy Body,
    Derry down, *&c.*

You see Forsooth, I'se no fine Singer, but i'faith I'se be th'
loudest ev'ry *Sunday* in our Church for all that; haugh.

Wood. Come *Belinda,* I'll relieve your Modesty the first
time; the Ladies enquire for you— Well, Sir, can you love
my Daughter?

Rey. Love her, ay, better than I do Beef and Pudding;
why she's a Boncritten— but i'faith we'se not part so— (*Kisses her.*) by my Troth as pretty a Morsel as a Mon wou'd
desire to feed on.

(Sings.) *And if thou dost not answer me Questions Three,*
    Thy Head shall be taken from thy Body.
    Derry down, *&c.*   [*Exeunt* Wood. *and* Reynard.

Enter Hillaria.

Hill. I have heard all, *Belinda,* and applaud my own good
Genius, but Intreagues of my forming generally prosper; I
often fancy I cou'd write a Play.

Bel. Why don't you try, *Hillaria.*

Hill. No really, *Belinda,* a Poetess is so scandalous a Character; for when a Woman has the Face to appear at Rehearsals, and teach Actors their Parts, her Assurance will scruple
nothing; besides, Women-Writers have quite lost their Reputation; for in Love Scenes their Thoughts are so loose, and
their Expressions so open, and unveil'd, the Ladies can't be
seen at a Performance of their own Sex; and Obscenity in a
                                Woman

48 Tunbridge-Walks: *Or,*

Woman is so odious— Well, *Belinda,* I long to see thee in a Lover's Arms, settl'd at *London,* and dress'd like other People: Lord ! How the Women o' Quality wou'd titter to see a high Crown-Hat in the Front-Seat o' the Box : Thou art good natur'd, Child, to suffer these Impositions ; shou'd any old Humourist force a Steeple upon my Head, I'de make more noise in his Ears than if 'twere a Church-Steeple with the whole Set o' Bells in't.

Bel. A ridiculous Habit reflects more on those that impose it, than on us, where dependance forces a Subjection ; but if I shou'd visit *London,* you'll instruct you Friend, *Hillaria* ; for tho' frequenting *Tunbridge* may render one not awkward, I shall be a perfect Novice in half the Town Airs.

Hill. Why truly, *Belinda,* tho' our Observation be all trifle, a Woman that's well vers'd in the Niceties of Behaviour, is thought no small Politician ; For in the first place, if you wou'd show a refin'd Education, you must be very timorous, and fearful, skream at the Jolt of a Coach, or the Pop of a Pistol, Die away at the Sight of a Rat ; All well-bred Ladies are frighted at ev'ry thing but a Man—— Then you must be taken Ill at publick Places ; tho' not like my Lady *Fullmoon,* that fainted away in a high colour ; but to Humour a Swooning, with a pretty Paleness, causes an agreeable Disturbance, and gives one an opportunity to be supported by the Man one likes ; Then the next Morning, there's such ratling with Footmen, which makes one considerable in the Neighbourhood, from this Lady and that Lady, tho' we hate one another mortally, to know how one's Head, and one's Stomach does, and how one rested that Night ; and I all the while in my Closet at a Couple of cold Chickens, and a Tankard o' Sherry.

Bel. But what Amusements have you there ?

Hill. Oh ! Innumerable ! My Head turns round with the promiscuous Enjoyment : There's the Play, Where I generally sidle in about the middle of the Second Act, that People may think I have been detain'd on some important Affair ; if 'tis a Tragedy, I turn my Rump, and talk to the Beaus behind;

The Yeoman of Kent. 49

behind; But a Comedy's very pleafant, if 'tis but Abufive; I love Satyr ftrangely: Then *Hyde-Park*, Oh! *Hyde-Park* does ravifh me.

Bel. But there you have no Converfation.

Hill. That's nothing, a world of pretty things may be done without Speech; but tho' our Tongues are filent, we Difcourfe ftill.

Bell. How fo?

Hill. With our Fingers; there's many an Intreague carry'd on that way, and that's fo pretty to appoint Time, and Place, and not a Word fpoke: That Art, they fay, was invented to oblige fome Men o' Quality, who wanted the Gift of Elocution; and are not thefe much preferable to the Melancholy Country; where you may walk a whole day, and not fee a Man: I'me fure I was fo Mop'd there once for want of Company, I was glad to talk to the great Bull-Dog.—— Come, Child, we'll fend for a Beau to carry us to *Southborrough*, and I'le tell you more.

Bel. I wonder, *Hillaria*, You'll appear with thefe Beaus, and always fpeak fo defpicably of 'em.

Hill. They give one Snuff, lofe their Money at Cards, and pay Coach-Hire. [*Exeunt.*

Loveworth *and* Squib *meeting.*

Squ. (*Afide.*) My Rival! Dear Spirit of *Burgundy* affift me.-- Mr. *Loveworth*, Draw.

Lov. Draw, Captain, Upon what Account? How long have we been Enemies.

Squ. Look you, Sir, I'me for Action, and not Words: In fhort, You have endeavour'd to deprive me of my Miftrefs, and muft either quit the Lady, or vindicate your Pretenfions.

Lov. (*Afide.*) Ha, ha, ha, *Hillaria* has Banter'd the Fool, I'le Humour him a little—— That matter, Captain, we may decide more Calmly— He who has Serv'd her longeft, beft deferves her: If we can't agree, let the Lady determine it by her own Inclinations.

Squ. (*Afide.*) Is he thereabouts, I'le purfue the point——

H

Sir,

50   Tunbridge-Walks: *Or,*

Sir, The Temple of the bright *Hillaria,* I have made the Repository of my Affections ; and whoever dares dispute the Legality of my Title, and not justifie what he says, Is a Son of an *Irish* Evidence, a Fool, and a pitiful Coward.

Lov. Nay, Captain, If you Brand me with the Name of Coward, my Honour's concern'd ; now I will Fight. [*Draws.*

Squ. (Looks Surpriz'd.)— Will you Fight— *(Puts up his Sword.)* Then gi'me thy Hand ; now I won't Fight with you ; we Men of Reciprocal Courage shou'd never Fight, but a Cowardly Rascal ought to be Kick'd and Posted.

Lov. No, Captain, I seldom draw my Sword ; but once provok'd, 'tis never drawn in vain ; now you shall Fight.

Squ. (Aside.) O Lord, What shall I do now—Come, come, Mr. *Loveworth,* Friends shou'd never quarrel— The Lady's yours ; I have a Stock of Mistresses, and can afford you half a Score at any time.

Lov. Nay, Captain, If you won't Fight, I must return you Coward, and Fool agen, with that, that, and that. [*Kicks him.*

Squ. 'Tis very well, Mr. *Loveworth,* mighty well, superlatively well ; indeed, look you, Sir, I shall meet you one dusky Evening in St. *James's* Park.

Lov. And what will you do then, Sir ?

Squ. Why, Sir, I'le order two or three of the Sentry to fling you into the Canal.

Lov. Will you so, Sir.   [*Kicks him agen.*

Squ. Nay, now—— I will walk off.   [*Exit.*

Lov. Thus flash of Valour, gilds the least Pretence,   ⎫
     Thus Lawyers Bawl, and Rise by Impudence,   ⎬
     Huffing for Courage passes, Noise for Sense,   ⎭
     By all Appearance, how the World's deceiv'd,
     Grave Dulness, Wisdom, Canting, Zeal's believ'd ;
     But were Desert, like Metal to be try'd,
     And each Pretender shou'd the Test abide,
     How many a Hero huffs without a Soul ?
     How many a Statesman wou'd be found a Fool.
        The End of the Fourth Act.

                                   ACT

ACT V.

SCENE, *Continues.*

Enter Woodcock, *and* Reynard.

Woodc. I Tell you, Mr. *Reynard*, My Daughter shall have no *London* Husband; I must have a Man that understands Farming, and will Improve my Estate, raise Portions for younger Children, and yet double it to the Eldest--- Whereas your Town Gentlemen Spend more in a Month than they Receive in a Quarter; know nothing of their Lands, 'till they come to Assign, and Set over; And I don't believe there's an Estate at Court, but is Mortgag'd to an Alderman in the City.

Rey. (*Aside.*) How perverse is Age? One may sooner Civilize a Satyr, Convert a *Jew*, or reduce a Woman from her Pride and Vanity, than persuade an Old Fellow out of a rooted Obstinacy--- But Mr. *Woodcock*, you have Reason, and shou'd Argue exceptionally, the Age may be Extravagant enough; But d'you think it impossible for the Town to afford Men of Conduct and good Management?

Woodc. Not impossible, I grant you; but you may as well look for Cleanliness in *Scotland*, Mony in *France*, or Wit and Manners at *Amsterdam*, as Sobriety in *London*— To be plain, You are People of Principles, you have neither Religion, nor common Morality; and I desire, Mr. *Reynard*, you'll desist your Pretensions: In short, I have engag'd a Person, fitter for my Daughter's Purpose, and more agreeable to my Temper.

Rey. What, The *Romney-Marsh* Gentleman, *Humphry Hobble* Esq; Ha, ha, ha.

Wood. (*Aside.*) How the Devil came he to know him?

Rey. Mr. *Woodcock*, to convince you; You have a wrong Notion of us bred in Town, I'le be Frank—— Your Daugh-

H 2 ter,

52   Tunbridge-Walks: *Or,*

ter, and I, are agreed; She receiv'd the Countryman only
to Humour you, and told me all that pass'd between 'em,
how he Loll'd in his Chair like a drunken Juſtice, Entertain'd
her with a wretched Old Song, and Grunted out his Love after
that Booriſh manner, ſhe fancy'd her ſelf in a Hogſty——
Since you ſee, Mr. *Woodcock*, I won't abuſe you, allow me.Ge-
nerous, and Ratifie our Affections.

Woodc. (*Aſide.*) The Curſe of Maidenheads light upon the
whole Sex—— Mr. *Reynard*, I muſt confeſs, you are a very generous Perſon, and to return your Generoſity, I will this moment Marry my Daughter to the Countryman—— I ſhall
ſpoil her Fop Intreague; that Women ſhou'd be ſuch Fools
to fall in Love with Perriwigs, and Lac'd Coats; but 'twill
be ſo, let a Man ſhow but a fair outſide, they don't care if he
has no more Brains than a Grand Jury.   [*Exit.*

Rey. Ha, ha, ha, Now for my Country Face agen.

Enter Loveworth.

Ned Loveworth ſauntring about like an Idle Courtier, or a poor
Poet in ſearch of a Dinner.

Lov. 'Tis true, *Frank*, I have no Heireſſes to follow, nor
croſs Miſers to attack; but I have a Miſtreſs too, and a very
whimſical one; for tho' ſhe admits me to Squire her about,
ſhe won't ſuffer me to mention Love.

Rey. She'll Conſent the ſooner; Women ſeldom care to talk
of Love, 'till they reſolve upon the Action, becauſe they hate
to be Tantaliz'd.

Lov. Well, my Dear Friend, and how go Matters?

Rey. Swimingly, ſwimingly, *Ned*; I aſſum'd all the Clow-
niſhneſs imaginable; No true Peaſant, bred amongſt Cattle
in the *Wild o' Kent*, or the *Peake* in *Derbyſhire*, cou'd have had
a more Ruſtical Air.

Lov. Thou wer't always a good Mimick *Frank*: But can'ſt
thou really lay aſide all Conſcience, and Honeſty, and have
the face to Marry this Lady, and Bubble the Yeoman out of
ſuch a prodigious Eſtate?   *Rey.* Con-

The Yeoman of Kent. 53

Rey. Confcience, and Honefty, ha hà ha, thou fhou'dft ha' been born feven Ages ago, thofe things are obliterated now-a-days, and for the Face o'the matter, a Man of Intreague muft have a Face for every thing, the Women indeed, are eafily fubdu'd, Coquet Ladies like *Hillaria,* you win with Mimicry and Scandal ; an Old Maid that's miferably pitted with the Small-pox, you muft praife her Youth, and Beauty ; to a young Creature you muft talk Modeftly, to a Widow, Mathematically, but to furprize Old Fathers that infpeftour Defigns, requires a Mafterpiece of Nature— To deceive a Country Yeoman, I'm a Clown you fee— To pleafe a rich Sergeant, I cou'd be a fpruce Barrifter, come to the Court powder'd beyond a Side-Box Beau, give a Hem, and cry, May it pleafe you my Lárd, and you Gentlemen of the Jury— Nay, to Curry with a Superftitious Old Uncle, I cou'd put on a precife, Conventicle-Face, and look as mortify'd as your Sneaking Citizens do of late, fince the Downfal of the Whig-Party. In fhort, *Ned,* If you wou'd rife in the World, you muft have a Face for ev'ry thing— Why the Women give us that Example, who, they fay, are arriv'd to that Perfeftion in Wafhes, Paftes, and Powders, they'll alter their Looks fo, you fhan't know 'em ; And I heard of a fine Town-Lady, who Painted her Face with that variety, fhe was pick'd up by a Purblind Lord, Six Nights together for a frefh Miftrefs— But, Dear *Ned,* excufe me, thou know'ft the Exigence of my Affairs, a Moment's trifling might be fatal.

Lov. Succefs attend you, Sir. [Exeunt *differently.*

Enter Woodcock *and* Belinda.

Woodc. Belinda, I muft talk with you— (*Afide.*) But why fhou'd I examine her ? She'll tell me a hundred Lies with as Grave a Face as a *Presbyterian* Divine, when he preaches up Confcience, and flides a filver Spoon into his Pocket—'Tis impoffible to know that Sex, they'll melt us with their Tears,
and

54　　Tunbridge-VValks: *Or,*

and in the fame Breath laugh at our Eafinefs; At Church, they'll be very Devout with one Eye, and Ogle a Fellow with t'other; and they have more Tricks, Querks, and Evafions to avoid Speaking Truth, than an Attorney has in drawing an Anfwer in *Chancery*——— *Belinda,* What think you of the new Gallant I brought you?

Bel. If my Approbation, Sir, wou'd not Create in you an Averfion to him, I cou'd tell you, I like him, like him infinitely, beyond any Man in particular, and the whole Sex in general.

Woodc. (*Afide.*) If fhe be real, this pleafes me indeed; this is News beyond an Exprefs from *Italy*——— 'Tis my Requeft then, that you Marry him inftantly.

Bel. Moft willingly: The Moment that I faw him, a fudden chilnefs feiz'd me ev'ry where; that chilnefs as fuddenly chang'd into a pleafing Warmth; the Warmth e're fince keeps fettl'd at my Heart, and my Thoughts fix'd on him.

Woodc. (*Afide.*) This is Love; but her Youth's unacquainted with thefe Symptoms, I have felt 'em formerly my felf——— This Hour then he fhall be yours——— (*Afide.*) But fhou'd'nt I firft fatisfy my felf with the Reality of this Eftate he pretends to have ——— It muft be fo, he lives too far from *London* to be a Cheat——— Now, what an impudent Rogue is this *Reynard,* to pretend a Contract with my Daughter, when fhe all the while Dies for Squire *Hobble*——— But then, how fhou'd *Reynard* know what pafs'd between the Countryman, and her, unlefs the Devil helpt him to't; like enough, truly, I believe moft o'your Town-Sparks are very intimate with Alderman *Belzibub*——— Come, *Belinda,*——— (*Afide*). Still I fufpect a Trick, but if fhe Marries him, there can be none; if fhe can Cheat the Prieft, fhe'll Cheat the Devil.　　　[*Exeunt.*

Enter Squib.

Squ. Pox of his Courage, I fay; I fhall be kick'd about by ev'ry *Chocolate*-Houfe Beau, now they know I won't Fight;

How

The Yeoman of Kent. 55

How fhall I be Reveng'd ? Shall I venture to Challenge him--- No, --- What fhall I do then ? Oh! I fhall meet him in the publick Dancing-Room, and I'le Sit above him.—— But now, How can I appear before my Miftrefs ? 'Tis no matter ; There's *Penelope* with a better Fortune ; and I cou'd like her were fhe not fo forward ; People naturally Slight thofe that are in Love with 'em, tho' fhou'd I have an Averfion to all the Women that are in Love with me, I might defpife the whole Sex ; therefore I will Marry her.

Enter Mrs. Goodfellow, *and* Penelope.

Mrs. *Goodf.* Sweet Captain, we have fought for you vehemently ; we wanted your Company with us to *Southborough.*

Squ. I have likewife, my fair *Penelope*, been upon the Chafe for you, to inform you fome Ladies here have a violent defign upon my Perfon ; and if you don't enclofe me prefently, I fhall be ravifh'd from your Arms.

Pen. Lofe my dear Captain, Aunt, Aunt, run for Doctor *Dromedary*, and let us be Married before the Sun repofes.
[*Exit* Goodf.

Squ. Now, Madam, we muft make a mighty Appearance, and have a ftately Bridal Equipage ; all new Marry'd People of any Figure, keep a Coach the firft year.

Pen. We muft go a Vifiting together, and to *Hyde-Park* together, and be extreamly Fond for a Month : Then, Captain, My Aunt, and I muft go to the *Artillery-Ground* o' Training Days, that the Soldiers may let off their Muskets, and cry, Heav'n Blefs the Noble Captain's Lady ; and fure nothing is fo pleafant as to frequent Places where one's Husband has an Authority, that one may be very rude, and Affront Folks—— But, Dear Captain, Let's make hafte ; for fhou'd you be Ravifh'd from me now, I wou'd be more concern'd, than if I were Ravifh'd my felf. [*Exeunt.*

Enter

56　　# Tunbridge-Walks : Or,

Enter Loveworth *and* Hillaria.

Hill. Sure no Courtier was ever worſe Plagu'd with a Petitioning Poet, than I am with you.

Lov. Sure no Poet was ever more coldly receiv'd by a ſtately Courtier, than I am by you; But to prove my Conſtancy, Madam, Be as Cruel as you pleaſe, I'le never leave you, I'me reſolv'd to follow you, Court you, and Addreſs you, 'till you yield.

Hill. And while you continue to follow me, Court me, and Addreſs me, I will never yield.

Lov. Why?

Hill. Becauſe we Women love dearly to be follow'd, Courted, and Addreſs'd; I muſt own, Mr. *Loveworth,* we do Cully your Sex ev'ry way; While you Court us, we make Spaniels of you; and when we have a Mind to render you more Contemptible, we make Husbands of you; and really you Lovers are meer Spaniels; for the worſe you are us'd, the more you Fawn.

Lov. You know, Madam, You have Pow'r, and are reſolv'd to Triumph.

Hill. We know you are Fools, and are reſolv'd to Laugh at you; but no more of this Chat, here's Company.

Enter Woodcock *Singing.*

Wood. Sing *Old Sir Simon the King tol tol, &c.*

Lov. I'me glad to ſee you ſo merry, Mr. *Woodcock,* ſhan't we rejoice with you too?

Woodc. With all my Heart, Mr. *Loveworth,* I have juſt Marry'd my Daughter, and am reſolv'd to Dedicate a whole Twelvemonth to Mirth, and Jollitry, I'le broach my ſix Hogſheads of Stout, that were Brew'd in the Days of King *Charles,* and make the whole Country as Drunk, as at an Election of Burgeſſes.

Hill. Shan't we ſee your Son-in-Law, Sir?　　*Woodc.* Pre-

The Yeoman of Kent. 57

Wood. Prefently, Madam, I left 'em but in the next Room to bill and coo a little--ha ha ha, what wou'd I give now Mr. *Reynard* were but here, to Laugh at him a little, and let him fee our Ale in the Country has infpir'd us with more Cunning, than all his Burgundy in Town.

Lov. Oh! Here they come.

Reynard, *and* Belinda, *Enter, and Kneel to* Woodcock.

Rey. Your Blefling Sir ?

Woodc. Mr. *Reynard* !

Rey. The very fame, Son-in-Law to you, and Partner. to this Lady, by your own Choice and Approbation.

Woodc. Here's a Son of a Copper-Smith——But, Daughter, *Belinda,* what means this Stuff, did not I give you to the Countryman, and did not the Prieft join your Hands, call in Doctor *Dromedary?*

Bel. You did, Sir, Commanded by you, and prompted by my own Inclination, with a double Joy I receiv'd him for my Husband.

Rey. To humour you, Sir, I was that Countryman, and to pleafe this Lady am now Mr. *Reynard* agen.

Woodc. Why then Mr. *Reynard* is the Devil incarnate.

Lov. I find, Mr. *Woodcock* your Country Ale has clouded your underftanding a little.

Woodc. (*Afide*) Hell and Furies, how have I been abus'd, impos'd on by a vain fluttering Fellow, and Jilted by my own Daughter——D'fdeath, I fhall be a Jeft to the whole Country. Mr, *Reynard,* I own you have been too hard for me, your Wit has gain'd her, now let your Wit maintain her, my Eftate deferves a better Ufage.

Hill. Nay now, Mr. *Woodcock,* I muft interpofe.

Woodc. You, I have a mighty refpeft indeed for your Sex.

Hill. I fancy, Sir, you never fpent much time in *France*— (*Afide*) A true *Englifh Clown.*

I

Lov. Ext

58   Tunbridge-Walks : *Or,*

Lov. But, Mr. *Woodcock*, your Experience fhou'd confider thefe frailties, fhe ftill refpects you as her Father, but neither Duty, Friendfhip, nor Intereft can prevail, againft the Force of Love.

Woodc. No, I have a Senfe of Money, and cannot bear to fee it us'd like Dirt; before my Eftate fhall be fpent in glaring Liveries, and feed an Empty Pride, I'le fit out a Regiment to help carry on the War, and Nobly fpend it in my Country's Service; this moment I difcard her; fince Blind Love chang'd her State, Blind Chance direct her Courfe—But whó am I thus Ufing? My Daughter? Who then muft Share my Wea'th? If I reject my Child, my only Child—Nature, Nature, why d' you rack me thus.

Bell. We'll fettle in the Country, Sir, Difpofe us as you pleafe, pardon but this Offence and own us yours.   [*Weeps.*

Woodc. How eafily Tears flow from Womens Eyes; after a Voluntary Difobedience, they Calm our Paffion with a feign'd Repentance; Her Sorrow moves me tho' I know 'tis falfe, Can I diffolve this Marriage? No, Mr. *Reynard,* take her; as you ufe her, you may hope my Favour. My Perfonal Eftate fhall defcend to her, my Real Eftate I'le Settle on your Eldeft Son, whom I expect to breed under my own Eye, and according to my own humour—'tis very hard, if you deny me that——On thofe Conditions, Heav'n blefs you both.

Rey. I have various reafons, Sir, to value your Efteem, and endeavour to oblige you, My Intereft, my Love to this Lady, and chiefly to perfuade you from a prejudice againft Men of Education——To gain a Miftrefs, we're allow'd deceit, in all things elfe you fhall find me a Man of Honour.

Lov. Now, Madam, we may Congratulate your Happinefs.

Hill. (*Afide to* Bel.) You, fee *Belinda,* my Words are verify'd, 'tis obferv'd, Fathers Love us better than we do them, thefe Eruptions will occafion fome Conflict, but 'tis foon over, except it be fome very crofs old Fellows, who when they're

difoblig'd

The Yeoman of Kent. 59

difoblig'd, won't part with their Money, but they Die the fooner, and one has it then——Mr. *Woodcock*, this A-&ion has won my Favour ftrangely; I muft extol your Goodnefs; nay, I fhall fpeak well of you behind your Back, (*Afide*) and that's what I never did of any body yet.

[*Mufick without.*

Rey. Blefs us, what mighty Proceffion have we here, that all the Mufick in the Place is mufter'd up?

The Muficians enter Playing, Squib *and* Penelope, *affectedly humouring Time, Mrs.* Goodfellow *following.*

Parturiunt Montes, nafcetur ridiculus Mus.

Squ. Gentlemen, and Ladies, my Dear, and I come to acquaint you with our Nuptials.

Hill. Penelope, and the Captain Marry'd!

Pen. Why really, Madam, my Dear, and I found our felves fo very fit for one another, Nature woudn't let us be any longer afunder.

Squ. Sure no Pair were ever fo well match'd as my Dear and I. [*Kiffing.*

Pen. Sure no Pair were ever fo fond as my Dear, and I.

Hill. (*Afide*) Sure no Pair were ever fo affected as my Dear and I, is there any thing fo fulfome as a new Marry'd Couple, that play the Fool, and kifs before Company?

Rey. (*Afide*) I fhall marr their Joy prefently—— But here comes foft Mr. *Maiden.* mortifi'd to the laft degree: for after all his Mufick, Painting, and other fine accomplifhments, he's difcover'd to have no Eftate.

All. No Eftate, ha, ha, ha.

Rey. fome Gentlemen it feems, pleas'd with his Vanity, buz'd a plaufible Story in his Ears, and brought him down hither to make him ridiculous

I 2

Hill. Poor

60   Tunbridge-Walks: *Or,*

*Hill..*Poor Mr. *Maiden*! But 'tis many a Beau's Cafe, to build a mighty Appearance on a very flender Foundation. The Greateft Beaus we have about Town, now are Milliners, Mercers Lawyers Clerks, and 'tis fuch upftart Fellows that ruine fo many poor Tradefmen; for amongft 'em all you'll fcarce find a Periwig that's paid for.

Enter Maiden.

Maid. What a Pox, muft *I* go to the *Change* agen, and fell Gloves and Ribbons?

Squib. No Eftate, O Lord, *Maiden*, what will become of your Airs now?

Bel. What Pity 'tis, the fine Mr. *Maiden*, who does ev'ry thing fo much like Quality, fhou'd be forc'd to turn Mechanick.

Wood. What will your Patchwork, and your Fillagree fignify now, Friend without an Eftate to keep your Follies in Countenance?

Hil. Come, come, Mr. *Maiden*, ne're be concern'd, Riches are only to fupply other Defeats; your Graces may command a Lady with an Eftate at any time.

Maid. Nay, whenever I marry, I don't doubt of a good Fortune yet; when I was at the *Change* before, People us'd to call me handfome Mr. *Maiden*. I have a Brother too, fo like me, no Body can diftinguifh us, and we us'd to cheat Folks, and lay it upon one another.

Rey. But the Captain here is more to be pitied, who inftead of marrying into a great Family, and with a great Fortune, has made an Alliance with Mrs. *Lime-Juice*, that keeps a Punch Houfe in *Long Acre*, and her Neice *Jenny Trapes*, who being known by ev'ry Body in Town, thought to pafs at *Tunbridge* for a Chaft *Penelope.*

Squib. *Jenny Trapes*——What that Carrotpated Jade that Lodges at the Corner of *White Horfe Alley.*

Rey. The

The Yeoman of Kent. 61

Rey. The fame indeed, only fhe has black'd her Hair with a Leaden Comb.

Squib. The Devil black her all over.

All. Ha, ha, ha, Give you Joy Captain.

Hill. Nay, really, I always took her for fome fuch Creature, fhe has made no fhow fince fhe came, but always trapifh and dirty, like an Actrefs at a Morning Rehearfal.

Maid. Marry'd her! O Lard, Captain, what will become of your Airs now?

Squib. Sir——(*afide.*) I have ftudy'd Intreaguing to a fine Purpofe, to be trick'd at laft, by an old Brandy-bottle.

Rey. Nay, they have cheated one another, for the Captain, whom I had a particular Reafon to enquire after, inftead of being a worthy Officer, and a Man of Subftance, is found to be one of the Handicraft Gentlemen that fit crofs'd Legg'd fix Stories high, fpoil a World of good Cloth, by putting it into an ill Shape, and ftuff up long Bills with Canvas, Buckram, and Stay-tape.

All. A Taylor, Ha, ha, ha.

Rey. We always fancy'd he had a fhambling Air, but Yefterday as he drew out his Handkercheif, he happen'd to drop a Meafure upon the Walks, and difcover'd all.

Wood. What a Misfortune 'tis fo renown'd a Warriour fhou'd dwindle into a Loufe Cracker.

Hill. I'm forry Captain, I cou'd'nt receive you for a Husband, a Taylor's Wife you know wou'd found but odly at *Tunbridge*, but I'll be fure to fend for you, when I have occafion for a new Jump.

Maid. A Taylor, nay, now I will banter him—— Captain, pray how many Yards o'Cloth muft you have to make my Monkey a pair of Breeches?

Squib. 'Dsblood, Sir.

Maid. (*Starts.*) Now the Duce take me if I an't afraid of him ftill, tho' I know he's but the Ninth part of a Man.

Rey. Well

62   Tunbridge-Walks : *Or,*

Rey. Well, Captain, you may keep your Title for all this,; Taylors, Shomakers, and Barbers may serve for Militia Officers, since you only fight Mock-battles, and represent what a Captain shou'd be.

Squib. Look you, Sir, 'tis natural for us that dwell in a Garret to be a little high minded, therefore I came down to *Tunbridge,* in hopes to make my Fortune, but since I find my Expectations frustrated, I candidly take my leave, and Gentlemen, and Ladies, when you come to Town, if you'l favour me with a Visit at the Doublet in *Barbakin,* 'twill be gratefully acknowledg'd by your very humble Servant *Ezekiel Cowcumber.*   [*Exit.*

All. Ha, ha, ha.

Wood. Come, good People, some Neighbours of mine shall divert you on this Occasion, tho' I design'd it an Entertainment suitable to a Rural Marriage.

Hill. (*To* Goodf. *and* Pen.) Ladies, Virtuous Ladies, you'll not deprive us of your Company, Ladies.

Goodf. I ne're was out of Countenance 'till now, I'll Ship off all I have, and run to *Ireland.*

Pen. I'll go hang my self in *White Horse Alley.* [Exeunt.

An Entertainment.

Lov. Well, Madam, now you see other People coupl'd, what say you to a Dance?

Hil. Marriage, Mr. *Loveworth,* is too solemn a Dance, I'm for a Frisk a Minuet or so, but I hate the Brawls, tho' really 'tis like a Feast, and to see People eat heartily wou'd make one fall to, tho' one had no Stomach——(*Aside.*) Now I find he's desperately in Love, I'll give my self an Air of Generosity——but Mr. *Loveworth,* since we come to talk seriously o'the matter, I must deal ingenuously with you, the Report you have of my Fortune is utterly False— My

Parents

The Yeoman of Kent. 63

Parents were mighty well-bred People, and what they fhou'd have laid up for my Portion, they fpent in my Education ; I have a great deal of good Humour, and all that, but no Money ; I'le tell you one thing, I am a Maid, but don't Expofe me ; therefore if you can like a Woman with only the Cloaths to her Back, and a Dozen good Smocks or fo, I muft own a very great Affection for your Eftate.

Lov. Hang Fortune, Madam, Your Wit and Beauty may Command the World, I'de Marry you tho' you had'nt fo much as Fig-Leaves.

Hill. That's very kind ; Take me then, and fince I bring you nothing, I'le manage your Eftate fo prudently, I'le fave you a Fortune, and in Twenty Years time you fhall know no difference—— Now did I depend upon Rambling about, Chaftity, and Clean-Linnen, and thought not of being that Sluttifh thing a Wife thefe Seven Years, but, ——ugh, Thefe Men, when they get an Afcendant over us, they turn and wind us juft as they pleafe.

Rey. Sifter, I approve your Choice, and wifh you much Satisfaction.

Lov. Hillaria, his Sifter.

Rey. My own Dear Sifter ; We were both caft in the fame Mould.

Bel. Hillaria!

Hill. Belinda!

Rey. There is an Eftate too belonging to our Family under fome Incumbrances, which a little of Mr. *Woodcock's* Affiftance might Difcharge, and raife a genteel Fortune for my Sifter.

Woodc, Not a Soufe, Mr. *Reynard,* 'till you have fhown your Skill, produce me a Grandfon, and you bind me yours.

Hill. (*Afide,* to *Rey.*) You muft reft contented, Brother, and refolve to Study his Temper : 'Tis not for the weak

to

64   Tunbridge-Walks: *Or,*

to oppofe the ftrong: We naturally Flatter and Diffemble for our Intereft; therefore Coaks him all you can, and when you have Wheedl'd him out of one half of his Eftate, go to Law with him for the reft.

Rey. (To *Woodc.*) You need not doubt my Performance, Sir.

> Beauty it felf fufficiently prevails,
> And Gold excites us oft, when Beauty fails,
> But, with a double force, our Skill we prove,
> When two fuch Charms unite to prompt our Love.

F I N I S.

The Women-Hater's Lamentation (1707)

The Women-Hater's Lamentation is a broadside ballad that would have been distributed in October–December 1707 during the pillorying of one or more sodomites who had been arrested by members of the Societies for the Reformation of Manners acting as *agents provocateurs*. According to the brief summary of *The TRYAL and CONVICTION of several Reputed Sodomites, before the Right Honourable the Lord Mayor, and Recorder of London, at Guild-Hall, the 20th Day of October, 1707* (1707), from mid-September eight members of the Societies walked up and down London Bridge (and also in the Royal Exchange), making themselves available to the sodomites who regularly cruised there. The entrappers operated in pairs, one man appearing to accept the solicitation, then giving a signal to his partner who stood nearby ready to make the arrest. The solicitation techniques were brazen and straightforward: the sodomite simply walked up to his proposed trick, offered to put his exposed penis into his hand, and thrust his own hand into the breeches of the other man. After a week or ten days, the Societies' agents had arrested more than forty sodomites. All of them confessed at their initial appearance before a magistrate, but at the actual trials they all pleaded not guilty except for one, who pleaded guilty. Eight men were convicted at the Guildhall trials: Thomas Lane, a foot soldier; John Williams, a youth; Charles Marriot; Paul Booth; Benjamin Butler; John Butler; James Brooke (who pleaded guilty); and William Huggins, a porter arrested at the Exchange, who said, when arrested, 'that he had hear'd there were such sort of Persons in the World, and he had a mind to try'. (At the trial, however, Huggins pleaded innocent and said that he was newly married and that his wife was pregnant.)

Augustin Grant, a woollen-draper in West Smithfield, hanged himself in prison before his trial came on. He left a suicide note proclaiming his innocence, which was mentioned by Lady Cowper in her diary for 10 October 1707. However, the account in the *Post-Boy* for 9–11 October 1707 emphasized that he had not denied the facts when brought before the magistrate, though claiming he was drunk, and that reputable witnesses made his guilt clear. A great concourse of people assembled before the Guildhall during the indictments (*Post-Boy*, 11–14 Oct. 1707). At Hicks's Hall, bills of indictment were found against three more persons 'on Account of Preposterous Venery' (*Post-Boy*, 14–16 Oct. 1707). On 18 October, seventeen more men were indicted by the Grand Jury for the City of London, and three more men were indicted by the Grand Jury for the County of Middlesex (*Post-Boy*, 16–18 Oct. 1707). At the same time, Thomas Vaughan, a foot-soldier, and Thomas Davis, a brandy-seller, were convicted of attempting to extort money by threatening to accuse men of sodomy (two other men in their blackmail ring escaped, and the fifth colleague turned King's evidence), and were pilloried and whipped (*Post-Boy*, 16–18 Oct. 1707; 21–3 Oct. 1707). (Vaughan had often discovered men using the Temple bog house, or public latrine, where a hole had been drilled through the partition wall which separated two stalls – what modern gay men call a 'glory hole'.) All of the prosecutions (for the misdemeanour of 'assault with attempt to commit sodomy') were brought and paid for by the Societies for the Reformation of Manners (*Post-Boy*, 16–18 Oct. 1707). The pilloryings of more than a dozen sodomites were reported in the newspapers through mid-December 1707.

The text is reproduced from the copy held by the Guildhall (Corporation of London) Library (shelfmark 2636). This is the only copy that exists. The broadside was re-used: on the back is printed *A Full and True Account of a Dreadful Fire* (1708).

The 𝕎omen-𝕳ater's Lamentation:

OR

A New Copy of Verses on the Fatal End of Mr. *Grant*, a Woollen Draper, and two others that Cut their Throats or Hang'd themselves in the *Counter*; with the Discovery of near Hundred more that are Accused for unnatural dispising the *Fair Sex*, and Intriguing with one another.

To the Tune of, *Ye pretty Sailors all.*

I.
YE injur'd *Females* see
  Justice without the Laws,
Seeing the Injury,
  Has thus reveng'd your Cause.

II.
For those that are so blind,
  Your Beauties to despise,
And slight your Charms, will find
  Such Fate will always rise.

III.
Of all the Crimes that Men
  Through wicked Minds do act,
There is not one of them
  Equals this Brutal Fact.

IV.
Nature they lay aside,
  To gratifie their Lust;
Women they hate beside,
  Therefore their Fate was just.

V.
Ye *Women-haters* say,
  What do's your Breasts inspire,
That in a Brutal way,
  You your own Sex admire?

VI.
Woman you disapprove,
  (The chief of Earthly Joys)
You that are deaf to Love,
  And all the Sex despise.

VII.
But see the fatal end
  That do's such Crimes pursue,
Unnat'ral Deaths attend,
  Unnat'ral Lusts in you.

VIII.
A Crime by Men abhor'd,
  Nor Heaven can abide
Of which, when *Sodom* shar'd,
  She justly was destroy'd.

IX.
But now, the sum to tell,
  (Tho' they plead Innocence)
These by their own Hands fell,
  Accus'd for this Offence.

X.
A Hundred more we hear,
  Did to this Club belong,
But now they scatter'd are,
  For this has broke the Gang.

XI.
Shop-keepers some there were,
  And Men of good repute,
Each vow'd a Batchelor,
  Unnat'ral Lust pursu'd.

XII.
Ye *Women-Haters* then,
  Take Warning by their Shame,
Your Brutal Lusts restrain,
  And own a Nobler Flame.

XIII.
Woman the chiefest Bliss
  That Heaven e'er bestow'd:
Oh be asham'd of this,
  You're by base Lust subdu'd.

XIV.
This piece of Justice then
  Has well reveng'd their Cause,
And shews unnat'ral Lust
  Is curss'd without the Laws.

Licensed according to Order.

LONDON: Printed for *J. Robinson*, in *Fetter-Lane*, 1707.

The He-Strumpets: A Satyr on the Sodomite-Club
(1707; 1710)

Like the previous selection, *The Women-Hater's Lamentation*, John Dunton's *The He-Strumpets* was prompted by the arrests of more than forty sodomites entrapped by members of the Societies for the Reformation of Manners which occurred in mid-September 1707. No copy exists of the first edition of *The He-Strumpets*, whose publication date is established by an advertisement in the *Post-Man* for 4–7 October 1707: 'This Day is published, / The He Strumpets; a Satyr on the Sodomite Club. Printed for B. Bragge at the Raven in Pater-noster-Row.' Benjamin Bragge published scurrilous pamphlets and early periodicals (such as the *Female Tatler* in 1709). I have found no references to the presumed second and third editions, and no copies exist. We reproduce 'The Fourth Edition, alter'd and much enlarg'd', from Dunton's collection of 'projects', *Athenianism*, published by T. Darrack in 1710 (I. ii. 93–9). The 1707 first edition of *The He-Strumpets* was followed by *Bumography: or, A Touch at the Lady's Tails, Being a Lampoon (Privately) Dispers'd at Tunbridge-Wells, in the Year 1707* (which Narcissus Luttrell says was published on 29 November 1707). In *Bumography*, Dunton has a note referring to 'the *Sodomite-Club*, in my Satyr Entituled the HE-STRUMPETS. Sold by *B. Bragge* in *Pater-noster-Rowe*' (p. ii).

Although *Bumography* is concerned primarily with female 'cracks' or whores, it also contains many references to sodomites, from Tunbridge Wells, where 'MEN grow so Obscene, / That a SHE-WAT'RING hardly cools the Flame, / The *SODOMITE* is now an *English* Name' (p. 53), to Grays Inn Walks, 'Where *Crack* oft sits disconsolate, / Cursing the Rigour of her Fate; (For SHE-TAILS now scarce Earn their Bread, / Since HE-WHORES learnt the *Sodom*-Trade)' (p. 8). A section of two dozen lines in *Bumography* (p. 17) is nearly identical to a section in the 1710 edition of *The He-Strumpets* (93.36–45, 94.1–14 in the text reproduced here). 'KEEPING-LADYS' and 'Preposterous *Venery*' in *Bumography* were changed to '*Stal[lio]n Ladies*', and '*unnat'ral Venery*' in *The He-Strumpets*, an indication of some of the changes that occurred from the first through the fourth editions of *The He-Strumpets*. Both satires have passages on lesbians, the lines in *Bumography* suggesting that women have copied men in their taste for same-sex love:

> Nor are their Flames to Man confin'd,
> But raging, seize on their own Kind.
> *Men's kissing Men* – has brought such Harms,
> Their Love springs now from Female Charms,
> And Man they mimick in each others Arms.
> And here such Deeds remain untold,
> Too gross for modest Ears to hold.
> Cou'd you but hear the *Fine Harangue*
> *In Private, to their Female Gang,*
> The Blood into your Cheeks wou'd rush,
> And *Creswell* (were she living) blush. (p. 18)

(The reference is to Madam or Mother Elizabeth Cresswell (*c.* 1625–84), the notorious Jacobean bawd.)

Dunton (1659–1733) was a bookseller, publisher and journalist whose early works appeared in his *Athenian Gazette* and *Athenian Mercury*. By the early 1700s he was having financial difficulties, and avenged himself upon his numerous creditors by writing *Dunton's Whipping-post, or A Satire upon Everybody* (1706). *Athenianism* (1710) was intended to contain 600 'projects' or essay-treatises, but only one volume appeared. After this, he wrote innumerable political pamphlets from the Whig point of view. He also wrote *King-Abigail: or, The Secret Reign of the She-Favourite* (1715), a mock sermon attacking Abigail Masham's influence over Queen Anne (see headnote to *A New Ballad*, pp. 107–8 below).

The text is reproduced from the copy held by the British Library (shelfmark G.14046).

PROJECT IV.*

The HE-STRUMPETS: *A Satyr* on
the Sodomite-Club.

The Fourth Edition, alter'd and much enlarg'd.

Having giv'n all the Whores a TOUCH*,
The CRACKS will rave and think it much,
If the New *Sodomitish* Crew
Han't a brisk Firking Bout or two,
Such MEN, such *Brutes*, I shou'd them call,
Whose TAILS are Sodomitical,
Shou'd make ev'n POETS to bewail :

* *In a* Satyr *I lately* publish'd, *entitl'd* The Rump; *or a* Touch
at the Ladies Tails.

Shou'd

94 *The* HE-STRUMPETS.

Shou'd wake the flowing Thoughts and Pen
Of *PRIOR*, *GARTH* and *ADDISON*.
But fince thefe *Firft Rates* en't aftride,
I'll try how my dull Mufe will ride.
It is indeed the fouleft Road
That ever POET's COURSER trod:
But *PEGASUS* be not afraid
That you fhou'd Founder, Trip, or Jade:
(No *Pound*, or *Club*, can ftop you long,
Unnatural Sights will make you run.)
Nor think becaufe the Day does waft,
My MUSE will fpur you on too faft,
For *Sodomy*'s fo vile a Crime,
'Tis LASH enough to name the Sin.

Lewd CRACKS repent, for 'tis the News,
Your Tails have burnt fo many Beaus,
That now *He-Whores* are come in Ufe.
Yes Jilts! 'tis prov'd, and muft be faid,
Your Tails are grown fo lewd and bad,
That now *Mens Tails* have all the Trade.
Yet CRACKS are Saints compar'd with them,
Who leave the Whores to pick up Men.
All CRACKS are found fo full of Ails,
A *New Society* prevails,
Call'd S——d——ites; Men worfe than Goats,
Who drefs themfelves in Petticoats,
To Whore as O——born did with O——tes.
Modefty fcarce can give a Name
To fuch a *Catamitifh* Flame;
This Luft as far as *Sodom* came.
In *Sodom* Men were fo unclean,
That when the Angels drefs'd like Men,
They'd afk to fornicate with them.
Then *Sodomy* is the Abufe
Of either Sex, againft the Ufe
Of Nature,—— that fhou'd Babe produce.
When Men with Men—— act what's unchaft,
Then Children (Nature's End) are loft,
And the main End of Woman's croft
When Tails thus Whore, and are uncivil,
They get no Children!—— but the *Devil:*
And yet fuch Tails are found of late
Who thus do Whore and Fornicate
With one another—— *Girls they hate.*

The Men who thus their Luft confine,
Do doat upon *He-Concubine*,

The HE-STRUMPETS. 95

Do Ply (that's Whore) near the *Exchange*;
Here Men turn C R A C K S——— 'tis wond'rous ftrange!
Yet very true——— for thefe exclude
All Women from their Interlude,
Yet act what's carnal, vile, and rude.
The very *Change* can fcarce efcape
This loathfome, nafty *Sodom* Rape.
But what's your Number Brutes? Be free:
'Tis faid your Gang is Forty Three,
That Whore (as 'twere) in *Sodomy.*
He-Whore! The Word's a Paradox;
But there's a Club hard by the *Stocks* *,
Where Men give unto Men the *Pox.*
Such Whoring——— (for I'll call it fo)
Is againft God and Nature too,
And makes Man's Tail a fort of *Stem.*
Such rob the Women of their Rights,
(Their Tails cou'd keep the Peace a' Nights)
But for——— this Club of *Sodomites.*
Thefe doat on Men, and fome on Boys,
And quite abandon Female Joys,
To act a Vice fo full of Shame,
That Brutes wou'd fly, and blufh to name:
For even Goats are grown fo poor,
That *He* with *He* does never Whore.
There's Mr. *Pufs* does caterwaul
With none but Sow-Cats on the Wall,
For Boar-Cats——— he does hate 'em all.
The *Town-Bull* he does never prove
His Mettle in the *He-Alcove,*
The modeft *Cow* has all his Love.
The very *Horfe* fo much does fmother
His wanton Tail from *Rampant Brother,*
That one Horfe never rides another.
And *Sparrow,* tho' a Whoring Tit,
Did ne'er *He-L———ry* commit,
Tho's Tail's a moft Salacious Bit.
  Thus, that the World might multiply,
And Tails might keep their Chaftity,
God did Ordain a *Marriage-Bed,*
That Male with Female ftill fhou'd Wed.
And for the *Goat,* *Pufs,* *Horfe,* and *Sparrow,*
And every Creature ftock'd with *Marrow,*
They do *He-L———ry* deteft;
'Tis only Man that is the Beaft.

---

* *Stocks-Market.*

96   *The* HE-STUMPETS.

'Tis only Men with Men will lie,
And burn their Tails with *Sodomy* ;
The higheſt Flight in *L———ry.*

   Sukey, (for ſo 'tis ſaid you greet
The Men you pick up in the Street)
En't you a MONSTER thus to quench,
And make Mens Tails a ſort of *Wench?*
In ſhort, (and worſe cannot be ſaid)
You are *He-Strumpets* in the Bed.
O fie! remember *Sodom's* MISS,
Unnat'ral Tails was all their Vice:
Your Flame is worſe, that thus rebel,
For *Sodomy's* the Flame of Hell.
O *J———nes!* O *Sodomitiſh* Wretch!
Shou'd you be damn'd you cou'd not grutch ;
You make your very Country bluſh.
He-Luſt! it looks ſo vile in Print,
There's none will ſtand a Trial in't.
They *J———nes* no ſooner did accuſe,
And Two i'th' Compter full as looſe,
But they ſtrait fly to Hempen Nooſe.
Jermain———a Clerk that liv'd i'th' *Eaſt,*
Ber———den a *He-Whoring* Beaſt,
And forty *S——d——ites* at leaſt,
No ſooner did their Lewdneſs flame,
But cut their very Throats for Shame.
Thus of all Tails Mens are the worſt,
Not but the *Females* vie in Luſt ;
For Womens Tails ſo wanton grow,
They breed *unnat'ral Vices* too.
They change the nat'ral Uſe and Feature
Into a Crime which ruins Nature:
Yea, *Sodomy* they will permit,
(A Vice they never can commit)
'Tho' kiſſing each other's ſomething like't.
There's *B———ry*, a Beaſtly Sin,
Is not a Vice too lewd for them:
For 'tis not forty Years ago,
A CRACK was hang'd or Whoring ſo ;
Her *Sparks* were but a Dog or two.
Sure Female Tails deſire to try
Who ſhall exceed in *l———ry!*
'Twas ſaid that *B———* (tho' near a Jayl)
Did Court a Monkey to her Tail ;

---

  * Jermain, *late Clerk of St.* Dunſtan's *in the Eaſt, who being*
charg'd with S——d——y, *cut his Throat with a Razor.*

And

The HE-STRUMPETS. 97

And S———— firſt truck'd her Maiden-head,
Then lov'd and kiſs'd her Huſband dead.
Nay, ſo unnat'ral is this Creature,
She'd almoſt gender with a *Satyr.*
But tho' her Lewdneſs we deplore,
There's none can match the *Common Whore.*

The *Brimſtone Crack* I here arraign,
Who's perfect Beaſt, and perfect Mange:
A *Night-Walker*—— we do her call,
But in the D A Y ſhe'll backwards fall;
She is a Proſtitute to all.
Chaſt Tails we ſafely may careſs,
That ſtrut it in a Paper Dreſs;
But for the Tails that ply for Hire,
They are perfect Brimſtone mix'd with Fire.
The *Common Whore's*——— an Hoſpital!
She muſt be Pox'd that lies with all,
She is not ſqueamiſh in Amour,
She'll lie with Man, with Dog, with Boar:
Who gives her moſt is valu'd beſt;
If it be either Man or Beaſt.
But yet ſhe's cheap in L————ry;
For Two Pence wet and Two Pence dry
Will make the ſtouteſt C R A C K comply,
That does in Street or Brothel ply.
She whores for Money, and wou'd thrive,
But is the pooreſt Slave alive.
The *Night-Walker* ſcarce earns her Breath;
Her Trade's a ſort of P O C K E Y D E A T H.
Then Sirs, who can enough deplore
That very Beaſt———— *A Common Whore?*
Who knows her Arts of drawing in,
And Tails made Broker to the Sin?
Then to the Hoſpital bequeath her;
'Tis there we found her, there we leave her.

But tho' ſhe breeds *unnat'ral* Vice,
There's as much B E A S T in *Keeping Miſs:*
For theſe tranſgreſs as much as thoſe
Who Jilt their Lovers, Pox the Beaus.
The *Stal————n Ladies* here I mean,
Whoſe Goatiſh Tails are ſo unclean,
They buy their Hell, do purchaſe Luſt,
And are of Proſtitutes the worſt.
They'll ſwear, perhaps, that they are Pure,
That none but needy Strumpets Whore;

G g   That

98   *The* HE-STRUMPETS.

That such do scarce of C R A C K partake,
Who only Whore for Whoring sake.
If they do Whore, 'tis with a Friend,
They take no Money, (rather lend)
Turn Tail to Tail and there's an End.
An End! No, Goats, take this from me,
There is no End of *L———ry.*
A Whorish Thought, a Lustful Eye,
And all *unnat'ral Venery,*
Is down-right *Heart Adultery* *.
And thus all Strumpets are the same,
They differ but in Face and Name ;
So early lewd, it may be said
That they scarce had a Maiden-head.
Some may be common, and some kept,
And some may hire what they affect,
But are *unnatural* alike.

Nay, ev'n modest Whores we find
Are to *unnat'ral Vice* enclin'd :
They'll blush for Guilt, smile to do ill ;
But kiss for nothing but to kill.
Modest when just on Whoring bent ;
They tempt when they seem innocent :
Their Coyness is a perfect Slight ;
They use to strengthen Appetite.
And thus unnat'ral and accurst,
They do legitimate their Lust.
Then *Naked Breasts* we shou'd deplore ;
When they heave up so high before,
They speak thus——— *Here Sir is a Whore.*
For why shou'd C R A C K S thus tempt the Men
With naked Breasts and charming Skin,
But that they know we love the Sin ?
Fam'd *C———ly, C———k—* and *L———son* too,
Have lately found (what *L———s* knew)
Below † there's nothing chast or true :
For L U S T you see does Rampant prove,
And then is Christned into L O V E.
So that tho' B E A S T S we are in Shame,
We must be L O V E R S all in Name.

Thus Tails have been unnatural,
In *Men*, in *Wives*, in *Cracks*, in all :

---

* *Mat.* 5. 28.
† Below——— *that's below the Girdle,*

But

The HE-STRUMPETS.

But ftill (as I obferv'd before)
The *Sodomite* does higheft foar ;
For *Men* with very *Men* will Whore.
With *Men!* they'll Whore with *Incubus* ;
If *He's* they care not what's the Curfe :
Their Tail's fo hot, they can't be worfe.
Nor Man nor Turkey can efcape ;
Scarce *J A C K* * himfelf avoid a Rape :
All muft go Padlock'd , if the Rogue
Should bring this *He-Vice* into Vogue.
If Men invent new *L———ry* ,
Sufpect thy Stable's **Chaftity** :
Or, which is yet a lewder Flight ,
Believe thy felf a *Sodomite.*

Thus Tail of Man (add Woman's to't)
When *Sodom's* Vice has burnt it out,
It is no Tail, but perfect Brute.
Brute! O no! It tempts to Evil ;
It is no Brute , but perfect *Devil.*

---

* *The Author of this* Satyr.

The Play of Sodom, A Tragedy (1707)

The title-page of *The Play of Sodom* claims that the play 'was lately Acted on the Stage of *France*, and now occasionally Translated into *English*'. This claim is probably to be understood metaphorically as a suggestion that sodomy has lately been imported into England from abroad. With five acts encompassed in only six pages, it is highly unlikely it was ever acted on any stage, and it does not read like a translation from the French. The topical 'occasion' being referred to is almost certainly the arrest and conviction of numerous sodomites in September–October 1707 (see headnote to *The Women-Hater's Lamentation*, pp. 83–4 above).

The Play of Sodom draws more closely upon the biblical story of Sodom and Gomorrah (Genesis 19) than the other items included in this volume: The Lord devises a test to determine if the inhabitants of Sodom are as wicked as they are said to be. Two angels disguised as men come to the house of Lot in the town of Sodom and are invited in as his guests. The wicked men of Sodom surround the house, demanding of Lot, 'Where are the men who came to you tonight? Bring them out to us, that we may know them.' Lot instead offers them his two virgin daughters: 'let me bring them out to you, and do to them as you please; only do nothing to these men'. The men of Sodom refuse, and attack the house, whereupon they are struck with blindness by the angels. The angels urge Lot and his family to leave the city before it is destroyed by the Lord. The two men who are to marry Lot's daughters think Lot is jesting about the future destruction of the city and stay behind while Lot, his wife and his two daughters flee for their lives. A rain of fire and brimstone consumes the cities of Sodom and Gomorrah. Lot's wife turns to look back, and is turned into a pillar of salt. Lot then has intercourse with his two daughters, begetting the races of the Moabites and the Ammonites.

Many modern biblical scholars argue that the sin of the Sodomites was a failure to recognize the duties of hospitality, rather than homosexuality. Various books in the Palestinian Pseudepigrapha specified the sins of Sodom and Gomorrah as fornication, uncleanliness, 'changing the order of nature' and 'going after strange flesh'. But the commonsense interpretation that the sin of the Sodomites was sodomy has prevailed since about 50 BC. Around AD 100 the interpretation solidified into the story about the homosexual rape of beautiful young men. Nevertheless, the ambiguous ideas of 'against nature' and 'strange flesh' continued to jostle with the specifically homosexual interpretation, as they do in *The Play of Sodom*.

Neither the Bible nor any apocrypha gives the names of Lot's wife or daughters or their husbands-to-be, or the angels, but our author manages to cobble together a set of names for his cast of characters.

The text is reproduced from the copy held by the Bodleian Library, University of Oxford (shelfmark Vet.A4f.480).

THE
PLAY
OF
SODOM,
A
TRAGEDY.

As it was lately Acted on the Stage
of *France*, and now occasionally
Tranflated into *Englifh*.

LONDON:

Printed in the YEAR, 1707.

(3)

The Play of *Sodom*, &c.

Names of the Persons in this Tragedy.

Lot, *a good Man living in* Sodom *for some Years.*
Mabellah, *his Eldest Daughter.*
Jeminah, *his other Daughter.*
Saphira, *the Wife of* Lot, *turn'd into a Pillar of Salt.*
Pharez, *one of* Sodom *that was* Mabellagh's *Husband.*
Jared, *another Person of* Sodom, *who was* Jeminah's *Husband.*
Raphael, Balthazar, *and* Melchior, *Three Angels.*

The P R O L O G U E.

NAY, *if our Sins are grown so high of late,*
  That Heaven scarce can long adjourn our Fate ;
By Raining scalding Showers of Brimstone down,
To burn us, as of old, the lustful Town :
Else a new Deluge overwhelm agen,
And drown at once our Land, our Lives, and Sin.
Judgments of other Kinds are often sent
In Mercy only, not for Punishment ;
But where Lust reigns, it shews a Nation's Fate
Is given up, and past for Reprobate.
Yet hoping, that the noble Reformation
Will soon in Triumph ride throughout the Nation,
And pious Magistrates will quickly quell
Those very Crimes which hatched were in Hell,
That Heaven may not scourge this latter Age
With all the Dregs and Squeezings of his Rage.

ACT

(4)

A C T. I.   *Seene* Sodom. *Enter* Raphael, Balthazar, *and* Melchior, *Three Angels.*

Rap. THIS, this is that defiled, luftful Place,
That's void of Shame, and quite as void of
This City has incenfed Heavenly Ire,   [Grace ;
And fhortly muft in Sulph'rous Flames expire.
   Balt. Were all the World fo wicked as this Town,
Our facred Sovereign Reafon has to frown
On all the Race of Man, and finite them too,
Tho' he was forced to create a new.
   Melc. God has too long born with their Infamy,
And fhould he let his Judgments ftill lie by,
His too much Mercy wou'd make Atheifts fay,
Chance guides the World, and has ufurp'd his Sway.
   Rap. their Guilt's fo great, that it makes Hell confefs
It felf out-done, and fcorn their Wickednefs,
Wherefore let's on our Meffage go, and tell
Old *Lot* to quickly leave this Second Hell,
For e're the Morrow's Sun do's dart his Beams,
This Town fhall drenching lie in Sulph'rous Streams.
                              [*The Angels go out.*

A C T. II.   *Scene a Houfe of Iniquity, where* Pharez *and*
Jared, *the Son-in-Law of* Lot *enter.*

Pharez. LET doating Age debate of Law and Right,
And gravely ftate the Bounds of Juft and fit ;
Whofe Wifdom's but their Envy, to deftroy
And bar thofe Pleafures which they can't enjoy :
Our blooming Years, more fprightly, and more gay,
By Nature were defign'd for Love, and Play :
Youth knows no check, but leaps weak Vertue's Fence,
And briskly hunts the Noble Chafe of Senfe :
Without dull thinking we'll Enjoyment trace,
And call that lawful, whatfoe'er does pleafe.
   Jared. Neither the Awe of Father's Frowns nor Shame,
Nor any gaftlier Fantom, Fear can frame,

                                        Shall

(5)

Shall frighten me into the Road of Bliſs,
But boldly let us ruſh on Wickedneſs :
Where glorious Hazards ſhall enhance delight,
And that, that makes it dang'rous, makes it great.

Phar. Nothing ſhall e're miſlead me from the Road
Of Glory nor infect my Heart with Good :
Never ſhall bold encroaching Vertue dare
With her grim Holy Fate to enter there.

Enters Lot.

Lot. Fie, fie, my Sons, what vicious Words are theſe
I hear, and which muſt Heaven ſore diſpleaſe ?
Leave off your vain Diſcourſe, and ſoon repent,
E'er heavy Judgments on your Heads are ſent.
Heav'n's not for ſuch, whoſe Crimes make Hell too good,
Too mild a Pennance for your curſed Brood ;
For whoſe unheard-of Deeds and damned Sake
Fate muſt below new ſorts of Torture make,
Since, when of old in fram'd that Place of Doom,
'Twas thought no Guilt like this cou'd thither come.

Jared. None but tame ſheepiſh Criminals repent,
Who fear that idle Bug-bear, Puniſhment :
Your gallant Sinner ſcorns that Cowardice,
The poor Regret of having done amiſs ;
Brave he, to his firſt Principles ſtill true,
Can face Damnation, Sin with Hell in view.

Lot. Religion ſure ſhould teach you better Things,
Than thus t'affront your God whole King of Kings ;
Your Maker ſurely cannot long diſpence
With ſuch unnatural Luſts and Impudence.

Phar. Religion ! we that idle Word declaim,
That frivolous Pretence, that empty Name ;
Meer Bug-bear Word, devis'd by States to ſcare
The ſenſleſs Rout to ſlaviſhneſs and Fear ;
Ne're known to awe the brave, and thoſe that dare.

Lot. Baſe filthy Leachers ! of all good bereft,
And ſurely by juſt Heav'n to Ruine left ;

Thy

(6)

Thy Company I loath, and foon I'll find
Some Place of Virtue to divert my Mind.

> [*Lot goes out, and his Two Sons
> in-Law follow him.*

ACT. III. *Scene a Garden, in which* Lot's *Two Daughter's* Mabellah *and* Jeminah *are walking.*

Mab. HOW Infamous and wicked is this Town,
Where Virtue moft young People do difown ;
I wifh my Refidence was in fome Ifle,
Where Grace an Virtue mutually do fmile
For fo abominable is this Place,
That dwelling here to Goodnefs is Difgrace.
    Jem. Was fome kind Guide to lead me on the Way,
No longer in this City wou'd I ftay ;
But wou'd feek out fome Solitude, wherein
I e're might fhroud me from this Place of Sin.
    Mab. Surely they don't confider, ev'ry Place
Offers a Road to cut off Human Race ;
Sometimes with Frowns, fometimes with fmiling Fate,
Th' Ambaffadors of Death our Ends do date ;
By open Force, or fweet Ambufcade
The ftrong ffaults on Human Life is made :
But knowing not how foon, they ought to dread
Their flocking the Plantations af the Dead.

Enter Saphira, *the Wife of* Lot.

    Saph. Seeing how Luft does here in Triumph reign,
From walking in the Garden pray refrain,
Ye are not fafe in this fad Town of Sin,
So Daughters with your Mother ftrait come in.

> [*They all go out.*

ACT.

(7)

A C T. IV. *Scene a Chamber: Enter* Lot *and his Wife* Saphira.

Lot. THE Beaftlinefs that's here my Heart do's grieve,
　　Wherefore the Place I am refolv'd to leave.
Peaceful is he, moft happy and fecure,
Whofe Heart, whofe Soul, and Actions all are pure;
How pleafant, fmooth and pleafing is his way,
Whilft Life's Meander daily flides away.
If a fierce Thunderbolt fho'ld chance to fly,
This quiet Man can unconcerned lie;
As knowing 'tis not levell'd at his Head,
So neither Noife or Flafhes does he dread.
Tho' a fwift Storm or Whirlwind tears in funder
Heaven above him, or the Earth that's under;
Nay, tho' the Maffy Rocks on heaps do tumble;
Or if the World fhould into Afhes crumble;
Tho' the ftupendious Mountains from on high
Drop down, and in their humble Vallies lie;
Or fhould the deep unruly Ocean roar,
And dafh its raging Foam againft the Shoar;
He finds no frightful Tempeft in his Mind,
Fears neither Billows, nor the bluftring Wind;
All is Serene, all very quiet there,
There's not one Blaft of troubled Air,
Old may often fall, or new ones blaze,
Yet none of thefe his Pious Soul amaze,
Such is the Man can fmile at irkfome Death,
And with an eafie Sigh give up his Breath.
　Saph. Then let us both endeavour ftrait to find
A Place, that may be peaceful to our Mind.
　　　　　　　　　　　　[*They both go off.*

A C T. V. *Scene reprefents* Lot's *Houfe.* Enter Three *Angels,* Lot, *his Wife, and Two Daughters.*

Raph. FROM Heaven we are on a Meffage fent,
　　To warn you of approaching Punifhment,

That's

(6)

That's near at Hand upon this Town to fall,
Because amongst this Num'rous People all,
Not Five Just Persons can be found to save
The Wicked from Destruction and the Grave.

    Lot. Where'er your Orders are, I shall obey,
And for such Grace to me shall ever pray.

    Bait. Oh! how excessive's the inglorious Lust,
That makes the filthy *Sodomites* accurst :
It eggs 'em on so much to slight the Rod
Of an All-seeing and revengeful God,
That in Conjunction they did strive to joyn
With Substances Ætherial and Divine ;
As if it was their Thoughts to get a Race
Of Demi-gods, to guard this cursed Place.

    Saph. Their filthy Crimes for Wrath Divine does call,
And now I see upon 'em it will fall.

    Melch. That God who batters Kingdoms with his Rod,
And makes the Mountains stagger with a Nod,
Has doom'd this lustful Town to Brimstone Fire,
Therefore from hence this Night *Lot* must retire,
With you, *Saphira,* his beloved Wife,
And both your Daughters ; so secure your Life.
                              [*Angels vanish.*

    Mab. Dear Father let us quickly shun this Place.
Which is so much a stranger unto Grace.

    Jem. Our safety don't let us too long delay,
Lest Heaven shou'd be angry at our stay.

    Lot. Prepare, prepare to bid this Town adieu,
For unto *Zoar* I'll go along with you ;
And since such Favour in my Maker's sight
I've found, I'll leave the Wicked Place this Night ;
And when the Morning in her Crimson's Drest,
Breaks through the glorious Windows of the *East,*
My Hymns of thankful Praises shall arise,
Like Incense, or the Morning Sacrifice.

F I N I S.

A New Ballad. To the Tune of Fair Rosamond (1708)

A New Ballad is an attack on Queen Anne's 'she-favourite', Abigail Masham (née Hill). Abigail's mother, Mary Jennings, was an aunt of Sarah Jennings, who married John Churchill, 1st Duke of Marlborough. Through the influence of Sarah, Duchess of Marlborough, Abigail was appointed a woman of the bedchamber to Queen Anne around 1704. In 1707 she privately married Samuel Masham, a groom of the bedchamber to Prince George of Denmark, Anne's consort. By that time she had supplanted Sarah in the Queen's favour. Sarah charged '*that Mrs.* MASHAM *came often to the* QUEEN *when the* PRINCE *was asleep, and was generally two hours every day in private with her*' (see her *Account of the Conduct of the Dowager Duchess of Marlborough* (1742), p. 184).

Abigail may also have been a distant cousin of the political intriguer Robert Harley, whom she helped to gain much influence at court. Even after his dismissal in February 1708, Harley remained in contact with the Queen through Abigail, and eventually helped the Queen to overthrow Marlborough's Whig ministry in 1710, two years after publication of *A New Ballad*.

Sarah knew of these intrigues from 1707 and bitterly resented that Abigail commanded the 'back way to the Queen's closet' (letter to David Mallet, 24 Sept. 1744, quoted in G. M. Trevelyan, *England under Queen Anne* (1932), vol. ii, p. 329). In 1711 Harley became 1st Earl of Oxford, Sarah was dismissed from office, and Abigail took control of the privy purse. In 1712 she was made a peer by the Queen (by making her husband the 1st Baron Masham), on condition that she continue as her bedchamber woman. In 1714 Abigail, now Lady Masham, quarrelled with Harley and procured his dismissal. However, the Queen died shortly afterwards, and Abigail went into retirement; she died in 1734. Jonathan Swift praised Abigail's plain understanding, her truthfulness and sincerity, and her unmitigated love for the Queen, whom she cared for in her long final illness. To some extent Abigail was a convenient tool for Harley and the Queen, but she was undoubtedly an assiduous intriguer herself, and clearly exercised the powers of a classic 'favourite'.

The lampoon *A New Ballad* was probably written by Arthur Maynwaring (1668–1712), the Duchess of Marlborough's private secretary and propagandist. His authorship seems confirmed by letters from him to

Sarah expressing sentiments expressed in the ballad, sometimes in the same words. Sarah went so far as to show the lampoon to the Queen and to follow it up with a belligerent letter (16 July 1708) to her, urging her to drop Abigail because of such publicity: 'I remember you said att the same time of all things in this world, you valued most your reputation, which I confess surpris'd me very much, that your Majesty should so soon mention that word after having discover'd so great a passion for such a woman, for sure there can be noe great reputation in a thing so strange & unaccountable, to say noe more of it, nor can I think the having noe inclination for any but one's own sex is enough to maintain such a character as I wish may still bee yours'.

A New Ballad was followed into print by *The Rival Dutchess; or, Court Incendiary* (1708), also probably by Maynwaring. Sarah described this pamphlet to the Queen in November 1709, saying that it contained 'stuff, not fit to be mentioned, of passions between women' (cited by Edward Gregg, *Queen Anne* (London, 1980), p. 295). In this imaginary dialogue, Abigail tells Madame de Maintenon that 'especially at *Court* I was taken for a more modish Lady, that was rather addicted to another Sort of Passion, of having too great a Regard for my own Sex, insomuch that few People thought I would ever have Married; but to free my self from that Aspersion some of our Sex labour under, for being too fond of one another, I was resolved to Marry as soon as I could fix to my Advantage or Inclination' (p. 6). Madame de Maintenon asks if the 'Female Vice, which is the most detestable in Nature' is as common in England as in the French convent schools, and Abigail assures her that 'we are arriv'd to as great Perfection in sinning that way as you can pretend to' (p. 6).

Harley's (failed) impeachment in 1715 is the subject of John Dunton's pamphlet *King-Abigail: or, The Secret Reign of the She-Favourite* (1715). He calls Abigail a '*Succubus*…who from the poor Degree of a *Chamber-Maid*, was at length made the Queen's Principal She-Favourite.…*Abigail the Favourite Reign's like a King*' (p. 15). Both *A New Ballad* and *King-Abigail* suggest that Abigail and Harley want to betray England to the Pretender, James Edward Stuart, and to Roman Catholicism.

The text is reproduced from the copy held by the British Library (shelfmark 162.m.70 (11)).

A New BALLAD.

To the Tune of *Fair Rosamond.*

I.

WHen as Qu---- *A*---- of great Renown
    Great Britain's Scepter ſway'd,
Beſides the Church, ſhe dearly lov'd
    A Dirty Chamber-Maid.

II.

O ! *Abi*---- that was her Name,
    She ſtarch'd and ſtitch'd full well,
But how ſhe pierc'd this Royal Heart,
    No Mortal Man can tell.

III.

However for ſweet Service done,
    And Cauſes of great Weight,
Her Royal Miſtreſs made her, Oh !
    A Miniſter of State.

Her Secretary ſhe was not,
    Becauſe ſhe could not write,
But had the Conduct and the Care
    Of ſome dark Deeds at Night.

V.

The Important Paſs of the Back-Stairs
    Was put into her Hand ;
And up ſhe brought the greateſt R----
    Grew in this fruitful Land.

VI.

And what am I to do, quoth he,
    Oh ! for this Favour great !
You are to teach me how, quoth ſhe,
    To be a Sl---- of State.

VII.

My Diſpoſitions they are good,
    Miſchievous and a Lyar ;
A ſaucy, proud, ungrateful B----,
    And for the Church entire.

VIII.

Great Qualities, quoth *Machiavel !*
    And ſoon the World ſhall ſee,
What you can for your Miſtreſs do,
    With one ſmall Daſh of me.

IX.

In Counſel ſweet, Oh ! then they ſat,
    Where ſhe did Griefs unfold,
Had long her grateful Heart oppreſs'd,
    And thus her Tale ſhe told.

X.

From Shreds and Dirt in low Degree,
    From Scorn in piteous State,
A Dutcheſs bountiful has made
    Of me a Lady Great.

XI.

Some Favours ſhe has heap'd upon
    This undeſerving Head,
That for to eaſe me, from their Weight,
    Good God, that ſhe were dead !

XII.

Oh ! let me then ſome means find out,
    This Teazing Debt to pay :
I think, quoth he, to get her Place,
    Would be the only way.

XIII.

For leſs than you ſhe muſt be brought,
    Or I can never ſee
How you can pay the Boons receiv'd,
    When you are leſs than ſhe.

XIV.

My Arguments lies in few words,
    Yet not the leſs in Weight ;
And oft with good Succeſs we uſe
    Such, in Affairs of State.

XV.

Quoth ſhe, 'tis not to be withſtood,
    I'll puſh it from this Hour :
I will be grateful, or at leaſt
    I'll have it in my Power.

XVI.

Quoth he, ſince my poor Counſel gains
    Such favour in your Eye,
I have a ſmall Requeſt to make,
    I hope you won't deny.

XVII. Some

XVII.

Some Bounties I like you have had
  From one that bears the Wand,
And very fain I would, like you,
  Repay them if I can.

XVIII.

Witnefs ye Heavens! how I wifh
  To flide into his Place;
Only to fhew him Countenance,
  When he is in Difgrace.

XIX.

Oh! would you ufe your Intereft great
  With our moft Gracious Q---,
Such things I'd quickly bring about
  This Land hath never feen.

XX.

Give me but once her Royal Ear,
  Such Notes I'll in it found,
As from her fweet Repofe fhall make
  Her Royal Head turn round.

XXI.

He fpoke, and ftraitway it was done,
  She gain'd him free accefs;
God long preferve our Gracious Q----,
  The Parliament no lefs!

XXII.

Now from this Hour it was remark'd,
  That there was fuch Refort
Of many great and high Divines
  Unto the Q-----'s fair Court.

XXIII.

Myfterious things that long were hid,
  Began to come to light;
And many of the Church's Sons
  Were in a Zealous Fright.

XXIV.

'Twas faid, with Sighs and anxious Looks,
  A General Abroad,
Had won more Battles than their Friends,
  The *French*, could well afford.

XXV.

That fo much Mony had been fent,
  Such needlefs things t' advance;
It fure was time, as in Reigns pafs'd,
  Some now fhould come from *France*.

XXVI.

At laft they fpoke it out, and faid,
  'Twas of the laft import,
That there fhould be a thorough Change
  In Army, Fleet, and Court.

XXVII.

For wicked *J*-----*y M*-----*b*
  So madly pufh'd things on,
That fhould he unto *Paris* go,
  The Church was quite undone.

XXVIII.

The Wife and Pious Q------ gave ear
  To this devout Advice,
And honeft fturdy *S*------*d*,
  Was whip'd up in a Trice.

XXIX.

A vaft! cry'd out the Admiral;
  No-near, you Rogues, no-near!
Your Ship will be amongft the Rocks,
  If at this rate you fteer!

XXX.

With that the Man that kept the Cafh,
  Slipt in a word or two;
Which made an old Acquaintance think
  This Game would never do.

XXXI.

He but one Eye had in his Head,
  But with that one he faw,
Thefe Priefts might bring about his Ends
  A thing we call Club-Law.

XXXII.

He on his Pillow laid his Head,
  And on mature Debate
With that, and what his Wife refolv'd,
  To play a Trick of State.

XXXIII.

Like Dr. *B*----*s* much renown'd,
  Of one he did take care;
Then flipt his Cloak, and left the reft
  All in moft fad Defpair.

XXXIV.

The Confequence of this was fuch,
  Our Good and Gracious Q-----,
Not knowing why fhe e'er went wrong,
  Came quickly right again.

XXXV.

However, taking fafe Advice
  From thofe that knew her well,
She *Ab*----*l* turn'd out of Doors,
  And hang'd up *Machiavel*.

F I N I S.

The Second Part, Of the London Clubs (1709)

Edward (Ned) Ward's *The History of the London Clubs, or, The Citizens Pastime*, part I, an eight-page chapbook published in 1701, described the Lying Club, the Yorkshire Club, the Thieves Club, the Beggars Club, the Broken Shopkeepers Club, and the Basket Womans Club. In 1709 another eight-page chapbook, *The Second Part, Of the London Clubs*, described the No-Nose Club, the Beaus Club, the Farting Club, the Sodomites or Mollies Club and the Quacks Club; the volume was published together with a reissue of part I. These pamphlets were printed by J. Dutton and identified as being 'By the Author of the *London Spy*' – referring to Ward's famous periodical. Before the end of 1709, expanded descriptions of the clubs in these two works were incorporated, together with additional clubs, into *The Secret History of Clubs*. This bears the date 1709, but no printer is given. In 1710, J. Phillips published *Satyrical Reflections on Clubs*, which is just a reissue of *The Secret History of Clubs*. In 1710 (or 1709) there appeared *The Second Part of the History of the London Clubs*, containing only the Farting, No-Nos'd, Misers and Atheistical Clubs, bearing no imprint, probably a pirated edition. Part I of *The History of the London Clubs* was republished in 1711, by J. Bagnall. In 1745 *A Compleat and Humorous Account of All the Remarkable Clubs and Societies in The Cities of London and Westminster* was published by Joseph Collier, which was a duodecimo reprint of *The Secret History of Clubs*; this was reissued in 1756 by J. Wren.

We have chosen to reproduce *The Second Part, Of the London Clubs* because it contains the first appearance of the Sodomites or Mollies Club. In its second appearance shortly thereafter, as 'Chap. XXV. Of the *Mollies* Club' in *The Secret History of Clubs* (1709), Ward more than doubled the length of the original prose sketch by adding a section on all the bustle of the mock christening, dressing the 'baby' and observing how closely he resembled his 'father'; and by greatly expanding the section on the tattle of the midwives (pp. 284–8). He also added a forty-three-line poem (pp. 288–90, misnumbered 288, 299, 300) characterizing sodomites as brutes:

> 'Tis strange that in a Country where
> Our Ladies are so Kind and Fair,
> . . . .
> That Men should on each other doat,

And quit the charming Petticoat.

. . . .

'Tis true, that Swine on Dunghills bred,
Nurs'd up in Filth, with Offel fed,

. . . .

But Men who chuse this backward Way,
Are fifty Times worse Swine than they:
For the less Savage four-leg'd Creature,
Lives but according to his Nature:
But the *Bug[ge]ranto* two leg'd Brute,
Pursues his Lust contary to't;

. . . .

But *Sodomites* their Wives forsake,

Unmanly Liberties to take,
And fall in Love with one another,
As if no Woman was their Mother:

. . . .

May he that on the Rump so doats,
Be Damn'd as deep as Doctor *Oates* [Titus Oates],
That Scandal unto all black Coats.

Dunton's *The He-Strumpets* (orig. pub. 1707), which also employs the rhyme 'goats / petticoats / Titus Oates', may have been a direct influence upon Ward.

Ward's decision to write about the Sodomites or Mollies Club may have been prompted by the arrest of a gang of nine sodomites after a raid on the back room of a brandy shop in Jermyn Street in 1709, organized by undercover agents of the Societies for the Reformation of Manners, to which Ward refers at the end of his sketch. The Societies' agents acted on the basis of information given by George Skelthorpe, a soldier and blackmailer of sodomites who was hanged at Tyburn on 23 March 1709 for assault and robbery. (He claimed these were false charges brought by two sodomites.) Two broadsheets were published in 1709, *A Full and True Account of the Discovery and Apprehending a Notorious Gang of Sodomites in St. James's*, and Paul Lorrain, *The Ordinary of Newgate His Account of…George Skelthorpe*.

The text is reproduced from the copy held by the Houghton Library, Harvard University (shelfmark EC7.w2113.709h).

The Second PART,

OF THE

LONDON CLUBS;

CONTAINING,

The No-Nose *Club*,	⎱ ⎰	The Sodomites, or
The Beaus *Club*,	⎰ ⎱	Mollies *Club*.
The Farting *Club*,	⎱ ⎰	The Quacks *Club*,

By the Author of the London Spy.

LONDON, Printed by *J. Dutton,* near *Fleet-street,* also the First Part.

(2)

Of the N O - N O S E - C L U B.

A MER R Y Gentleman who had often hazarded
his own Boltſplit, by ſteering a Vitious Courſe
among the Rocks of *Venus*, having obſerv'd in
his walks thro' our *Engliſh Sodom*, that abundance of both Sexes had Sacrificed to the God *Priapus*, and
had unluckily fallen into the *Æthiopian* Faſhion of Flat-Faces,
pleas'd himſelf with an Opinion, it muſt prove a comical ſight
for ſo many maim'd Leachers ; ſnuffling old Stallions; young
unfortunate Whoremaſters ; poor ſcarify'd Bawds ; and ſali-
vated Whetſtones, to ſhew their ſcandalous Vizards in one
Noſe-leſs Society ; To accompliſh which, he made it his buſineſs, for ſome time, to ſtrole about the Town, on purpoſe
to pick acquaintance with all ſuch ſtigmatiz'd Strumpets and
Fornicators, as he thought might be proper Members of the
Snuffling Community, pretending ſome thing or other that
carry'd a face of Intereſt to all that he talk'd with, appoint-
ing every one apart to meet him at the *Dog-Tavern* in *Drury-
Lane*, upon a certain Day, a little before Dinner-time, that
they might Eat a bit together, and he would then acquaint
them with the Secret. Being a well-bred Gentleman, and a
Perſon that behav'd himſelf, to all he ſpoke to, with an un-
ſuſpected Gravity ; when the Day appointed came, every
one was curious to know the upſhot of the Matter. The Gentleman, againſt the time, having order'd a very plentiful Dinner, acquainted the Vintner, who were like to be his Gueſts,
that he might not be ſurpriz'd at ſo ill-favour'd an appearance, but pay them that Reſpect, when they came to ask for
him, that might encourage them to tarry. When the Morning came, no ſooner was the hand of *Covent-Garden* Dial upon the ſtroak of the Hour prefix'd ; but the No-Noſe Company began to drop in apace, like Scald-Heads and Cripples to
a Mumper's Feaſt, asking for Mr. *Crumpton*, which was the
feign'd Name the Gentleman had taken upon him, ſucceed-
ing one another ſo thick, with jarring Voices, like the brazen Strings of a crack'd Dulcimore, that the Drawer could
ſcarce ſhew one up Stairs before he had another to conduct ;
the anſwer at the Bar being, to all that enquir'd, That Mr.
Crumpton had been there, and deſir'd every one that ask'd for
him

(3)

wuold walk up Stairs, and he would wait upon them present-
ly. As the Number encreas'd, the Surprife grew the greater
among all that were prefent, who ftar'd at one another with
fuch unaccuftom'd Bafhfulnefs, and confus'd Odnefs, as if e-
very Sinner beheld their own Iniquities in the Faces of their
Companions.

The Dinner being now brought to the Table, and the
Scare-Crows feated according to their Seniority, as foon as
their Food was fanctify'd with a fhort Grace, they all fell to
Grinding and Snuffling, for want of clear Paffages, like fat
Aldermen at my Lord-Mayor's Feaft, who when tir'd with
their Journy from *London* to *Weftminfter*, commonly eat their
Cuftard between fleeping and waking. Among the reft of
the Entertainment, there happen'd to be a couple of fat Pigs,
which the Cook to make a Jeft had merrily fent up with both
their Snouts cut off: The Gentleman being offended to fee
the Pigs Heads fo ftrangely mangl'd, fent for the Cook up
ftairs to know the Reafon of it, who anfwer'd, ' He had cut
' off their Snouts to put the Pigs in the Fafhion ; for that he
' thought it not fit for two fuch fqueamifh Creatures, to run
' their unmannerly Nofes into fuch good Company that had
' but one amongft them. A Pox take you, *Reply'd an old Snuf-*
' *fler*, for the Son of a Dripping-pan! The fewer Nofes there
' are in the company, the more there ought to be in the
' Feaft, for the Ladies know that flat things always love long
' Snouts.

As foon as they had eaten off the Edge of their Appetites,
being all highly pleas'd with their plentiful Entertainment,
the Founder's Health was difh'd about in a Bumper, till they
all grew as Frolickfome as fo many Jugs and Bumkins at a
Country Houfe-Warning; and then they began to Jeft, and
be Merry with one another's Iniquities, as if their Sins were
their Pride, and their Sufferings their Glory, every one being
as free of their paft Vices and Intrigues, as Goffips o er their
Ale, are of their Husbands Infirmities, that the fingle-Nos d
Gentleman was fo delighted with his Guefts, that he gave
them his Company moft part of the Day, and fat like *Don*
John among his gaftly Affembly of defac'd Monuments, juft
ftarted from their Pediftals to take a Dinner with the Libertine.

But the bountiful Promoter, within lefs than a Year hap-
pening, in fpight of his Nofe, to Die in a Salivation, the

A 2   Flat

(4)

Flat- Fac'd Community were unhappily Diſſolv'd : The laſt of their Meeting, at the requeſt of the Deceas'd, being to Solemnize his Funeral, where every one had a Ring, in *Pia Memoriᴀ* of their Generous Benefactor, whoſe Remains were Honour'd with the following Elegy,

Mourn all ye No-Nos'd Bullies of the Age,
Whoſe batter'd Snouts the World's decay preſage,
And ſhew, whilſt Living, how the faireſt Faᴛ,
Adorn'd by Nature with each Charming Grace,
Tho' a Chaſte ſtranger to the Joys of Love,

Muſt Rot when Underground, like yours Above ;
And that fair Bridge, which in ſuch form does grow,
Beneath whoſe Griſtly Arch ſuch Juices flow,
When Dead, like your fallen Noſes, e'er you die,
Muſt tumble, and in Flat Diſorder lie.

The BEAUS CLUB.

THis Finikin Society, or Ladys Lap-Dog Club, is now kept at a certain Tavern near *Covent-Garden*, where every Afternoon the Fantaſtical Idols, aſſemble themſelves in a Body, to compare Dreſſes, invent new Faſhions, talk Bawdy, and drink Healths to their Miſtreſſes. At the upper end of their Club-room, ſtands a Side-board Table, which is conſtantly furniſh'd with a Dozen of Flannel Muckinders, folded up for rubbing the Duſt off of their Upper-Leathers, or an unfortunate Speck off their Scabbards of their Swords. Next to theſe cleanly Neceſſaries, ſtands an Olive-Box, full of the beſt perfum'd Powder, crown'd with three or four mighty Combs, that their Wigs may be continually new ſcented, and every ſtragling Hair that has been rufled by a Storm of their Miſtreſſes Breath, may be carefully put into Orders. Round the Edges of the Table lies ſtrew'd by way of Garniſh, Sciſſars. Tooth-pickers, and Tweezers : Patches, Eſſences, Pomatums, Paſtes, Patches, and Waſhes, with all the artful impliments Woman can invent, to turn Men into Monkeys: So that the Sir Foplings are no ſooner met, but they are as buſie as ſo many Stage-Players before a Comedy, dizening their ill ſhap'd Carcaſſes, and Apes Faces. Then down they ſit to their *Champaigne, Burgundy,* and *Hermatige,* pull out their gilt Snuſh-Boxes, with Orangeree, *Brazil,* and plain *Spaniſh,* that each may feed his Elephants Trunk with Odoriferous Duſt, and make his Breath as ſweet as an *Arabian* Breeze, to the Noſtrils of a Seaman ; and when they are thus ſcented, down goes a delicious Health to ſome Celebrated Harlot, nay Houſe Punk ; or Court Courtezan.   When

(5)

When the Modifh Fops, *Amoretta*'s have drank fo many fe-
lect Healths to their Miftreffes, without the danger of raifing
Pimples on their Faces, then they pay their Reckonings, tiff
up the Fore-tops of their Wiggs, with their Alabafter Figures,
and walk bare-headed to the Play-Houfe, where they commonly arrive about the Third Act, by which time the Ladies,
who care not much to appear by Day-light, are bolted from
their Stews, and *Drury-lane* Alleys, to fneak into the Pit, and
Eighteenpenny Gallery, without Tickets, at the Courtifie
of the Door-keepers, when thefe gaudy Cringing Coxcombs
have thus met with their Matches, they tattle away the Play
time among their Half-Crown Punks, till one of the Fraternity of fham Heroes, makes an humble Bow to the Box Ladies, and the reft follow him according to their Cuftom, to
Drinking, Whoring and Gaming, till next Morning.

To be a Modifh Fop, a Beau compleat,
Is to pretend to, but be void of Wit :
'Tis to be Squeamifh, Critical, and Nice
In all things, and Fantaftick to a Vice ;
'Tis to feem knowing, tho' he nothing
(nows:
And vainly lewd to pleafe his Brother
[Beaus;
'Tis in his Drefs to be profufely Gay,
And to affect Whore-like, a wanton way;
'Tis to be charm'd with each new fafhi-
(oh'd Whim,
And to be modifh to a vain extream,
That each gay Punk a luftful Eye may

[rowl,
And for his Shapes admire the pretty fool;
'Tis to attack the Ladies with a Grace,
And ftill tranfer his Love to each new
[Face,
Flutter about his Charms, till like a Fly,
Burnt by the Flame, he's fcorch'd amidft
[this Joy ;
Then Curfing of the B----ch, is forc'd to
[cool
The Pocky Heat, by running oft to Stool;
Till with repeated Purges, by degrees,
The pricking pains and Inflamations ceafe

The Sodomites, *or* Mollies C L U B.

There are are a particular Gang of Sodomitical Wretches
in Town, who call themfelves *Mollies*, and are fo far dege-
nerated from all Mafculine Deportment, or Manly Exercifes, that they rather fancy themfelves Women, imitating all
the little Vanities that Cuftom has reconcil'd to the Female
Sex, affecting to fpeak, walk, tattle, curtfy, cry, fcold, and
mimick all manner of Effeminacy. At a certain Tavern in
the City, whofe Sign I fhall not mention, becaufe I am un-
willing to fix an *Odium* on the Houfe, they have a fettled and
conftant Meeting. When they are met together, their ufual
Practice is to mimick a Female Goffiping, and fall into all
the impertinent Tittle Tattle, that a merry Society of good
Wives

(6)

Wives can be fub'ect to : Not long fince they had cufhion'd up the Belly of one of their Sodomitical Brethren, or rather Sifters, according to Female Dialect, difguifing him in a Woman's Night-Gown, Sarfenet-hood, and Night-rail, who when the Company were met, was to mimick the wry Faces of the Groaning Woman, to be deliver'd of a Jointed-Baby, they had provided, and to undergo all the Formalities of a Lying-in. The wooden Offspring to be afterwards Chriften-ed, whilft one in a High Crown'd Hat, I am old Beldams Pinner, reprefenting a Country-Midwife, and another di-zen'd up in a Hufwife's Coif for a Nurfe, and all the reft of an impertinent *Decorum* of a Chriftening.

And for the further Promotion of their unbecoming Mirth, every one was to talk of their Husbands and Children, one extolling the Virtues of her Husband, another the Genius and Wit of their Children ; whilft a third would exprefs himfelf forrowfully under the Character of a Widow.

Thus every one in his turn makes Scoff of the little Effemi-nacy, and Weakneffes, which Women are fubject to : when Goffiping o'er their Cups, on purpofe to extinguifh that Na-tural Affection which is due to the fair Sex, and to turn their Juvenile Defires, towards preternatural Polotions. No foon-er have they ended their Feafts and run through all the Cere-monies of Theaterical way of Goffiping, then they begin to enter upon their Beaftly Obfcenities, that no Man who is not funk into a State of Devilifm can think on without Blufhing : Which Practice they continu'd till they were happily routed by the conduct of fome of the under Agents, to the Reform-ing Society ; fo that feveral of them were brought to open Punifhment, which happily put a Period to their Scandalous Revels.

The Quacks *Club.*

THE Empericks of the Town, *alias,* Licens'd Phyfici-ans as to Scandal of the College, they are pleas'd to call themfelves, that they might be the better able to pro-mote the Intereft of Quackifm, thought it neceffary fome Weeks fince, to hold a Weekly Correfpondence at a certain Tavern near the Change, that they might not only be able to be of mutual Service to each other, but defend their

Pre-

(7)

Pretenfions ro Phyfick, Chymiftry, &c. againft all oppo-
fers : Upon their firft meeting, Dr. *Saffold's* Succeffor had
the Honour to be chofen by the Majority of High-German
Coblers, Dutch-Tumblers, and Englifh Rope-Dancers,
Prolocutor to the Society, and took his Place at the Board
in an Elbow-Chair accordingly : every formal Student in
the Twin Sciences or Pedentry of Phyfick and Aftrology,
having fo ftrict a regard to the Gravity of their Profeffion,
that they grac'd the folemn Junto with their Ebony Canes,
Bands, and all their Querpo Formalities, as if they were going to Dine with my Lord, and to beg leave of the City to
pull down the Statue of King *Charles* II. and to erect a
Monutebanks Stage in the middle of the Exchange, that
by felling Packets of a Noble Cathartick, call'd *Pitula Ho-
nefta*, they might purge all manner of Knavery out of the
canker'd Confciences of Change-Brokers and Stockjobbers.
When thefe Medicinal Coxcombs have exemplified at large
the infallible Virtues of their Popular Pills, Univerfal Powders, and fundry forts of Panaceas, Noftrums, Hodge-
Podges, and Cathalicons, then the wonderful Cures they
have performed are feperately difcanted on : Such inimita-
ble Miracles upon Country Chubs, Old Nurfes, fick Cham-
ber-Maids' and Lame-Mumpers, that are never to be for-
gotten, whilft we have a Sir *Will--m* in his Coach and Six,
or a famous Dr. *Gately* with his numerous Retinue of Vaul-
ters, Tumblers and Rope-Dancers, to fupport the Memory
of their Emperical Predeceffors. For when our Modern
Operators mount their Country Scaffolds, with their Train
of *Bartholomew*-Fools, furrounded with a gaping Crowd of
Dairy Drudging Jugs, and Rural *Coridons* ; then, that their
Packet Speeches may be larded with fomething that may feem
Learned, *Ceffante Tollitur, caufa Effectus*, fays the Plufh Jacket Doctor, was the good faying of that famous Phyfician
Dr. *Kerleus*, who, for his Countries good, Travell'd as I do ;
which is as much as to fay, if you take my Phyfick you may
be fure of a cure.

For the fake of thefe, and fuch like Advantages, they
continu'd their weekly Meeting, during one whole Winter ;
but Summer coming on, the greateft part drawing off, to
their country Circuits, and the reft in their cups contending
about their skill, and the Excellency and Efficacy of their

never

(8)

never failing Remedies, fell together by the Ears on the first of *April* last, and so like April Fools, put an End to their Society, verifying the old Proverb, That two of a Trade can never agree.

Of all the Plagues with which our Land is Curst,
The Frauds rf Physick seem to be the worst.
For tho' the Law, 'tis true, abounds with Weeds,
And from Astrea's Rules too oft receeds,
Yet those keen Foxes of such sundry sorts,
Who hang in Swarms about her awful Courts,

By their Male Practice, and Prolix Debates,
Can only hurt our Pockets and Estates;

But baneful Quacks, in Physick's Art un-read,
To Weaving, Cobling, or to Tumbling bred,
Or else poor Scoundrels, who for Scraps and Thanks
Swept Stages for their Master Mountebank.
These to the World destructive Slops com-mend,
And do their poys'nous Cheats to Life ex-tend;
By vain Pretences pick the Patent's Purse,
And with sham Med'cines make 'em ten times worse.

Of the FARTING Club.

OF all the fantastick Clubs that ever took Pains to make themselves Stink in the Nostrils of the Publick, sure no ridiculous community ever came up to this windy Socie-ty, which was certainly Establish'd by a parcel of empty Sparks, about thirty years since, at a Publick-House in *Crip-ple-Gate* Parish, where they us'd to meet once a Week to poi-son the Neighbouring Air with their unsavoury *Crepitations,* and were so vain in their Ambition to out Fart one another, that they us'd to Diet themselves against their club-Nights, with cabbage, Onions, and Pease-Porridge, that every one's Bumfiddle might be the better qualified to sound forth its Emulation.

Since he who by deceitful Arts,
With Arms instead of Arse lets Fart,
Shall be Dispis'd, because his Fun,
Can't fairly call the Sound its own.

Then what must he deserve who Steals
His Wit, and treads on others Heels?
Whose busie Tongue makes publick use
Of what his Brains could ne'er produce.

FINIS.

Love-Letters between a Certain Late Nobleman and the Famous Beau Wilson (1723)

According to Narcissus Luttrell, in his diary for 10 April 1694, towards the end of 1693 Captain Edward Wilson, whose good looks and extravagance earned him the sobriquet Beau Wilson, was living at the astonishing rate of £4,000 per annum, without any visible estate. John Evelyn similarly wondered how this younger son of a man of only middling wealth had managed to live 'in the Garb & Equipage of the richest Noble man in the nation for House, Furniture, Coaches & 6 horses, & other saddle horses; Table & all things accordingly' (diary, 22 Apr. 1694).

These diary reflections arose because on 9 April 1694 Wilson was killed in a swordfight by John Law (1621–1729) following a heated exchange of letters between them. Law claimed that Wilson had taken his sister from a lodging house in which Law's mistress resided, thereby suggesting that the house was a brothel. One day Law forced a quarrel with Wilson as he was drinking with his friend Captain Wightman at the Fountain Inn on the Strand. Wightman and Wilson left the tavern and got into a carriage. Law followed and stopped the carriage in Bloomsbury Square. Wilson alighted and drew his sword. Law drew his sword and killed Wilson with the first thrust. It was a premeditated assault, unfairly fought, without any of the niceties of a duel. Law was tried for murder, convicted on 19 April and sentenced to death on 20 April (*Trial of John Lawe*, in *Proceedings in the Old Bailey* for 18–20 Apr. 1694). The sentence was commuted to a fine, but Wilson's family appealed that decision. While awaiting the outcome, Law filed through the bars of his prison window and fled abroad.

The Plot Discover'd: or Captain Wilson's Intreigues Open (1694) revealed that Captain Wilson served for a short time in Flanders before his uncle, a colonel of a regiment, sent him home because 'his Comliness and Presence' were judged 'to be much fitter for a Courtier than a Soldier' (p. A3r). After only six months in England, he was observed to 'appear in that Pomp and Grandieur becoming the Quality of a Peer' (p. A3v), living in ever-increasing magnificence until his death. According to *The Plot Discover'd*, many people believed that Wilson was maintained by a woman, and 'there is but one Dutchess in the Kingdom able to support a Gallant in the expensive Grandeur of his Living' (p. A4r). That was

Elizabeth Villiers (1657?–1733), sister of the 1st Earl of Jersey (afterwards Countess of Orkney) and mistress of William III. After Wilson received his mortal wound, he is said to have given his keys to a friend with instructions to burn his writings, but 'all they found was a Receipt left to him by his Grand-mother, to cure Old Women of the Tooth-ach' (p. A4v).

In her fictional letter 'The Unknown Lady's Pacquet of Letters' (published in 1708 as an appendix to the second edition of the English translation of Mme de La Mothe's (D'Aulnoy) *Memoirs of the Court of England in the Reign of Charles II*), Delariviere Manley speculated that Wilson was secretly supported by Villiers, and supposed that when he became too acquisitive Villiers arranged his murder and subsequently helped Law to escape from prison.

Law went on to become a famous fiscal administrator and financial theorist. He worked for a while as an officer of the bank of Amsterdam, then tried to persuade European powers to adopt his financial projects for state banking and paper money. With the help of the Duke of Orleans he founded the first bank in France and established the pre-eminence of paper money over metallic, resulting in the expansion of French industry by a system of credit. But his great plans for the Mississippi Scheme collapsed in 1720, ruining the economy of France. Law returned to England in November 1721, and was granted a royal pardon for the murder of Beau Wilson (Abel Boyer, *The Political State of Great-Britain* for Nov. 1721, vol. xxii, pp. 445–53).

In 1720 Charles Spencer, 3rd Earl of Sunderland (1674–1722), First Lord of the Treasury (i.e. Prime Minister), had formed the South Sea Company, using Law's Mississippi Scheme as a model. Sunderland was blamed for the collapse of this bubble in 1721, which had a devastating impact on the British economy. The business of Parliament during 1721–2 was almost wholly occupied with laying the guilt at the doors of the South Sea Directors; some fled and had their estates confiscated, some were imprisoned, some committed suicide. Sunderland was accused of conspiring to make a great deal of money from the affair and of deliberately destabilizing the nation in support of the Jacobite cause (see parliamentary debates in Boyer, *Political State* for 1721–2, vols xxi–xxiii). He resigned in March 1721. On 19 April 1722 he was found dead, at the age of only 47. An autopsy was ordered to dispel the widespread belief that he had poisoned himself, and duly detected pleurisy, a polyp in the heart, and an inflamed kidney (Boyer, *Political State* for Apr. 1722, vol. xxiii, pp. 452–3).

Thomas Gordon (1691?–1750), together with his patron John Trenchard (1662–1723) the radical Whig journalist, wrote a series of letters by 'Cato' attacking the government for the South Sea Bubble crisis, from 5 November 1720 through September 1722. In 1721 'Britannicus' published *The Conspirators; or, The Case of Catiline*. This was pointedly and sarcastically addressed 'To The Right Honourable The Earl of S—d.' *The Conspirators* portrayed Sunderland as 'Catiline', the leader of a conspiracy to defraud people of their money through a corrupt financial scheme, and a sodomite: 'He married several times, but chiefly, as People suspected, for the Convenience of strengthening himself by *Alliances* with *Great Men*, rather than out of any Affection for the *Ladies*. For if we may believe some Authors, he had a most *unnatural* Tast [*sic*] in his *Gallantries*: And in those Hours when he gave a Loose to Love, the Women were wholly excluded from his Embraces....some of his *Ganymedes* were pamper'd and supported at a high Rate at his Expence' (pp. 24–5). The pamphlet was denounced in Parliament, the printer Mist was imprisoned, the publisher Peele absconded, and the author – identified as Thomas Gordon – 'kept out of the way'. However, Gordon soon repeated his charge in part II of *The Conspirators* (1721): '*CATILINE* was *publick* and *preposterous* in this Sort of Gallantry: Nor was he alone or singular in the Practice of it. For the *Pathicks*, and *Cinædi*, began to be in the greatest Request in those Times, and to be look'd upon as the fine Gentlemen of the Age. Of these, Numbers resorted to *CATILINE*'s House, and found Entertainment, who were publickly reported not to have any Regard to their Modesty' (p. 44).

Gordon was probably the author/editor of *Love-Letters*. His main publisher was J. Roberts, but some of his works (e.g. *The Craftsman*, 1721) were published by A. Moore, who published *Love-Letters* and innumerable pamphlets during the South Sea debates. The printer's device that designates the first letter of *Love-Letters* is identical to the letter 'I' in Gordon's *Francis, Lord Bacon: Or, the Case of Private and National Corruption...Addressed to the South Sea Directors* (J. Roberts, 1721); in both cases it may be intended to represent Sunderland's great mansion Sunderland House. And the decorative portrait in a cartouche flanked by winged cupids at the top of the first letter in *Love-Letters* is identical to one in Gordon's *A Collection of the Proceedings in the House of Commons against the Lord Verulam* (pub. 'A. More', 1721).

Love-Letters Between a Certain Late Nobleman and the Famous Beau Wilson appeared in June 1723 (see 'New Miscellaneous Pamphlets', *Monthly Catalogue* (1723–30), vol. i, no. 4 (June 1723)); it was republished in 1745. The 1745 edition was republished in 1990 with a lengthy analysis by

George Rousseau, which begins with a false premise: 'if these letters were *authentic*, the nobleman (whoever he was in 1723) would have taken action' ('An Introduction to the *Love-Letters*: Circumstances of Publication, Context, and Cultural Commentary', in Michael S. Kimmel (ed.), *Love Letters between a Certain Late Nobleman and the Famous Mr. Wilson* (New York, 1990), pp. 58–9). Rousseau has overlooked the reference on the title page to 'a certain *late* Nobleman', i.e. one who was recently deceased, and who of course could *not* have taken action. This nobleman was probably Sunderland.

Another candidate is James Stanhope, 1st Earl of Stanhope (1673–1721) but he died in February 1721, making him less likely to be called 'late' in June 1723. Rousseau argues that the author intended Stanhope to be recognized as 'the noble Lord' because he was catering to popular knowledge of Stanhope as a sodomite (in lampoons, etc.), but this was also true of Sunderland (e.g. in *The Conspiracy*). And Sunderland, like Stanhope, was rumoured in private to be a sodomite, as in the diary of Revd Robert Wodrow: 'Profaneness never abounded more at London, and throu England, than nou. The abomination of Sodomy is too publick. My Lord Ross tells what he heard; but, as he is highly disobliged, so it's probable it was a story of his enemies, of whom he had many, that the Earle of Sunderland was the first who set up houses for that vile sin, and, when this was like to break out, poisoned himself, to prevent the discovery. This is so horrid, that it's not to be believed till vouched' (20 Sept. 1727). (William Ross, Lord Ross of Halkhead, worked with Sunderland on official commissions in 1689 and 1704.) In 1694, Stanhope was married and in debt, whereas Sunderland was unmarried and rich (though readers in 1723 would not necessarily know facts of thirty years earlier). Wilson was about the same age or even a year or so *older* than Sunderland, whereas readers of *Love-Letters* may see an older sodomite seducing a younger minion. (Stanhope, less than a year older than Sunderland, would also be about the same age as Wilson.) But presumably 'Beau' Wilson looked younger than his age, and would have been treated as a subordinate by his powerful 20-year-old patron. (The story of Cloris in the 'Observations', which portrays an old Lord wearing false calves, is a fictional parable and should not determine any decision about the authenticity of the actual twenty-nine letters.) In the Introduction to the present volume, I review internal evidence that suggests that the letters are genuine (see pp. xiv–xvi).

The text is reproduced from the copy held by the British Library (shelfmark 1080.i.35).

LOVE-LETTERS

Between a certain late

NOBLEMAN

And the famous

Beau *WILSON.*

Price One Shilling.

LOVE-LETTERS

Between a certain late

NOBLEMAN

And the famous

Mr. *WILSON*:

DISCOVERING

The true H I S T O R Y of the Rife and furprifing Grandeur of that celebrated BEAU.

Pro Venere *fæpe, pro* Adonide *femper.*

L O N D O N:

Printed for *A. Moore,* near *St. Paul's.*

THE
PREFACE.

*T is to be expected, that up-
on the reading the Title of
thefe Letters, the Curious
will not be a little alarm'd
at a Piece of Hiftory which
has lain fo long in the Dark,
and is now, more by Chance than any other
Means, coming to a fair and open Light.
The only Conteft among the politer Part of
Mankind will be, Whether the Facts are
true, and the Letters genuine; or only a
fictitious Scene of the worft Sort of Gallantry, and the Product of a mercenary Pen.
To obviate the firft Objection, we fhall only
fay, that we have not as yet had one tolle-
rable Difcovery, how the Party who is the
Subject of thefe Memoirs, kept up that pro-*
fufe

The PREFACE.

fufe Grandeur, in which he liv'd within the Memory of Multitudes ftill furviving. The Reader will find, in the Courfe of the Letters, the fame dark Gueffes and Con-jectures concerning this Meteor of Mortality, as are now publifh'd from Mouth to Mouth, without the leaft Foundation of Truth, and he has been the fame Myftery fince Dead, as he was when living. But the Difcovery made in the following Papers, fets the Mat-ter quite upon another Bottom, and gives it all the Probability that an Affair of fo odious and criminal a Nature can poffibly have. Had there been more faid, it might have render'd the whole fufpected; and therefore the Editor has been obliged to connect the broken Parts of the Story by fome additional Remarks, which have come to his Knowledge from feveral Hands, with whom the Parties were very familiar.

As to the fecond Part of the Objection, That it might be a Work of Fancy or Ima-gination, fuch as are every Day obtruded upon the World, under the Notion of true Hiftory: He takes the Liberty to affure the World, that the Originals were found in the Cabinet of the Deceas'd, which had pafs'd thro' fome Hands, before the private Drawer, the Lodgment of this Scene of Guilt, was difcover'd. How, or by what Means this was done, or from what Hand

they

The PREFACE.

*they are made publick, is a Point too tender
and consequential to relate. But we can
appeal to a better Taste for these Letters
being genuine, especially to such who have
any Taste of Style, or Delicacy of Writing.
They are too polite, and written with an
Air too peculiar not to be distinguish'd from
the Productions of a feigned Intrigue :
The Thing speaks itself ; and any one,
without Preface or Commentary, might easily see by the naked Letters, that they could
not come from any Person, but one of Birth
and Figure, and many other Court-like Accomplishments.*

*There is still behind another Objection to
the Publication, which we will not dissem-
ble, and that is, the Scandal of the Vice
here described thro' the Course of these
Papers. The dead Languages are full
enough of luscious Pictures of this Kind,
and we don't find the Moderns scruple to
translate them, in order, as we may suppose,
to raise a greater Abhorrence of a Sin
which is not familiar to our Northern Climate. It is easy enough to take away all
Offence of this Kind, by applying the Passion of these Letters to distinct Sexes, which
we desire the Reader to do, and then he'll
be a better Judge of the Spirit of the Writer. All the Weeds will then vanish, or be*

turn'd

The PREFACE.

turn'd into Flowers, and in that View let them be seen.

We muſt beg Pardon for not publiſhing one Letter, which relates to a Perſon now living, of too great an Intereſt and Figure in this whole Concern, to be meddled with at preſent.

All that can be ſaid is, that no Reader of common Senſe can miſtake the Party, and we have no Reaſon to help his Conjectures, when the Caſe is ſo evident. Another Opportunity may make that Supplement both a neceſſary and uſeful Key to the whole Adventure, till when, farewell.

LOVE.

[1]

LETTER I.

To Mr. WILSON.

A Y, was it a cold In-fencibility that caufed you to fhun a Challenge, where to give and receive excefs of Pleafure, was to have been the only Combat be-tween us ; or confcious of your own matchlefs Charms, are you refolv'd with peevifh, coy Pride, to be won at the Ex-pence of a thoufand Inquietudes and reft-lefs fond Defires, you Force me to en-dure ?

If you are of a Turn infencible to Plea-fure, I know Gold has the greateft afcen-dant over you ; for all covet it for what it purchafes: This Bill may convince

B you

[2]

you, I have that in my Power : I can be Fortune to you, and, with many Bleffings, I'll crown the chiefeft Wifhes of your Heart ; only haften to gratify the eager Impatience of mine, that longs to fold you in thefe Arms, where you may fecure me, ever yours.

> Greenwich-Park, *be behind* Flamftead's *Houfe, and I fhall fee you, to Morrow Nine at Night, don't fail to come.*

LETTER

[3]

LETTER II.

To ⸺

YOU might juftly have reproach'd my backwardnefs in meeting a Challenge, had it been poffible to have difcern'd, that either Love or Rage had dictated thofe ambiguous Phrafes, which lay liable to variety of Conftructions : I was convinced it came from no mean Hand, and for me to fix it, might be Prefumption ; but you have done me the Honour to difclofe the Miftery by the fofteft and moft agreeable way in Nature : For tho' I'm not afraid to meet a brave Man's Sword, the Indearments of a fine Lady are infinitely preferable. Then how great muft be her Power, to infpire the Souls of others with that dear bewitching Paffion, who can herfelf exprefs it with fo much Force and Delicacy : After all this, and the many delightful Ideas my fond Imagination has rais'd, how needlefs is the Charge of not failing to be at the Time and Place appointed.

B 2 LETTER

[4]

LETTER III.

To Mr. WILSON.

I Had not above an hundred Pieces by me when I receiv'd yours, which made me fend, fwift as the Minutes, to the Bank to fetch this. I would have my *Willy* believe, I am never fo delighted, as when I am doing that which may convince him, how very dear he is to his nown Love : Then come away, the Bath is ready, that I may Wreftle with it, and pit it, and pat it, and————it ; and then for cooler Sport, devour it with greedy Kiffes; for *Venus*, and all the *Poet*'s Wenches are but dirty Dowdies to thee.

Put on the Bruffels *Head and* Indian *Atlafs I fent yefterday.*

LETTER

[5]

LETTER IV.

To the same.

My dearest Dear,

L AST Night I was in Company with
fome of thy Acquaintance; amongft
other ftrange Wonders, it was ftarted how
you liv'd; drowzy *N———k, faid,* He
thought it was fo extraordinary, it would
not be amifs, if the Parliament took it
into Confideration : That, *replied fqueak-
ing J———s,* I believe Mrs. *V—l—s*
will prevent : Several Conjectures were
made ; as *French* Money, the Jew's Jewels, Miftreffes ; or elfe, a Contract with
the Devil, which occafion'd a learned Difpute, Whether there is fuch a Gentleman, or no ? At laft it was agreed, *nemine
Contradicente,* to make you Drunk, and
then try to fift you, they knowing you intend for *Tunbridge* on *Tuefday.* At Night
the Plot is laid, which I would have
you give into ; pretend you are giddy
before the Reft ; I fhall be the activeft

in

[6]

in this *Farce*, and, perhaps, rudely prefs
for the Secret : Be wary ; How hard will
it be to treat you fo different from the
fond Sentiments my Heart has for you ?
who are all, all, the Delight of it.

Don't let us meet, nor be
feen together, 'till this Bu-
finefs is over.

✿ ✿ ✿ ✿ ✿ : ✿ ✿ ✿ ✿ ✿ ✿ ✿ ✿ ✿ ✿ ✿ ✿

LETTER V.

To the fame.

THey are all devilifhly puzzled about
you ; it is pleafant to fee how the
Ideot's Curiofities are raifed by this Dif-
appointment ; do you retire to Town as
refenting it : In two or three Days I will
follow, not being able longer to flay
from Thee, the fofteft, lovelieft Joy, my
doting Heart e'er poffeft : But begone
then, and when the dull three Days are
over, I'll fly to my Deareft, in whofe
Arms, I fhall be recompens'd for fo tedious an Abfence, and there laugh at all their
ridiculous Conjectures.

Wednefday nine a Clock.

LETTER

[7]

≈≈≈≈≈≈≈≈≈≈≈≈≈≈≈≈

LETTER VI.

To the LORD.

My LORD,

AFTER I had parted from your Lordship laſt Night, I was ſtop'd and
accoſted in a very extraordinary manner,
and in ſpite of all the Reſiſtance I was
able to make, under the Diſadvantage of
my Female Dreſs, was carried off by a
Crew of Ruffians, under the Pretence of
Debt, by a ſham Name and Action. A Fellow who had diſcover'd my Viſits to you,
endeavour'd, firſt with flattering Means,
and then by bullying me with a Piſtol
at my Breaſt, to make me reveal what
thoſe private Meetings between us meant ;
but finding I deſpis'd all his Threats,
in Conſideration of what an Injury it might
be to my deareſt LORD : I, at laſt, found
a Way to work on him, by fair Promiſes
of Rewards, ſo as to get out of him,
that a certain GREAT LADY who
knows

[8]

knows all her Actions are back'd by a fuperiour Power, had a Hand in it. When
your Lordſhip permits me the Honour of
relating the Particulars more at large,
your diſcerning Judgment will not only
diſcover the Motives that induc'd her
to it, but direct me how to deceive her,
as to the Knowledge ſhe already has got,
having made her Engine my Creature,
who waits my Orders, as I do your
Lordſhip's, with great Impatience; that
Indulgence, my dear Lord, has, at all
Times, been pleaſed to extend towards me,
will, I hope, pardon my Dread of loſing
it, and condeſcend to give me your Commands how to avoid it.

LETTER

[9]

LETTER VII.

To Mr. WILSON.

IT was one a Clock before I receiv'd
Yours, being, till then, with the King,
or I had flown to you as foon as I had
heard the News of my dear *Willy*'s being
ill; a thoufand dreadful Apprehenfions
about your Health made me as reftlefs
as I am afraid your Diforder did you:
Should envious Death take Thee, my deareft Bleffing, from me, I am undone: I can't
be eafy till I fee you; therefore let
every Body be out of the Way, that I
may come with more Freedom, to my only
beloved, which will be in half an Hour.

C LETTER

[10]

❦❦❦❦❦❦❦❦❦❦❦❦❦❦❦❦❦❦

LETTER VIII.

To Mr. WILSON.

Id I not ſtrictly charge my deareſt Boy, at parting, not to omit one Opportunity of accquainting me with his returning Health, by which alone my Joys can be reſtored ? ſix Poſts have paſt, and yet no Notice taken of its forlorn expecting dying Lover : Tell me the Cauſe of this, if thou art able ; but I'm afraid thou can'ſt not, or dur'ſt not do it; either thy Illneſs is relaps'd with a malicious Bent to make eternal Separation, and thou haſt too much Tenderneſs to kill me with the Knowledge of it ; or I have been remiſs, or overfond, and cloy'd thee ; that thou doſt artfully withdraw thyſelf from theſe loathed Arms ; or doſt thou vilely deſcend to the low Subtilties of the inferiour Sex, who, to enhance their Price, play at faſt and looſe, inſult and idly triumph over the Sot that does more idly ſuffer ſuch a Drab to gain the aſcendant. Forgive me, my dear *Willy*, if I wrong Thee ; lay all

the

[11]

the Blame on this unruly Paſſion : A Plague confound thoſe lying Dogs of Poets, who to delude and torture all Mankind, would palm it on us as a Heaven of Pleaſure ——Damn'd Spite, ——It's Hell to love and doat to Madneſs, as I do on Thee. Anſwer me quickly if thou canſt ; ſay ſomething to me ; if it be a Lye, let it be a well invented one ; and it will pleaſe.

You ſee I'm mad by G——
I had forgot to bid you
incloſe to Her at Park-
Corner ; direct mine for
Mrs. Gray.

C 2   LETTER

[12]

LETTER IX.

To the LORD——

My LORD,

AFter a long, long fruitlefs Expeċt-
tation of your Command how to
direċt to you, which your Lordſhip may
remember was not fix'd on, tho' I often
urged it, I have been ſo wretched to con-
ſtruċt it as a Mark of your declining Favour : as the Tortures of my Soul are
inexpreſſible under ſuch bitter Affliċtion,
ſo are my Joys as full to find them cauſe-
leſs : Thoſe ſoft complaining paſſionate
Expreſſions tranſported me beyond my
Strength to bear, and then revived me with
your kind Rebukes ; what followed rai-
ſed an Extaſy too great : The paſt Con-
fliċts of my Mind, under the imaginary
Diſpleaſure of my deareſt Lord, made
me regardleſs of the Diſorders of my Body, which ſince your Lordſhip has enjoyn'd
ſhall be more my Care ; my Fate is who-
ly in your Power, and you have vouchſafed to bleſs me above all Men. Com-
                                    mand

[13]

mand me to be well and live; but not (for Oh! I cannot) live without you : Recall me from this reftlefs Banifhment, or honour me with your loved Prefence here; the Beauties of the Place have fuch Enticements, which, with other Reafons, I am inform'd, have long detained fome Perfons of Diftinction on odd Intreagues, perhaps, not unworthy your Lordfhip's Notice.

I am,

My LORD, *&c.*

LETTER

[14]

LETTER X.

To the LORD——

My LORD,

EAger to acquaint your Lordſhip with my Return to Town, I diſpatched a Meſſenger that Moment with a Letter, who failing of the wiſh'd Opportunity, to deliver it as uſual, I went immediately to the Play, in Hopes to gratify my Impatience by ſeeing you there ; but contrary to that, had the Mortification to find one Misfortune attended by a ſtill greater ; when as ſometime to diſguiſe my ſecret Affection, I ſurvey Beauty with as much ſeeming Delight as other Men ; Curioſity led me to make Enquiry of a fine dreſs'd Lady, I had never before obſerv'd to adorn any publick Place ; but how was I confounded, and what racking Thoughts poſſeſt me, when I underſtood ſhe was a new favourite Miſtreſs of your Lordſhip, obtain'd, with much Difficulty ; ſo that, my Lord, my miſſing you laſt Night, which then

[15]

then only feem'd Chance, may probably hereafter appear to be your Lordfhip's Choice : I refer to your own Judgment, which never errs in Matters of far higher Importance than my Happinefs, and who are fo well acquainted with all the Paffions that can affect human Nature, that it would be Prefumption to fend you my feeble Difcription, of what I fuffer on this hateful Difcovery. I only flatter myfelf with one Hope, attended by a thoufand Doubts, which two or three Lines from your Lordfhip will confirm or difperfe : I long, yet dread to have your Anfwer, which I am certain you won't fail to fend, as foon as this comes to your Hands, If you have any Regard for,

My LORD,

Your moft entirely,

moft paffionately devoted Servant,

W. WILSON.

[16]

LETTER XI.

To Mr. WILSON.

Did it fret and teafe itfelf .becaufe I have got a Wench, but don't let one Fear perplex it : When I have Thee in my Arms, thou fhalt fee how I defpife all the Pleafures that changeling Sex can give compared to one Touch of thine ; it's true, I had her dirty Maidenhead, which I took fome Pains for ; not fo much to amufe the dull Time in thy tedious Abfence, which no Confideration but your dear Health, could have made me comply with ; as to ftop fome good natur'd Reflections I found made on my Indifference that way. But thou alone art every, and all the Delight my greedy Soul covets, which is heigthned to fuch Excefs, that even pains me, to find my dear *Willy* has fuch a Tendernefs for its nown Love ; then haften to my fond Heart, that leaps and bounds with Impatience to fee Thee, and devour thee with greedy Kiffes.

LETTER

[17]

LETTER XII.

To the LORD ——

My LORD,

IT is not to be express'd with how much Rapture I receiv'd your Lorplhip's Commands to attend you, and if it were poffible that could increafe with me, it is even now, when the different Tranfports of my Soul prevent my ready Obedience to them. Can I fupport your adored Prefence with the Torture of not feeing you entirely my own. No, my *Lord*, the Greatnefs of my Paffion created and infpired by you, has difdained to fhare a Pleafure with that bafe, low, dull, infinuating Sex; let not one of them prefume to hope the leaft Thought, in your exalted Mind, or noble Appetites, and contemn the idle medling infipid World; but I forget myfelf, and rave with the diftracting Thought, that any thing in Nature fhould be able to interpofe between us; pardon, my deareft Lord, when I affume to joyn myfelf with you; remember, it is a Crime you firft defcended to encourage me

D in,

[18]

in, and impute it to no other Spirit of Ambition, but that of being inseparably,

Your Lordship's

most obedient Slave,

W. WILSON

❀ ❀ ❀ ❀ ❀ ❀ ❀ ❀ ❀ ❀ ❀ ❀ ❀ ❀ ❀ ❀ ❀ ❀ ❀

LETTER XIII.

To Mr. WILSON.

ARe these my *Willy's* Raptures, that instead of hisself, sends me only Words ? Why this Difficulty about a Trifle I despise ? For all Things are so, compared to Thee ; she shall be turn'd a-drift, and I will contemn the idle medling World, and nothing shall interpose between us ; for thou canst be guilty of no Crime to me, but that of this peevish Absence, which I shall chide it for, and beat it, and then eat it up with greedy Kisses. I have got the six pretty Horses, it said it liked before it left the Town, and something it san't know of till it comes. Make Haste.

LETTER

[19]

LETTER XIV.

To the LORD.———

My LORD,

WHen your Lordſhip paſt me yeſterday in the *Mall*, it's probable, you might ſee me take up a Pocket-book, which I found with ſix and thirty Letters from a very great Man to a Lady, who muſt have dropt it juſt then; they, diſcovering an Amour of ſome Continuance between 'em, and wherein was an Order for fifty Pounds payable to the Bearer, under his Grace's Hand. I ſaw it abſolutely neceſſary to return it entire to the Lady, but with ſuch Caution, as ſhe can never be ſenſible who it is has had the Peruſal of her Paquet. The Spirit of 'em throughout, to me, ſeems low and wrangling, but ſuppoſe 'em writ with infinitely more Force than even this great celebrated Man is ſaid to be Maſter of, What muſt they appear to thoſe who have

D 2

[20]

the Honour to have a frequent Correſ-
pondence with your Lordſhip.

I took Time to copy four the moſt remarkable Letters, and only wiſh they may
prove as inſtrumental to divert your preſent Shagreen, as the Secret you were ſo
well entertain'd with ſome Time ſince,
concerning that noble Peer who lay in.

I flatter my ſelf it wont be
long, before I have Or-
ders to attend your
Lordſhip.

LETTER

[21]

LETTER XV.

To Mr. Wilson,

IS this thy Faith? Is this thy Return to all my foolish lavish Fondness? It seems I have taught you a Trade, and Harlot-like you intend to be as common and as despicable as those abject Wretches [*We must beg Pardon of the Reader for omitting here some Lines which are in the Original of this Letter, being too obscene to be inserted*] May every Disease incident to them infect and destroy thee. What, couldst thou find none but that old nauseous Dog to kiss and slobber thee? Don't pretend to deny it, for by ———— I saw him: Had not a little Regard to my self prevented, I had stabb'd thee that Moment.

I suppose you intend to hide your detested Head in some Hole, to escape my Rage; but my Revenge shall find thee, and punish thy black Ingratitude:

an

[22]

an Ingratitude fo vile, that thou de-
ferveft to be a terrible Example to all
that bafe Frye : Did not I take thee from
a wretched neceffitous Life, perplex'd
with petty Duns, and have raifed thee
to be the Nation's Wonder ? Have I deny'd thee any thing ? but have been fo
lavifh to make thee (or thou pretendeft)
to blufh at my Excefs of Bounty : But
now I will be as boundlefs in my Hatred
as I have been profufe in my extravagant
Love. May all ·——————— torture
thee, as thy Bafenefs does me.

Letter XVI.

To the Lord ————

MAY all the deteftable Curfes your
Lordfhip has been pleafed to pronounce, with ten thoufand more, inflict
—————————————————— if I
know or can guefs what you mean.

Is

[23]

Is it to try the Bent of my Mind, under the moſt calamitous of all Circumſtances, your Lordſhip's dread Diſpleaſure? as you have before done the other Way, in raiſing me from that abject Fortune to your high Grace, diſpenſing Favours beyond my own aſpiring Hopes, or vaineſt Deſires; which when I ceaſe moſt gratefully to acknowledge, as is my Duty, or give juſt Cauſe of Offence, either by Action or Omiſſion, may all the Valuable World, nay, what is infinitely preferable to all, your Lordſhips ſelf, continue to hate, deſpiſe, and brand me, for the moſt villanous of all that black and loathſome Herd you have already rank'd me with.

Am I not the Creature of your Framing, to riſe, to fall, to live or die, to mould and faſhion as you pleaſe? And ſhould I dare to repine at, or more baſely endeavour to hide my ſelf from the Fate you have allotted me? It is thinking too poorly of the Wretch, your Lordſhip once vouchſafed to honour with your Love and Eſteem, which, perhaps, you'll ſee was not wholly miſplaced, when I have an Opportunity to throw myſelf at your Feet; in the mean Time, deviſe as many

Tortures

[24]

Tortures to rack this hated Body, as at present my Soul endures, and let both fall a willing Sacrifice to gratify your Pleafures.

I am,

My L O R D,

Your Lordſhip's moſt

faithfully moſt entirely

devoted Slave,

W. W I L S O N.

LETTER XVII.

To Mr. W I L S O N.

SUre thou art falſe for theſe Eyes ſaw you ſuffer G———n to kiſs and ſlobber you, you have diſarm'd my Anger, wou'd you could my Doubts : Let me ſee you, but come with certain Proofs of thy Faith, that I may not be fatal to Thee and myſelf : Swear never to ſee that hated Dog, and I'll believe Thee ; You have a powerful Advocate within, that would

fain

[25]

fain would find Thee true ; the very Hope,
is a Joy, great as ever fill'd my Breaſt; then
what muſt the Certainty be ? Add that
to the many Raptures thou alone could'ſt
give, and I will be thy humble Slave
for ever ; but take Heed or you'll find my
Wrath terrible, exceeding even the Malice
of Women.

LETTER XVIII.

To the LORD——

My LORD,

WIth longing Expectation of the
coming Joy, I was flying to attend your Appointment; when taking
my Tour, according to Cuſtom, I obſerved ſome Perſons, well known to your
Lordſhip, who took the Pains to dog me ;
the Particulars of which whimſical Adventure I'll relate when I have the Honour to approach you next in private,
in the mean Time your Lordſhip I hope
will not blame my cautious Retreating ;
and give me leave to ſay, I wait your
freſh Orders with the utmoſt Impatience.

E   LETTER

[26]

🙢🙢🙢🙢🙢🙢🙢🙢🙢🙢🙢🙢🙢🙢🙢🙢🙢🙢

LETTER XIX.

To Mr. WILSON.

My deareſt Boy.

THis impertinent Letter I have ſent
Thee, was brought me up this
Morning; they told me the Fellow would
not give his Name but preſs'd to have it
deliver'd as ſomething of Conſequence
to me; could I be angry with my darling
Rogue, I ſhould chide it from this Neglect
that you did not contrive with me or
ſome other Way to get rid of him; go
or ſend to him immediately without taking Notice you have heard from me,
and be very ſmooth with him, till I be
able to manage it ſo as to make the Impudent Raſcal wiſh he had been ignorant,
or at leaſt not ſaucy in my Affairs; after
you have been with him come away to
me; for one melting Extaſy, thou alone
can'ſt give, will recompenſe a thouſand
ſuch

[27]

fuch Uneafineffes. ———— D——n this confounded Hurry of Bufinefs, which has debarr'd me of Thee thefe five Days, and forced me laft Night to make ufe of my Pillow which was as infipid as a ————.

LETTER XX.

To Mr. L——

SIR,

IS it poffible that a Man of Honour and good-Nature, as Mr. L—— fhould be ftirr'd by imaginary Injuries to treat his Friend after fo furprizing and inhuman a Manner, as the taxing me with Crimes to him whofe Welfare you muft needs be fenfible I have ever had, and fhall continue, the moft tender Regard for. I proteft folemnly, fo far have I been from harbouring a Thought of Difhonour to your Family, that I prefer it every Way to my own; and would fooner run on my Damnation than offer Injuries, or omit

E 2 Opportu-

[28]

Opportunites of paying my grateful Ac-
knowledgements for your fingular Favours;
I am not infenfible the real Offence taken
was more juftly grounded, unhappily,
by one we are unable to contend with.
And it is a great Misfortune to have it
placed to my Account, which I fhall ufe
my fpeedieft Endeavours to acquit my
felf of, by ftraining my utmoft Intereft
to give you all the Satisfaction you can
require, as a Gentleman who have fo
much obliged, and may fo entirely command,

Your moft humble Servant.

W. WILSON

Obfervation

(29)

Observations on the foregoing
LETTERS.

I T is evident by the Beginning of the first Letter, that there was a preceeding one from his Lordship, but wrote in so ambiguous a Manner that *Wilson,* who was as yet a Stranger to his Passion, could not by that be induc'd to accept the Challenge; which put his Lordship on another Project, and naturally led him to imagine that a Cash-Note must be the only Bait to draw this *cold Insensible.* Yet even this Letter was not open enough to discover the Sex of the Writer; for *Wilson* in the following one appears with all the Extasies of an impatient Lover, in the delusive Expectations of meeting a fine Lady; which, undoubtedly, were rais'd from the Words of the unknown, who says, *Where to give and receive excess of Pleasure was to have been the only Combate between us.* But had he consider'd how awkwardly the polite Softness of that Sex is imitated, the most lascivious of them generally expressing themselves, tho'

in

(30)

in as Paffionate, yet in a much decenter
Manner, he would foon have been convinc'd of his Error, efpecially, by the laft
Line, where he fays *you may fecure me e-
ver yours,* which is different from the
Sentiments of the Fair, who know their
chief Power is in gaining, and all their
Hopes to keep depends only on the Faith
of the Lover, What the Confequence of
that interview was, appears through the
whole courfe of thefe Letters ; but the
next of them muft furprize the Reader,
where he fees fo unnatural an Appetite
exprefs'd in fo tender, paffionate, and obfcene a Manner ; but what will appear
moft ftrange is his Lordfhip's Orders to
Wilfon to be drefs'd for this amorous
Encounter in the Habit of the Sex he
fhews fo great a Contempt for:

By this Time we perceive their Intimacy was very great, and that it was
the Intereft of both to prevent the leaft
Difcovery ; for *Wilfon* became the Wonder of the whole Town, who from being a private neceffitous Dependant on
Fortune, feem'd now to be the Ruler
of her ; the Eyes of all were turn'd on
him ; his Splendor, Gayety, and Drefs
was the Delight of the Fair, and the
Envy of his own Sex ; fome were refolv'd

to

(31)

to find out the hidden Source of all his Grandure, and destroy this Meteor of Profuseness ; the several Conjectures made on him, and their Resolutions were discover'd by his Lordship, as we find in Letter IV. Who to frustrate their Designs agrees to be at the Head of the Conspiracy, and press to know the Secret of his Living ; *Wilson* being thus apprised of their Designs, guarded himself against them at their Meeting, where his Lordship, as before agreed, insisted on the Discovery of it, but he, pretending a Resentment, left *Tunbridge,* and, shortly after, in order to prevent the least Suspicion of his Lordship's being in the Secret, sent word by some of his Friends, in a publick Manner, that he thought himself injur'd by this Treatment ; and, in particular, by his Lordship ; that it did not become a Person of his Lordship's Character to be concern'd in such an Affair, tho' to One so much his Inferior ; his Lordship, in as publick a Manner, own'd himself in the wrong, and, at the same Time, hinted that somebody very powerful must support him. This was their first Plot to destroy suspicion ; the rest which I shall relate, must, by all, be own'd to be Masterpieces in their kind, and to excel the most

Jesuitical

(32)

Jefuitical Defigns that ever were known; this Management may convince the World that his Lordfhip was no lefs a Politician in his private Affairs, than he was in the Publick; he feems himfelf highly pleas'd with it, becaufe by that he had left them in a greater Perplexity than ever.

But tho' no light could be gain'd from thence, yet not long after, an unlucky Accident fell out, which had it not been counter-manag'd with abundance of Art and Cunning, muft inevitably have difcover'd their Intimacy, and caft an everlafting Odium on them; for it having been conjectur'd that Mrs. *V———l———s* (who is the *great L A D Y* mention'd in Letter VI.) was the Perfon who had thus rais'd him, and coming to her Knowledge, fhe was very uneafy, believing if fuch a Report fpread, it might Occafion a Difference between her and the Power who fupported her; but certainly nothing but a fecret Efteem for him with that Curiofity, natural to her Sex, could induce her to fo formidable an Attempt to difcover his myfterious Affairs. In order to this, fhe fet Spies to watch him from Place to Place,

who

[33]

who found he ufually din'd with different People of Quality, and faunter'd
away the Afternoon at Court, Park, or
Play, with fuch other Amufements;
and that often about ten at Night he
difmifs'd his Equipage, and took a Chair,
which carry'd him to a private Houfe
near *Hyde Park* Corner, into which he
enter'd by a Key he had with him;
where they waited to obferve who elfe
went in or out; but nothing was feen
to move or ftir in or about the Houfe
'till about Five the next Morning, at
which Time he generally return'd.

After this Mrs. *V—ll—s* fent one of
her Spies there to enquire for Lodgings;
a Bill being on the Door for that Purpofe, who was anfwer'd by an old Woman who kept the Houfe, that fhe did
not care for Men; the next Day fhe fent
another Spy, who enquir'd for Lodgings
for a young Lady, who was told by the
fame old Woman, that Women Lodgers
fhe could by no Means fatigue herfelf
with; which plainly convinc'd them
that her Bill was only a Blind.

Mrs. *K—ll—s* Curiofity was heighten'd
by all this to that Degree, that fhe could
not reft 'till farther Difcoveries were
made; they found a back Paffage to the
Houfe, by which they fuppofed fome Per-

F   fon

[34]

fon gave him a Meeting there; accordingly, the Houfe being on both Sides carefully watch'd, *Wilfon* went in the Street
Way, as ufual, and in lefs than an Hour
after, the Old Woman provided a Chair
at the Back-Door, which was immediately fill'd by one in the Habit of a Lady,
whom they follow'd to the Nobleman's;
about four Hours after, they faw the fame
Perfon return to the Back-Door, and
fhortly after, *Wilfon* went out at the Street-
Door directly Home.

Mrs. *V—ll—s* finding it to be a frequent Practice, concluded, this fine Lady who made her Midnight Vifits fo
conftantly to my Lord, could be no
other than *Wilfon* himfelf, but was refolved to be thoroughly fatisfy'd, and
as Women are quick at Invention, fhe
and her chief Engine, whom I fhall call
Johnafco, contrived to have him arrefted
in his Chair; which was accordingly
done, to the great Surprize of the feeming Dame, who alledg'd that the Name
and Action were falfe, and dared them
to detain him at their Peril; but they
infifted they were not afraid to anfwer
what they did, and if fhe would not
pay down the Debt, which was laid
vaftly high, they muft do their Duty
in fecuring her 'till fhe gave in Bail; and

not-

[35]

notwithſtanding he ſtrenuouſly inſiſted
they were miſtaken, they carry'd him to
a Spunging-houſe, and lock'd him up by
himſelf, where he was a ſhort Time left
to reflect on this ſurpriſing Uſage, when
Johnaſco came into the Room, who with
the Pretence of taking him for a Lady,
after a Preamble of Complements gave
him to underſtand he was violently in
Love with him ; and that judging by
his Midnight Viſits to my Lord ————
his Affections (unfortunately for him)
were there pre-engag'd, he had contriv'd
this Stratagem to get him in his Power,
which he was reſolved not to part with
'till his Happineſs was compleated ; by
Degrees he began to preſs for indecent
Liberties, which was repuls'd with great
Modeſty on *Wilſon*'s Side, but in ſpite of
all his Strength and Reſiſtance, the Lover ſoon found a Cure for his pretended
Paſſion, by diſcovering him to be of his
own Sex, which chang'd his amorous
Addreſſes into as ſeeming furious a Rage,
threat'ning to kill him unarm'd, unleſs
he would confeſs what all thoſe dark
Doings meant ; but finding him too ſtea-
dy to be moved by ſuch Menaces, he
ſhifted the Scene of Fidelity to Mrs.
V—ll--s, ſtaggering at the Sight of *Wilſon*'s Gold and Promiſes, which out-

F 2   weigh'd

[36]

weigh'd his Hopes from the other Quarter; thus began the Acquaintance between *Johnasco* and *Wilson*, which in the End prov'd fatal to the latter, tho' for the present he had secur'd him his Creature.

Johnasco returned to Mrs. *V—ll—s*, who was on the Rack of Expectation to know the Event of her Plot; when seeing him, with eager Impatience she ask'd him his success; he reply'd, I have discover'd, Madam, that the Person whom you suspected to be *Wilson*, is really so; but tho' I have us'd my utmost Endeavours, both by Threats and Promises, to disclose the Mistery of these midnight Visits, I could by no Means prevail; he behav'd himself with so resolute an Obstinacy, that I fear if he is longer detain'd, it may be very injurious to you; I believe he would be glad to excuse what is past, to be set at Liberty; however, I have yet some Hopes of prying into the Cause of this Intrigue. Mrs. *V—ll—s* reflecting on what *Johnasco* had said, which I suppose *Wilson* had order'd him to say, intending by that Means to confound and blind her in what she had already found out, gave Orders for his Release, leaving the entire Management of it to *Johnasco*.

Not

[37]

Not long after this, my Lord addrefs'd
to Mrs. *V—ll—s*, to obtain a Trifle of
the King, with fuch a Complaifance and
an infinuating Refpect, that fhe readily
comply'd with his Requeft, being willing to oblige a Perfon of his Intereft,
thinking at the fame Time, that her Civility in that Affair would prevent his
fufpecting her to have a Hand in the
Defign againft *Wilfon.*

Some little Time after, my Lord being out of Town, *Johnafco* inform'd her
that he had made one of my Lord's Servants his Friend, but could not find by
him that any Lady came to my Lord in
that private Manner ; but that one Night,
walking in the Garden, which he had
frequently done, both before and fince
my Lord went out of Town, to make
Difcoveries, he perceiv'd a Lady, the
Shape and Height as *Wilfon* appeared to
be of in his Female Drefs, come in at
the Garden Door, go to one of the
Parlour Windows, and give a fmall Rap,
which immediately open'd for her Reception ; fome Time after fhe was got
in, he crept clofe to the Window, and
heard low talking, but could not diftinguifh either the Words or Voices ; on
Enquiry, he found it was the Steward's
Apartment, who was a *French* Gentleman

[38]

man who pretended to have left his E-
ftate and Country on the Score of Religion, and with his Daughter fled into
England. When he had told Mrs.*V—ll—s*
this, with other Circumftances, which he
thought would confirm her Belief of it,
he gave his Opinion, that he thought it
could not be my Lord that *Wilfon* came
to, he being at that Time out of Town;
that perhaps the Steward might. not be
fo great an Enemy to the *French* Intereft
as he pretended, therefore there muft
be fomething extraordinary in that mi-
fterious Procceding; which if, fays he,
my Lord is ignorant of, as I am inclin'd
to believe, he wou'd be the propereft
Perfon in finding it out, having a Power
over his Steward to call him to an Account, it being his own Houfe in which
the Defign is carry'd on.

    Mrs. *V—ll—s,* who believ'd all he
faid to her, according to his Advice, acquainted my Lord with it as foon as he
came to Town, who pretending a great
Surprize, made a thoufand fufpicious
Conjectures, with a Refolution to fearch
into the Meaning of it; and confulting
with her concerning the beft and fureft
Method for Difcovery, it was at laft a-
greed, that *Johnafco* and another of her
Creatures fhould be on the Watch in the
Garden,

[39]

Garden, as ufual, till they faw *Wilfon* approach, which they did not 'till the fourth Night; *Johnafco* immediately ran to acquaint my Lord; after fome fmall Time the Steward was order'd to be call'd for, who was not to be found; my Lord then pretending that he wanted fome Papers that were in his Cuftody, went to his Apartment with *Johnafco* and the other Perfon, broke open the Door, where they found *Wilfon* confufed, and his Female Drefs very much ruffled; the Steward's Daughter, furpriz'd at the unexpected Coming of my Lord, and for the Shame of being thus expos'd, ran to the Bed, endeavouring to hide herfelf in the Cloaths; my Lord turning to *Johnafco* faid, *I perceive this is only a Plot on a* French *Petticoat:* So left the Lovers, and went with *Johnafco* and the other to Mrs. *V—ll—s,* where he fhow'd a Fund of Wit, and diverted himfelf in a Ridicule on the Pains they had all taken about fuch a Trifling Intrigue. Thus, by the private Help of *Johnafco,* was fhe brought to believe fhe had found out the real Truth of *Wilfon's* Defigns; when, in Fact, 'twas only a Counter-Plot to deftroy her juft Sufpicions.

How *Wilfon* got into the Favour of the *French* Girl I know not; but we may eafily

[40]

eafily fuppofe that my Lord, who took
fuch Pains to deceive Mrs. *V—ll—s*, contriv'd with him that the Girl fhou'd be
firft gain'd e'er they put in Execution this
artful Project.

I know not whether to impute the Defign of this furprizing Counter-Plot to
his Lordfhip or Mr. *Wilfon*; but certain
it is, that without it they had been difcover'd. I have often heard that the
World would never allow *Wilfon* to be a
Man of any Parts or Capacity; but by
thefe few Letters of his, efpecially by
Letter IX, he feems to be perfectly fkill'd
in the Art of Infinuation; whether infpir'd by my Lord's excellent Genius,
or his Gold, I will not pretend to determine, perhaps it was the latter, made
him feel all thofe Pangs we find he expreffes in fo lively and refpectful a Manner to his Lordfhip.

While *Wilfon* was out of Town for
the Recovery of his Health, from whence
he wrote the abovemention'd Letter, my
Lord was diverted in fome Meafure from
his Paffion for *Wilfon*, by a young Lady
whom he had feduced from her Friends;
and in Order to excufe himfelf to *Wilfon*,
fays, *It was not fo much to amufe the dull
Time in his tedious Abfence, as to ftop the
World's good-natur'd Reflections on his Indifference*

[41]

difference that Way; but I fhould be inclined to believe he diffembled with him,
did not the following Story, which I had
from a Relation of my Lord's, fhew he
ftuck at nothing tho' ever fo vile to ac-
complifh his Ends; and as the Circumftances agree with this Letter, I am convinc'd it is the fame Perfon he hints at
therein.

This Lady, (my Lord's Relation) at
the Requeft of *Cloris*'s Parents, brought
her to Town, that fhe might have the
Advantage of a genteeler Education than
the Country could afford; in order to
which, no Expence was fpar'd, by which
fhe might be improv'd; fhe introduc'd
her into the Company of moft People in
Town, and at the fame Time took Care
to inftill into her the Principles of Modefty and Vertue, as the fureft Guards
againft the too frequent Temptations of
Men.

Cloris was tall, tho' very young. a
lively Vivacity in her Looks, and a
Sprightlinefs in her Words and Actions,
that rather inclin'd to ill-natur'd Satire,
than a well-bred Politenefs. My Lord,
who ufed frequently to vifit there, was,
when not reftrain'd by Policy or Civility,
of a troublefome peevifh Temper; and
poor *Cloris*, who retain'd, in Spite of

G   her

[42]

her Dancing - Mafter, fome awkward
Country Airs, had her Patience perpetually exercis'd by his fplenatick Reflections, which fhe did not fail to return
with a Tartnefs that occafion'd fuch
Clafhings between them, as created a
thorough Hatred for each other.

She had often heard that his Lordfhip's handfome Perfon formerly made
great Impreffions on the Ladies, and was
refolv'd to let him fee he had outliv'd
that Attraction, by taking an Opportunity before Company, to run Pins in his
falfe Calves, to fhew them that Age had
depriv'd him of his natural ones ; which
childifh Trick he refented fo deeply,
that from that Moment he ftudy'd to be
reveng'd on her to which he was encouraged likewife by a particular Incident :
A Lady who was there vifiting, falling
into Difcourfe with him about the Virtues and Vices of the Female-Sex, he af-
ferted that Vice was the moft predomi-
nate in them on his own Knowledge ;
the Lady as warmly maintaining the contrary : The Argument was heighten'd
'till they came to Particulars, he affirm-
ing no Woman was Proof againft the
Importunities of a Man abfolutely refolved to gain her, be it ever fo difadvan-
tageous to her Reputation or Intereft:
Upon

[43]

Upon which the Lady (piqu'd with what he faid) made Anfwer, And do you believe that even your Lordfhip, fupported by the mighty Treafures you poffefs, with that powerful Addrefs you are Mafter of, could obtain *Cloris* in a difhonourable Way ? Grounding her Challenge on the Hatred fhe had obferv'd the Girl conceiv'd againft him : To which he made fome trifling Reply, and turn'd the Difcourfe ; but was refolv'd within himfelf to convince them both he had Youth enough left, as well as fafhionable Galantry, to work her Ruin. From that Time he began to pay more frequent Vifits than ufual, and fo foften'd his Manner to his intended Prey, that he foon infinuated himfelf into her Favour ; he readily inclined to any one that feemed to admire her Perfon or Parts, willing to gratify her little Pride and Vanity, by fhewing her Acquaintance fhe deferved to be diftinguifh'd above them, as fuperior in Wit and Beauty. Thus prepar'd by the natural Failures of her Sex, and wrought up by his Artifice, it will appear no mighty Difficulty, if one of lefs Skill than this great Statefman, fhould carry off a Prize of higher Value than it feems he ever efteem'd her to be. Having thus obtain'd a Conqueft he had

[44]

no further Regard to than that of making
it fubfervient to his Ends, as the amufing
the dull Time in the Abfence of his beloved Minion, and to fhew his irrefiftible
Power with the Fair, but more particularly to make good his Affertions with
the Lady who prefumed to difpute his
Influence: Thefe, with fome few other
Reafons, induced him to keep *Cloris* in fo
grand a Way, as might make the Lofs of
her Reputation the more remarkable,
which the poor deluded Wretch attributed to the Effects of his Lordfhip's violent Paffion for her Perfon. By this
Time *Wilfon* returned to Town, and was
alarm'd at fo feeming a dangerous Rival
getting into his Lordfhip's Favour while
he was abfent; but when he found by
the Anfwer his Power was not diminifh'd,
his Jealoufy abated; and the Fondnefs
his Lordfhip expreffes in Letter XIII,
fhew'd him how ready he was to comply
with any Thing he defir'd, tho' of more
Difficulty than turning off a Miftrefs.
She had now ferv'd all the Defigns he
had on her; and not being willing to
fupport an Expence he had no farther
Occafion for, he thought fit to let her
know by a Letter he was thoroughly fenfible of her ill Conduct, and fecret Correfpondence with another; which Ingratitude

[45]

titude had fo difobliged him, that fhe
muft not prefume to think of him any
more, nor attempt to be troublefome by
impertinent Meffages, or complaining
Scrawls. The poor Girl was Thunder-
ftruck at this unexpected Expulfion from
his Lordfhip's Favour, at a Time when
fhe thought her felf fully fecur'd of it.
All the delightful Idea's fhe had form'd
of her future Grandeur, and the fplendid Way of Living fhe was juft arrived
at, were now changed to the dreadful
Apprehenfions of future Shame and
Wants : Now fhe began to think her
Character and Intereft with her Friends
were blafted and ruin'd for ever. Some
Time fhe remain'd under the greateft
Diftrefs of Mind, without Courage to
endeavour her Juftification to my Lord,
or Reconciliation to the Lady fhe had fo
rafhly eloped from ; 'till by Degrees fhe
rally'd up Spirit enough to attempt the
former, tho' fhe could not the latter,
not being confcious of his Accufations;
but finding all her Proteftations, and
fofteft Submiffions, nay even her ac-
quainting him with her moving Condition of being pregnant, and the Diftref-
fes fhe was reduced to, not only fruitlefs, but return'd with Contempt and
Hatred, fhe refolved to revenge herfelf
on

[46]

on the Author of her Miferies; fhe provided herfelf with a Man's Habit, and
according to the Intelligence fhe had got,
fhe watch'd an Opportunity of meeting him as he return'd from *Kenfington*,
which fell out to her Defire toward the
Dufk of the Evening; fhe made Signs
to ftop the Coach, and approaching his
Lordfhip with great Refpect, begg'd fhe
might be admitted to a private Audience
with his Lordfhip about a Matter of high
Importance to him, which requir'd his inftant Knowledge of; tho' fomewhat furpriz'd, his Lordfhip's Curiofity was rais'd
to know what it was; and not fufpecting
any ill Defign, nor being at all prejudic'd
to a Youth fo beautiful, he very readily
comply'd with his Requeft, and walking
with her to a more retir'd Place in the
Park, where they could difcourfe with
Freedom. the poor Girl, fully bent on
her rafh Undertaking, began to upbraid
him with bafely deluding her from her
Parents and Family, deftroying her Virtue and Reputation, and then thrufting
her forth to fuch Infamy and Mifery, as
muft infallibly fall on one left in her a-
bandon'd Condition; then prefented a
Piftol to his Breaft: His Lordfhip, who
had a Spirit above being furpriz'd with
Fear, pufh'd it by with as much Contempt,

[47]

tempt, as if fhe had rapt his Knuckles
with her Fan, feeing her manage it after
fo timorous and awkward a Manner, he
eafily wrench'd it out of her Hand, and
pretending to take her for a Bully (tho'
her Voice, Difcourfe, and effeminate
Fears muft needs difcover her to him)
fhe had fent to affaffinate him, fwore he
would chaftize him with his own Hands,
which he did in fo unmerciful a Manner,
that fhe quickly funk down at his Feet
under the Violence of his repeated Blows
and Kicks, where he had the Inhumanity
to leave her expofed to what Chance or
Providence allotted. This barbarous U-
fage to a Woman, and with Child by
himfelf, plainly fhews what a Hatred he
had to the whole Sex; for no Man that
was not given to the moft abandon'd Vices could treat them whofe tender Delicacy courts and invites our Protection,
with fuch unheard of Cruelty. The
forlorn *Cloris* having lain fome Time
without Senfe or Motion, recover'd fo
far as to feel extreme Pains, which fhe
exprefs'd in melancholy Groans, that
were heard by a Soldier who accidentally
came that Way, who with great Humanity took Care to get her into a Hackney
Coach, that drove according to her Orders to the private Lodging fhe had taken
to

[48]

to fhift her Female Drefs. The Agonies
which this brutal Treatment flung her
into, brought the Pains of Labour ftrong
upon her ; and believing her miferable
Life was near it's End, fhe gave Directi-
ons to the Soldier to go to the Lady
from whom fhe unfortunately abfconded,
and defire her to come immediately ;
who much furpriz'd with fuch a Meffage
from a Gentleman at the Point of Death,
knew not what to do, being apprehenfive of fome ill Defign ; 'till being prefs'd
by the Meffenger, who told her the dif-
mal Condition he had found him in, and
that he conjur'd her to come, not being
able to die in Peace without feeing her,
fhe went under the Guard of a Gentleman. No fooner had fhe enter'd the
Chamber, but cafting her Eyes on *Cloris*
then in Bed, fhe knew her ; upon which
fhe difmifs'd the Gentleman that came
with her, and approaching near the Bed,
all her Refentment for *Cloris'* ill Conduct
gave Place to Compaffion, at feeing her
in that deplorable Condition ; which the
Girl perceiving by her Tears, faid, Is it
poffible that you, who have fo juft a
Right to reproach my Guilt and Folly,
can pity a Wretch whofe Life you fee
thus miferably torn from her by the cruel Author of her Crimes? The Lady
anfwer'd

[49]

anfwer'd her very mildly, finding both her Griefs and Pains extream ; which gave fome Eafe to her diftracted Mind, tho' to her Pains it was impoffible ; for after a Continuance of them for three or foun Days, fhe was deliver'd of a dead Child, two Months before its Time, and immediately expir'd.

Thus fell the unfortunate *Cloris*, a Sacrifice to one who had not even the Excufe of once liking her ; but work'd her Ruin, to gratify his own Pride, and mortify hers.

F I N I S.

An Epistle from Signora F----a to a Lady (1727)

An Epistle from Signora F[austin]a to a Lady was the product of a feud between two prima donnas, Signora Faustina and Signora Cuzzoni. It was probably published in London (the imprint 'Venice' is false) around June 1727, at the height of the battle between their rival factions. Francesca Cuzzoni (*c.*1700–70), born in Parma, made her debut as Dalinda in *Ariodante* in Venice in 1718, and would soon conquer most soprano roles. She married the harpsichord master and composer Pietro Giuseppe Sandoni and used 'Signora Sandoni' as her stage name. Handel and Heidegger invited her to London for the 1722–3 season for their Italian Opera venture; her triumph was as Rodelinda in 1725. The mezzo-soprano Faustina Bordoni (1700?–81), whose stage name was Signora Faustina, made her debut in *Ariodante* in Venice in 1716 and was an immediate success. She was also invited by Handel to London, and made her debut there as Rossana in Handel's *Alessandro* in May 1726. Facing her on stage in this opera were Signora Cuzzoni as Lisaura, and the great castrato Senesino (stage name of Francesco Bernardi) in the title role. All three singers were paid the same high rate, £2,000 for the season. They were fiercely competitive – had any one of them received one penny more than the others, the others would have withdrawn – but they did not exceed the bounds of decorum until the following season.

By January 1727 factions had developed, with their patrons alternately cheering or hissing Cuzzoni or Faustina. Cuzzoni's partisans were led by Mary, Countess of Pembroke, and the opposite camp was led by Dorothy, Countess of Burlington, and Lady Delawar. That month, Cuzzoni was nearly hissed off the stage during a performance of *Astianatte* while Princess Amelia was present; Cuzzoni remained on stage by royal command and endured the catcalls. A near-riot broke out at the King's Theatre in the Haymarket on 6 June during another performance of *Astianatte*, when Princess Caroline was present: 'The Contention was at first carried on by Hissing on one Side, and Clapping on the other; but proceeded at length to Catcalls, and other great Indecencies' (*British Journal*, 10 June 1727). Very shortly afterwards, at a joint performance of both prima donnas, Faustina and Cuzzoni had a hair-pulling fight on the stage. This scandal was lampooned in *The Devil to Pay at St. James's: or, A full and True Account of a Most Horrible and Bloody Battle between Madam*

Faustina and Madam Cuzzoni, which appeared in June 1727, and in *The Contre Temps; or, Rival Queans* (1727): '*The Queen and Princess again engage; Both factions play all their warlike Instruments; Cat-calls, Serpents and Cuckoos* [wind instruments] *make a dreadful din.* F—s—na *lays flat* C—z—ni's *Nose with a Sceptre; –* C—z—ni *breaks her head with a gilt-leather crown:* H[ande]l *desirous to see an end of the battle, animates them with a kettle-drum*' (pp. 15–16). *An Epistle* was republished in *The Twickenham Hotch-Potch* (1728, pp. 22–5). The continuing discord brought about the downfall of the Royal Academy of Music's new opera company, which found itself unable to pay its debts and which was formally disbanded in June 1728, when Faustina, Cuzzoni and Senesino returned to the Continent. Faustina married the composer Johann Adolph Hasse in 1730 and had her base at the Dresden court opera for many years. Cuzzoni, however, had to sing for her freedom from a debtors' prison in 1751, and ended up making buttons and selling greens in Bologna, where she died in poverty.

The third great prima donna of the age, mentioned by name in *An Epistle*, was Margherita Durastanti (Signora Casimiro Avelloni; born *c.*1685). Her debut was in the title role of Handel's *Agrippina* in Venice in December 1709. Handel engaged her for the 1720–1 London season, usually for breeches parts. Contemporaries referred to her as 'an elephant', and she was known as 'Black Peggy' because of her complexion. She retired from the stage at the end of the 1723–4 season, having been ousted by her rival Cuzzoni; she returned briefly in 1733–4, then disappeared.

Faustina was the only one of these prima donnas who was unmarried at the time *An Epistle* was published. *An Epistle* is presumably written by a supporter of Cuzzoni, and the 'Lady' to whom Faustina is imagined as making a declaration of lesbian love is perhaps intended to be her patroness, the Countess of Burlington or Lady Delawar.

The text is reproduced from the copy held by the British Library (shelfmark 841.m.26 (2)).

AN
EPISTLE
FROM
Signora F—A
TO A
LADY.

They do Let Heav'n see the Pranks,
They dare not shew their Husbands.

OTHELLO.

VENICE:
Printed in the Year M.DCC.XXVII.

[2]

CONDEMN not, *Madam*, as I write in Hafte,
My Thoughts confus'd, or any Word mifplac'd.
Of cens'ring Tongues I fcorn the little Spite,
In wild Diforder, as I Love, I Write.
In Hafte I write to eafe your tortur'd Mind,
Spite of your Jealoufy, I ftill am kind.
Unfpotted as the Sun, my Love fhall rife,
And foon difpel the Fears that cloud your Eyes.

Let others for dear Scandal fearch the Town,
Or with fuperior Fancy chufe a Gown:
Others their Heads with learned Volumes fill,
Or boaft of deeper Science at Quadrille:
In the gay Dance let other Nymphs excel;
F----------na's Glory lies in Loving well.
Of Pleafure all the various Modes I know,
Its different Degrees, its Ebb and Flow.
Ladies, unpractis'd in the Art of Love,
A living *Aretin* in me may prove.
Propitious *Venus* grant me Power to give
Joy to fair --------, 'tis for her I Live.
Ceafe then to let your jealous Fancy rove,
Nor give me fuch a cruel Proof of Love.

Am

[3]

Am I in Fault, that Crouds obfequious bend,
And rival Beauties for my Love contend?
That fierce *Thaleſtris* has attack'd my Heart?
Or gentle *Chloe* caſt a milder Dart?
To fierce *Thaleſtris* I diſdain to yield,
And gentle *Chloe* ne'er ſhall gain the Field.
In vain ſhe breathes her Paſſion in my Ear,
For when you ſpeak I nothing elſe can hear:
In vain with Tranſport to my Feet ſhe flew,
All Joys are taſtleſs, but what come thro' you.
Before your fatal Face I chanc'd to ſee,
No Cynick ever laugh'd at Love like me.
Inconſtant as the Wind, free as the Air,
I rang'd from Man to Man, from Fair to Fair.
I rov'd about like the induſtrious Bee,
Firſt ſuck'd the Honey, then forſook the Tree.
In *Venus'* Combats, I have ſpent the Day,
Swiſs-like, I fought on any Side for Pay.
But now I Love, and your bewitching Face
Has well aveng'd the Cauſe of Human Race.
Do Juſtice to your ſelf, review your Charms,
Nor fear to ſee me in another's Arms.
Have you not Beauty equal to your Youth?
Look in your Glaſs, and then ſuſpect my Truth.
No Paſſion tramontane in you I've found,
By Love and Gratitude I'm doubly bound.
You firſt of all the Britiſh Fair declar'd,
I ſung unrival'd, e'er my Voice you heard.

You

[4]

By Sympathy you felt each Charm, each Grace,
And lov'd my Perfon, e'er you faw my Face.
Nor was I coy, or difficult to move,
When you reveal'd the Story of your Love.
With fuch pathetick Mirth you play'd your Part,
You found an eafy Conqueft of my Heart.
I felt a thrilling Joy, 'till then unknown,
And Lov'd with Ardour equal to your own.
Witnefs the Tranfports of that happy Day,
When melting in each other's Arms we lay.
With Velvet Kifs your humid Lips I prefs'd,
And rode triumphant on your panting Breaft.
Thus rode St. *George*, thus fearlefs thruft his Dart
Up to the Head in the fell Dragon's Heart.

In Extafy you cry'd, What Joys are thefe?
Not *Dureftanti*'s felf fo well cou'd pleafe.
This is no fleepy Husband's feeble Mite,
The taftelefs Tribute of an ill-fpent Night.

Such were our Joys, O cou'd they always laft!
But greateft Pleafures are the fooneft paft.
O did my Power and Will in Concert move!
And were my Strength but equal to my Love!
Th' incredulous Philofopher fhou'd fee
Perpetual Motion verified in me.

F I N I S.

Plain Reasons for the Growth of Sodomy, in England (1730?)

The anonymous satire *Plain Reasons for the Growth of Sodomy* is generally dated *c.*1728, but it is likely that it was published in 1730. The author says that '*Comedy* and *Tragedy* died with *Addison* and *Congreve*, and *Action* with *Booth* and *Oldfield*': the death dates of these playwrights and actors were, respectively, 1719, 1729, 1733 and 1730. If we take 'died' to refer to when these people ceased to write for the theatre or to act on stage, I would opt for the date 1730. Anne Oldfield was still appearing on the stage of Drury Lane in 1730, the year of her death; and Barton Booth, though he did not die until 1733, had retired from the stage in 1727. In an earlier section the author observes that 'our *Sessions-Papers* are constantly stain'd with the *Crimes* of these *Beastly Wretches*'. The *Proceedings in the Old Bailey* published reports of only six trials for sodomitical offences from 1715 through 1725. There were ten sodomitical trials in 1726, five in 1727, six in 1728, three in 1729, four in 1730; then only one or two (or none) each year for the next dozen years and more. All of the 1728 trials took place in October that year, a datum that might seem to suggest that *Plain Reasons* was published in late 1728. However, another satire, *Hell upon Earth*, published in 1729 for Dodd and Roberts (*Plain Reasons* was published for Dodd and Nutt), makes a similar observation on the rise in prosecutions, which *Plain Reasons* seems to echo: 'The late proceedings in our Courts of Law have furnished us with ample Proofs, that this Town abounds too plentifully with a Sect of brutish Creatures called SODOMITES; a Sect that ought to be excluded from all civil Society and human Conversation. They exceed the worst Beasts of the Field in the Filthiness of their Abominations' (p. 41). This passage is a nearly verbatim plagiarism of a letter published in the *Weekly Journal; or, The British Gazetteer* for 14 May 1726, which had referred to four trials for sodomy in April 1726. So documents cannot always be dated conclusively according to the dates of the trials they refer to. However, a date later than mid-1730 is unlikely, because in June and July that year the newspapers widely reported the execution of more than fifty sodomites in Holland, which the xenophobic author of *Plain Reasons* would surely have exploited.

Plain Reasons was subsequently plagiarized. *Satan's Harvest Home*, published in 1749, contains a verbatim copy of the original *Plain Reasons* (under a separate half-title, 'Reasons for the Growth of Sodomy') and the poem 'Petit Maître', as well as a verbatim copy of *Pretty Doings in a Protestant Nation* (1734; reproduced in vol. i of the present set, see pp. 349–410) and a verbatim reprint (acknowledged) of a two-page story from A. G. Busbequius, *Travels into Turkey* (1744), with a perfunctory remark about 'the Game at Flats'. *Satan's Harvest Home* has become an important benchmark for historians of the perception of the homosexual, and is treated as an important marker of a significant shift by 1749, without recognition that this work is wholly plagiarized from earlier works (see my comments in the Introduction, pp. xvi–xvii).

The text is reproduced from the copy held by the British Library (shelfmark 1080.i.38).

PLAIN
REASONS
FOR THE
Growth of Sodomy,
IN
ENGLAND:
To which is added,

The PETIT MAITRE,
An Odd Sort of
An Unpoetical P O E M,
IN THE
Trolly-Lolly Stile,

LONDON:
Printed for *A. Dodd*, near *Temple-Bar*,
and *E. Nutt*, at the *Royal-Exchange*.
(Price Six-Pence.

(3)

REASONS

FOR THE

Growth of SODOMY, &c.

CHAP. I.

The general Contempt of Learning, and Abuse in the Education of our Youth.

UR Fore-Fathers were train'd up to Arts and Arms; The Scholar embellish'd the Hero; and the fine Gentlemen, of former Days was equally fit for the Council, as the Camp ; the Boy, (tho' perhaps a Baronet's Son) was taken early from the Nursery and Sent to the Grammar-School, with his Breakfast in his Hand,

and

(4)

and his Satchel at his Back : fubject to Order and Correction, he went regularly through
his Studies; and, if Tardy, fpurr'd up: The
School-Hours over, and his Exercife made,
he had his Moments of Play allotted him, for
Relaxtion ; then fought he the refort of
other Boys, either in the Fields,- or publick Squares of. the City ; where he hard'ned
himfelf againft the inclemency of Weather,
and innur'd himfelf to athletic Exercifes ;
wholfome, as well, as pleafant : this has
fent him home with his. Blood in a fine Cir-
culation, and his Stomach, as fharp as a Plow-
man's : Supper over, and jogg'd down with
t'other Frolick, he went to Bed, and flept
fweetly ; after which he rofe early the next
Morning, frefh, and fit for Study, hurry'd on
his Cloaths, and away to School again : No
matter if his Hands and Face were now and
then a little Dirty, fo his Underftanding was
clean : If his Cloaths were fometimes torn
with fome Skirmifh, his Heart was whole,
and the frequent Battles between School and
School ; (which were then in Vogue) innur'd him to Courage, gave him a Thirft after Honour, and a Pronenefs to warlike Exercifes.

I would not from this have my little Hero
efteem'd a Bully ; no, his Learning temper'd
his Paffions ; with all this Spirit, the Boy was
bafhful to the laft Degree ; Dutiful and Humble

(5)

ble to his Parents, Mannerly to his Elders and Superiours ; he knew no Vice, being train'd up in a series of Virtue; the Authors he read infpir'd him with Notions of Honour; the Heroes and Sages, whofe Lives he found tranfmitted with fuch Applaufe, through fo many Ages, fill'd him with an Emulation to Knowledge, and a Thirft after Glory; fami-liarized to Temperance and Exercife , he was no Valetudinarian in his Conftitution, but a Stranger to Debauch; and as he grew to riper Years, where the virtuous Object of his firft Wifhes crown'd his virtuous Love, there, in the Flower of his Health, and Vi-gour of his Youth, ftampt he his Maker's Image: Behold our School-Boy now become a Father, bleft with an endearing Wife, and a dutiful, beautiful Off-fpring; his Love and care for them, now makes him ready to purfue whatever State of Life Heaven has alotted him, his abilities of Mind and Body, render him capable of ferving his King, his Country, and his Family : His Appli-cation to Bufinefs keeps him from Debauch, and his fuccefs fo Spurrs him on, that he foon fees a fine Provifion made for himfelf and Family; and his (perhaps fmall) Patri-mony amply augmented: this fhews the Advantages of a proper Education; 1 am forry to fay an old fafhioned One.

Now

(6)

Now let us take a Sketch of the modern Modish way of bringing up Young Gentlemen.

Little Master is kept in the Nursery 'till he is Five or Six Years Old, at least, after which he is sent to a Girl's School, to learn Dancing and Reading, and, generally speaking, gets his Minuet before his Letters ; for whereas Boys of Old went to School at Six in the Morning and came home at Eleven ; Master goes at Eleven and stays till Twelve ; for the poor Child must not get up till all it's Things are aired, and 'tis Barbarous to let him Breakfast without his Mamma ; so that if he is Drest by Tea time, 'tis well enough : to let him have Milk-porridge, Water-gruel or such like, spoon Meats is vulgar and Unpolite : well, by Eleven or a little after Breakfast is over, and Master e'en to School, though very often Breakfast is drilled on till it is too late, unless they Dance in a Morning, and then the whole Family is up sooner than Ordinary. When he comes to School he stands by his Mistress, who is generally working and looking another way all the while, he repeats the Alphabet after her not without some Interruption, though without the least Attention ; for the Child is looking at it's School-fellows, and the Mistress directing
the

(7)

the young Ladies in their Samplers, or other Fiddle Faddles.

Here he continues till the Age at which Boys formerly went to the Univerfities, at laft (with great Reluctance) he is fent to a Mafter, probably to a writing School, for fear he fhould break his Head with *Latin*, befides *Gramamr-Mafters* are harfh; and the Child is of a tender Conftitution: well may it be fo when the Tone of his Stomach has been fpoiled with Tea, when his Blood is curdled with now and then a Dram, to keep the Mother in Countenance; when the Boy's Conftitution is half torn to pieces with Apothecary's *Slip Slops*, occafioned by early Intemperance, fitting up late on Nights, eating Meat *Suppers*, and drinking Wine, and other ftrong Liquors of moft pernicious Confequence to Infant Conftitutions.

Befides his whole Animal Fabrick is enervated for want of due Exercife; and he is grown fo chilly by over nurfing, that he gets Cold with the leaft Breath of Wind; for 'till he went to the *Girls School*, he feldom or never was out of the Nurfery, unlefs to pay a Vifit, in a Coach, with his Mamma : For at the Miftrefs's *School* he was brought up in all refpects like a *Girl*, (Needleworks excepted) for his Mamma had charg'd him not to play with rude Boys,

for

(8)

for fear of fpoiling his *Cloaths*; fo that hither-to our young Gentleman has amufed himfelf with Dolls, affifted at mock Chriftnings, Vi-fits, and other girlifh Employments, inviting and being invited to drink Tea with this or that School-fellow; infomuch, that his whole Life hitherto has been one Series of Igno-rance, Indolence, and Intemperance.

But here the Mafter being doubly bri-bed, by the Father to bring him forward, and by the Mother not to *Correct* him; with much a do, makes a fhift to teach him to Read and Write a little *Englifh*, by which time he is almoft too big to go to School; however, for form's fake, 'tis fit he fhould learn his Accidence before he goes to the Univerfity, or to Travel.

The Boy, thus fpoil'd, becomes *Company* for none but Women, and even of thofe, on-ly the Fantaftical and Impertinent; for, to the Glory of the Sex be it fpoken, the genera-lity of 'em feeing the depravity of *Men*, have fet themfelves to thinking, and got the upper-hand of our *Petits Maitres*, not only in common underftanding, but even in liberal Acquirements and polite Converfation; and are, in all Refpects, fitter for the manage-ment of publick and private Affairs, than the *Milkfops* beforemention'd.

Far

(9)

Far be it from me to arraign all Mankind
for the Faults of a few ! No, Our publick
Schools, such as *Weſtminſter, Eaton,* &c.
ſtill retain the ſame manly Spirit : A Milk-
ſop there, is like an Owl among the Birds :
'Tis juſt the ſame at our Univerſities ; There
are real Students, as well as Fops ; the former being the Glory, as the latter are the
Shame of their Age, or Country.

When our young Gentleman arrives to
Marriage ; I wiſh I could ſay fit for it,
What can be expected from ſuch an enervated effeminate Animal ? What Satisfaction
can a Woman have in the Embraces of this
Figure of a Man ? Should ſhe at laſt bring
him a Child, What can we hope from ſo
crazy a *Conſtitution?* but a feeble unhealthy
Infant, ſcarce worth the rearing ; whilſt the
Father, inſtead of being the Head of the
Family, makes it ſeem as if it were govern'd
by two Women : For he has ſuck'd in the
Spirit of *Cotqueaniſm* from his Infancy : As
for ſupporting them, his Indolence won't let
him undertake any thing laborious ; his Ignorance denies him all Hopes of any thing
of *Conſequence* ; and his Pride won't accept
of what is mean: (at leaſt what he thinks
ſo.) Thus, unfit to ſerve his King, his Country, or his Family, this Man of *Clouts* dwin-
dles into nothing, and leaves a Race as effeminate as himſelf ; who, unable to pleaſe

B   the

(10)

the Women, chuſe rather to run into unnatural Vices one with another, than to attempt what they are but too ſenſible they
cannot perform.

CHAP. II.

*The Effeminacy of our Men's Dreſs, and
Manners, particularly their Kiſſing
each other.*

I AM confident no Age can produce any
thing ſo prepoſterous as the preſent
Dreſs of thoſe Gentlemen who call themſelves pretty Fellows : Their Head-Dreſs,
eſpecially, which wants nothing but a Suit
of Pinners to make 'em down-right Women.
But this may be eaſily accounted for, as they
would appear, as ſoft as poſſible to each other
any thing of *Manlineſs* being diametrically
oppoſite to ſuch unnatural Practices, ſo they
cannot too much invade the Dreſs of the
Sex they would repreſent. And yet with
all this, the preſent Garb of our young Gentlemen is moſt mean and unbecoming. 'Tis
a Difficulty to know a Gentleman from a
Footman, by their preſent Habits : The low-
heel'd Pump is an Emblem of their low Spirits ; the great Harneſs Buckle is the Height
of

(11)

of Affectation; the Silk Waftcoat all belac'd, with a fcurvey blue Coat like a Livery Frock, has fomething fo poorly prepofterous it quite enrages me ; I blufh to fee 'em Aping the Running Footmen, and poifing a great Oaken Plant, fitter for a Bailiff's Follower than a Gentleman. But what renders all more intolerable is the Hair ftrok'd over before and cock'd up behind, with a *Comb* fticking in it, as if it were juft ready to receive a Head-Drefs: Nay, I am told, fome of our Tip Top Beaus drefs their Heads on quilted *Hair Caps,* to make 'em look more Womanifh; fo that Mafter *Molly* has nothing to do but flip on his *Head-Cloaths* and he is an errant Woman, his rueful Face excepted; but even that can be amended with Paint, which is as much in Vogue among our Gentlemen, as with the Ladies in *France.*

But there is no *Joke* like their new-fafhion'd *Joke Hats,* equally priggifh as foppifh; plainly demonftrating, That notwithftanding the *Buftle* they make about *Jokes,* they have 'em only about their *Heads.* But to fee 'em drefs'd for a *Ball,* or Affembly in a *Party-colour'd Silk Coat,* is the Height of my Averfion: They had better have a *Mantua* and *Petticoat* at once, than to mince the Matter thus, or do Things by Halves.

But of all the Cuftoms *Effeminacy* has produc'd, none more hateful, predominant, and

per-

(12)

pernicious, than that of Men's *Kissing* each other. This *Fashion* was brought over from *Italy*, (the *Mother* and *Nurse* of *Sodomy*); where the *Master* is oftner *Intriguing* with his *Page*, than a *fair Lady*. And not only in that *Country*, but in *France*, which copies from them, the *Contagion* is diversify'd, and the Ladies (in the *Nunneries*) are criminally *amorous* of each other, in a *Method* too grofs for *Expreffion*. I muft be fo partial to my own *Country-Women*, to affirm, or, at leaft, hope they claim no Share of this *Charge*; but muft confefs, when I fee two Ladies *Kissing* and *Slopping* each other, in a *lafcivious Manner*, and *frequently* repeating it, I am fhock'd to the laft Degree; but not fo much, as when I fee two *fulfome* Fellows *Slavering* every Time they meet, *Squeezing* each other's Hand, and other like *indecent Symptoms*. And tho' many Gentlemen of Worth are oftentimes, out of pure good *Manners*, obliged to give into it; yet the Land will never be purged of its *Abominations*, till this *Uumanly*, *Unnatural* Ufage be totally abolifh'd: For it is the firft *Inlet* to the deteftable Sin of *Sodomy*.

Under this Pretext vile *Catamites* make their prepofterous *Addreffes*, even in the very *Streets*; nor can any thing be more fhocking, than to fee a Couple of *Creatures*, who

(13)

who wear the Shapes of *Men*, *Kifs* and *Slaver*
each other, to that Degree, as is daily practifed even in our moft publick Places; and
(generally fpeaking) without Reproof; becaufe they plead in Excufe, *That it is the
Fafhion*. Damn'd *Fafhion!* Imported from
Italy amidft a Train of other *unnatural
Vices*. Have we not *Sins* enough of our
own, but we muft eke 'em out with thofe
of *Foreign Nations*, to fill up the Cup of
our *Abominations*, and make us yet more
ripe for *Divine* Vengeance.

’Till of late Years, *Sodomy* was a *Sin*, in
a manner unheard of in thefe Nations; and
indeed, one would think where there are
fuch *AngelickWomen*, fo foul a Sin fhould
never enter into Imagination : On the contrary, our *Seffions-Papers* are conftantly
ftain'd with the *Crimes* of thefe *Beaftly Wretches*; and tho’ many have been
made Examples of, yet we have but too
much Reafon to fear, that there are Numbers yet undifcover'd, and that this *abomina-
le Practice* gets Ground ev’ry Day.

Inftead of the *Pillory*, I would have the
Stake be the Punifhment of thofe, who in
Contradiction to the Laws of *God* and *Man*,
to the Order and Courfe of *Nature*, and to
the moft fimple Principles of *Reafon*, pre-
pofteroufly *burn* for each other, and *leave*
the *Fair*, the *charming Sex*, neglected.

But

(14)

But as Loſs of Appetite is inſeparable from a feeble and depraved *Stomach:* ſo is this *Vice* moſt predominant in thoſe, to whom *Nature* has been ſo ſparing of her Bleſſings, that they find not a Call equivalent to other *Men.* And therefore, rather than expoſe themſelves, they take the *contrary Road*; and, like Eunuchs, out of meer Madneſs and Diſappointment, loath the Dear Sex they have no Power to Pleaſe.

This muſt be the Caſe, if we conſider that the Majority of Perſons ſuſpected of this Vice, are antiquated Leachers; who have out-lived the Power of Enjoyment: are ſo Conſcious of their own Inſufficiency, they dare not look a Woman in the Face.

But ſo Numerous are they Grown, it is high Time to put a Stop to them, leſt the growing Generation be corrupted; and *England* Rival *Italy*, in this moſt unnatural and wicked Practice.

No Step will be more Effectual than at once to Aboliſh the Fulſome Cuſtom of *Men Kiſſing* each other, and to admit of no Plea or Exception in Favour of ſo Deteſtable a Practice.

Is not the old Cuſtom of ſhaking Hands more Manly, more Friendly, and more Decent? What need have we of *Judas* like a Practice? For my Part, I hold it ſo ridiculous fooliſh Cuſtom for a Man to *Kiſs* even his

own

(15)

own Brother, it Savours too much of *Effe-minacy*, to say the best of it. I know some worthy Gentlemen so Scrupulous, they will not on any Account *Kiss* any Friend or Relation of the same *Sex* ; and I saw myself, two Brothers take a very solemn Leave of each other without one *Kiss*, though not without Tears ; and I dare say with more Friendship than Ten Thousand *Kisses* could Express. I am of a Society of Gentlemen, and with Pride I declare it ; who have made a solemn Vow, never to give, or take from any Man a *Kiss*, on any Account whatever ; and so punctual have we been in Observation of this Injunction, that many times at the Expence of a Quarrel, this Rule has been most inviolably kept among us.

If such a Resolution was more Universal the Sons of *Sodom* would lose many *Proselytes*, in being baffled out of one of their principal Advances ; for under Pretence of extraordinary Friendship, they intice unwary Youth from this first Step, to more detestable Practices, taking many Times the Advantage of their Necessities to Decoy them to their Ruin.

I know a Thousand Objections will be brought against what I say, I shall be laught at by all the Votaries of Sodom and Effeminacy ; but I hope the Manly and Generous *Britons*, who yet Survive will take what;

I say,

(16)

I say, into Confideration, and fhow themfelves *Friends to the* F A I R S E X ; by op-
pofing all inlets to the Sin of *Sodomy*, of
which *Man-Kiffing* is the very Firft.

With this, all other *Effeminacy*'s fhould
be abolifhed ; and each Sex fhould maintain
it's peculiar Charaȼter : I hope the Ladies
will not ftand in need of any Advice from
me ; yet I could wifh that fome among
them would feem lefs Amorous of one Another ; for tho' Woman *Kiffing* Woman, is
more fuitable to their Natural Softnefs, and
indeed more excufable than the like Praȼtice
in the contray Sex ; yet it ought to be done
(if at all) with Modefty and Moderation,
left Suggeftions, which I hope are falfe, and
which to me feem Improbable, fhould bring
fuch Ladies under Cenfure ; who give themfelves too great Liberties with each Other :
for as the Age encreafes in Wickednefs, new
Vices may Arife ; and fince they themfelves fee how Fulfome it is in Gentlemen, I hope they will abftain *from all Appearance of Evil,* and Contribute to the intended Reformation ; not only by fcorning
and deriding fuch *Wretches* of *Men,* who
fhall openly Affront them, by *Kiffing* each
other in their Prefence : but that they will fet
the Gentlemen a Pattern, and fhame them

out

(17)

out of it by ufing a *Kifs*, if it muſt be uſed in ſo decent a Manner, and with ſo great Reſtraint, that the moſt Envious ſhall find no cauſe of Cenſure.

C H A P. III.

The Italian OPERA's, *and Corruption of the* Englifh *Stage, and other* Publick Diverfions.

HOW famous, or rather how infamous *Italy* has been in all Ages, and ſtill continues in the Odious Practice of *Sodomy* needs no Explanation, it is there eſteemed ſo trivial, and withal ſo modiſh a Sin, that not a Cardinal or Churchman of note but has his *Ganymede*; no ſooner does a Stranger of Condition ſet his Foot in *Rome*, but he is ſurrounded by a Crowd of *Pandars,* who ask him if he chuſes a *Woman* or a *Boy,* and procure for him accordingly; this Practice is there ſo General, they have little elſe in their Heads or Mouths, than *Caſto* and *Culo* which they intermix with almoſt every Sentence, (a beaſtly and withal a moſt ſtupid Interjection!) for, let them be talking

C   on

(18)

on never fo ferious a Subject, thefe two Syllables muft come in, though never fo foreign to the Purpofe ; thefe they ufe juft as the *French* do the Word *Foutre*, which muft come in by Head and Shoulders in every Company and Sentence. Nay, there are thofe who will intermingle it Word for Word, to the no fmall Improvement of Converfation, we are not yet arrived to this pitch of Perfection ; but much may be hoped in time : For fince the Introduction of I T A L I A N O P E R A S here, our Men are grown infenfibly more and more *Effeminate* ; and whereas they ufed to go from a good *Comedy,* warm'd with the Fire of Love ; and from a good *Tragedy,* fir'd with a Spirit of Glory ; they Sit indolently and fupine at an O P E R A, and fuffer their Souls to be Sung away by the Voices of *Italian Syrens* ; 'twas juft the fame in *Greece,* when they left their Noble warlike Moods, and ran into foft Compounds of *Chromatic Mufic* ; of this the *Philofopher* complains, and to this Attributes the lofs of fo many Battles and Dwindling of the *Grecian-Glory*. *Rome* likewife fank in Honour and Succefs, as it rofe in *Luxury* and *Effeminacy* ; they had Women Singers and Eunuch's from *Afia,* at a vaft Price : which fo foftned their Youth, they quite loft the Spirit of Man-hood, and with it their Empire. For they grew fo

Womanifh

(19)

Womanish in Mind, Gesture, and Attire; and withal so fearful of hurting their sweet Faces, which were nurs'd up with all the *Cosmetics* Art or Nature could invent or produce, that their Enemies kill'd 'em with their very Looks, and for Fear of having their *Faces* gash'd, or their *fine Cloaths* spoil'd, they turn'd their Backs upon those *ugly dirty Fellows*, and gave up their Liberty to preserve their *Effeminacy*. Heav'n grant the Application may never extend to *England*; but I leave any reasonable Person to judge, if the *Similitude* is not too close.

As the ITALIAN OPERA's have Flourish'd, the *English* Stage has diminish'd. Where is that Life, Fire and Spirit which adorn'd our *Plays* of old? Look over the Productions of this last Age (Mr. ADDISON's *Cato* excepted) and you will see nothing worthy to be called a *Play*, or proper to be exhibited to a *British* Audience: They are rather *Drolls* or *Farces*, than *Tragedies* and *Comedies*; so that it may be well said *Comedy* and *Tragedy* died with *Addison* and *Congreve*, and *Action* with *Booth* and *Oldfield*. Our *Players* are now turn'd *Ballad-singers*; our *Theatres* are transform'd to *Puppet-Shews*, improperly called *Pautomimes*; for the *Pantomimes* of the Antients were clever Fellows, that would exactly mimic, or imitate, the Voice

C 2   and

(20)

and Gefture of any Man they had an Intent to to *ridicule.* But in thefe *Pantomine Entertainments* there is neither Head or Tail, Meaning or Connection : *Gods, Harlequins, Priefts,* and *Sailors,* are all jumbled together, even in *Temples,* in the moft incoherent Manner, ten times more extravagant than the moft extravagant Dream that ever was yet dreamt : However, thefe *Drolls* have *crowded Houfes,* while the beft *Plays* of *Shake-fpear* are exhibited to *empty Boxes.*

This fhews the Tafte of the Town, and the Genius of the People ; who, grown quite *Lethargic* with *Luxury,* and in a State of *Perdition,* dare not *think,* and only feek to be *diverted.*

The *Mafqerades, Ridotto's,* and *Affemblies,* of late fo much the Mode, at once explain and condemn themfelves. 'Tis the greateft *Reproach* imaginable to the *Britifh* Nation, that they have fuffer'd themfelves to be bubbled at this rate by a vagabond *Swifs,* who has liv'd *profufely* for many Years paft, at the Expence of *Englifh* Fools ; a publick *Cock-Bawd,* who while others of his *Profeffion* have been punifh'd by Juftices, *&c.* has gone on with Impunity, carefs'd by the *Chief* (I was about to fay beft) of our *Quality ;* but for what Reafons may be eafily imagined.

Next

(21)

Next to the Abuse of *Public Diverfions,* is that of *private Converfation,* which is now reduced to thefe two important Heads, *Tittle Tattle* and *QUADRILLE.*

This *Whiling* away of Time renders us fuch ufelefs *Animals,* that we feem to live to no Purpofe; for as our *Senfes* grow depraved, fo will our *Appetites* and *Inclinations:* For it is evident to Men who have the free Ufe of their *Faculties,* that as there is no Pleafure on Earth equal to the Poffeffion of an *agreeable Woman*; fo it muft be confefs'd, that whoever runs into any *Extreme* of a contrary Nature, it is becaufe he is neither *worthy* or *capable* of enjoying fo great a *Bleffing.*

C H A P.

(22)

C H A P. IV.

The Persecution of Prudes, *and Barbarity of* Women *one to another.*

NOW I have given the *Gentlemen* due Discipline, the *Ladies* must excuse me if I caution them against the malicious Insinuation of *Prudes,* whose Pride is to demolish every one's *Character* to set up their own, when at the same Time they themselves are most voluptuous private *Libertines,* sinning with the utmost Secresy and Security, and yet are maliciously prying and magnifying into *Crimes* every little unguarded Liberty taken by *unwary Persons,* who too secure in their own good *Intentions,* are oftentimes represented as *Devils,* by these much greater *Devils,* whose only Aim is to blacken whatever *Reputation* is fairer than their own,

An old *Proverb* says, *There is no Harm done where a good Child's got.* Faults of this Nature must be confess'd to proceed from a Richness in *Constitution,* and therefore are more excuseable than *base* and *unmanly Practices.*

(23)

ctices. It is the Action of a *Man* to *beget* a *Child*, but it is the Act of a *Beast*, nay worfe, to———I fcorn to ftain my Paper with the Mention; but how many too fearful Perfons are there, who dread more the *Scandal* of a *Child*, than the *Charge*? How many *Murders* have been committed! How many innocent *Babes* perifhed by *Parifh-Nurfes*, becaufe their *Fathers* have not had *Fortitude* enough to ftand the Shock of common *Scandal*? many Men having but too often feen their own Flefh and Blood ftarv'd to Death, and their Eftates left to Strangers. I write not this to encourage *Licentioufnefs*, but to alleviate the thing when an Irrecallable *Accident* has happen'd. Let us fuppofe a *Man* and a *Woman* in the Flower of their *Youth*, paffionately fond of each other, indulging themfelves in the utmoft Latitude of Love; admit the *Woman* become *pregnant*, muft fhe be expofed, ftigmatized, eternally ruin'd for this *Slip*? Muft the *Man* be turn'd out of all Bufinefs, and banifh'd Society for loving a Woman? Muft the poor innocent *Babe* be deem'd an *Outcaft*, upon whom Almighty GOD has thought fit to ftamp his *Sacred Image*?

If 'tis a Sin to *beget* a *Child*, 'tis a much more worfe not to *provide* for it; if 'tis a Sin to *debauch* a Woman, 'tis a much worfe
to

(24)

to *expose* her; if 'tis a Sin for a Man to *love* a pretty Girl, 'tis a much worfe to *burn* for his own Sex.

Let then the *Ladies* be more *merciful*, the *Gentlemen* more *manly*. Let a Harmony between the two *Sexes*, and an univerfal Charity (the greateft of *Perfections*) reign among us, teaching us to walk in the *Paths* of *Virtue* ourfelves, without being fo uncharitably *vain-glorious* of our own Merits, to lofe all Compaffion for the *Venial Offences* of our Fellow Creatures.

POSTSCRIPT.

THE following Piece having fomething very whimfical in its Nature, being an agreeable Mixture of the *Ode* and *Epigram*, is communicated to me by a worthy Friend, whofe Name I would gladly publifh with his Performance, but his Modefty will not permit it; yet I doubt not but it will pleafe the Publick as much as it has done me.

THE

The PETIT MAITRE,

An Odd Sort of

An Unpoetical P O E M,

IN THE

Trolly-Lolly Stile,

By a Gentleman Commoner.

I.

 ELL me, gentle Hob'dehoy!
Art thou Girl, or art thou
Boy ?
Art thou Man, or art thou Ape ;
For thy Gefture and thy Shape,
And thy Features and thy Drefs,
Such Contraries do Exprefs :

D   I ftand

The PETIT MAITRE.

I ftand amaz'd, and at a Lofs to know,
To what new Species thou thy Form
   doft owe?

II.

By thy Hair, comb'd up behind,
Thou fhould'ft be of *Womankind*:
But that damn'd forbidding Face,
Does the charming Sex difgrace;
Man, or Woman, thou art neither;
But a Blot, a Shame to either:
Nor dare to *Brutehood*, even to make
   Pretence;
For *Brutes* themfelves, fhew greater
Signs of Senfe.

III.

By thy *Jaws* all lank and thin;
By that forc'd unmeaning grin:
Thou appear'ft to Humane Eyes,
Like fome Ape of monft'rous Size;
Yet an Ape thou can'ft not be,
Apes are more Adroit than thee;
               Thy

The PETIT MAITRE.

Thy Oddittys fo much my Mind
  perplex ;
I neither can Define thy Kind or
  Sex.

IV.

Art thou Subftance, art thou Shade ?
That thus monft'rouly Array'd,
Walking forth in open Day,
Doft our Senfes quite Difmay ?
Unghaftly yet, thou only can'ft pro-
  voke,
Our Rage, our Deteftation, and our
  Joke.

V.

If thou art a Man, forbear
Thus, this *motly Garb* to Wear ;
Do not Reafon thus difplace,
Do not Man-hood thus Difgrace ;
But thy Sex by Drefs impart,
And appear like what thou Art :
Like what thou Art, faid I, pray
  Pardon me ;
I mean appear, like what thou ought'ft
  to be.

F I N I S.

Advertisement.

AT Monsieur *Babillard*'s *French* Board-ing-School, near *Foppington-Square*, Young Gentlemen are politely edu-cated after the newest Fashion, and carefully taught Dancing, Dressing, Carving and Qua-drille, by the best Masters. They shall be subject to no Hours, Study, or Correction; but us'd tenderly, like Gentlemen; and not brought up Slovers, as at other Schools.

Each Gentleman finds his own Tea; and for the Convenience of those who drink Ass's Milk, Asses attend twice a Day.

N. B. If any Gentleman brings his dry Nurse, she is taken in as an Half Boarder.

College-Wit Sharpen'd; or, The Head of a House, with, A Sting in the Tail (1739)

Dudley Rider, in his diary for 1715–16, advised that 'among the chief men in some of the colleges sodomy is very usual and the master of one college has ruined several young handsome men that way,…it is dangerous sending a young man that is beautiful to Oxford' (ed. W. Matthews (London, 1939), p. 143). This is borne out by the anonymous satire *College-Wit Sharpen'd*, which was prompted by a homosexual scandal that shook Wadham College, Oxford, in February 1739 – hence the alternate title on the first page of the text: 'The Wadhamites'. The major document resulting from this scandal, *A Faithful Narrative of the Proceedings in a Late Affair between The Rev. Mr. John Swinton, and Mr. George Baker,…to Which is Prefix'd, A Particular Account of the Proceedings against Robert Thistlethwayte…for a Sodomitical Attempt upon Mr. W. French* (1739), is reproduced in set I of *Eighteenth-Century British Erotica* (London, 2002) together with my notes and comments (vol. v, pp. 355–90).

Revd Robert Thistlethwayte, Warden of Wadham, was in the habit of making homosexual advances to students and employees of the College. He seems to have forced his sexual attentions (just short of sodomy) upon a Commoner of the College, Master William French, on 3 February 1739. After about a week of silence, French's friends persuaded him to make his accusations public, despite his fears that he would be expelled. A committee of prominent officials of the University began investigating the affair. Robert Langford, the butler, was subpoenaed and testified that Thistlethwayte had invited him to supper, and while drinking a bottle of wine Thistlethwayte had tried 'to kiss and tongue him, and to put his Hand into his Breeches' (*Faithful Narrative*, in set I of *Eighteenth-Century British Erotica* (London, 2002), vol. v, p. 374) and told him 'I would not give a Farthing for the finest Woman in the World, for I love a Man as I do my Soul' (*Faithful Narrative*, p. 375). William Hodges, the barber, was subpoenaed and testified that 'Whilst he was shaving him,…he found the Warden trying to introduce his Hand into his Breeches. Whereupon he asked him what he meant…the Warden answered, "There is no Harm in this, my Dear"; and talked to the same effect so long, that the Barber swore he would never shave him again, for he knew what he wanted, and that he was the wrong Person for his Purpose' (*Faithful Narrative*, pp. 375–6). Thistlethwayte resigned all his offices on 22 February 1739 and fled to Boulogne, where he died five years later.

Revd John Swinton, French's tutor, was also drawn into the scandal. French's friend George Baker gathered evidence from Swinton's servant Bob Trustin, who claimed that 'he used to lie in the Bed with Mr. *Swinton*; that Mr. *Swinton* used to tickle and play with him in the Morning; that he used to play with Mr. *Swinton*'s Cock, which used to stand;…that he used to put his Cock into his A[rse] H[ole], and that he felt something warm came from him, and he sometimes made him wet between his Thighs' (*Faithful Narrative*, pp. 379–80). Baker made these accusations public, but Swinton and a University committee forced Baker to sign a recantation, which was published in the newspapers on 21 March. This seems to have prompted the satirical pamphlet, *The State of Rome, under Nero and Domitian* (1739), which referred to the scandal in stereotypical rather than specific terms: 'Say *Dear Swintonius* what detested Clime, / Taught *Latium*'s learned Sons so dire a Crime? / … / Here *Sporus* live – and once more feel my Rage, / Once and again I drag thee on the Stage, / *Male-female* Thing, without one Virtue made, / Fit only for the *Pathick*'s loathsome Trade' (pp. 8, 9). Shortly afterwards, Baker published *A Faithful Narrative* to justify his accusations, and in 1740 Baker successfully sued Swinton at the Court of King's Bench for defaming his character. The author of *College-Wit Sharpen'd* refers to names and incidents recounted in *A Faithful Narrative*, which was probably his source rather than any first-hand knowledge of the affair. Despite all this adverse publicity, Swinton not only retained his post, but steadily advanced in his career. He married *c*.1743 and migrated to Christ Church in 1745. He was appointed keeper of the University archives in 1767 and became famous as an antiquary and scholar on Asian, Etruscan and Arabic subjects.

The text is reproduced from the copy held by the Bodleian Library (shelfmark G. A. Cambs 80 194 (9)).

COLLEGE-WIT *Sharpen'd:*

O R,

The HEAD of a HOUSE,

W I T H,

A STING in the TAIL:

BEING, A

New *English* AMOUR,

OF THE

EPICENE GENDER,

DONE INTO

BURLESQUE METRE,

FROM THE

I T A L I A N.

ADDRESS'D TO THE

TWO FAMOUS UNIVERSITIES

OF

S-d-m and *G-m-rr-h.*

L O N D O N:

Printed for J. WADHAM, near the Meeting-House in *Little-Wild-Street*, where the SUPPLEMENT, which will shortly be published, may be had; and Sold at the Pamphlet-Shops of *London* and *Westminster*. M.DCC.XXXIX.
(Price Six-pence.)

[1]

The WADHAMITES:

A

BURLESQUE

POEM.

T length, the *Quære* is decided;
And Difputants, long fince di-
(vided,

Muft now in one Opinion join,

OXFORD does CAMBRIDGE far out-fhine.

B   There

[2]

There reigns, and thrives, an antient ART,

T'improve the Health, and chear the Heart.

O! *Whitefield*, had you tarry'd longer,

Your Party might have been much ſtron-

(ger.

Could you, dear Sir, abet this Cauſe,

You'd ſkreen your ſelf from penal Laws;

W-rd-ns, and *C---ll--r*, would be-friend

(you;

B-ſh-ps at *Kennington* attend you:

Nay, in their holy Arms embrace,

Squeeze your white Hand, and kiſs your

(Face:

Nay,

[3]

Nay, more, they'd grope your virgin ------

(Breeches,

And lign your Pockets well with Riches.

I only Hint, I don't advife;

(Since ev'ry Man's not born to rife:)

For fhould your Genius prove too low,

Your Skull too thick, your Wit too flow;

Should *Sw-nt-n* after taking Pains,

T'infufe his Skill into your Brains,

For want of Taft, mifpend his Time,

Your heavy Soul would be your Crime.

ATTEND, I'll paint you out a Cafe,

Which happen'd, in that learned Place.

B 2   Not

[4]

Not *Pembroke*'s *Warden*; no, 'tis *W-dh-m*,

The Word, Ifaith, founds much like *So-*

dom:

Deeply in this rare ART acquainted;

Virtuous; no Vice his Soul e'er tainted:

Nay, more, abhors a pretty Wench.

Pleas'd with the fprightly Air of *Fr--ch*,

Kindly determines to impart

To him, the Secrets of his ART.

Straightway the *Manciple* he fends,

That Dr. *Th-ftle-th-te* intends,

The choiceft Favours to beftow

On pretty *Fr--ch*; that he muft go

Directly to the *Warden*'s Chamber.

The Truth can never be a Slander.

AWAY

[5]

Away comes *Fr--ch*, the *W-rd-n* meets
(him,
And with the greateſt Friendſhip, treats
(him;
But ſad Neglect, ne'er aſks his Mind,
If he was to the ART inclin'd:
But *Nolens Volens*, learn he muſt,
And at him makes a potent Thruſt.

Fr--ch, tho' a Youth of ſolid Parts,
Well read in many uſeful Arts,
Could not the *W-rd-n*'s Science reliſh;
But baſely, often call'd it Helliſh.
This muſt be owned, no Diſgrace is,
Since Gifts are various as Faces.

Some

[6]

Some are for one Thing, fome another;

This a Divine, a Lawyer t'other:

What one efteems a ufeful ART,

Another values not a Fart.

Thus *W-dh-m*'s *W-rd-n*, learned, wife,

Extols this ART above the Skies.

THE worthy *Dr.* kindly try'd,

T'inftruct the Youth, (who ftill deny'd,)

With all the Symptoms of Affection;

And Promifes of his Protection:

To which he adds, an ardent Kifs,

As Earneft of that future Blifs

He might expect, would he but once

Submit to learn; yet ftill a Dunce.

Hard

[7]

Hard Fate, O! *Th-ftle-th-te*, is thine,

To caft thy Pearls, before fuch Swine.

L--g f--d, and *H-dg-s*, are the next,

The *Warden* preach'd to, from that Text;

Lab'ring with more than human Skill,

His wholfome Doctrine to inftil;

Defcrib'd it in its proper Light,

As yeilding Profit with Delight:

And to eradicate each Doubt,

That might fubfift, he ftrait pull'd out,

An *Inftrument*, moft finely fram'd,

(I cannot fay I hear'd it nam'd:)

To give a Demonftration plain,

He taught them not, in Hopes of Gain.

                              Then

[8]

Then eagerly he went to work.

I'm told, there hardly is a *Turk*,

In that moft fpacious Tract of Land,

But what this ART does underftand.

THAT by the Bye. This Man of *W-d-*
(*h-m*,

Whofe ART exifted firft in *Sodom*,

Began to fhew his Skill moft truly,

Hard Fate! The Wretches prov'd unruly.

H-dg-s bawl'd out, forbear, be Civil:

L--gf--d cries, Fury, Hell, the Devil.

THIS ftopt a while his Demonftration,

And fill'd his Soul with great Vexation.

Then

[9]

Then both in one Petition join'd,

Dear Mr. *W-rd-n*, pray be Kind,

We cannot learn: O pray give o'er,

And we'll provide you with a *Wh-re*.

The *W-rd-n* fays, I pray don't hollow:

Your Inference, can never follow;

My ART may feem moft ftrange to you,

Your Ign'rance, that's the Caufe; 'tis true.

But you are not to Old to learn;

Will Riches do you any Harm?

THEN took he *L--gf--d* in his Arms,

My Dear, you are all over Charms.

Oh! Why fo Coy, my pretty Jade;

Why, of my facred ART afraid?

C   Difcard

[10]

Difcard your Doubts, difperfe your Fears,

Joy fhall attend your future Years;

You I'll fecure, from ev'ry Woe,

Then change for Yes, the dreadful No.

View but how *Sw-nt-n* fpends his Time;

Pleafure and Profit, both combine,

To make his Days one fingle Scene,

Of perfect Blifs; then what d'ye mean?

Embrace the prefent happy Time;

Int'reft can never be a Crime.

This faid, he made a frefh Attack,

His Skill to prove, upon his Back.

What fhall we fay, this bafe Ingrate,

With Stick of Oak, he broke his Pate;

Leaving

[11]

Leaving the *W-rd-n* on the Floor,

To rowl and wallow in his Gore:

Rend'ring for Good, the greateſt Evil,

Sure, their ſome Kin unto the Devil.

But let me crave your cloſe Attention,

To what I farther have to mention.

After they had this Faƈt committed,

For which they ſhould have been *De Wit-*

(*ted*,

Conſcience diſturb'd, for the Tranſgreſſi-

(on,

Fear of their Spirits took Poſſeſſion.

What might be done, with Speed, to ſkreen

('em,

Was often argued between 'em.

C 2 Schemes

[12]

SCHEMES are advanc'd, again rejected,

For fear they both fhould be detected.

At laft, as Fortune often Smiles,

On Knaves, and honeft Men beguiles,

They heard by Chance, Oh happy Day!

That *Fr--ch* as ftupid was, as they;

That after all the *W-rd-n*'s Pains,

He curs'd the ART, and call'd him Names,

WITH Joy they fpeedily repair,

T'acquaint him with the whole Affair;

Tell him their Cafe, and what they fear'd,

The which, when *Fr--ch* had fully hear'd,

Courage

[13]

Courage (fays he) keep but all Quiet,

We'll ruin him, they both cry'd, *Fiat.*

THIS is the Scheme, (and we'll declare

(it,

Nay, more than that, we'll roundly fwear

(it,

Before the Jury-Men with Speed,

Which if by you, 'tis but agreed,

My Life for't, when they've heard the

(Cafe,

They'll foon expel him from this Place;)

That being void of Holy Fear,

And ev'ry Grace, to *Chriftians* dear,

Holds Converfation with the Devil;

Deals in black ARTS, and ev'ry Evil;

Raifes

[14]

Raiſes up Spirits, horrid, frightful;

In ſhort, that he is grown ſo ſpiteful,

As to deſtroy the Health and Eaſe,

Of all, who dare him to diſpleaſe.

THIS Scheme contriv'd, with helliſh ART,

They to the Jury-Grand impart,

Back'd with an Oath, to bind it ſton-

(ger;

The Jury could contain no longer,

But ſend immediately a Proctor,

To cite before them, *W-dh-m's Doctor.*

BUT he withdrew; for having hear'd,

Their baſe Deſigns, he wiſely fear'd,

That

[15]

That Right, or Wrong, he might be Caft;
Thus they were Conquerors at laft.

THIS you well know, fometime's the
(Cafe,

Virtue and Learning meet Difgrace;
Yet very often gets the beft
Of Vice and Falfhood,: Hear the reft.

Sw-nt-n, a Man, to moft fuper'our,
To none in *W-dh-m* is infer'our,
In the fame ART the *W-rd-n* taught;
Blefs'd with a happy Turn of Thought,
To fkreen himfelf fecure from Spight:
In that he certainly is Right;

For

[16]

For tho' as harmless as a Dove,

Yet surely it does well behove,

For to assume the Serpent's Wit.

Least like the *W-rd-n* he is Bit.

Sw-nt-n's Success in *S-d-m's* ART,

Should animate each fearful Heart,

To cultivate, and spread the Science,

And bid each env'ous Dunce defiance.

If their dull Souls cannot attain

This ART, promoting Health and Gain;

Why should they envy brighter Mind?

This was the Cafe, as you will find,

Sw-nt-n desiring for to spread

The Skill, in which he's deeply read,

To

[17]

To all around, both Rich and Poor;

No Indication can be truer,

Of a diffufive publick Spirit,

Which few are born for to inherit;

After his ART with great Succefs

He'd taught to twenty, more or lefs,

Some Rich, fome Poor, as he could find

Their Genius was thereto inclin'd;

Beheld with Sympathy a Youth

Poor, yet unprejudic'd to Truth;

Of foft Behaviour, pregnant Wit:

This Lad he inftantly thought fit,

To well inftruct in ev'ry Part,

Of this his late revived ART.

Then took him Home to Board and Bed,

And daily Lectures to him read,

D   That

[18]

That by **Degrees** he might prepare him,

For fear the firſt Attempt might ſcare

(him;

And between whiles, he ſtrok'd his Face,

And felt him over in each Place,

And cloſely hugg'd him in his Arms,

Swore none alive poſſeſs'd ſuch Charms.

In ſhort Sir, *Sw-nt-n* by Degrees,

Taught him the MYSTERY with Eaſe.

BUT as it often is the Fate

Of Virtuous, Fortunate, and Great,

To be by envious Tongues defam'd:

This was the Caſe of him juſt nam'd.

A

[19]

A Man there was of Genius mean,

Crafty and bafe, as will be feen;

Not born to taft fuch ARTS as thefe,

Him Nature had not form'd to pleafe;

With hellifh Malice views the Boy,

Carefs'd by *Sw-nt-n*; call'd his Joy:

Forms a moft bafe and vile Defign,

To fwear on *Sw-nt-n* the fame Crime,

Charg'd on the *W-rd-n* by his Foes:

This done, away the Traitor goes;

Prevails on *Bob* the Fact to Charge,

Before the *C-----ll-r* at large,

Upon the very beft of Mafters,

Virrue will not prevent Difafters.

This wicked Boy, of Grace devoid;

All Senfe of Gratitude deftroy'd,

D 2   Affirms,

[20]

Affirms, and aggravates the Cafe,

With mimmick Probity in's Face;

Declares, that fhould the human Race,

His wicked Mafter's A R T embrace,

Mankind would foon become no more,

Things would be juft as heretofore.

Thus far the Scheme did well fucceed,

And *Sw-nt-n* would have been decreed

At leaft, to leave that famous Place,

With Deteftation and Difgrace,

Had he not plainly made appear

His Innocence: Once more give Ear.

What is't that Promifes won't do?

He fends to *Bob*, I vow 'tis true,

Upbraids him with his bafe Defigns;

Bob's Confcience pricks him for his Crimes:

What

[21]

What can he do to make Amends,

His injur'd Mafter, beft of Friends?

No more's required on this Score,

Unfay what you have faid before;

Declare that *B-k-r* mov'd you to't,

By Cafh and Promifes to boot.

Bob acts his Part, the Tables change,

(My Friend, there's nothing new or ftrange;)

B-k-r before the *C------ll-r*'s cited,

Who tells him that he is indicted,

Upon the Defamation Act,

And prefs'd him warmly to retract;

And own, that Malice was the Caufe,

Againft all Juftice, Truth and Laws

That moved him to forge this Story,

To blaft forever *Sw-nt-n*'s Glory:

And

[22]

And adds with domineering Note,

That he muft fign, what they had wrote;

Or he'd commit him, and expel him :

Thus Sir, you fee, what has befel him.

WHAT could he do, who dare with-ftand,

The Stroke of his vindictive Hand?

He fign'd the Scrowl; own'd Truth a Lie,

My Tale is told: Dear Sir, Good-bye.

THUS thrives an ART, none dare op-

(pofe,

Unlefs he'll forfeit Food and Cloaths.

F I N I S.

The Pretty Gentleman: or, Softness of Manners Vindicated (1747)

The author of *The Pretty Gentleman* was Nathaniel Lancaster (1701–75), a protégé of George Cholmondeley, 2nd Earl of Cholmondeley. In the year of his patron's death, 1733, he was appointed chaplain to Frederick, Prince of Wales. From 1737 until his death he was the rector of a small parish near Ongar, Essex. Cholmondeley had introduced Lancaster into polite society, and Lancaster was said to be a brilliant conversationalist. His only other writings were *Public Virtue, or The Love of our Country* (1746), *The Plan of an Essay upon Delicacy* (1748) and a kind of sermon-in-verse, *Methodism Triumphant* (1767). *The Pretty Gentleman* was published in 1747, and reprinted in *Fugitive Pieces* published by R. and J. Dodsley in 1761, which was reprinted in 1762 (Dublin edn), 1765 and 1771.

The attribution to Lancaster is made on the basis of a manuscript note by Isaac Reed on the flyleaf of the 1771 edition of *Fugitive Pieces* (British Library shelfmark 12315.bb.40): '1762 | Extract of a Letter from Mr. Robert Dodsley to Mr. [William] Shenstone "– The name of the concealed Authors in The Fugitive pieces are as follow....The pretty Gentleman by Dr Lancaster & the plan of the Essay on Delicacy by the same."' The letter has not been traced, but there is no reason to doubt Reed's statement of its existence or contents (Reed went through Dodsley's papers after his death). But was Dodsley himself misinformed? Lancaster's *Plan of an Essay upon Delicacy* was published under his own name in 1748, with a dedication to the Earl of Cholmondeley. Why should Dodsley call Lancaster a 'concealed Author' with respect to this latter work, whose authorship was never in doubt?

The *Plan of an Essay upon Delicacy* (1748) is very polite and very learned, illustrating a familiarity with the classics also shown in *The Pretty Gentleman*. However, it lacks the irony and forcefulness of *The Pretty Gentleman*. It also lacks the italics and dashes that strew the latter. Whatever the internal evidence may indicate about the latter, the *Plan* could have been written *by* a Pretty Gentleman. It is a serious praise of elegance, politeness, comely manners and the beauties of delicacy and refined delights, as opposed to 'SAVAGE MERRIMENT' (p. xxi). It consists of a dialogue between Sophronius and Philocles, two men who 'have long lived together in the strictest intimacy, and most unreserved communication of sentiments' (p. 4).

It is not clear why Lancaster would have been stimulated to contribute to the debate about effeminacy or why he would have strong feelings against Garrick such as those expressed by the pseudonymous 'Philautus' in *The Pretty Gentleman*. Further, it does seem odd for the author of *Methodism Triumphant* to rejoice in coarse puns such as the names of his characters Molliculo ('soft arse') and Amoriculus ('arse-lover'), and to quote Juvenal rather than the Scriptures, or at least the less scurrilous of the Ancients. But we must remember that Georgian rectors were not Victorian parsons.

The text is reproduced from the copy held by the British Library (shelfmark 1081.m.27).

THE
Pretty Gentleman :

OR,

SOFTNESS of MANNERS
VINDICATED

From the false RIDICULE exhibited
under the Character of

WILLIAM FRIBBLE, Esq;

LONDON:
Printed for M. COOPER at the *Globe* in *Pater-
noster Row.* 1747.
[Price Six-Pence,]

T O

Mr. GARRICK.

S I R,

AS in the *Wantonnefs* of your petulant
Fancy, you have fallen upon a Set
of Gentlemen, who cannot' poffibly have
given you any perfonal Provocation; I
have thought proper to prefix your Name
to this their Defence, and call upon you
thus publickly to juftify your Behaviour,
if it be poffible. But furely, Sir, it
muft have been a fecret Admiration of
their Elegant and Refined Manners, that
called forth your Spleen, to turn into Ridicule thofe foft Accomplifhments you de-
fpaired to equal; and, as a Comic Writer
did by the Divine Socrates, mimic and
burlefque upon the Stage what you had not
the Face to imitate in real Life. But your
Wit was as impotent as your Malice was
ftrong. Your Farce was no fooner feen,
than it was laugh'd at; you know, Sir, it
was laugh'd at; moft prodigioufly laugh'd
at: A plain Proof, that it was judged to
be very ridiculous.

A 2　　　　　　B E-

(iv)

BELIEVE me, Sir, you have fallen most miserably short in your Attempt. And how should it be otherwise? You pretend to exhibit a Representation of The Pretty Gentleman, *who are by no means an* Adept *in the Character!* You! *that are an entire Stranger to those fine Sensations, which are* requisite *to give a thorough Notion, and true Relish of the Enjoyments it affords! How should you paint what Nature has not given you Faculties to feel? As far as* SHE *leads you by the Hand, you may perhaps succeed: But to leave her* behind, *and tread those secret Paths to which her Guidance never points;* This, *Mr.* Garrick, This *is far beyond the Power of your limited Genius.*

SO wishing you more fortunate in your next Essay, and wise enough never to expose yourself again to Derision, by endeavouring to laugh out of Countenance a Character which all sensible Men look upon with Admiration *and* Astonishment, *I take leave to subscribe myself, as much as I ought to be,*

  SIR,

   Your Humble Servant,

     PHILAUTUS.

THE

Pretty Gentleman, &c.

 H E Theatre is said to be the proper School for correcting the little Irregularities and Foibles of Mankind ; and no Method is held more likely to check the Growth of Folly, than to bring it to full View in Scenes of humorous Representation. But then the Comic Writer should be certain, that what he endeavours to expose, be really an Object of Ridicule ; otherwise he not only offends against the Rules of the *Drama*, but the Precepts of *Virtue*.

I AM

[6]

I AM led into thefe Reflections, by a late Performance exhibited on our Stage, wherein the Author attempts to laugh out of Countenance that *mollifying Elegance* which manifefts itfelf with fuch a bewitching Grace, in the *refined* Youths of this *cultivated Age.* It is in Defence of thefe injured Gentlemen that I have taken up my Pen ; and how well qualified I am to exeöute fuch an Undertaking, the Reader will be convinced, if he has but Patience to perufe carefully the following Sheets.

AMIDST all my Refearches into the Hiftory of this Country, I do not find one PRETTY GENTLEMAN, till the glorious Reign of King *James* I. This Prince had an odd Mixture of contrary Qualities. In fome refpects he retained the Rufticity of *Gothick* Manners ; in others, he was very refined.

LORD *Clarendon* affures us, " That His " *Moft Sacred* MAJESTY was fo highly de- " lighted with a Beautiful Perfon and Fine " Cloaths, that thefe were the chief Recom- " mendations to the Great Offices of State." A convincing Proof (begging the noble Hif-
torian's

[7]

torian's Pardon) of that Monarch's fuperiour Talents for Government.

'In the Reign of *Charles* I. this Refinement funk in Reputation : For how indeed was it poffible, that a genuine Tafte could be cultivated, when *Falkland* was beheld with general Admiration, and *Waller* read with general Delight ?

Harder ftill was her Fate, under the Rebukes of an auftere Republic, and a four Protector. The very *Loyalifts* themfelves were treated with lefs Rigor, and not a Man of any Elegance durft even fhow his Head.

But when Monarchy was reftored, *Tafte* emerged from her Obfcurity, and fhone with fome Degree of Luftre. For tho' the Prince was fomewhat inelegant in Himfelf, yet that *downy Eafe*, which was cherifhed under his aufpicious Influence, was highly favourable to the Cultivation of *foft Manners*; notwithftanding the malicious Efforts of *Milton, Denham. Dorfet, Buckingham* and *Dryden.*

FROM

[8]

FROM this Period, to the Beginning of the prefent Century, her Progrefs was now and then checked by the Blafts of Envy; yet, upon the whole, fhe made fome tolerable Shoots; when at laft, a Set of malevolent Spirits arofe, who * with a cruel and bloody-minded Zeal, entered into a Combination to deftroy this lovely Plant, both Root and Branch. The better to effect their barbarous Refolution, they fet up an *Idol* of their own Fancy, afcribed to it all the Attributes of the *Graces*, and with the Artifice of deceiving Blandifhments, allured the Majority of the Nation to fall down and worfhip the *Image* which they had fet up.

HENCE it was that *Elegance* became a neglected Character, and the *pretty Gentleman* an Object of general Contempt, and barbarous Raillery.

BUT no fooner were thefe Enemies removed, than the Sons of Delicacy made an Attempt to rife again: And how fuccefsful they

* Under the Forms of *Tatlers*, *Spectators*, and *Guardians*.

[9]

they have been, every Place of polite Resort does fully witness; and notwithstanding all Opposition, they are determined to push on their Designs, and polish the *British* Manners. Now the better to carry on this glorious Scheme of Reformation, these Gentlemen have erected themselves into an amicable Society, and from the Principles on which it is founded, have very pertinently stiled it,

The Fraternity of PRETTY GENTLEMEN.

As no associated Body can possibly subsist, unless they are cemented by an Union of Hearts, the grand Principle of this Fellowship is mutual Love, which, it must be confessed, they carry to the highest Pitch. In this Respect, they are not inferior to the Ιερα φαλαγξ, *The sacred* Theban *Band*, so illustrious in Story. Such an Harmony of Temper is preserved amongst them, such a Sameness is there in all their Words and Actions, that the Spirit of *One* seems to have passed into the *Other*; or rather, they *all* breathe the *same* Soul. This is the secret Charm, that the *Platonists* talk of, the intellectual Faculty,

B which

[10]

which connects one Man with another, and
ties the Knot of virtuous Friendship. But I
need not dwell any longer on a Subject,
which can admit of no Debate; the Notoriety
of the Fact is even become *Proverbial* amongst
us, and every one cries out;

Magna est inter Mollies *concordia!*

I shall now open another Scene, and
present to the Reader a View of their Studies
and Employments; where he will find them
no less worthy of his Admiration and Regard.

They do not indeed consume their Hours
in such Points of vain Speculation, wherein the *Pride* of *Reason* and *Learning* has
Room to operate. And indeed there is
something in the Drudgery of *Masculine* Knowledge, by no means adapted to Youths of so
nice a Frame, that it cannot be said, they are
ever invigorated with perfect Health. The
enfeebled Tone of their Organs and Spirits
does therefore naturally dispose them to the
softer and more refined Studies; Furniture,

Equi-

[11]

Equipage, Drefs, the Tiring Room, and the Toy-fhop.----What a Fund is here for Study! And what a Variety of eafy Delights! Or, if the Mind is bent upon Manual Exercife, the *Knotting-Bag* is ready at Hand; and their fkilful Fingers play their Part. Notwithftanding the Ridicule, which is thrown upon this Part of the Character, it appears to me, rather to merit our *Applaufe*, than to provoke our *Laughter*. With what Satisfaction have I beheld five or fix of thefe elegant Youths interfperfed with an equal Number of Ladies, almoft as delicate as themfelves, and vying with them in their own Accomplifhments! Rouzed by the Ardor of Emulation, they work for *Glory*, and affert the Prize of *Feminine Merit*.

With equal Skill their practifed Fingers apply the Needle, and rejoin the Lace: With equal Facility they convey the gliding Shuttle thro' the opening Thread, and form the various Knots. Pretty Innocents! How virtuoufly, how ufefully are their Hours employed! Not in the wrangling Squabbles of the Bar, or the unmannerly Con-

B 2 tentions

[12]

tentions of the Senate; not in the robuft
Sports of the Field, or, in a toilfome Appli-
cation to ungentlemanlike Science; but in the
pretty Fancies of Drefs, in Criticifms upon
Fafhions, in the artful Difpofition of *China*
Jars and other Foreign Trinkets; in fowing,
in knitting Garters, in knotting of Fringe,
and every gentle Exercife of Feminine Oeco-
nomy.

IF from their Studies we turn our Attention to their Converfation, we muft be convinced, that in this Refpect likewife they
are fo far from meriting Contempt, that nothing in the World can be more refined, or
more engaging.

IT is an eftablifhed Maxim in this School
of Manners, never to oppofe the Sentiments
of the Company. Every Gentleman affents
to every thing that is faid. Sometimes indeed, you may hear what appears, at firft,
like a Difference of Judgment: But have a
little Patience, and you will find, it is only
the genteel Interchange of Sentiments: For
Sippius will go over to the Opinion of *Fannius*,
rather

{ 13 }

rather than be fo rude to contradict him; and *Fannius* will allow his Friend to be in the right, rather than be thought fo ill-bred as not to give up fuch a Trifle as his own Judgment. Whereas your unrectified Spirits are eternally infifting upon the natural Right of maintaining their Opinions, and the Liberty of fpeaking their Minds.

THE Liberty of fpeaking your Mind! A pretty Affertion truly! I know not what Arguments may be drawn, in favour of it, from the mufty Precepts of antiquated Sages, but I am certain, that Good-breeding abfolutely difallows it : Neither indeed is it reconcileable with common Senfe and Difcretion ; for he who difapproves my Sentiments, does in Effect tell me *I am a Fool.* Confequently, let him talk ever fo well, and reafon (as you call it) ever fo juftly, he is fure to give Offence : Whilft the yielding Companion, the well-bred Affenter, never fails to conciliate Favour ; for there is not a more engaging Compliment to the Underftanding, than to facrifice *your own* Vanity to That of *another*.

A

[14]

A PRETTY GENTLEMAN therefore scarce ever dissents. He will indeed sometimes say, " *Oh! pard'n me, mi Dear! I ke'n't* " *possibly be of that Apinion!* " But then this is only a polite Artifice, that he may flatter your Judgment with a finer Address, when he afterwards suffers himself to be convinc'd by your superior Reasoning. To give him his Due, he has no Attachment to any one Opinion in the World, but *that* of preserving the Rules of Good-breeding. In all other Cases, he has an Assent entirely at your Service; and you cannot change Sides oftner, than this most obsequious humble Servant will follow you. A Transgression of *Decorum* is indeed so shocking to his Nature, that he cannot let it pass without Correction; but then it is always inflicted with a gentle Hand. The severest Animadversion never rises beyond this,

O! fie! ye filthy Creter!

THE Epithet *filthy*, as it appears upon Paper, may seem somewhat coarse and unclean: **But**

[15]

But were you to hear how he liquidates the Harſhneſs of the Sound, and conceals the Impurity of the Idea by a ſweetned Accent, you would grow enamoured of his Addreſs, and admire the enchanting Beauties of refined Elocution. *Oh! fie! ye filt-by Creter!* How eaſy, how gentle, how humane a Chaſtiſement for the higheſt Offence!

It has been obſerved (but I don't remember by what Author) that there are two Kinds of Converſation: The one, cloſe and continued; the other, looſe and unconnected. The *Firſt* was practiſed amongſt us whilſt the Enemies of Elegance prevailed: But now the *Latter* has deſervedly gained the Aſcendant, as it is perfectly ſuited to the Turn and Caſt of our polite Aſſemblies of every Denomination.* The Gravity of dull Knowledge is at laſt happily exploded: *Maſculine* Senſe and Wit are rejected as obſolete and unfaſhionable Talents; and better ſupplied by the more engaging Charms of the contrary Qualities. Nothing is now heard, but ſweet Chitchat,

* Drums, Kettle-Drums, Drum-Majors, Routs, Hurries, Riots, Tumults, and Helter-Skelters, the ſeveral Appellations by which the modern Aſſemblies are aptly characterized and diſtinguiſhed.

[16]

chat, and tender Prittle-Prattle, Shreds of
Sentiments, and *Cuttings* of Sentences, all
foft and charming, elegant and polite.

By this fhort Abftract of the prevailing
Turn in polite Converfation, the Reader fees,
that the *Pretty Gentleman* muft neceffarily be
the beft Company ; becaufe he will neither
offend by the abominable Coarfnefs of *manly*
Reafon, nor the ungrateful Poignancy of keen
Repartee : But tho' he is not fuch a *Fool*, or
fo ill-bred as to be down-right *Witty*, he will
now and then indulge himfelf in what he
calls, *The little Efcapes of Fancy*, which I
will not injure fo much as to rank them under the Denomination of *Wit*. If the Company happens to grow languid, *Fannius* has
an admirable Talent at reviving their Spirits
by fome pretty familiar Remark or other ;
which, obvious as it is, would never have entered into the Head of an unrefined Mortal.
On fuch an Occafion this little Wag will pat
a Lady over the Shoulder, and tell her with
the moft facetious Leer,

    " I vew, Me'me, yur'e immoderately en-
" tertaining."   AND

[17]

AND tho' this is all he fays, yet there is fome-thing in the *Manner*, in the *Accent*, and in the---*I don't know what* ; that the Company inftantly revive, and begin again to exchange their *Words*. Nor let any Man imagine that this is a trifling Talent, which can raife Some-thing out of ---Nothing, and reftore a Society to Chearfulnefs and Pleafantry ; for good Man-ners require that Converfation fhould be kept up at any Rate.

BUT when I told you that their Raillery was the moft inoffenfive thing in Nature, and operated fo finely, that it could fcarce be felt ; yet as there are no general Maxims but what have fome Exceptions, I confefs that *Lepidulus* now and then fteps beyond the Rules of the Community, and like a little Wafp as he is, leaves his Sting in the Wound he inflicts.. A certain Lady, who affects a mafculine Senfe and Spirit of Jocularity, gave herfelf the Li-berty to rally the modern Refinement, and in the Ardor of her Zeal was tranfported fome-what beyond the Limits of *Decorum*. Upon this, *Lepidulus* was fo exafperated, that he

C   could

[18]

could not, for the Soul of him, contain any
longer, but fteps towards her with a nettled
Air, looks her full in the Face, and with a
rebuking Countenance, mixed with Fear, gave
Vent to his Spleen.---" I vew, Me'me ! it-it-
" it's not--without infinite Pains --that yu're
" able---to make yurefelf lefs am'able."

THIS cutting Reproof, juft and feafonable
as it was, would hardly have paffed uncenfur-
ed by the Fraternity, had it not been excufed
by the high Provocation, which occafioned it.

THE other Day, when the whole Body
was affembled, they had the Patience to-per-
ufe that abominable *Farce* now under my Correction. " It is the moft aftonifhing Thing
" in Nater, cries *Tenellus*, that fo low a Per-
" formence fhould meet wi' fuch pop'ler Ap-
" plaufe ! --- O Lard ! Oh Lard ! as I hope
" for Mircy, replies *Lepidulus*, there's re'lly
" now nothing at all fupprizing in the Cafe ;
" for pop'ler Fame is nothing but *Air* ; and
" *Air* (as your Scholars tells us) nat'rally
" preffes into ------ a Vac'uum. He---he---
" he--he !

THO'

[19]

THO' this was a keen Conceit, yet as it reflected Honour on the Community, it was fo highly relifhed, that they had certainly broke out into a loud Laughter, were it not that fuch *Burfts* of Mirth are looked upon as the Marks of favage Manners. A *governed* Smile, or fo---they judge to be not at all ungraceful. Nay, an *Half-Laugh* upon a very extraordinary Occafion, is not efteemed a Departure from Decorum. But then, the utmoft Caution imaginable is taken, that it proceed no farther. And it is pleafant enough to fee the the little Difficulties they ftruggle with in fupprefling the Inclination. The tick-'ling Senfe of the home-felt Conceit, puts the rifible Features into Motion ; but then it is inftantly checked by the quick Impulfe of fine Senfation. The one prompts to give full Vent to the rifing Joy ; the other bids---forbear. It is this pretty Altercation, which produces that *tempered Laugh*, which plays with fuch a Grace on the Countenance of a Pretty Gentleman.

Bʏ what I have already advanced, the Reader may probably perceive, that their

C 2   Language

[20]

Language and Diction has the moſt eſſential
Requiſite of Style, and that *the Sound always
eccho's to the Senſe*.　But ſince this Part of the
Character has been a Subjeċt of our Mimic's
Raillery, I ſhall produce ſuch Inſtances, as
will inconteſtibly demonſtrate the Truth of
my Aſſertion.

SOME time ago, four or five of theſe elegant Youths were invited to dine at Lady
Betty ----'s.　The firſt Diſh that was ſerved
up happened to ·be a Leg of *Lamb and Spinage*; at the Sight of which *Fannius* inſtantly
fainted away.

　" OH Lard! ſays *Timidulus*, fetch ſome
" Draps.---Take away the Diſh, cried *Molli-
" culo*---Perhaps he has ſome 'Tipathy **to**
" Lamb.　No, no, replies *Tenellus*, he has
" evermore his Hyſterics at this Time of the
" Year.---Let him alone, for He'vns Sake!
" don't croud about'm ;---he'll come to him-
" ſelf preſently.---Fetch a little Pepper Mint-
" water, ſays *Cottilus*, it is------

By

[21]

B v this Time, *Fannius* finding his Spirits
return, gently lifted up his Head,---and after
half a Dozen Sighs—— " Heigh ! Hob !
" Where am I ? ——Well—I proteſt — I
" am quite ——— aſhamed to —— to——
" But——do you know, whenever I ſee a
" Leg of *Lamb* and *Spinage*, it is ſo like——
" that it puts me in mind of—" [*Here he
burſt out into a Flood of Tears*]— " It puts me
" in mind of my dear, — dear Bitch *Chloe*
" ——— ſunning herſelf upon a *Graſs-Plot !*"
' What a dull Creter was I, *replied the Lady,*
' that I could not think of this ! But upon
' my Veraçity ! I never heard a Syllable that
' *Chloe* was———. It was ſure the moſt
' engaging Company ! And had the ſofteſt
' Coat ! Well ! It was an infinitely pretty
' Creter !

" Oh dear Me'me ! replied *Fannius*—Not
" a Word more, I intreat you.—Your Favor
" is an Antidote againſt all Misfortunes."
Upon this he dried up his Tears ; the Company ſat down again, and all was well. I
have given this Narrative not only as a beautiful

[22]

tiful Specimen of their Language, but as
an exemplary Inſtance of great Humanity of
Temper.

Nor are they leſs excellent in what is commonly called the *Epiſtolary Style*, but more
properly Missive Conversation : The Reader will be fully convinced of this, if he gives
his Attention to the following Specimens.

A CARD.

" Lord *Molliculo's* Compliments to Sir
" *Roley Tenellus*—hopes did not ketch Cold
" laſt Night when he went from th' Oppera--
" ſhall be proud of his Cumpany at Cards
" nex Wenſday fennit,—to meet Lady *Betty*,
" and begs will not fail.

When the Sentiments are committed to
Paper, the Diction riſes to an higher Pitch,
preſerving at the fame time a great Degree of
the *kindred* Form.

Copy

[23]

COPY of a LETTER from Sir *Tho-maſin Lepidulus*, to *Narciſſus Shadow*, Eſq;

Mi Dere· *Neſſy*,

I Expected yu wud ha' retorted upon that brootal Monſtir, who atak'd yu laſt Nite at *Lady* Betty's.—You certinly had it in yure Pour ;—but upon matuer D'liberation, I vew, I think yu was in the Right to turn it off, and treat the Retch wi' good Manners. Yu fine Geniuſſes who 'clypſes every Body, certainly for that Reſon ows every body inf'nite Civility. Pour Puſs is better this Morning—Fever pretty much abated. Pray, mi Dere, how is yure Cold? I tho't yu was vaſtly hoarſe laſt Nite. Better not ſtir abroad — Weather's extremely piercing. I hate this deteſtable Climate, as much as ——, You will ſupply the reſt——

Adieu, dere *Neſſy*,

Yours infinitely,

T. LEPIDULUS.

[24]

Narciſſus read this Letter to his Valet ; and having talked the Subject over with him, not perhaps to borrow any of the Fellow's Sentiments, but to give Riſe to ſome in himſelf, wrote the following Anſwer—

I Proteſt to you, my dear Leppy, *I was ſeveral Times upon the Point of breaking out with the Sharpneſs of Rebuke. Was there ever ſuch a nauſeous Creter? To confeſs the Truth,—I ſhud certainly have been ſevere upon him, but that ---- it is much more becoming a Gentleman, not to ſay any thing ſubject to inconvenient Interpretations. The Fellow is ----- what you call ſprightly ---- but has not the leaſt Tincture of Delicacy about him. Pray, have you ſeen the New Play? I ſhe'n't be eſy till I have yure Opinion.*

MY Suſpicions are confirmed. Amoriculus (wud You believe it?) the abominable Man is, bona fide, *become a Parent by his Criminal Gratifications.*

Adieu Deery! Love me, as I do You---- and more ---- if You can.

Yours for ever,

P.S. *Half Hour paſt 2.*
Going to Dreſs.

N. Shadow.

[25]

AND what now have the Sons of *Momus* to object against the Style of a *Pretty Gentleman?* Here is every Requisite in Fine Writing : Here is Brevity, Softnefs, Propriety, and Eafe. Happily freed from the Shackles of *connecting* and *restraining* Rules, the Diction roves and wanders, now here, now there, and with a wond'rous Facility glides so imperceptibly from one Flower to another, that the moft fubtile Penetrator would be at Lofs to find, where *This* ends, and where *That* begins. Some Negligences there are indeed ; but they are fuch as muft be allowed the trueft Ornaments of Speech.----Let any Man examine the Letters I have here faithfully tranfcribed, and tell me whether he does not admire the little Carelefineffes which are beautifully interfperfed in thefe pretty Compofitions. If thefe are *Faults*, it muft be owned that they are truly charming : One cannot but delight in the lovely Errors, and fay of this Style what *Quintilian* did of *Seneca*'s,

Abundat Dulcibus Vitiis.

D   It

[27]

IT is a common Obfervation, that nothing has fpoiled more Authors than the affected Imitation of another Man's Diction. Every one has fome natural Bent, fomething *peculiar* in his Genius, which if he does not follow, he will never be able to fpeak or write with any Succefs. The *Pretty Gentleman* carefully avoids this Error, and follows his natural Genius. He neither writes like *Addifon*, nor talks like C--------: but nobly difdains all fervile Imitation. His Language is Original: It is his Own: and I defy the fnarling Critic to produce any thing like it. I fpeak only of the *Style*; for I will not deny, that fometimes he will condefcend to *fteal* an *Hint* from another, as may be feen in the Specimens I have given. But how does he *fteal* it? No otherwife than like thofe, who (as *Garth* fays of *Dryden*) fteal Beggars Children, only to cloath them the better.

ANOTHER Object of this Mimic's Raillery, is that fweet Placability of Temper, which obliges a refined Gentleman to put up even repeated Injuries and Affronts, rather than avenge them by the ufual Method of demanding Satisfaction.

I AM

[27]

I AM not apprehenfive that this Part of his Character is lefs defenfible than the reft. I could produce fome tolerable Arguments againft Duelling, drawn from certain Principles, which were once looked upon to be the Rules of Human Conduct. I could eafily prove, that the fingle Combat is derived from *Gothic* Manners, and is abfolutely inconfiftent with the Character of a Gentleman. But fuch Reafonings as thefe are neither fo well adapted to the Times, nor fo pertinent to the Caufe I have undertaken. Waving then this kind of Defence, upon this fingle Argument I lay my whole Strefs—— " The *Pretty* " *Gentleman* will not fight,---- becaufe---- He " is not *able*."

AND can any Man produce a better Reafon for not doing a Thing, than to make it manifeft ---- that he *cannot ?*

BEHOLD that tender Frame ! thofe trembbling Knees ! Thofe feeble Joints ! Obferve that fine Complexion ! Examine that fmooth, that Velvety Skin ! View that *Pallor* which fpreads itfelf over his Countenance ! Hark, with what a feminine Softnefs his Accents fteal their Way

D 2

thro'

[28]

thro' his half-opened Lips! Feel that foft
Palm! thofe flender Fingers, accuftomed only
to handle Silks and Ribbons, the eafy-pierc-
ing Needle, or foft-gliding Shuttle; but un-
practifed in the rough Exercifes of Warlike
Weapons! Mark all thefe, and a Thoufand
other gentle Imbecillities, and then tell me,
impartial Reader, whether fuch a Being is
formed for Battle? ------You cannot think it:
You will not fay it. I will therefore venture to
affirm, that He is fo far from deferving Com-
tempt and Ridicule, when he declines the Combat, that he merits our Efteem and Applaufe.
He therefore who is fo bafe as to affront, or
fend a Challenge to *fuch* a Perfon, is an arrant
Coward.   For would a Man of Honor draw
his Sword upon a *Lady?* And to fay the
Truth, *The Pretty Gentleman* is certainly formed in a different Mould from that of Common Men, and tempered with a purer Flame.
The whole Syftem is of a finer Turn, and
fuperior Accuracy of Fabric, infomuch that
it looks as if Nature had been in doubt, to
which Sex fhe fhould affign *Him*.

Now this Contexture of his Organs, and
the Tone of his Spirits approaching fo very

near

[29]

near That of the *Fair*, has rendered Him
liable to the fame gentle Impreffions, and
Alarms of Fear. Does *Cælia* fet up a Scream
at the Apprehenfion of the leaft Danger?
Delicatulus is as eafily intimidated, and fcreams
with as pretty an Accent. Do the Weaknefs
of Lady *Betty*'s Nerves fubject her to Fits and
Swoonings? *Tenellus* likewife has his Hyf-
terics, and dies away with as foft a Grace.
It is to attain thefe and fuch like Accomplifhments, that they make frequent Vifits to the
Ladies ; though fome flanderous Perfons would
make us believe, that they have another Motive, and intimate I know not what, *vitious*
Defigns, that are too indecent even to be
mentioned. But I can affure the World,
there is not the leaft Foundation for the bafe
Suggeftion. This Attendance, I know, takes
its Rife from Caufes, with which the Appetite for *That* Sex has no manner of Connex-
ion. So pure are their Morals! So inviolable
their Modefty! Amazing Continence! And
yet, our Wonder is leffen'd, when we confider what Methods they purfue to fence
againft the Allurements of Female Charms.
They are certainly the moft fober and tem-
perate Beings that ever exifted. It is an invi-

olable

[30]

olable Maxim with them, to refrain from every Indulgence, which is apt to irritate the Blood, and excite the Pruriency of Defire.

Old *Englifh* Roaft-Beef is indeed properly adapted to Old *Englifh* Manners ; fince, as all Phyficians obferve, the Quality of our Food communicates itfelf to the Mind. Therefore at the Table of a *Pretty Gentleman,* you never fee the Flefh of a full-grown Animal. Chickens of a Week old, Veal Sweet-breads, or a Leg of Lamb, and now and then Pigs-petitoes, are their higheft Indulgence. But the ufual Food, is Cheefe-cakes, White-pot, Tanzeys, and Flommery. And can it be thought that this Abftemious Reftriction is a proper Subject of Raillery, when a certain celebrated Writer, amidft the Praifes he beftows on his noble Patron, mentions *this* as his finifhing Excellence, " That he lived upon *Panada* and Water-gruel." * I mention this, becaufe it is the Obfervation of one who never fhew'd any Favour to Modern Elegance.

As to Wine, it is abfolutely their Averfion. And indeed, fo Delicate is their Frame, that even

* *Middleton's* Life of *Cicero.* Dedication.

[31]

even the Moderate Indulgences of the *Fair*
would ill-agree with thefe more tender Males.
" The *Firft* Glafs, *faid a Pretty* French *Author,*
" I may drink for myfelf; a *Second* for my
" Friend; but if a *Third*, it is for my Ene-
" my." *Our* Youths feldom go fo far as a
Second; and when ever That happens, 'tis
fure to be followed with bitter Reflections.
" What do you think? (faid *Umbratilis* to
" Lord *Molly*.) I was the moft abominable
" Rake laft Night! Do you know? I drank
" *Two* Glaffes of Claret after my Flom-
" mery.

" O H fie! you naughty Child! what a
" *Paw* Trick was that! as I hope for Mercy,
" you deferve to be foundly Wh---t, fo you
" do.

Two Glaffes only! No more! And yet me-
rited fuch a rigorous Animadverfion. But perhaps even that fmall Quantity might be too
much for the Infantine Conftitution; to which
Nature points out a more fuitable Liquor, of
a Soft and Delicious kind, emulged from the fa-
lutiferous Cow, or the thin Juices of the *Gentle*
Afs; the Temperament of whofe Fluids is pro-
ductive

[32]

ductive of a correspondent Temperament in the Person, who accustoms himself to these assimilating Draughts.

I HAVE already detained the Reader so long, that I shall not trespass upon his Patience by giving a Detail of the numerous Artifices, which are exhibited in the important Hours that are employed in decorating their Persons. Were you to behold *Narcissus* at his Toilet, how would you be charmed with the Order and Disposition! Did you view this lovely Youth whilst he takes his exterior Form into a most exact Adjustment, you must stand amazed at all the Pretty Wonders of his Art. What Pains! What Care! What Study! What Address! To arch that Eye-brow! To soften that Hand, and to Curl those lovely Locks! Whilst all the Graces attend as Invisible Handmaids, to finish the Work of Elegance. And when the busy Scene is over, and he is decorated in every minute Circumstance with the most Perfect Concinnity ; behold, with what a soft Air and sweet Complacency he presents himself to View, and like *Horace's Barine* coming from her Toilet,

——————————— *enitescit*

Pulchrior multò, Juvenumq; *prodit*

Publica cura.   THUS

[33]

THUS have I prefented to the Reader's
View an Enumeration of the feveral Qualities
which conftitute

A PRETTY GENTLEMAN:

FROM whence it is eafy to collect the true
Notion of *Genuine* Elegance ; which, without
any apprehenfion of being difproved, I do not
hefitate to define thus-----

" *ELEGANCE* is the Abfence or Debi-
" litation of *Mafculine* Strength and Vigor,--
" Or rather, The Happy Metamorphofis, --
" Or, The Gentleman turn'd Lady ; that is,
" Female Softnefs adopted into the Breaft of
" a *Male,* difcovering itfelf by outward Signs
" and Tokens in Feminine Expreffions, Ac-
" cent, Voice, Air, Gefture and Looks.
" Or, as the *French* more clearly define it,
" *A je ne fçai quoi.*

AND now I appeal to the Judgment of
the Impartial, whether This be a Character
which deferves that Contempt and Ridicule
fome rude and undifciplined Spirits have endeavoured to throw upon it? It is impoffible

E   that

[34]

that any *ferious* Perfon can entertain fuch a Thought,

I CALL therefore upon the Wifdom of the Nation : I call upon the L--ds, K----ts, and B----s, now, affembled in P--------t, to interpofe in this important Caufe, this truly *National* Concern.

THE Queftion is, Whether we fhall become more than *Men*, that is, *Pretty Gentlemen*; or worfe than Brutes, *i. e.* Mafculine, Robuft Creatures with unfoftened Manners. The latter will infallibly be the Cafe, if an effectual Stop be not put to that licentious Raillery, which would laugh out of Countenance the generous Endeavors of a Race of virtuous Youths, to polifh our Afperity, mollify us into gentle Obfequioufnefs, and give us a true Relifh of all the dulcet Elegancies of Life? I will fpeak without Referve : Should not the Theatres be *abfolutely demolifhed?* We have already in vain tried the lenient Meafures of Reftriction. Why then fhould we not now have Recourfe to the laft Remedy, and cut down the Tree, which

[35]

which after all our Pruning and Culture, ftill continues to produce *poifonous Fruit ?*

THE indulgent Reader, I dare fay, will approve the Method I prefcribe. But perhaps fo many Difficulties may arife to his Imagination, that he will conclude it impracticable.

DIFFICULTIES there are, no doubt; but *One* there is, which if *He* can furmount, I my felf will undertake to remove all the reft.

HERE lies the grand Impediment! How can we expect the Favour of the *Learned* or the Protection of the *State,* to cherifh and fupport *This Refinement,* when its moft inveterate Enemy is the *very Man,* who has always been the *Standard of Tafte* with the Former; and is now raifed to a Poft, which gives him fuch an unhappy Influence in the latter? Unhappy indeed for the Sons of Elegance! For what can the moft Sanguine expect from one, who has made it the Bufinefs of his Life, to bring into Repute the falfe Refinements of ancient *Greece* and *Rome?* Will a Perfon of

his

[36]

his *Masculine* Talents become the Patron of soft and dulcified Elegance? Will *He* give up that *Attic Wit*, which has gained him such high Applause, and made him the Delight of a mif-judging World, to cultivate Qualities, in which he is not formed to excel?

WHAT then remains, but that the *Sons of Elegance* wait with Patience (for they are too *gentle* to ufe any *violent* Methods) till the kind Fates fhall remove this implacable Adverfary out of the World. And then, my foreboding Heart affures me, true Politenefs will thrive and profper, and fpread her fweet mollifying Influences over the Land, till nothing fhall be heard of or feen, but Softnefs and Complaifance, Prettinefs and Elegance, Infantine Prattle, Lullaby Converfation, and gentle Love; and every well-educated *Male* amongft us, fhall become

Mollis & parùm Vir;

that is,

A PRETTY GENTLEMAN.

F I N I S.

A Letter to David Garrick, Esq. from William Kenrick, LL.D. (including Love in the Suds; A Town Eclogue) (1772)

The satirical lampoon *Love in the Suds*, by the writer and actor William Kenrick (1725?–79), alleges a homosexual relationship between the actor and playwright David Garrick and the Irish dramatist Isaac Bickerstaffe. From the production of numerous comic operas, including the very successful *Love in a Village* (1762), Bickerstaffe earned a great deal of money, which he spent on frequent trips to the Continent. His last trip abroad was prompted by a blackmail notice published in the *Daily Advertiser* on 30 April 1772: '*Whereas* on Tuesday Night last, between the hours of Eight and Ten, A Gentleman left with a Centinel belonging to Whitehall Guard, a Guinea and a half, and a Metal Watch with two Seals, the one a Cypher, the other a Coat of Arms, a Locket, and a Pistol Hook. The Owner may have it again by applying to the Adjutant of the first Battalion of the first Regiment of Foot-Guards at the Savoy Barracks, and paying for this Advertisement.' Other London newspapers, such as the *St James's Chronicle*, quickly made the meaning of the advertisement clear: 'The History of this Watch, &c. is this: A *Gentleman* grew enamoured, the other Night at Whitehall, with one of the Centinels, and made Love to him; the Soldier being of that rough cast, who would rather act in the Character of *Mars* than *Venus*, not only rejected the Lover's Suit, but seizing him, threatened to take him immediately to the Guard-Room. The Affrighted Enamorato, to avoid the consequences of Exposure, with the greatest Precipitation gave the Soldier his Watch, Rings, and other Valuables, for his Liberty.' One of these valuables, a mourning ring, established the identity of the owner. On 18 May the *Northampton Mercury* reported that a celebrated literary character had absconded, and the following day everyone knew this was David Garrick's good friend Isaac Bickerstaffe. Mr Thrale told Dr Johnson that Bickerstaffe had long been a suspected sodomite. Dr Johnson was shocked, and replied, 'By those who look close to the ground, dirt will be seen, Sir. I hope I see things from a greater distance.' Bickerstaffe sailed to St Malo, where he assumed the name Burrows and took lodgings in a bookshop near the cathedral. He wrote to Garrick on 24 June: 'ayant perdu mes amis, mes esperances; tombé, exilé, et livré au desespoir comme je suis, la vie est un fardeau presque insupportable…' ('Having lost my friends, my hope, fallen, exiled and delivered into despair as I am, life is a burden almost unbearable…'). Garrick wrote on the letter: 'From that poor wretch Bickerstaffe. I could not answer it' (quoted in P. A. Tasch, *The Dramatic Cobbler* (Lewisburg, 1971), p. 225, my translation).

Love in the Suds was published in early June 1772, with a second edition mid-July, and three more editions by mid-August. It is unclear why Garrick did not immediately issue a writ against Kenrick, but he did not initiate legal action until 7 July. The court case was postponed until Kenrick, on 21 November, issued a public retraction in the *London Evening Post* and agreed to suppress the pamphlet. Kenrick privately admitted to Thomas Evans, the publisher of the *Morning Chronicle*, that 'I did not believe him [Garrick] guilty, but did it to plague the fellow' (John Forster, *The Life and Adventures of Oliver Goldsmith* (1848), p. 491; also reported in *General Evening Post*, 2–4 July 1772). He did, however, believe that Garrick knew about, and tolerated, Bickerstaffe's homosexual affairs. Kenrick felt he had been ill-treated by both Bickerstaffe and Garrick, who had rejected his plays for production. Libels and counter-libels raged on for five years: in 1777 Bickerstaffe wrote to Garrick, from Vienne in France, to complain that the libel controversy was destroying his (Bickerstaffe's) reputation more than the original scandal. Impoverished, he begged Garrick for £10, but Garrick never replied. The 1782 edition of *Biographia Dramatica* noted that Bickerstaffe 'is said to be still living at some place abroad…where he exists poor and despised by all orders of people' (i. 28). The newspapers reported that Bickerstaffe was drinking two pints of spirits a day, that he died in Sussex in 1783, that he had drowned himself, that he had hanged himself, that he was living in Milan, that he had been sighted in Charing Cross in 1811, that he was writing for the Marseilles stage. He did send a play to Mrs Jordan for one of her benefits in 1790. He probably died at the age of seventy-five in 1808, the last year in which he drew his half-pay pension.

The pamphlet that we reproduce was published on 8 August 1772 (according to notices in *Morning Chronicle*, 6 and 8 August 1772). The text is reproduced from the copy held by the British Library (shelfmark 11641.l.13).

A

LETTER

TO

DAVID GARRICK, Esq.

FROM

WILLIAM KENRICK, LL.D.

Meo deo irato. Ter. Phor.

LONDON:

Printed for J. WHEBLE, Pater-noster-Row.

MDCCLXXII.

To DAVID GARRICK, Efq.

S I R,

THE author of the following Eclogue, having requefted my affiftance to introduce it to the world ; it was with more indignation than
furprize I was informed of your having ufed your extenfive influence
over the prefs to prevent its being advertifed in the News-papers.
How are you, Sir, concerned in the Lamentation of *Rofcius* for his
Nyky ? Does your modefty think no man entitled to the appellation
of Rofcius but yourfelf? Does Nyky refemble any nick-named favourite of yours? Or does it follow, that if you have cherifhed an unworthy favourite, you muft bear too near a refemblance to him ? *Qui
capit ille facit* ; beware of felf-accufation, where others bring no
charge ! Or, granting you right in thefe particulars, by what right or
privilege do you, Sir, fet up for a licenfer of the prefs ? That you
have long fuccefsfully ufurped that privilege, to fwell both your fame
and fortune, is well known. Not the puffs of the quacks of Bayf-
water and Chelfea are fo numerous and notorious : but by what authority do you take upon you to fhut up the general channel, in
which writers ufher their performances to the public ? If they attack either your talents or your character, *in utrumque paratus,* you
are armed to defend yourfelf. You have, befides your ingenuous
countenance and confcious innocence ; *Nil confcire fibi, nulla pal-
lefcere culpa* ; Befides this brazen bulwark, I fay, you have a ready
pen and a long purfe. The prefs is open to the one, and the bar
is ever ready to open with the other. For a poor author, not a
printer will publifh a paragraph, not a punning pleader will utter
a quibble. You have then every advantage in the conteft : It
is needlefs, therefore, to endeavour to intimidate your antagonifts
by countenancing your retainers to threaten their lives ! Thefe in-
timidations, let me tell you Sir, have an ugly, fufpicious look. The
genus irritabile vatum want no fuch perfonal provocation ; they
are befides needlefs; Heav'n knows, the life of a play-wright, like
that of a fpider, is in a ftate of the moft flender dependency. It
is well for my rhiming friend that his hangs not on fo flight a
thread. He thinks, neverthelefs, that he has reafon to complain,
as well as the publick, of your having long preferred the flimzy,
tranflated, patch'd-up and mif-altered pieces of your favourite com-
pilers, to the arduous attempts at originality of writers, who have
no perfonal intereft with the manager. In particular, he thinks

A   the

[ii]

the two pieces, your are projecting to get up next winter, for the emolument of your favorite in difgrace, or to reimburfe yourfelf the money, you may have advanced him, might, for the prefent at leaft, be laid afide. Put on your begging face, tell the town your unluckly fituation, and it will certainly allow you principal and intereft for your money.

But you will afk me, perhaps, in turn, Sir, what right I have to interfere with the bufinefs of other people, or with yours. I will anfwer you. It is becaufe I think your bufinefs, as patentee of a theatre-royal, is not fo entirely yours, but that the publick alfo have fome concern in it. You, Sir, indeed have long behaved as if you thought the town itfelf a purchafed appurtenance to the theatre; but, tho' the fcenes and machines are yours; nay, tho' you have even found means to make comedians and poets your property; it fhould be with more caution than you practife, that you extend your various arts to make fo fcandalous a property of the audience.

Again I anfwer, it is becaufe I have fome regard for my friend, and as much for myfelf, whom you have treated as ill as you have behaved to any other writer; while under your aufpices, fome of the wretches ftigmatifed by the fatirift, have frequently combined to do me the moft effential injury. But *nemo me impune laceffit.* Not that I mean now to enter into particulars which may be thought to relate too much to myfelf and too little to the publick. When I fhall have leifure to draw a faithful portraiture of Mr. Garrick, not only from his behaviour to me in particular, but from his conduct towards poets, players and the town in general, I doubt not to convince the moft partial of his admirers that he hath accumulated a fortune, as manager, by the meaneft and moft meretricious devices, and that the theatrical props, which have long fupported his exalted reputation, as an actor, have been raifed on the ruins of the Englifh ftage.

In the mean time, I leave you to amufe yourfelf with the following jeu d'efprit of my friend; hoping, tho' it be a fevere correction for the errours of your paft favouritifm, it may prove a falutary guide to the future. With regard to its publication I hope alfo to ftand excufed with the reader for thus interpofing to defeat the fuccefs of thofe arts, you fo unfairly practife to prevent, from reaching the public eye, whatever is difagreeable to your own.

I am, Sir,

Yours, &c.

W. K.

LOVE in the SUDS;

A

TOWN ECLOGUE.

BEING THE

LAMENTATION of ROSCIUS

FOR THE

LOSS of his NYKY.

Dixin' ego vobis, in hôc eſſe Atticam elegantiam? TER.
O me infelicem! ——
—— *quæ laudâram quantum luctus habuerint!*

PHÆD.

With ANNOTATIONS by the EDITOR.

LONDON:

PRINTED FOR J. WHEBLE, PATER-NOSTER-ROW.

MDCCLXXII.

L O V E in the S U D S;

A

T O W N   E C L O G U E.

W HITHER away, now, George* ? into the city,
And to the village, muſt thou bear my ditty.
Seek Nyky out, while I in verſe complain,
And court the Muſe to call him back again.

Bœotian Nymphs, my favorite verſe inſpire ;
As erſt ye Nyky taught to ſtrike the lyre.
For he like Phœbus' ſelf can touch the String,
And opera-ſongs compoſe—like any thing !
What ſhall I do, now Nyky's fled away ?
For who like him can either ſing or ſay ?

I M I T A T I O N S.

Quo te, Mœri, pedes ; an quò via ducit in urbem ?
Nymphæ, noſter amor, Libethrides, nunc mihi carmen,
Quale meo Codro, concedite ; proxima Phœbi
Verſibus ille facit.——
                    Quid facerem ?

N O T E S.

* The brother and conſtant companion of Roscius ; the Mercury of
our theatrical Jupiter, whom he diſpatches with his divine commands to
mortal poets and miſerable actors.

B   For

[2]

For me, alas ! who well compos'd the fong

When lovely PEGGY * liv'd, and I was young ;

By age impair'd, my piping days are done,

My memory fails, and ev'n my voice is gone.

My feeble notes I yet muft ftrive to raife ;

Bœotian Mufes ! aid my feeble lays :

A little louder, and yet louder ftill,

Aid me to raife my failing voice, at will ;

Aid me as loud as Hercules did bawl,

For Hylas loft, loft NYKY back to call ;

While London town, and all its fuburbs round

In echoes, NYKY, NYKY, back refound.

Whom

IMITATIONS.

—— —— Sæpe ego longos
Cantando puerum memini me condere foles
Nunc oblita mihi tot carmina : vox quoque Mœrim
Jam fugit ipfa ———
Omnia fert ætas, animum quoque.
——— Mufæ paulò majora canamus.
——— Hylan nautæ quo fonte relictum
Clamaffent ; ut littus, Hyla, **Hyla**, omne fonaret.

NOTES.

* PEGGY WOFFINGTON, on whom our ROSCIUS, then her inamorato, made a famous fong, beginning with the following ftanza :

> *Once more I'll tune the vocal ſhell,*
> *To hills and dales my paſſion tell,*
> *A flame which time can never quell,*
> *That burns for thee, my Peggy.*

Time

[3]

Whom flieft thou, frantic youth, and whence thy fear ?

Bleft had there never been a grenadier !

Unhappy NYKY, by what frenzy feiz'd,

Couldft thou with fuch a martial thing be pleas'd ?

What, tho' thyfelf a gentle horfe-marine,*

Couldft thou with foot-foldiers at land be feen ?

Not fabled Nymphs, by fpleen turn'd into cows,

Low'd to the nafty bulls their amorous vows;

Tho' turn'd their loving horns upon each other,

Butting in play, as brother might with brother.

Unhappy NYKY, whither doft thou ftray,

Loft to thy friends, o'er hills and far away ?

IMITATIONS.

Quem fugis ? Ah demens !——
Et fortunatam, fi nunquam armenta fuiffent,
Pafiphaen nivei folatur amore juvenci.
Oh, virgo infelix, quæ te dementia cepit ?
Prœtides implérunt falfis mugitibus agros:
At non tum turpes pecudum tamen ulla fecuta eft
Concubitus : quamvis collo timuiffet aratrum,
Et fæpe in levi quæfiffet cornua fronte.
Ah, virgo infelix, tu nunc in montibus erras !

NOTES.

Time, however, effects ftrange things, as the poet fays, and many have been the paffions which have fince agitated, and have been alfo quelled-in the bofom of ROSCIUS.

* NYKY is an half-pay officer of marines. The term horfe-marine is well known to fome kind of failors. *Modò vir modò fœmina.*

Ye

[4]

Yet to Euryalus as Nifus true,

So fhall thy Roscius, Nyky, prove to you ;

Whether by impulfe mov'd, itfelf divine,

Or fo I'm bound to call it, as it's mine.

A mighty thing prefents itfelf to view,

Which by your aid I yet projeʄt to do.

Mean time do thou beware, while I bemoan,

How far thou trufteſt feas or lands unknown.

To Tyber's ſtream, or to the banks of Po,

Safe in thy love, fafe in thy virtue go ;

Yet even there with caution be thou kind,

And look out ſharp and frequently behind.

But ah beware, nor truſt, tho' native mud,*

The banks of Liffy or of Shannon's flood ;

Or there, if driv'n by fate, be huſh'd thy ſtrain ;

Nor of thy wayward lot nor mine complain.

IMITATIONS.

Nifus ait, " Diine hunc ardorem mentibus addunt
Euryale ? An fua cuique deus fit dira Cupido ?
Aut pugnam, aut aliquid jamdudum invadere magnum
Mens agitat mihi ——
Hàc iter eſt ; tu ne qua manus fe attollere nobis
A tergo poſſit, cuſtodi et confule longè.

NOTES.

* Nyky it feems was born and bred in Ireland ; where his chriſtian name
was *John* How he came by the Jewiſh appellation of *Ifaac* is not generally known. Whether it was beſtowed upon him for his refemblance to
the chofen *people*, or given him by poetical licence, may poſſibly be a matter of difquifition for future fcholiaſts.

Left

[5]

Left female Bacchanals, when flush'd with wine,

Serve thee, like Orpheus, for thy song divine ;

Nay back return, left my too plaintive verse

Entail on me the same Orphean curse ;

Left Venus' train of Drury and the Strand

Attack my house by water and by land ;

Hot with their midnight orgies, madly tear

My little limbs, and throw them here and there ;

Casting, enrag'd at my provoking theme,

Th' inditing brain into the neighbouring stream :

When, as my skull shall float the tide along,

Thy much-lov'd name, the burthen of my song,

Shall still be stutter'd, later than my breath ;

NYKY---NYK---NY---till stopt my tongue in death :

Through London-bridge shall Wapping NYKY roar,

And NYK be even heard to Hampton's shore.*

IMITATIONS.

—— —— Spreto Ciconum quo munere matres
Inter sacra deûm, nocturnique orgia Bacchi,
Discerptum latos juvenem sparsere per agros.
Tum quoque marmoreâ caput à cervice revulsum,
Gurgite cum medio portans Oeagrius Hebrus
Volveret, Eurydicen vox ipsa et frigida lingua
Ah miseram Eurydicen anima fugiénte, vocabat :
Eurydicen toto referebant flumine ripæ !

NOTES.

* The celebrated villa of ROSCIUS.

C   On

[6]

On Hebrus' banks fo tuneful Orpheus died ;

His limbs the fields receiv'd, his head the tide.

Nor more its ftream renown'd than Thames in fame :

Here Catherine Hayes ferv'd Goodman Hayes the fame.*

Here, on this fpot, where now th' Adelphi ftands,

Was thrown her hufband's noddle from her hands ;

His fcatter'd limbs left quiv'ring on the fhore ;

As Thracian wives had play'd their part before.

Oh, horrour, horrour ! NYKY back return ;

Nor more for grenadiers imprudent burn.

And yet, ah why fhould NYKY thus be blam'd ?

Of manly love ah ! why are men afham'd ?

A new red-coat, fierce cock and killing air

Will captivate the moft obdurate fair ;

What wonder then if NYKY's tender heart

At fuch a fight fhould feel a lover's fmart :

No wonder love, that in itfelf is blind,

Should no diftinction in the difference find ;

No wonder love fhould NYKY thus enthrall ;

Almighty love, we know, fubdues us all ;

IMITATIONS.

Omnia vincit amor et nos cedamus amori.

NOTES.

* See the Tyburn Chronicle and Newgate lamentations *pro tempore* ; particularly that famous ballad, entitled A merry fong about murder, beginning with, " In Tyburn road there liv'd a man," &c.

While

[7]

While, vulgar prejudices foar'd above,

Nyk gave up all the world,—well loft for love.

Yet flight the caufe of Nyky's late mifhap ;

Nyk but miftook the colour of the cap :

A common errour, frequent in the Park,

Where love is apt to ftumble in the dark.

Why rais'd the haughty female head fo high,

With the tall caps of grenadiers to vie ?

Why does it like tremendous figure make,

To fubject purblind lovers to miftake ? *

Or rather why, in thefe enlighten'd times,

Should rigid Nature call fuch errours crimes ?

" Thou Nature art my goddefs," faith the play :

But even Shakefpeare's text hath had its day.

More gentle cuftom no fuch rigour knows ;

And cuftom into fecond nature grows.

Let vulgar paffions move the vulgar mind,

Superior fouls feel motives more refin'd :

Among the low-bred Englifh flow advance

Th'. Italian *gufto* and *bon ton* of France.

Strange to the claffic lore of Greece and Rome,

And rudely nurs'd in ignorance at home,

N O T E S.

* Nyky is near-fighted.

The

[8]

The taftelefs herd e'en conftrue into fin,

That poets fhould in metaphor lie in,

While I, their beft man-midwife, muft be fham'd

Whene'er the Fafhionable Lover's nam'd.*

But Candour's veil love's foibles ftill fhould cover

And NYK be ftil'd a FASHIONABLE LOVER.

　　To polifh'd travellers is only known

That tafte which makes the ancient arts our own ;

Which fhares with Rome in every gem antique ;

Which blends the modern with the ancient Greek ;

Improves on both, and greatly foars above,

In pure philanthropy, Platonic love ;

That love, which burns with undiftinguifh'd rage,

And fpares in fondnefs neither fex nor age ?

N O T E S.

*　*If any author of prolific brains*
　In this good company feels labour-pains ;
　If any gentle poet big with rhyme
　Has run his reckoning out and gone his time :
　Know fuch that at our bofpital of mufes
　He may lye in, in private, if he chufes ;
　We've fingle lodgings there for fecret finners,
　With good encouragement for young beginners."
　　　　　　　Prologue to the FASHIONABLE LOVER.

　　It is indeed now plain enough that ROSCIUS has given great encouragement to *fecret finners* ; but I would advife none of our poets to lie-in
again in private ; but to remember the fate of a late tragedy and farce.
Poor Clementina, and the lady *An hour after marriage,* both privately lay-in
and mifcarried.

Ah !

[9]

Ah! therefore why in thefe enlighten'd times

Sould rigid Nature call fuch errours crimes?

Muft not the tafte of Attic wits be nice?

Can antient virtue be a modern vice?

The Mantuan bard, or elfe his fcholiaft lies,*

Virgil the chafte, nay Socrates the wife,

The gay Petronius, fophifts, wits and bards,

Of old, beftow'd on youth their foft regards;

In modifh dalliance pafs'd their harmlefs time

Ev'n modifh now in foft Italia's clime.

Could lightenings ever iffue from above

To blaft poor men for fuch a crime as love;

When the lewd daughters of inceftuous Lot

Were both with child by their own father got?

Poor goody Lot indeed might be in fault,

And juftly turn'd to monumental falt:

The matrimonial emblem of a wife:

Needs muft be falt a difh to keep for life!

A fable Sodom's fate: in Heav'n above

All is made up of harmony and love;

IMITATIONS.

Formofum paftor Corydon ardebat Alexin.

NOTES.

* The Jefuit Ruæus begins the argument of Virgil's fecond Eclogue with the following explicit declaration, *Amabat Virgilius puerum.*

D   That

[　10　]

That ſuch its vengeance I believe not, I ;

Hiſtorians err and Hebrew Jews will lie.

　　Sing then, my Muſe, a more engaging ſtrain

To lure my Nyky back to Drury-lane.

Tell him the fancied danger all is o'er ;

Home he may come and love as heretofore.

In vain the vulgar ſhall for vengeance call,

Or move the juſtices at Hickes's-hall ;

In vain grand juries ſhall be urg'd by law

In his indictment not to leave a flaw.

Ev'n at the bar ſhould Nyky ſtand arraign'd,

No verdict 'gainſt him ſhould be there obtain'd ;

Nay, by the laws and cuſtoms of the land,

Tho' trembling Nyky ſhould convicted ſtand,

The candid jury ſhall be mov'd t'acquit

A gentleman, an author, and a wit.

For liberal minds with candour ever ſee

The milder failings of humanity !

IMITATIONS.

　　—— Deos didici ſecurum agere ævum
Nec ſi quid miri faciat natura, deos id
Triſtes ex alto cœli demittere tecto.
　　—— —— Credat Judæus Apella,
Non ego.——
Ducite ab urbe domum mea carmina ducite Daphnim,

　　　　　　　　　　　　　　　Smooth-

[11]

Smooth-fpoken MANSFIELD,* with his vacant face,

In foftening accents firft fhall ope his cafe;

Which to defend, the want of Merlin's cunning

Shall be fupplied by that of Grimbald Dunning. †

E'en at th' Old-Bailey they for Nyk fhall plead;

Where would they not, if they were largely fee'd?

Were Nyky fummon'd to the bar below,

Well-fee'd thefe faithful barrifters would go;

Their tale to Minos would they glibly tell;

Minos the MANSFIELD, or Chief Judge, of Hell. ‡

   Nor need my Nyky fear a London jury

Will e'er be influenc'd with a female fury.

Can they who let a prov'd affaffin 'fcape

Hang up poor Nyky for a friendly rape?

If in the dark to ftab, be thought no crime,

What may'nt be hop'd from jurymen in time?

Soon Southern modes, no doubt, they'll reconcile

With the plain manners of our Northern ifle;

N O T E S.

* Not the Judge of that name; but the barrifter, who is by no means a judge of any thing.

† See King Arthur, lately revived at Drury-lane Theatre, and attend the pleadings in our courts of law and equity at Weftminfter, Guildhall, and Lincoln's-inn.

‡ Minos is reported by the poets to have been raifed to this high office for his impartiality in the adminiftration of juftice here on earth: what a pity that office is not foon to become vacant; as it might be moft luckily filled by as worthy a fucceffor.

                                                            And

[12]

And e'en new-married citizens be brought

To reckon S——y a venial fault:

When if GEORGE BELLAS,* cruel and unkind,

Blaſt not their loves, with rude tempeſtuous wind,

In common-council Corydon may burn,

And Corydons for Corydon in turn,

Till every alderman about the chair

Find his Alexis in a new lord-mayor.

    Sing then, O Muſe, a more pathetic ſtrain,

To lure my gentle NYKY back again:

For, ſure as Thames reſembles Tyber's tide,

Shall Macaronis ſoon poſſeſs Cheapſide ;

As petty-jury-men in judgment fit,

And ev'ry Corydon, with NYK, acquit.

Yes by this knife, this uſeful † knife, I ſwear,

Which for my lov'd B——TTI's ſake I wear ;

IMITATIONS.

Ex illo Corydon, Corydon eſt tempore nobis.

———   ———   ———

Ducite ab urbe domum, mea carmina ducite Daphnim.

Ἀλλ' ἐκ τοι ἐρέω, χ̔ ἐπι μέγαν ὅρκον ὀμᾶμαι,
Ναὶ μὰ τόδε ζκῆπ]ρον, τὸ μὲν ἄπο]ε φύλλα χ̔ ὄζυς
Φύσει, ἐπειδή πρῶτα τομὴν ἐν ὅρεσσι λελοιπεν,
Οὐδ' ἀναθηλήσει.   HOM.

NOTES.

* A boiſterous mock-patriot, ſuppoſed to be deſcended from Eolus and Amphitrite, being famous for his mackarel expeditions, his muſical knowledge of the fundamental baſe and public performances on the baſſoon.
† See the utility of this knife in a late Seſſions-paper.

This

[13]

This knife, whofe haft, at Stratford Jubilee,

For ever left its parent mulberry tree;

For thence it grew, tho', tipt with fteel fo fine,

It now will ferve to ftab with, or to dine; ..

That tree, which late on Avon's border grew;

By Shakefpeare planted; Warwick lads fay true;

By this moft precious relick, here I pledge

Myfelf to fave him from the halter's edge:

And not myfelf alone, but ev'ry friend

Shall all his intereft and affiftance lend.

Quaint B————K, holding the rude mob in fcorn,

Shall tell how Irifh bards are gentle born;

Next I, to captivate the learned bench,

Will ftrait affirm that NYKY writes good French; *

IMITATIONS.

Ut fceptrum hoc (fceptrum dextrâ nam fortè gerebat)
Nunquam fronde levi fundet virgulta nec umbras;
Cùm femel in fylvis imo de ftirpe recifum,
Matre caret, pofuitque comas et brachia ferro
Olim arbos, nunc artificis manus ære decoro.
Inclufit patribufque dedit geftare Latinis.   VIRG.

Hanc ego magnanimi fpolium Didymaonis haftam,
Ut femel eft avulfa jugis à matre perempta,
Quæ neque jam frondes virides neque proferet umbras,
Fida minifteria et duras obit horrida pugnas
Teftor.   VAL. FLAC.

NOTES.

* See the Seffions-paper; in which this admirable plea is made ufe of by ROSCIUS to exculpate a culprit, accufed of murder.

E   Thy

[14]

Thy timid nature Johnson fhall maintain, †

In words no dictionary can explain.

Goldfmith, good-natur'd man, fhall next defend,

His fofter-brother, * countryman and friend :

Shall prove, the gentler paffions, now and then,

Are incidental to us little men ;

And that the part our gentle Nyky play'd

Was but philofophy in mafquerade. ‡

Let

N O T E S.

† See the fame ; in which this pompous pfeudo-philofopher affects to fuppofe cowardice incompatible with the character of an Italian bravo.

* So called from having not long fince made one in a poetical trium-virate, which gave occafion to the following verfes, in imitation of Dry-den's famous epigram on Milton ;

"Three poets in three diftant ages born," &c.

> *Poor Dryden ! what a theme hadft thou,*
> *Compar'd with that which offers now ?*
> *What are your Britons, Romans, Grecians,*
> *Compar'd to thorough-bred Milefians ?*
> *Step into Griffin's fhop, he'll tell ye*
> *Of Goldfmith, Bickerftaff, and Kelly,*
> *Three poets of one age and nation,*
> *Whofe more than mortal reputation,*
> *Mounting in trio to the fkies*
> *O'er Milton's fame and Virgil's flies.*
> *Nay, take one Irifh evidence for t'other,*
> *Ev'n Homer's felf is but their fofter-brother.*

‡ It feems indeed to be growing into fafhion for philofophy to go in mafquerade, if there be any truth in the fubject of the following ; which lately appeared in the public prints.

To Doctor Goldsmith, on feeing his name in the lift of the mummers at the late mafquerade.

> "Say fhould the philofophic mind difdain
> "That good which makes each humbler bofom vain ;
> "Let fchool-taught pride diffemble all it can,
> "Such little things are great to little man."   Goldsmith.

How widely different, Goldfmith, are the ways
Of doctors now, and thofe of ancient days !

Theirs

[15]

Let me no longer then my lofs deplore,

But to his ROSCIUS, Mufe, my NYK reftore!

For who like him will patch and pilfer plays,

Yielding to me the profit and the praife.

Tho' cheap in French tranflations MURPHY deals;

For cheap he well may vend the goods he fteals;

Tho' modeft CRADDOC fcorns to fell his play,

But gives the good-for-nothing thing away;

What tho' the courtly CUMBERLAND fucceeds

In writing ftuff no man of letters reads;

Tho' fenfe and language are expell'd the ftage;

For nonfenfe pleafes beft a fenfelefs age;

IMITATIONS.

Ducite ab urbe domum mea carmina ducite Daphnim.

NOTES.

Theirs taught the truth in academic fhades,
Ours haunt lewd hops and midnight mafquerades!
So chang'd the times! fay philofophic fage,
Whofe genius fuits fo well this tafteful age,
Is the Pantheon, late a fink obfcene,
Become the fountain of chafte Hippocrene?
Or do thy moral numbers quaintly flow
Infpir'd by th' Aganippe of Soho?
Do wifdom's fons gorge cates and vermicelli
Like beaftly Bickerftaff, or bothering Kelly?
Or art thou tir'd of th' undeferv'd applaufe
Beftow'd on bards affecting virtue's caufe?
Wouldft thou, like Sterne, refolv'd at length to thrive,
Turn pimp and die cock-bawd at fixty-five,
Is this the good that makes the humble vain,
The good philofophy fhould not difdain
If fo, let pride diffemble all it can,
A modern fage is ftill much lefs than man.

MORNING CHRONICLE.

What

[16]

What tho' the author of the New Bath Guide

Up to the skies my talents late hath cried ; †

Tho' humble HIFFERNAN in pay, I keep,

Still my fast friend, when he is fast asleep ;

Tho' long the Hodmandod my friend hath been,

With the land-tortoise earth'd at Turnham-Green : *

Tho'

N O T E S.

† The compliments passed between these celebrated geniuses indeed were mutual ; Mr. A. commending Roscius for his fine acting, and Roscius in return Mr. A. for his fine writing. The panegyric on both sides was equally modest and just ; and yet some snarling epigrammatist could not forbear throwing out the following ill-natured jeu d'esprit on the occasion.

On the poetical compliments lately pass'd between
Mess. G. and A.
When mincing masters, met with misses,
Pay mutual compliments for kisses ;
Miss Polly sings no doubt divinely,
And master Jacky spouts as finely.
But how I hate such odious greeting,
When two old stagers have a meeting.
Foh ! out upon the filthy pother !
What ! men beslobber one another.

* Two amphibious monsters, well known in the republic of letters as editors of the Critical and Monthly Reviews. The latter seems to be compared by the poet to a land-tortoise buried in the earth, on account of the slowness of its motion and the clouds of dust and dullness with which it is surrounded : the former hath been long known by the above appellation from the following humorous description.

LUSUS NATURÆ TYPOGRAPHUS.
Monstrum horrendum informe ingens cui lumen ademptum. VIRG.
I thought some of Nature's journeymen had made men, and not made them
well ; they imitated humanity so abominably. SHAKESPEAR.
In Nature's workshop, on a day,
Her journeymen inclin'd to play,
Half drunk 'twixt cup and can,
Took up a clod, which she with care
Was modelling a huge sea bear,
And swore they'd make't a man.

They

[17]

Tho' Harry Woodfall, Baldwin, Evans, Say, ‖

My puffs in faireſt order full diſplay ;

Impartially inſert each friendly PRO,

Suppreſſing every CON of every foe ; †

For well, I ween, they wot that *cons* and *pros*

Will tend my faults and follies to expoſe :

Tho' mighty Tom doth ſtill my champion prove,

And Lockyer's gauntlet be a chicken-glove ;

Tho'

NOTES.

They tried, but, handling ill their tools,
Form'd, like a pack of bungling fools,
    A thing ſo groſs and odd ;
That, when it roll'd about the diſh,
They knew not if 'twere fleſh or fiſh,
    A man or Hodmandod.

Yet, to compleat their piece of fun,
They chriſten'd it Arch Hamilton ;
    " *But what can this thing do ?* "
Kick it down ſtairs ; the devil's in't
If it won't do to write and print
    The Critical Review.   KENRICK.

‖ Editors and printers of news-papers, well known to the public for their impartiality in regard to Roscius.

† A recent inſtance of this muſt not paſs unnoticed. In the Public Advertiſer appeared lately the following quaint panegyric, ſuggeſted probably to Roscius himſelf by his brother George the attorney.

Nature
againſt } Notice of Proceſs.
G------

    Dame Nature againſt G------ now by me
    Her action brings, and thus ſhe grounds her plea.
      " *I never made a man but ſtill*
      You acted like that man at will ;
      Yet ever muſt I hope in vain
      To make a man like you again."
    Hence ruin'd totally by you,
    She brings her ſuit, &c. &c.   B. Solicitor for the Plaintiff.

F

In

[18]

Tho' ſhambling BECKET, ‡ proud to ſoothe my pride,

Keeps ever ſhuffling on my right-hand ſide ;

What tho', with well-tim'd flattery, loud he cries,

At each theatric ſtare, " See, ſee his eyes !"

What tho' he'll fetch and carry at command,

And kiſs, true ſpaniel-like, his maſter's hand ;

With admiration NYK ne'er heard me ſpeak,

But preſs'd the kiſs of love upon my cheek ; *

Inceſſant clapp'd at th' end of every ſpeech ;

And, had I bidd'n him, would have kiſs'd my br——— !

NOTES.

In reply to this notice, it is ſaid, the *defendant's plea* would have appeared in the ſame paper ; but the cauſe was obliged to be removed by *certiorari* to another court ; when it appeared thus :

Nature
againſt } Defendant's Plea.
G——

> *For G—— I without a fee*
> *'Gainſt Nature thus put in his plea.*
> " *To make a man, like me, of art,*
> *Is not, 'tis true, dame Nature's part ;*
> *I own that Scrub, fool, knave I've play'd*
> *With more ſucceſs than all my trade ;*
> *But prove it, plaintiff, if you can,*
> *That e'er I acted like a man."*
> *Of this we boldly make denial.——*
> *Join iſſue, and proceed to trial.*
>
>   A. Attorney for the Defendant.

‡ The famous THOMAS A BECKET, feigned by the poets to have been drown'd, when, being half ſeas over, in claret, he endeavoured to return to land : on which occaſion a wicked wit of the town made the following epitaph for his tomb.

> *Here lies*
> *That ſhuffling, ſhambling, ſhrugging, ſhrinking ſhrimp,*
> *Tom Becket, Mammon's moſt induſtrious imp !*

* A cuſtomary method it ſeems, of NYKY's expreſſing his admiration of the acting of the immortal ROSCIUS.

Let

[19]

Let me no longer, then, my lofs deplore,

But to his Roscius, Mufe, my Nyk reftore.

But hah ! what difcord ftrikes my liftening ear ?

Is Nyky dead, or is fome critic near ?

Curfe on that Ledger and that damn'd Whitehall,*

How players and managers they daily maul !

Curfe on that Morning-Chronicle ; whofe tale

Is never known with fpightful wit to fail.

Curfe on that Foote ; who in ill-fated hour

Trod on the heels of my theatric power ;

Who, ever ready with fome biting joke,

My peace hath long and would my heart have broke.

Curfe on his horfe—one leg ! but one to break !

" A kingdom for a horfe"—to break his neck !

Curfe on that Stevens, † with his Irifh breeding,

While I am acting, fhall that wretch be reading ?

Curfe on all rivals, or in fame or profit ;

The Fantoccini ftill make fomething of it ! ‡

Curfe

IMITATIONS.

Ducite ab urbe domum mea carmina ducite Daphnim.

NOTES.

* News-papers fo called, in which Roscius is not a fharer, and hath not yet come up to the price of their filence.

† George Alexander Stevens the lecturer, not the Macaroni editor of Shakefpeare.

‡ What formidable rivals to the immortal Roscius ? Harlequin, Scaramouch, Chimney-fweeper, Bafs-viol, Aftrologer, Child, Statue and Parrot !

But

[20]

Curfe on that KENRICK, † with his cauftic pen,

Who fcorns the hate, and hates the love of MEN ;

Who with fuch eafe envenom'd fatire writes,

Deeper his ink than aqua-fortis ‡ bites.

Stand

N O T E S.

But ROSCIUS having received a formal challenge from Mr. Punch and his merry family, a pitch'd-battle, for which great preparations are now making, will be fought between them next winter ; when there is no doubt but the triumphant ROSCIUS will, even at their own weapons, rout them all. There is the lefs reafon to fear this, as he hath already exceeded even Mr. ———'s activity in King Richard. It is but three or four years ago fince this mock-monarch died fo tamely that he was hiffed off the ftage ; on which occafion the following epigram appeared in the papers.

> ROSCIUS REDIVIVUS.
>
> *George ! did'nt I hear the critics hifs,*
> *When I was dead ?---" Yes, brother, yes,*
> *" You did not die in high rant."*
> *Nay, if they think a dying king*
> *Like Harlequin convuls'd, fhould fpring,*
> *Let ——— be hence their tyrant.*

ROSCIUS, however, hath chang'd his mind, and acquired new elaftic powers ; in fo much that the following complimentary verfes appeared on the agility, which he lately difplayed in the performance of that character.

> *Be dumb, ye criticks, dare to hifs no more,*
> *While crowded boxes, pit and galleries roar.*
> *Who fays that Rofcius feels the hand of Time,*
> *To blaft his blooming laurels in their prime ?*
> *With ever fupple limbs and pliant tongue,*
> *Rofcius, like Hebe, will be ever young.*
> *See and believe your eyes----did e'er you fee*
> *So great a feat of pure agility ?*
> *Nor Hughes nor Aftley, vaulting in the air,*
> *Like Rofcius makes the ftruck fpectators ftare.*
> *Nor Lun nor Woodward ever gave the fpring,*
> *He gave laft night in Richard, dying king !*
> *Th' immortal actor, who can die fo clever,*
> *In fpite of fate will live to die for ever !*

† A Briton blunt, bred to plain mathematics,
  Who hates French b--gres, and Italian pathics.

‡ The plaintive ROSCIUS feems here to have an eye to the following lines :
  The wits who drink water, and fuck fugar-candy,
  Impute the ftrong fpirit of Kenrick to brandy.
  They are not fo much out : the matter in fhort is
  He fips aqua-vitæ and fpits aqua-fortis. PUBLIC ADV.

[21]

Stand his perpetual-motion § ever ftill;

Or, if it move, oh, let it move up hill.

The curfe of Sifiphus, oh, let him feel;

The curfe of Fortune's ftill recurring wheel;

That upward roll'd with anxious toil and pain,

The fummit almoft gain'd, rolls back again.

Ne'er fhall his FALSTAFF † come again to life;

Ne'er fhall be play'd again his WIDOW'D WIFE; ‡

IMITATIONS.

Aut petis aut urges ruiturum, Syfiphe, faxum.

NOTES.

§ This multifarious genius pretends to have difcovered the Perpetual motion, but it muft be a mere pretence; as he is weak enough to think the public ought to reward him for his difcovery, and offers to difclofe it on the fimple terms of no purchafe no pay.

† Falftaff's Wedding, a play written in imitation of Shakefpeare; at firft rejected, as unfit for the theatre, on account of having fo many of Shakefpeare's known characters in it; tho' the manager himfelf afterwards brought on a pageant, in which were almoft all Shakefpeare's known characters; when finding it difficult to make any of them fpeak with propriety, he contented himfelf with inftructing them to bite their thumbs, fcrew up their mouths, and make faces at each other, to the great edification of the audience.— This play indeed was afterwards performed, and tho' received with the moft confirmed and general applaufe, has however never fince been acted, either for the author's emolument or the entertainment of the publick.

‡ Another comedy, nearly under the fame predicament with refpect to the town: having been performed but once fince its firft, run, tho' received with fimilar approbation; the manager in the mean while having brought on, and repeatedly acted, the performances of his favourite play-wrights, to almoft empty houfes: and yet ROSCIUS hath all the while pretended to have the higheft opinion of the talents, and the greateft regard for the intereft of the writer.——The manager claims a legal right, indeed, as patentee, to perform what plays he pleafes; but tho' the play-houfe and patent be his property, he has no liberal right to make, at pleafure, a property of the players, the poets and the publick!

G   Ne'er

[22]

Ne'er will I court again his ſtubborn Muſe,
But for a pageant would his play refuſe.
While puff and pantomime will gull the town,
'Tis good to keep o'erweening merit down ;
With BICKERSTAFF and CUMBERLAND go ſhares,
And grind the poets as I grind the players.
Curſe on that KENRICK, ſoul of ſpleen and whim !
What are my puffs, and what my gains to him ?
If poor and proud, can he of right complain
That wealthier men and wittier are as vain ?
Why muſt he hint that I am paſt my prime,
To blaſt my fading laurels ere their time ?
Death to my fame, and what, alas, is worſe,
'Tis death, damnation, to my craving purſe ;
Capacious purſe ! by PLUTUS form'd to hold,
(The God of Wealth) the devil and all of gold.
Inſatiate purſe, that never yet ran o'er,
But ſwallows all, and gapes, like Hell, for more.
A vaſt abyſs, that would with eaſe devour
Great JOVE, deſcending in a ſilver ſhower !

　　And yet, alas ! how much the world will lye !
They call me miſer ; but no miſer I ;
He, brooding o'er his bags, delighted ſits,
And laughs to ſcorn the jeſts of envious wits ;

If

[23]

If faft his doors, he fets his heart at reft,
And dotes with rapture on his iron cheft;
No galling paper-fquibs his fpirits teize,
But ev'n the boys may hoot him if they pleafe.
He fcorns the whiftling of an empty name,
While I am torn 'twixt avarice and fame;
While I, fo tremblingly alive all o'er,
Still bleed and agonize at every pore;
At ev'ry hifs am harrow'd up with fear,
And burft with choler at a critic's fneer.
Rack'd by the gout and ftone, and ftruck with age,
Prudence and Eafe advife to quit the ftage;
But Fame ftill prompts, and Pride can feel no pain;
And Avarice bids me fell my foul for gain.

Bring N Y K Y back, O Mufe! by verfe divine,
The Trojan-Greeks were once transformed to fwine.
By verfe divine B——T T I 'fcap'd the rope:
Now love is known, what may not lovers hope!

IMITATIONS.

Sordidus ac dives, populi contemnere voces
Si folitus: populus me fibilat: at mihi plaudo
Ipfe domi, fimul ac nummos contemplor in arcâ.

Ducite ab urbe domum, mea carmina ducite Daphnim:
Carminibus Circe focios mutavit Ulyffei:
Carmina vel cœlo poffunt deducere lunam.
Nunc fcio quid fit amor ——————
—————— —————— *quid non fperemus amantes?*

Ev'n

[24]

Ev'n as with *Griffins* * ftallions late have join'd

With blood-hounds goats may litter, as in kind;

Nay wanton kids devouring wolves may greet,

And wolves with loving lyoneffes meet.

By different means is different love made known,

And each fond lover will prefer his own.

Strange lot of love ! two friends, my foul's delight,

Men call that M———r, this a Catamite !

Yet bring him back ; for, who chafte roundelay

Shall fing, now B———ST—FF is driv'n away ?

Who now correct, for modeft Drury-Lane,

Loofe Wycherly's or Congreve's loofer vein ;

With nice decorum fhunning naughty jokes,

Exhibit none but decent, dainty folks,†

Ah

IMITATIONS.

Jungentur jam *Gryphes* equis, ævoque fequenti
Cum canibus timidi venient ad pocula damæ.
Torva leæna lupum fequitur, lupus ipfe capellam,
Te Corydon, O Alexis : trahit fua quemque voluptas.

NOTES.

* Fictitious and unnatural monfters, familiar only with the poets.

† NYKY was employed by ROSCIUS to correct the Plain-dealer of Wycherly ; which he accordingly attempted, and infcribed the attempt to his
patron, " as a tribute of *affection* and efteem for his many fhining and
amiable qualities." " The licentioufnefs of Wycherly's mufe," fays this
modern corrector, " rendered her fhocking to us, with all her charms : or,
in other words, we could allow no charms in a tainted beauty, who brought
contagion along with her." Of the play of the Plain-dealer, in particular,
he

[25]

Ah me! how wanton wit will fhame the ftage,

And fhock this delicate, this virtuous age!

How will *Plain-dealers** triumph, to my forrow!

And Paphos rife o'er Sodom and Gomorrah!

N O T E S.

he intimates that it had been long excluded the theatre; becaufe, to the honour of the prefent age, it was immoral and indecent: that on a clofe examination, he found in it exceffive obfcenity; that the character of Manly was rough even to outrageous brutality; and that he thought it neceffary to work the whole materials up again, with a mixture of alloy agreeable to the rules of modern refinement! See Preface to B———ff's Plain-dealer. What a champion for decency and delicacy, morality and humanity! What improvement may not fterling wit receive from the mixture of fuch alloy! What an idea may we not hence acquire of modern refinement!

* A character thus admirably depicted by Wycherly, in the fcene between Manly and Plaufible.

Manly. I have more of the maftiff than the fpaniel in me, I own it: I cannot fawn, and fetch and carry; neither will I ever practife that fervile complaifance, which fome people pique themfelves on being mafters of.———— I will not whifper my contempt or hatred; call a man fool or knave by figns and mouths, over his fhoulder; while I have him in my arms: I will not, as you do———

Plaufible. As I do! Heaven defend me! upon my honour! I never attempted to abufe or leffen any one in my life.

Manly. What! you were afraid?

Plaufible No: but ferioufly I hate to do a rude thing. No, faith, I fpeak well of all mankind.

Manly. I thought fo: but know that this is the worft fort of detraction, for it takes away the reputation of the few good men in the world by making all alike! Now I fpeak ill of many men, becaufe they deferve it.

F I N I S.

Sodom and Onan. A Satire (1776)

In *Sodom and Onan*, the Reverend William Jackson (1737?–95) attacked the Irish dramatist Samuel Foote (1720–77), known in his day as 'the English Aristophanes'. As a law student in the Temple, Foote was regarded as a great beau, spending most of his time in coffee houses and taverns. He soon gave up law, and wrote a series of successful satirical plays, notably *The Minor* (1760), an attack on Methodism in which he played the skirt role of Mother Cole. In 1766, while on a chase with the Duke of York and his (Foote's) intimate and inseparable companion Sir Francis Blake Delaval, Foote fell and broke his leg. This had to be amputated and replaced by a cork leg – giving rise to many 'foot' and 'leg' jokes. Later that year the conscience-stricken Duke of York helped him to secure the royal patent for a summer theatre. Foote accordingly purchased the Haymarket Theatre, which he rebuilt. In 1768 he cleared nearly £4,000 with *The Devil upon Two Sticks*, in which he played the lame Devil, but he lost it all gambling in Bath. *Dr Last in His Chariot* (1769) was co-authored with Isaac Bickerstaffe (the subject of the previous selection).

In 1775, in *The Trip to Calais*, Foote satirized Elizabeth Chudleigh, Duchess Dowager of Kingston, in the character of Lady Kitty Crocodile. She protested, fearing that its presentation would affect her forthcoming trial for bigamy – she had married the Duke of Kingston after abandoning, rather than divorcing, her husband Augustus Hervey, who had succeeded to his title as the Earl of Bristol by the time of the trial. Foote published a sarcastic apology, only half-heartedly denying his intentions, and alluding to her bigamy. He also exposed her *eminence grise*: 'Pray, madam, is not J—n the name of your female confidential secretary? and is not she generally cloathed in black petticoats made out of your weeds?' (*The Works of Samuel Foote*, ed. Jon Bee (1830), vol. i, p. clvi). This was a reference to her male secretary, Jackson. The Chamberlain refused to license the performance of *The Trip to Calais*. The Duchess was convicted of bigamy in April 1776. She claimed privilege of peerage to escape branding or flogging, and was discharged upon payment of her court costs (she had already gone abroad).

On 13 May 1776, Jackson in the journal the *Public Ledger* accused 'Aristophanes' of being a sodomite. Foote took out a libel suit, which he won, but Jackson renewed the attack in late-June and published, under the pseudonym of Humphrey Nettle, *Sodom and Onan*, whose title page bears a recognizable portrait of Foote, together with an illustration of a large naked foot. An advertisement appeared in the *Morning Post, and Daily Advertiser* for 22 June 1776: 'This Day is published, Price 2s. SODOM and ONAN, A SATIRE. Embellished with a striking likeness of the patron, engraved by an eminent Artist. Printed for the Author, and sold at No. 23, opposite St. Dunstan's Church, Fleet-Street.'

A warrant was issued for Foote's arrest and on 8 July he was indicted for assault with an attempt to commit sodomy. The trial was postponed to December. Foote rewrote *The Trip to Calais* as *The Capuchin* in August, portraying Jackson as Dr Viper. The prosecution, before Lord Mansfield at King's Bench on 9 December 1776, was paid for by the Duchess of Kingston and organized behind the scenes by Jackson. Foote's former footman John Sangster charged Foote with an attempt to commit an unnatural crime upon his person in 1775, first at his townhouse in Suffolk Street and later in the stables of his country house at North End, Hampstead. Circumstantial details confirmed by the gardener and coachman supported Sangster's evidence. But Lord Mansfield judged that there was a conspiracy to blacken Foote's character, and Foote was acquitted. Foote's health broke under the strain. He reappeared on the stage in *The Devil upon Two Sticks* in 1777, lank and emaciated, and then had a series of paralytic strokes. He sold his patent to George Colman and went to Brighton. His physician advised him to go to France for a change of air. He reached Dover on 22 October, but the winds were unfavourable for a crossing. The next morning he had a shivering fit, and died that afternoon. His contemporary Hester Lynch Piozzi observed that 'Doctor Johnson was not aware that Foote broke his heart because of a hideous detection; he was trying to run away from England, and from infamy, but death stopped him' (*Autobiography Letters and Literary Remains of Mrs Piozzi (Thrale)*, ed. A. Hayward (1861),vol. i, pp. 310–11). Some newspapers reported that he died from an overdose of laudanum. He left legacies to two alleged natural sons, but there is no evidence to support the rumour that he married his washerwoman. Jackson later became committed to the French and American revolutions and in 1794 was arrested in Dublin as a spy; he poisoned himself and died while in court.

The text is reproduced from the copy held by the British Library (shelfmark 11642.g.15).

SODOM and ONAN,

A SATIRE.

INSCRIB'D to

Esq.

-- alias, the *DEVIL* upon two Sticks

MOST INFERNAL SIR,

I Have long obferv'd with admiration, the vaft Variety of unnatural Characters you have *enter d into ;* not only in this Metropolis, but every other that has been infefted with your diabolical prefence.

Your laft capital *Man-œuvre* cannot be fufficiently applauded :—the World is now convinced, that no Female, (not even THALIA,) has charms fufficient to enflave fo extenfive a Genius. The rapid progrefs you have made in the fcience of Alchymy, aftonifh'd your moft fanguine admirers, but the Oath of an honeft Man has fatisfied them, that you have (by a Progrefs far fuperior, in point of pleafure and expedition, to any ever difcovered by our elaborate Fore-fathers,) extracted the moft precious *Mettle* in the world out of Stone.

The Satisfaction your important difcovery has afforded the State, is fufficiently teftified by the countenance of your S— and his Minifters ; more efpecially that of the amiable Minden Hero ; who by the ftrange mifreprefentation of *unrefin'd* Men of Valour, was degraded as a Coward, for turning his back towards his Enemies ; of which charge he muft now ftand acquitted, fince it is known he diftinguifhes his *deareft Friends* by receiving them in the fame Manner : And as you have the honour to rank among the number of his Favourites, I prefume you have been often gratified by a fimilar mode of Reception.

What may not this difordered Nation hope for, when the Minifter of the moft convuls'd Department is affifted and *prick'd* on to Action by a Genius like you? whofe *extenfive* Abilities are calculated for the *Deepeft Penetration ;* whofe
internal

ii

internal Acquaintance with, *and practical Essays on Man*, claim precedence even of the immortal POPE, who had neither *personal Strength*, nor mental Courage sufficient to explore the *dark* and *difficult Recesses* into which you have immerg'd.

Lest your immense skill should remain unknown to any Member of that Community whose good opinion you are ambitious of, I assume the character of your Herald, and challenge Europe to produce so great a Master of *Fundamental* Knowledge in the *refin'd and polite* Arts.

Unable to restrain my zeal for your service, the following Pages will be found to want that high finishing which the Elegance of the Subject wou'd admit of.—But your known candour and impartiality, I know will readily pardon all defects in a laudable Intention.———That this work may appear in that light to the Public, is the wish of their

and your INFERNAL HIGHNESS's,

moft obedient Servant,

HUMPHREY NETTLE.

SODOM and ONAN,

A

SATIRE.

CRIMES, and the Man I fing,---
Whofe callous Heart, infenfible of Shame,
Admits each glaring Vice, and damns his Fame;
Whofe mind-corrupted Dealings, are portray'd
In ftronger Colouring than Gold can fhade.

Oh! that offended Genius wou'd infpire
Me, with one Note from Churchill's well-ftrung Lyre,
To fatirize thofe Fiends, who unconfin'd,
Will ftop the Propagation of Mankind.---

Genius, who kindly took the Mifcreant's Part,
When Poverty had levell'd every Dart,

And

(2)

And overwhelm'd his Mind in Exigence,
The juſt Reward of *mean* Extravagance.
Genius! --yet why thy gen'rous aid implore?
Juſtice alone can all his ways explore:
Let him rave on in frantic extaſy,
Forſook by Friends, by Fortune, and by thee.

Nature provides each Son with armour good,
To fight the Cauſe of Love and Gratitude;
To execrate that Fiend of Sodom's Race,
Who Manhood, Friendſhip, Honor dar'd diſgrace;
Who choſe of Crimes moſt capital the worſt,
Reſolv'd in Infamy to rank the firſt.
He, who ne'er lov'd his Friends * whoſe worth he knew,
Their virtues leſſen'd, and their foibles drew,
And Natures failings held to public view.

Curs'd be the Wretch who, joining hand in hand,
Smiles in my face,---ſeems all at my command,---
My Table his,---no Stranger to my Purſe,---
He meditates my death; or what is worſe,

Forgets

* Mr. Ap--price, &c.

(3)

Forgets the harveſt and the field he reap'd,
And ſtabs my Name, with Tongue in venom ſteep'd.

Ingratitude! fell Monſter! when poſſeſt,
Sedition raiſes in the human breaſt,
And every· ſpark of virtue ſhe can find
Quickly eradicates; and leaves the Mind
A prey to paſſions, vile and rankeſt luſt,
And moulders Reputation into duſt:
Relieves the heart from conſcientious fear,
And mocks all ſentiments to honor dear:

Often my ardent pen have I reſtrain'd,
To learn if his obdurate heart contain'd
One palliative merit, --- vain controll!
Reſearch unprofitable!--- In his foul
Ingratitude had firmly·fix'd her ſeat,
And troops of crimes march in without defeat:
Sodomy old, ſee at the van appear,
Polluting Onan ſly, brings up the rear.

At

(4)

At their approach, his fiery blood forfakes
Its natural channels, and frefh courfes takes ;---
Sudden, a glow unufual fills his veins
New form'd, and his inverted Eye difdains
'Objects of Female foftnefs.--- with pleafure
He beholds, (like Ganeymede) that Treafure
Exquifite, a lovely Youth, whofe Innocence
'Gainft his prevailing Arts, prove weak defence;
E'en age attractions has ; but Youths a Prize!
An-handfome Boy's a *Jewel* in his Eyes.---
Ignorance juvenile, ne'er 'fcapes his Snares,
But when he aims at one of riper Years;
He Tampers in fubordinate degree,
And Onan, introduces S -d--y.

Raging with Luft, (forgetful of difgrace
Which muft attend repulfe,) he fought a place,
To vent imagination kindled Fires,
And fell a facrifice to rank Defires :---
In fplendid Manfion finding no refource,
Fain he'd defile the Chamber of his Horfe.---

Yet

GANYMEDE.

(5)

Yet in mean Garb, he met a ftrong defence,

To Decency, and a Virtuous Senfe

Of good, and felf-fuftaining Innocence.---

Boldly the Man repell'd the vile Effay,

Judging it wrong in all things to obey ;

A Mafter, fo inflam'd with ftrange Defires,

And Eyes betraying wrong directed Fires.——

From Nature's paths the wholefome Hind ne'er

And hop'd by Juftice they might be preferv'd. [fwerv'd

To Juftice flys for aid, devoid of Guile,

Leaving the Brute, to meditate fome while,

By which he might evade the Law, and try

Like his Compeer Drybutter, to defy

The Hand of Equity.--- I truft in vain

Ne'er let him act the Shameful part again ;

The blind Difpenfer of each penal Law,

Soon in the Mimic's 'Scutcheon found a Flaw :

And wifely bound him to fuperior Court,

Tho' often there the worft find beft fupport,

And Juftice frequently is leaning caught.

Yet

(6)

Yet in a caufe like this, when horrors fieze
Th' attentive Auditors, and blood doth freeze
Of Old and Young.   In all there will appear,
Each Hair partic'lar ftarted in it's Sphere :
Each Eye, will watch the tendence of the Chief,
Whofe quick difcernment, wou'd cut caufes Brief ;
But pleadings muft be heard to try confufions,
Lawyers are much averfe to fhort Conclufions :
They'll Brow-beat, Twift and Torture Evidence,
Cancelling meanings, 'till the whole condenfe,
And thick as Head of Jury Man (who laid
In good ftore of Solid Viands, afraid
Of Dunning, for when longer winded,
Of three good Meals his Belly he'd refcinded.)
Bewilder'd in a maze of contradiftions,
Unknowing how to feperate the Fiftions,
Or t' inveftigate the clue Sophiftic,
Gapes on thefe Orators, as dealers Myftic,
'Till learned Judge the Evidence repeats,
Which well fum'd up chicanery defeats.

But

(7)

But much depends upon his clear conception,

Mansfield ne'er errs, unlefs 'tis in fubjection,

To mandate vile of a court party faction.

There Ariftophanes has friends, we know,

Who *fellow-feelings* fuffer for the blow

That wounds his reputation, — *fore before*,

Which cataplafm rare can ne'er reftore.

They for their Favorite will interfere

Behind the curtain, — fhunning public ear.

Mansfield beware, a caufe like this is nice ;

No tongue hath dar'd to taint your name with vice.

Like this ;— or reprobate been heard to fay,

That for fuch practice you e'er found a WAY.

With honeft candor, weigh in equal fcale

The pros and cons, and let the truth prevail.

A-t-n we know is partial to the Fair ;

Married he is, —— (*but that's nor here nor there.*)

With care-tir'd thoughts, domeftic feuds to quench,

He folaces abroad with buxom wench,

And

(8)

And cracks Commandments with no more remorfe
Than I crack nuts, or merrily difcourfe.
A Judge in Commons he had rather been,
There he might patronize his darling Sin ;
Adultery's no *Camel* in his eyes,
For what he fpeaks in confidence, implies,
That Man the Crime of Marriage may commit,
But who diflikes his Wife, is not a wit
If in one inftance he'll to her fubmit.
His doctrine and his dealings well agree,
For Spoufe and him you ne'er together fee :
Impartiality we fure may hope
From one whofe paffion takes fo fair a fcope.

In laughter-loving W-ll-s lurks fome difguife,
Momus he looks like, *tho he's wond'rous wife* ;
Above being dubb'd, remains a *fimple* 'Squire,
A thorough Englifhman, with no defire,
Save wine, girl, beef, and eafe by fea-coal fire.

Refembling

(9)

Refembling A—t—n, (not in his grimace,)
He fain in wenching would keep equal pace;
But left in cups he fhould be led aftray,
His Wife the Circuit goes as well as he;
She gives the Man no chance to play the fool,
When warm abroad, fhe takes him home to cool.
Such prudent Dames, keep Hymen's torch alight,
Who TRIM it regularly day and night.
Of W-ll-s I think there's little caufe to doubt,
Mansfield will put him in when he is out.

Now laft, not leaft in our dear love, appear,
We nothing hope from thee, nor nothing fear,
Afhurft, the grave, the gentle, and ferene,
Nought from his words can lift'ning ftudents glean;
Nay, had he wifdom of a Solomon,
His Elders arrogant wou'd keep him down;
Whene'er he wou'd be heard, the pointed thiftle,
Quick interrupts, and he as well might whiftle.
'Tis hard to judge without a full difplay,
But candour guides, no malice I'll betray:

He

(10)

He may be what Pope calls, Beſt work of GOD ;
He's neither wit nor feather, chief nor rod.

'Fore ſuch a Bench, who'd fear to ope his cauſe,
Aided by rhetoric of grave Counſellors ;
Who never fail to plead with energy,
When brief's made heavy with a proper fee.
F——te knows the law too well to ſtarve a Cauſe,
Money well tim'd will cover many flaws.
A recent inſtance he, of Fortune's whim,
The law he follow'd once, now follows him.
If his ſupplies are ſcanty from the town,
E'er trial he muſt melt his ſilver down ;
Diſhes and plates from Villa muſt be brought,
And for a while ſuſpended be his Court.
Sollicitors are chary of their fame,
For dirty work, an higher price they claim.
Dunning three hundreds got to plead for Lead,
Which Pomfret loſt with aching heart and head.

Black

(11)

Black was the matter fued for, but compare,
Black Lead with B —y, I'll engage you'll fwear
Black Lead is White, and B——'s Devils are.

Dunning will be retain'd, if Money'll buy
His Talents in behalf of Sodomy,
But he's too generous to proftitute
Shining abilities: or to difpute
For Punifhment the fmalleft mitigation,
He'd rather fee the Tribe in conflagration,
A Burning Sacrifice to fave the Nation.

Wallace, the favorite of the chief, no fear,
Will be diftinguifh'd in this Sable War,
Not for his Wit, or Declamation,
They often meet with refutation.
But for broad northern Accent, vacant Face
Might fuit a Murd'rer, but not gain him Grace;
In this no *Grieve*-ous challenges there'll be,
Ariftoph' Coward is no lefs than he.

Bearc—t

(12)

Bearc—t can ne'er refift the ftrong Temptation
Of current Gold, nor fhew a deteftation,
To whate'er nature, fort, or kind the Sin is
If Client's rich, and Lards it well with Guineas.

When Juftice lingers, Villains may defeat her,
An Error that in Britifh Legiflature,
Since fuch Exotics her attention draw,
Their Turkifh Crimes, fhou'd feel the Turkifh Law.
Which Inftant at the Populace requeft,
Th' accufed punifhes; or if oppreft
Acquits. But here the Laws leave Avenues,
Which pow'rful Sod'mites frequently abufe;
Tamper with Gold, and terrify with Threats,
'Till the aftonifh'd Ignorant forgets
His Injuries. Alarm'd at all he hears,
Amaz'd, diftracted with a Thoufand Fears,
He fells his Country, quits his virtuous fhield,
And artful B——s Glory in the Field.

Beware

(13)

Beware young Man, avoid the Fatal Snare
By Treach'ry laid, nor fingle venture near
The Demon's haunts, Devices rare he'll try,
Affifted by Colleagues in Infamy,
Your meritorious efforts to fubdue,
And drive you from the Path you now purfue;
Which once effected, the juft calumny
Now crufhing him, will all be thrown on thee.
If motive good hath urg'd thee to declare
What fhudd'ring Juftice was compell'd to hear;
If from the line of truth you ne'er have ftep'd,
In this dire 'Count, nor confcience have o'erleap'd,
Boldly maintain the ground whereon you ftand,
You'll find protection from the public hand.

Ariftoph' mercenary hackney'd Scribe,
Worfe than newfpaper Rhymers, or the tribe
Of Grub ftreet Poets, (who when hunger calls,
Trump up a bloody murder for the walls
Of Palaces,—hung round without,—no Sin,
Where murders daily are contriv'd within)

Offal-

(14)

Offal-fed wretches, hid in alley rank,
Whether in Garret high or Cellar dank,
They weave their humble ditties into rhyme,
(Ne'er rais'd by gen'rous wine to the fublime,)
With Thee, Arifloph', vie for fpotlefs Name,
Unpamper'd by the Price of plunder'd fame.
What fhall preferve thee from the fatal Tree?
Or from the rogue-exalting pillory?
If Afhurft helps thee not with fpecial plea?

Vile Slanderer, the Crifis of thy fate
Approaches;—now Intereft 'mongft the great
Thofe tender-hearted Privy Counfellors,
Who late for Jones expanded Mercy's doors.

Infamy fure her higheft pitch has foar'd,
And virtue's banifh'd from the Council Board,
When fawning fycophants in royal Ear
Pour ftrains pathetic for their trembling Dear;
In whofe Society they have enjoy'd
Soft Converfe, fuch as Females would have cloy'd.

Tender

(15)

Tender remembrance, fprings of Little **Sports**,
Unrival'd in Chinefe or Turkifh Courts :
Their Chrift'nings, Lyings-in, Abortions ;—
Their Caudle-makings,—fifty foul **Diftortions**,
Unfit for public repetition,
Shou'd be refer'd to Spanifh Inquifition.
Who knows what Honours Ariftoph' may claim?
He·may a Peerefs be, and to his Shame,
Have borne an Heir or Heirefs at the Game.

If 'tis confirm'd, that in *their* Marriage Bed,
A virtuous Peer obtain'd his Maidenhead,
Confiderable 'vantage he will get,
Of what in Kingfton he derided.   Yet,
To Peerefs' priveledge there s no pretence,
He went beyond a Clerg' able offence,

Now Briftol's Countefs victory compleats,
Two thoufand fav'd, with Honour fhe retreats;
The Female Circle, jointly feel th' attempt,
To fpurn at all through her; but with contempt

And

(16)

And Indignation juft, they all confpire
To Crufh the Woman hater, and retire
To Scenes, where Bronze like his muft ne'er appear,
Not *Female* Proftitutes, they're fo fevere
Will condefcend to Grace his Theatre.
Male Whores of Quality, before Conviction
May yeild fupport to countenance the Friction.
And if by curs'd chican'ry he can boaft
Acquital, they'll erect him ftanding Toaft:
Lord Robert Gallery mounted 'mongft the Gods,
Aims Luftful, difconcerting, Winks and Nods.
Nobility degrades to prowl for prey,
Plump Heifers flights, and Steers conveys away
To fome dark Alley, where the Sun difdains
To fhine obliquely, or exhale the Stains,
Which fwelt'ring Sodomites accumulate
And their attendant Fiends, loud execrate.

Ambition was the fall'n Angels Crime,
High Heav'n offended, plung'd them from fublime

To

(17)

To fcorching Regions, deftitute of eafe,

A painful Purgatory to appeafe

Their Maker's Wrath.---Then where will he commit

Th' infernal Crew, or when remit

Their Tortures? who regardlefs of command,

With Sodomy contaminate the Land?

The wife Creator, ne'er remifs, furveys

The fprings of action : in due time conveys

Rewards and punifhments:---Then George beware,

Be vigilant, and recollect his care

Supreme, when finally refolv'd to free

The land of Sodom by a a juft decree,

And from the face of land the crime to chace,

Sent fire to extirpate the guilty race.

Again they rife, nor here will be fupprefs'd

While at the Court the Actors are carefs'd.

As heaven's Vicegerents Kings on Earth are plac'd,

But G —-e the feal majeftic hath difgrac'd ;

Inveigled by Scotch Infinuation

To pardon Sodomites and damn the Nation.

S———e

(18)

S——e, both Coward, and Catamite, commands
Department hon'rable,---and kiffes hands,
With lips that oft' in blandifhment obfcene
Have been employ'd, yet now, (oh fhame!) he's feen
An haughty headftrong Minifter of State,
Controuling Men of minds immaculate.

View ftradling B-rt--, that Bedchamber Lord,
(Felon in Gyves as well might grace a fword,)
Leering he eyes when M———'s undreft,
And on a **** cou'd make a princely feaft :
Yet fuch divinity doth hedge a King,
That Catamites their off'rings dare not bring :
But as I'm lefs than King, I fhall take care
E'er I undrefs, that B-t-e is not there.
Ne'er in my houfe a welcome Gueft he'll be,
Ent'ring my doors, he'll want to enter me.

· Chefter and Holderneffe difmifs'd, concern
Sits on the Monarch's brow ; with afpect ftern

He

(19)

He ruminates on Men,--- and gloomy weighs

Their different talents ; but difcerns few rays

Of worth intrinfic, 'mongft the jealous tribe

Of purfe-proud Bifhops, who defpife a bribe,

But---when Death removes an old Incumbent

Of Archbifhopric,------meanly recumbent

The Right Reverends fall,---pant for Tranflation,

Praifing the doƐrine of tranfmigration.

Their objeƐ gain'd, in eafe and affluence blefs'd,

Religion, Mitre, Key and Crozier reft.

In vain the mif-led, pond'ring Parent ftrives

To learn the manners of their private Lives :

Refolv'd no more to rack his-ftubborn brain,

To Favorite's controul refigns the rein :

Let Bute pronounce the word, and ftraight you'll fee,

Sackville and Bertie fhall Præceptors be.

Ye free-born Cits, who kneeling 'fore the throne,

Congratulate, petition and bemoan ;

Demonftrating the Mis'ries of this Land,

Yet only meet with churlifh reprimand ;

Hafte

(20)

Hafte to Apollo, there make fupplication,
With care explain the dreadful complication
Of Diforders, raging in crown-fhelter'd brain ;
(Accumulation vaft for few years reign,)
Beg him of wifdom to lay in, a ftore,
Where not a fingle gleam e'er fhone before :
Men and their meafures then will be infpected,
Merit will rife, and Villains be detected.

Where is the Author of the village Love ?
Sweet Ifaac Bickerftaff, who never ftrove
To wipe away the ignominious ftain,
Convinc'd that kicking 'gainft the *Pricks* was vain.
For Safety flown to foft Italia's fhore,
Where Tilney, B——l, Jones and many more
Of Britain's caft outs, revel uncontroul'd,
Who for their Beaftial luft their Country fold,
Who diffipate Eftates in Foreign Climes
To buy indulgence, for their darling Crimes.

In times like thefe conduct yourfelf with Care,
For virtuous Company is very rare ;

If

(21)

If with convivial Friends, you chance to paſs
The Ev'ning tide, and take a chearful Glaſs,
Merrily glide the Laughter ſeaſon'd Hours,
'Till drowſy Somnus exerciſe' his Powrs ;
Then for ɐ Female rouſe and beat the round,
And if no yielding fair one's to be found,
In ——'s Hotel you ſeek a Friendly Roof,
Obſerve this rule :-- ne'er pull your Breeches off.---
From Health reſtoring Slumbers ſtrive to keep,
Or ten to one your are B——'d in your Sleep.

Benignant Heav'n hath wiſely ſet his ſeal
Indelible, on all who chooſe to deal
In this dark commerce.—The conſpicuous ſtamp
Their practice Indicates, as true as Lamp
The Quacking Doctors, ſignify'd in Bill;
Pendant in paſſage, where he vends his Pill;
They both allay for raging Fires provide,
In different conſtitutions; unally'd.

'Gainſt

(22)

'Gainſt Nature in one inſtance I exclaim;
In dealing puniſhments ſhe miſs'd her aim;
Diſeaſe corroſive ſhe hath miſapplied;
Maiming her votaries, who have comply'd
With her wiſe dictates, in firm confidence
Of milder treatment for obedience.
The Race of Catamites, devoid of ſhame,
Conclude that ſhe is partial to their flame;
Urging as argument for their deſires,
That they're exempted from venereal Fires.

Transfer the curſe, dear Goddeſs, and applauſe
Command, from all who venerate thy Laws;
Exempt poor Proſtitutes from foul infection,
And uſe it to bring B---ers in ſubjection.
Where'er the Letchers meet to recreate,
Let the rank poiſon ſieze them at the gate;
That none may 'ſcape, who but in thought deſign'd
To gratify ſuch paſſions-unconfin'd.

                                    Commons

(23)

Commons and Lords, to quell domeſtic ſtrife,

Are daily ſeperating Man and Wife:

Will no wiſe Member dare to frame a bill,

Effectually to cruſh this growing ill?

Some Youth of *Parts* ſhou'd ſuch an act prepare,

'Twou'd be an introduction to the Fair.

No Law provides 'gainſt funeral obſequies;

The Dead are puniſh'd not for crimes like theſe:

But if deſponding Mortal, who withſtood

Fortunes Severities, by Land and Flood,

A ſmall reſerve committed to the care

Of Friend,—with reaſon he might think ſincere,—

(For when Proſperity, which ſeldom fails,

In ſome kind hour, to ſend us thriving Gales,

Had crown'd him with ſucceſs, his foſt'ring hand,

Delighted in its power to raiſe that Friend

From poverty, which taunting proud men mock,

And Fools and Knaves make a deriding ſtock;

From priſon dread, and heart-corroding cares,

To liberty, and gay revolving Years.)

Yet

(24)

Yet by a feries of concurring ills,

With which capricious Chance Life's checquer fills,

He is reduc'd to claim his fcant Eftate,

And in retirement calmly wait on fate,

Patient he hies him to the well-known door,

---Approaching,---hears the table in a roar ;---

His name announc'd, the honeft Servant's chid

For interrupting laughter, and forbid

T' admit within th' ungrateful wall

The Man that rais'd it ;——for his quick decline

Had reach'd the Monfter's manfion; who, in wine

Caroufing, feels no pang, but noify quaffs

The healths of Profp'rous men,---at others laughs.

    Few Minds are calculated to endure

Th' affaults of Indigence,---and end obfcure

The remnant of a life in pleafure flown,

When age and forrows weigh the fpirits down.

But

(25)

But if ingratitude affliction joins,
And in rash hour the wretch his Life refigns,
Then ill-digefted Laws exert their power
O'er Suicide,— that Alkali for four
Misfortunes fhafts,) and punifh in the grave,
Which e'en from perfecution cannot fave:
While the triumphant engine of thefe woes
Revels. in affluence,—nor repentant throws
A bribe to Coroner; who for paltry fee,
Wou'd change his verdict into Lunacy.

But heinous S———s no law controuls;—
When Hell's difgrac'd with their malignant Souls,
Like Chriftians they're depofited in earth,
And cunning Priefts, refpectful of their *worth,*
After the Gallows happ'ly is reliev'd
Of their convicted Bodies, (*unrepriev'd,*)
With countenance indiff'rent and ferene
As when they're praying for their King and Queen,
Wickedly

(26)

Wickedly proftitute the folemn pray'r,
Like perjur'd Jew, or love-protefting Play'r.

Curs'd be fuch flaves to foul-corrupting Ore,
Who treat Religion like a painted whore ;
Refembling Confeffors, her price enhance
When Sodomy demands her countenance.

Oh ! that with legal pow'r I were endued
To punifh fodomitic turpitude ;
Spaniards and Portugueze fhou'd both refign,
And Dutch the Inquifition at Amboyn',
When they but hear the tortures I'd invent,
unnatural-tranfgreffions to prevent.

Pandora I invoke to ope' her ftore,
And add fome plagues fhe never us'd before ;
Pour them on Ariftoph', nor e'er relent,
He merits all their pains in full extent :
Let his whole mafs with poifon be condens'd,
And for each pang of his, one Whore be cleans'd ;

Let

(27)

Let rank corruption, mining all within,

Confume his vitals, e'er the caufe is feen;

'Till noifome ftench prevents the Faculty

Approaching near, their Cauftics to apply:

And may he one tormenting B--boe feel,

From the Corona veneris to the heel;

While fhankers perforate his mouth and nofe,

That not a fingle want he may difclofe:

Let an inceffant itch attack the part

Where the infection enter'd, 'till with fmart.

Enrag'd, he openly expofe the Caufe,

Intreating mitigation, or the jaws

Of Hell to clofe the horrid fcene,

Where burning convicts feel inferior pain.

Indulge him then, and *tenderly* enforce,

To finifh Life, the dread Free-mafons curfe:

Gnafhing his teeth, he'll reprefent Defpair,

And his laft breath infect the wholefome air.

If in a grave he's fuffer'd to confume,

Drybutter'll crawl chief mourner to his tomb.

Bick-

(28)

Bick-----ff, B--t-e, B——l, Bu——rs all,

Jones, S——e, D--v-is ſhall ſupport the pall ;

And as a requiem to his burning Soul,

Lamenting Niky'll chaunt the Iriſh howl.

Thus from the world his mangled coarſe convey'd,

Shall reſt 'till night's dull murder-ſcreening ſhade,

Encourages thoſe hounds (whoſe vile employ

Is robbing Worms e'er they a meal enjoy,)

By Sheldon ſent to ſeize e'er it decays,

The forfeit Body of late limping Bayes,

Which in becoming Sackcloth he ſecures,

And in his Limb-deck'd Surgery immures ;

There Guards the Prize, like two headed Janus

Reſolv'd to Inveſtigate, the Furor Anus.

In vain the dreadful object he'll explore,

As ſome ingenious Men have done before ;

Barowby ne'er the Matter cou'd define,

Nor give one reaſon, human or divine :

The Theory was far beyond his Art,

Tho' well he knew the practicable Part.

On

(29)

On the fame fubject, Sheldon might have try'd
Experiments, nor waited till he died ;
Eafy of accefs, he cou'd ne'er refufe
An Artift any part he wifh'd to ufe.

But Sheldon, Young and Handfome, was afraid
To truft himfelf too near till he was dead.

Puzzled, perplex'd, and dreading fome Infection
From Flefh, fo much inclin'd to putrifaction,
Sheldon extends the Law and ftraight diffects
The bloated Carcafe, and the flefh ejects
On Neighb'ring Dunghill, where lean porkers feed ;
(An half-got, hungry, Scottifh, mealy Breed.)
Joyful he cries the Garbage I confign,
And fend the Devil once more into the Swine.
Ariftoph' cou'd he feel wou'd die with Glee,
Enjoying one more Beaftiality.

Ariftoph' plung'd in darknefs for his Luft,
Good Men ne'er hear his Name, but with difguft.

F I N I S.

A Sapphick Epistle, from Jack Cavendish to the Honourable and Most Beautiful Mrs. D★★★★ (1778?)

The British Library Catalogue suggests the date '1771?' for *A Sapphick Epistle*, but several of the Bluestockings and members of the Twickenham set referred to in the satire would have been unknown to the public in 1771. The poem refers to 'Miss Aikin', who would be Anna Laetitia Aikin, whose first publication was not until 1773 (*Poems*, and also *Miscellaneous Pieces in Prose* with her brother John Aikin). Miss Aikin married Rochemont Barbauld in May 1774, and was for a time described as 'Mrs Barbauld (late Miss Aikin)' and then as 'Mrs Barbauld'. The earlier form nevertheless persisted. For example, in 1780 she was called 'Aikin' in *Sketches of the Lives and Writings of the Ladies of France* by Ann Thicknesse, and in a poem published in the *Gentleman's Magazine* in March 1786 (but possibly written earlier) she is called 'Miss Aikin (now Mrs Barbauld)'.

In any case, a brief 'Review of *Sapphick Epistle*' appeared in the *Monthly Review* for March 1778: 'Were a court of criticism to be held by the rakes and debauchees of this wicked town, a *Sapphick Epistle* would afford them matter for a capital investigation: nor should we, queer old Square-toes! presume to approach the verge of their jurisdiction' (cited by Andrew Elfenbein, *Romantic Genius* (New York, 1999), pp. 101–2). The publisher, M. Smith, also published in 1778 *The Court of Adul[ter]y: A Vision*, a twenty-four-page quarto like *A Sapphick Epistle*, which went through at least six editions that year (expanded to thirty-two pages), plus a Supplement; and several scandalous pamphlets including *An Adieu to the Turf: A Poetical Epistle from the E[ar]l of A[bingdo]n to His Grace the A[rchbisho]p of Y[or]k* and *An Epistle from Mademoiselle d'E'on to…L[or]d M[ansfiel]d*. In later years he published *The Devil Divorced; or, The Diablo-Whore* (1782), political cartoons and some trials for 'criminal conversation' (i.e. adultery) up to about 1790. Another copy, with missing pages, bears a different title page with the false imprint 'T. Southern'. The unknown author (who seems to have a special familiarity with law courts) may have chosen the pseudonym 'Jack Cavendish' to libel the sometimes-controversial Whig politician Lord John Cavendish (he resigned as Chancellor of the Exchequer in 1782, together with Fox's Whig government, but was reappointed in 1783). One possibility may be William Combe, who in *The First of April; or, The Triumphs of Folly* (1777), in the course of an attack on the Marquis of Hertford, libelled Hertford's relative Anne Damer for showing no grief after her husband committed suicide in 1776 and for looking forward, together with her comforter Lady Harrington, to the 'joys which blooming Widows share'.

It is clear from puns on 'Dame' and 'D—R' that its subject is Anne Seymour Damer (née Conway; 1749–1828), an amateur actress and a sculptor who frequently exhibited her work at the Royal Academy. She married in 1767 but soon separated from her husband and never remarried after he killed himself. Much later, Hester Lynch Piozzi denounced Anne Damer as a 'Sapphist' in her diary (17 June 1790): 'Mrs. *Damor* a lady much suspected for liking her own Sex in a criminal Way, had Miss Farren the fine comic Actress often about her last year; and Mrs. Siddon's Husband made the following Verses on them. "Her little Stock of private Fame / Will fall a Wreck to public Clamour, / If Farren leagues with one whose Name / Comes near – Aye very near – to *Damn her*."' Lord Derby's pursuit of the actress Elizabeth Farren (1759?–1829) was satirized in Charles Pigott's *The Whig Club* (1794): 'superior to the influence of MEN, she is supposed to feel more exquisite delight from the touch of the cheek of Mrs. D—r than the fancy of any *novelties* which the wedding night can promise with such a partner as his lordship' (p. 55). Anne Damer's probable lover was Mary Berry (1763–1852), who became Horace Walpole's literary executor and inherited his Gothic folly, Strawberry Hill. The two women travelled together on the Continent and in England, and Miss Berry performed in the amateur theatricals that Mrs Damer organized at Strawberry Hill. Joseph Farrington in his diary (19 Aug. 1798) commented: 'The singularities of Mrs. Damer are remarkable – She wears a Mans Hat, and Shoes, and a Jacket also like a mans – thus she walks abt. the fields with a hooking stick.…The extasies on meeting, & tender leave on separating, between Mrs. Damer and Miss Berry, is whimsical. On Miss Berry going lately to Cheltenham, the servants described the separation between Her & Mrs. Damer as if it had been parting before death.' *A Sapphick Epistle* also alludes to the actress Catherine 'Kitty' Clive, a friend of Mrs Damer and Miss Berry and a neighbour of Walpole, whom she frequently visited and by whom she was supported in her retirement after 1769.

The text is reproduced from the copy held by the British Library (shelfmark 11630.e.9 (4)).

A

SAPPHICK EPISTLE,

FROM

JACK CAVENDISH

TO THE

Honourable and moſt beautiful Mrs. D****

———————————

Printed for M. SMITH, and ſold by the Bookſellers near *Temple-Bar*, and in *Paternoſter-Row*.

[5]

A

SAPPHICK EPISTLE,

FROM

JACK CAVENDISH, to the Honourable Mrs. D---R.

WAS there a Maïd of Lesbos * Isle,

That ever did refuse to smile,

     When Sappho deign'd to woo?

And yet she left their rosy cheeks,

And all their little modest freaks,

     For Phaon---most untrue.

* Lesbos, an Isle of the Ægean Sea, famous for the birth of Miss Sappho, who was the first young classic maid that bestowed her affections on her own sex : She wrote better poesy than either Mrs. Mohtague, Mrs. Greville, Miss Carter, or Miss Aikin, but yet her verses failed when she came to address the cold Phaon. So when an old maid, and unfit for man's love, she pursued the young girls of Mytelene, and seduced many. She was the first Tommy the world has upon record; but to do her justice, though there hath been many Tommies since, yet we never had but one Sappho.

     No more the Lesbian dames my passion move,
     Once the dear objects of my guilty love.

Mr. Pope, and Mr. Publius Naso Ovid, the first a waspish English Poet, the latter the most accomplished Roman Gentleman in the reign of Augustus, have given evidence to this heterogeneous passion of Sappho.

           B   Ah !

[8]

Ah! haplefs woman, to confide

In man, and figh to be the bride;

A veffel full of care:

Would you the wifer Sappho learn,

You might your happinefs difcern,

And fhun a fharp defpair.

When Sappho, the fair Lefbian belle,

Had gain'd the knack to read and fpell;

She woo'd the Graces all:

No wench of Mytelene's Town,

Or black, or fair, or olive brown,

Refus'd her amorous call.

By Penny-poft fhe fent her odes,

To matrons, widows, whores and bawds,

And won them to her will:

For who, Ah tell me cou'd refufe,

The pow'r of fuch a pleading mufe,

The language of her quill?

Thus

[7]

Thus happy Sappho paſt her time,

In making love, and making rhime,

      To all the Leſbian maids :

Who were more conſtant and more kind,

More pure in ſoul, more firm of mind,

      Than all the Leſbian blades.

Thrice ſenſible, diſcerning dame,

That firſt purſued the hallow'd flame,

      Of chaſtity and joy :

That left the brutal claſp of man,

Jove's trite, dull, delegated plan,

      And e'en his Gany-boy.

When this pure ſcheme the dame purſued,

There was no ſin in being lewd,

      It brought no mean diſgrace:

'Twas

[6]

'Twas chafte platonick love and law,

As taught in France by * Jacques Roufleau,

That wonder of his race.

His † Eloifa was a wife,

A pattern of domeftic life,

Moft pious fage and true:

And Mr. Wolmar was a man,

Made on the old, tame, ftale, cold plan,

And cuckolded by St. ‡ Preue.

* Jean Jacques Roufleau, a fingular wit and philofopher, the author of the new Eloifa, wherein, to prove the excellence and elegance of his pen, he attempts to unite all contrarities, to make drunkennefs amiable, and vice, virtue. He came to England to fee the celebrated Scots Hume, (a greater philofopher in another way) he lodged at a little Chandler's Shop in Chifwick, under the pretence of learning the manners of the people, and the Englifh Language; he always appeared in the Armenian drefs, and his fellow traveller and companion, was, a Pomeranian cur dog. He quarreled with the fenfible Hume, and returned to Paris; were he now copies mufic, prefering that ftile of poverty and independance to elegant retreat.

† Dans ce Roman on apprendra à fuborner philofophiquement une jeune fille, et elle lui donnera la prémiére un baifer fur la bouche, & elle l'invitere à coucher avec elle, & il y couchera, & elle deviendra groffe de metaphyfique; & fes Billets-doux feront des Homilies philofophiques.

‡ Puis il ira faire le tour du monde pour donner le tems aux enfans de fa maîtreffe de croitre, & devenir en Suiffe, pour être leur préceptuer, & leur apprendre la vertu comon à leur mere.

But

[9]

But now my mufe hath ta'en a dance,

And led me off, full frifk to France,

  Which was not my intention;

To Lefbos Ifle I meant to ftick,

To praife, and vifit every nick,

  By help of fome invention.

Ah tell me Lady (for you can)

What little joy there is in Man,

  The rough, unweidly bear:

Ah Sappho! I adore thy name,

That did the vulgar * Wretch difclaim,

  For the more lovely Fair.

O! think how Phaon us'd the dame,

Curfe on his impious heart and name,

  Curfe on his cold difdain:

* But ah beware Sicilian nymphs! nor boaft
That wand'ring heart which I fo lately loft.
       POPE.

  C   A cruelty

[10]

A cruelty, like his, would prove
To me a perfect cure for love,

    Of ev'ry vig'rous fwain.

But thank my ftars, I have no caufe,
To rail at man, or human laws,

    To me they're kind and true:

But I deteft the jealous race,
I'd rather fee * Almeria's face.

    Or gaze on pretty C---.

Oh wou'd the fex purfue my plan,
And turn upon the monfter man,

    What would they not efcape :

A thoufand woes, a thoufand pains,
Swellings, diftortions, cramps and ftrains,

    The ruin of each fhape.

* Nature never produced fo amiable a female, nor endowed her with greater beauties.

Tell

[11]

Tell me, for you are vers'd in love,

Did you from man sweet transports prove,

　　To counterpoise the pain?

Can one so slender and so mild,

Support the torments of a child,

　　Nor reprobate the chain.

The marriage chain, Oh hell on earth!

The iron shackle of all mirth,

　　Life's purgatory here:

For woman had been gay, if free,

Nor curs'd to raise up pedigree,

　　To peasant and to peer.

Dear Lady, such is woman's state,

With Charlotte, or with Ruffia's Kate,

　　Or Moll, or Peg, or Nan:

All sigh, as soon as fledg'd, to have

Some mere, male creature for a slave,

　　To prime their little pan.

　　　　　　　　　　　　　Small

[12]

Small's then the touch-hole, not being old,

The colour lead, or carrot gold,

Or brown, or white or black:

But think, what a fair maid muſt bear,

When ſome rough markſman to a hair,

Shoots at the little crack.

Behold that noble Jockey Fool,

He's neither made by line or rule,

But form'd to wound and lame:

Miſs F--k--, as † Propontis wide,

Where veſſels beat from ſide to ſide,

Squals at the ‡ Aſs's name.

† It is thus wittily deſcribed by the *Ovidian* author of the Meretriciad.
       'Tis like the Heleſpont, on whoſe high ſtrand,
       The love-ſung Seſtos, and Abydos ſtand:
       The deepeſt ſtream pent in the cloſeſt lea,
       For all within's Propontis and the ſea:
       Nay could you croſs this ſea, you'd find again,
       Another Boſphorus and another Main.
In fact, it is as much without an end as the Globe, tho' more variable in its motions.

   ‡ Vers ſon amant elle avance la main
     Sans y ſonger, puis la titre ſoudain.
     Elle rougit, s'effraie & ſe condamne,
     Puis ſe raſſure, & puis lui dit : " belle âne!"
     Mais ce bel âne eſt un amant céleſte;
     Il n'eſt héros ſi brillant & ſi leſte:
     Nul n'eſt plus tendre & nul n'a plus d'eſprit,
     Il eut l'honneur de porter J--- C---.
                      Voltaire.   Ah !

[13]

Ah! Kitty, Kitty, buxom wench,

To let this creature make a trench,

    Where Heav'n but made a flit:

'Tis martyrdom fmall wits declare,

To torture fuch a beauteous fair,

    On fuch a monftrous fpit.

To decency they've no pretence,

The want of that, is want of fenfe;

    For fay, what woman fhou'd,

In fuch a cafe devote her life,

'Tis worfe than ftabbing with a knife,

    To rip up flefh and blood.

But delicacy's fled the land,

They'll any thing now take in hand,

    If they can fhut their eyes:

Tho' it might make the dumb to fpeak,

It cannot even make them fqueak,

    So well they manage fize.

       D   Ah!

[14]

Ah! were the gentle fex like you,

Joy wou'd be rational and true,

  And women might have fame:

You are a pattern of a wife,

That could refign a hufband's life,

  To raife a Sapphick name.

Ah! Mytelene's beauteous maid,

Could I poffefs thee in the fhade,

  And fober D----- by:

You ne'er fhould wifh for puerile joy,

Nor whimper for the fcornful boy,

  Like Mrs. Chicken † ***.

Curfe on my ftars, that I was born,

In fuch an age of luft and fcorn.

  Oh, Sappho, had'ft thou been

---

† A certain military fwain, who ufed to prefer the pleafures of his wife to his own honour, and therefore procured her a ftage Romeo to play the garden fcene; and in fuch a manner as fatisfied the expectations of one, and the defires of the other.

               Alive

[15]

Alive in thefe rude, filthy days,

Thy verfes had been all in praife

    Of me and beauty's queen.

Oh! had it been my wretched fate,

That Phaon had made me his hate,

    What then had been my cafe?

Like D---- I had fcorn'd the youth,

Kifs'd every female's lovely mouth,

    And follow'd ev'ry face.

Look on that mountain of delight,

Where grace and beauty doth unite,

    Where wreathed fmiles muft thrive;

While Strawberry-hill at once doth prove,

Tafte, elegance, and Sapphick love,

    In gentle Kitty *****.

Have

[16]

Have I not feen (the tale how juft)

Upon his knees, Imperial duft,

    With all the Royal look :

The fond embrace, the heaving figh,

The hand's foft fqueeze, the melting eye

    Of gentle B****b**ke ?

Let envious talkers babble forth,

He woo'd to gain my arms for worth ;

    The thought---was far from Harry.

Too oft' my ears have heard the fong,

That he hath rid too hard and long,

    To be *the* man---to marry.

                              He

[15]

He woo'd me for my parts and merit,

With true Equeſtrian---Britiſh ſpirit,

   Not like the wanton punk.

He wants the jovial, buxom wife,

One that can chear his ebbing life,

     And every night get drunk.

Far, far from me be ſuch a ſpouſe,

With ſuch a rake I'll never nooſe,

     Nor ever once get hockey:

Good Heavens! how all the world would ſtare,

To ſee me turn the old brood-mare

    Of ſuch a broken jockey!

Ye

[16]

Ye Sapphick Saints, how ye muſt ſcorn

The dames with vulgar notions born,

Who proſtitute to man :

Who toil and ſweat the tedious night,

And call the male embrace delight,

The filthy marriage plan,

Ah worſe, far worſe, are they who prowl,

And ſacrifice th' ethereal ſoul,

And murder conſtitution :

See Lady G-------r run a muck,

And all the Vernon virtue truck,

For luſt and proſtitution.

View

[17]

View M---, Bird of Paradife,

Rais'd on the painted wings of Vice,

In every folly mad:

There * T--r--r's gold unties the noofe

And while Mifs R----l takes her fpoufe,

She flies to Sir John L---d. ‡

Such Birds of Paradife as thefe,

Are the fell Syrens of the feas,

With faces not their own:

* This Spark of the Park paid the Piper for his adultery, though Pioneers and all had worked in the Covert-way before him. But the fenfible fpoufe bought a bargain, and was determined to fell one; fo, like Sir G--- C---, he lay perdue for an Hefperian Dragon, and took the golden fruit for his difhonours.

‡ A thing of a lad about Town, more abfurd than any boy fince Icarus.

E

[18]

They may awhile allure the beau,

For in the morn they come and go,

       Then wither on the Town.

So have I feen in winter hour,

A very beauteous, hot-houfe flow'r,

       Difplay'd to court the eye:

But e'er that it had fhown it's bloom,

The fatal blight declar'd it's doom,

       To wither, **fade, and die.**

In all, how hard is Woman's fate,

For ev'ry thing's too fmall, or great,

       And fcarcely fit to hint-on:

                                               For

[19]

For pretty * S--p--y ftill is chafte,

Virtue can never be difgrac'd,

   By L--n-- or C--t--n.

The little they can do in life,

Will not or fpoil a maid or wife,

   Or foil a reputation :

Exert themfelves, do all they can !

There's not in them, enough of man,

   To rife to fornication.

 * This beautiful female hath been deferted by an unfeeling hufband, and fhe has only ftooped to the addreffes of a certain Lord, who hath not in the leaft difpoiled her conjugal reputation, by any exertion of fornication.

May

[20]

May I not hope---dear, lovely Fair,

Of you to have some little fhare ?

For if report is right,

The maids of warm Italia's Land,

Have felt the preffure of your hand,

The preffure of delight.

Nor, D---, let me plead in vain,

Thee faireft of the fifter-train,

With pureft, fweeteft charms :

No more, dear Dame, my fuit refift,

Jack Cavendifh cannot exift,

A moment from your arms.

" Say

[21]

" * Say lovely Dame, that do'ft command,

" Jack Cavendifh's heart and hand,

  " And elegies of woe;

" Afk not the caufe why fhe doth chufe,

" The founding lute and lyric mufe,

  " Love taught her tears to flow.

" I burn, I burn," like Portfmouth Dock,

" I have no heart as hard as rock,

  " I now confume with flame?

---

* Something of this fort was Mifs Sappho's addrefs to the fcornful Phaon, who very properly judged, that fhe was not a proper object of love to him, who had feduced moft of the pretty girls of Mytelene.

F   " Not

[22]

" Not Ætna's fires, or pitch or tar,

" Or hoſtile ſhips engag'd in war,

　　" Blaze like thy burning dame.

" Thou'rt all my care, and my delight,

" My ſigh by day, my dream by night,

　　" Round thee in wreaths I twine:

" A thouſand tender words I ſpeak,

" A thouſand melting kiſſes take,

　　" And feel thee all divine.

　　　　　　　　　　　　　　　" Pride

[23]

" Pride of the age, and of thy race,

" Come, come and melt in this embrace,

" And all my vows receive :

" But if obdurate you will prove,

" Deaf to the language of my love,

" Take *that* you cannot give."

F I N I S.

Notes to the Texts

NB: Unidentified allusions and references are not generally noted.

Tunbridge-Walks: or, The Yeoman of Kent

5.10–11. '*Ridentem dicere verum / Quid vetat?* Horat.': 'What forbids us to tell the truth while laughing?' (Horace, *Satires*, I. i. 24). This Latin tag was frequently used by satirists as a justification for their method.

7.2. 'John How, Esq': John Grubham How or Howe (1657–1722), commonly called Jack How, active Member of Parliament, especially for Gloucester. In 1699, when the size of the army was reduced, How succeeded in obtaining half-pay for the disbanded officers, referred to at 9.4–5. He became a member of Queen Anne's ministry and was appointed paymaster general in January 1703. Swift in 'On the Game of Traffick' satirizes How's vanity and French leanings.

11.10. '*Searchers*': people (mainly old women) hired to report recent deaths to the parish authorities and the coroner.

15.2. 'Mr. *Pinkethman*': William Pinkethman or Penkethman (d. 1725), actor at the Theatre Royal, Drury Lane, favoured especially by the lower classes for his variety shows and other forms of 'low' entertainment. Many 'drolls' were staged at Penkethman's Theatrical Booth at Bartholomew Fair; he played the part of Squib in *Tunbridge-Walks* (see note to 18.9).

15.6. 'French *Disease*': venereal disease.

15.10. 'Quest-*Ale*': probably ale served at 'quest-houses' where official inquiries (i.e. 'inquests') were held; one of the rewards for undertaking parish duties.

18.1. 'Dramatis Personæ': All the actors and actresses in the play were members of Christopher Rich's United Company at the Theatre Royal, Drury Lane (and the company's second theatre, Dorset Gardens Theatre). See note to 39.7–8.

18.4. 'Mr. *Mills*': John Mills (d. 1736), actor and manager.

18.6. 'Mr. *Wilks*': Robert Wilks (*c.* 1665–1732), actor, dancer, singer, manager, who also performed in Thomas Baker's *Humours of the Age* (1701). He was very popular in his role as Sir Harry Wildair in George Farquhar's *The Constant Couple* (1699) from 1699 through the 1720s; the audiences wouldn't let him give up the role even when he tired of it. He was the United Company's leading actor and director of rehearsals. See also note to 18.14.

18.7. 'Mr. *Johnson*': Benjamin Johnson (1665–1742), actor.

18.9. 'Mr. *Pinkethman*': William Pinkethman (see note to 15.2), was also a good singer and dancer, and, by 1703, was highly paid. Pinkethman and William Bullock (see next note) often appeared together, playing off one another as buffoons noted for horseplay and tomfoolery.

18.12. 'Mr. *Bullock*': William Bullock (*c.* 1667–1742), actor and, from 1703, manager of a booth with Pinkethman as a sideline (see preceding note). For the first ten or twelve years of his career he specialized in playing 'skirt roles', then became noted for playing fops, bumpkins, comic Irishmen and hotheads. Due to his playing of women's parts, in contemporary records he is sometimes mistakenly listed as 'Mrs Bullock'. His two sons also became actors noted for their female roles. See also preceding note.

18.14. 'Mrs. *Rogers*': Jane Rogers (d. 1718), actress, singer. She was the lover of Robert Wilks (see note to 18.6), and always played the heroine when he played the hero; their illegitimate daughter married Christopher Bullock, son of William Bullock (see preceding note).

18.16. 'Mrs. *Verbruggen*': Susanna, Mrs John Baptista Verbruggen (*c.*1667–1703), actress. She also performed in Baker's *Humours of the Age*. She died in August of the year that *Tunbridge-Walks* was first performed. Her husband was also a well known actor.

18.19. 'Mrs. *Powell*': Mary, Mrs George Powell (fl. 1686–1723), actress.

18.21. 'Mrs. *Moor*': Henrietta Moore (fl. 1698–1730), actress.

18.22. 'Trapes': slut, slattern.

18.22. 'Mrs. *Lucas*': Jane Lucas (fl. 1693–1707), actress, dancer, singer. She occasionally sang and danced in entr'acte entertainments.

20.11. 'Atlasses': silk-satin dresses imported from the East, damaging the home-grown trade.

21.13. 'High-Crown-Hat': an old-fashioned or provincial survival of a 17th-century fashion.

22.13. 'Ptysichy': pthisic, a cough, a lung disease.

22.20. 'Kickshaw': something fancy and frivolous, from a dainty dish in cookery.

22.33. 'Topes': dozes.

22.36. '*Italian* Eunuchs': castrato singers in the Italian operas.

23.27. '*the City Train-Bands*': trained companies of citizen soldiers, in this instance raised by the City of London.

24.30. 'a true Country Put': a bumpkin.

25.34–6. 'Green-Sickness': anaemia, giving a greenish tinge to the skin, supposed to be caused by a lack of sexual intercourse, alleviated by the calcium gained from eating chalk; likened to a disease of poultry.

25.17. 'D'slife': 'God's life' (exclamation).

25.19. 'Leveret': a young hare.

25.20. 'Auls': awls, tools for piercing leather, bodkins.

26.6. 'Oyster Women': women who hawked oysters in the streets, sometimes regarded as being little more than street-walkers.

26.21. 'Projectors, Stock-Jobbers': schemers, speculators, dealers in stocks (equivalent to 'wheeler-dealers').

26.29. 'has a Nose on her Face': has not been infected with syphilis, which eats away the fleshy part of the nose.

27.6. 'the *Bear-Garden*': arena or amphitheatre for the sport of bear-baiting set up in Bankside, Southwark, and elsewhere, noted for encouraging the cruder manifestations of manliness.

28.31. 'bubbl'd': duped.

28.32. 'Groom-Porters': officials of the Royal Household who regulated gambling.

29.9. 'decay'd': financially distressed in old age.

29.10. 'Mantoes': mantuas, dresses or gowns.

31.2. '*The Walks*': Tunbridge was famous for its arcaded walkways in front of the shops (today called 'The Pantiles'), permitting the fashionable to promenade.

31.18. 'Noncon-Preacher': Nonconformist preacher.

32.7–8. 'the *Bath*': the fashionable spa resort of Bath.

32.31. 'fleering Air': a grinning, fawning, obsequious manner.

33.5. '*D'Oyley* Stuff-Suits': cheap, lightweight woolen clothes.

34.6–7. 'high full Rumps': buttocks emphasized with cork pads, or bustles.

35.2. 'Raffling-shop': shops where lottery tickets were sold.

36.25–6. 'the Pewterer's Wife in *Bedlam*': shorthand for the traditional ballad 'The Seven Merry Wives of London: or, The Gossips Complaint against Their Husbands, for Their Neglect' (the Pewterer's Wife was one of the seven). Bedlam is Bethlehem Hospital, the lunatic asylum in Moorfields.

37.24. 'These late Mournings': Court mourning following the deaths of William III on 8 March 1702 and Queen Mary II on 29 December 1694.

38.16. '*the Small-Coal Musick Meeting*': musical gathering of the lower classes (i.e. those who could afford only the cheaper waste coal).

39.7–8. 'more trouble…the *Drury-lane* players': Christopher Rich (*c.* 1657–1714), manager of the United Company at the Theatre Royal, Drury Lane and Dorset Gardens Theatre, had an interest in the company from about 1688 and acquired full control in 1693. In April 1695, after a dispute between patentees and actors, he became sole manager of the rump of the United Company. Rich seems to have enjoyed wrangling. Tom Brown in one of his *Letters from the Dead*, wrote: 'Mr. *Rich* finds some trouble in managing his mutinous Subjects, but 'tis no more than what Princes must expect to find in a mixt Monarchy, as we take the Play-house to be. The Actors jog on after the old merry rate, and the Women drink and intrigue' (10 Jan. 1701). Baker's joke with this line is that the actors performing *Tunbridge-Walks* were of course Rich's Drury Lane players.

40.18. 'Shock': poodle.

41.4. 'Stockjobb it away at *Jonathans*': waste it in speculation at Jonathan's Coffee House, Exchange Alley, Cornhill, where stock was traded.

41.33. 'Geers': finery.

41.34. 'Furbulo's': flounces, pleated borders of a petticoat.

42.3. 'Smooth-fac'd Fellow': one lacking facial hair, hence a eunuch.

42.8. '*Cremona*': town in Lombardy famous for its school of violin-makers.

42.26. 'a pair of Horns': the sign of a cuckold.

47.12. 'Kit-Cat Club': politico-literary club in London whose members included Joseph Addison, Richard Steele, William Congreve, Sir John Vanbrugh and others.

47.23. 'Prince *Eugene*': Prince Eugène of Savoy, Austrian general (1663–1736) who would join Marlborough in England's war against France.

48.34–6. 'There's Beau *Simper*…the prettiest Company': The type has gone askew at the beginnings of these three lines, which should read 'There's Beau *Simper*…Colonel *Coachpole*, and Count *Drivel*, that sits with his Mouth open, the prettiest Company'. Count Drivel may be modelled on Algernon Capel, 2nd Earl of Essex (1670–1710), holder of many public offices, thus lampooned in other satires.

49.3. 'Burridge': borage, plant used for making a cordial.

49.4. 'talk of *Venlo* and *Vigo*': important sea battles in 1702 at which the British were victorious during the early stages of the War of the Spanish Succession (1701–14): the siege of Venlo on the Meuse and the battle of Vigo harbour in Spain.

50.19. 'Flamboys': flambeaux, torches.

53.9. 'Bagnio': bath-house.

54.8. 'D'sdeath': 'God's death' (exclamation).

55.31–2. 'Lord *Leadenhall*...Earl of *Stocks-Market*': named after the major commercial streets in the City of London.

57.4–5. 'Impudence of *Fuller*': William Fuller (1670–1717?), famous impostor, associate of Titus Oates, revealer of alleged Jacobite plots, was imprisoned in 1692–5 and pilloried in 1702.

60.8. 'Son of a *Sucubus*': equivalent to 'son of a bitch' (a succubus is a demon who assumes human shape and has sex with people while they sleep).

64.8. 'Burgamy Payre': bergamot pear, a variety of pear with a red tinge.

65.18. 'Boncritten': good creature.

71.16. 'Conventicle-Face': a solemn expression suitable for a church meeting.

74.3. 'Petitioning Poet': a poet who begs money from his patron.

77.11. '*Parturiunt Montes nascetur ridiculus Mus*': 'Mountains labour to bring forth mice' (Horace, *Ars Poetica*, 139).

78.8. 'the *Change*': commercial streets near the Royal Exchange, City of London, such as Exchange Alley.

79.13–14. 'Mechanick': a common workman or labourer.

79.6–7. 'trappish': cheap and showy (clap-trappish).

79.24. 'Louse Cracker': one who picks and kills lice by pinching them (which produces a loud cracking sound).

79.28. 'Jump': under-bodice (later producing 'jumper', short jacket).

80.10. 'the Doublet in *Barbakin*': the Doublet public house in the Barbican, an area once near an outer fortification of the City of London.

The Women-Hater's Lamentation

85.3. 'Mr. *Grant*': Augustin Grant, a woollen-draper in West Smithfield (see headnote).

85.31. 'in a Brutal way': like an animal.

The He-Strumpets: A Satyr on the Sodomite-Club

89.6. 'CRACKS': lewd term for prostitutes.

89.8. 'Firking': shagging, fucking.

89.10. 'TAILS': arses in particular, and, more generally, 'pussies'.

90.2. '*PRIOR, GARTH* and *ADDISON*': the writers Matthew Prior (1664–1721), Sir Samuel Garth (1661–1719) and Joseph Addison (1672–1719).

90.9. '*Pound*': enclosure for keeping stray animals.

90.16. 'Your Tails have burnt so many Beaus': Your sexual organs have infected so many men with venereal disease.

90.27. 'To Whore as *O—born* did with *O—tes*': Titus Oates (1648–1705), famous for fomenting rumours about a Papist Plot in 1678, was alleged in contemporary satires to have been a sodomite; e.g. the ballad *Titus's Exaltation to the Pillory, upon His Conviction of Perjury* (1685) has him say 'A curse on the day, when the *Papists* to run down, / I left buggering at *Omers*, to swear Plots at London.' Thomas Osborne, 1st Earl of Danby (1631–1712) and chief minister, was impeached in 1679 when his role in handling secret financial dealings with Catholic France was revealed.

90.29. '*Catamitish*': from 'catamite', passive partner of the sodomite (derived from 'Ganymede', the Trojan prince ravished by Zeus).

91.1. 'the *Exchange*': the Royal Exchange in the City of London, a centre for prostitution as well as other forms of commercial activity.

91.6. '*Change*': the Royal Exchange; see previous note.

91.16. '*Stew*': the baths, noted for sexual licence.

91.36. '*He-L—ry*': he-lechery.

92.4–5. '*Sukey*, (for so 'tis said you greet / The Men you pick up in the Street)': Sukey was a slang name for a female prostitute, but this form of address to a potential homosexual pick-up is occasionally documented, and the mollies occasionally called themselves by this nickname for Susan or Susanna. In James Dalton's *A Genuine Narrative of All the Street Robberies, Committed since October Last* (1728, reproduced in set I of *Eighteenth-Century British Erotica* (London, 2002), vol. v, pp. 297–54), Sukey Haws was Dalton's guide through the homosexual underworld, and Sukey Bevell kept a molly house in the Mint, while another molly was nicknamed Sukey Pisquill. In *The Ordinary of Newgate, His Account of the Behaviour, Confession, and Dying Words, of the Malefactors, Who Were Executed at Tyburn, on Monday the 9th of This Instant October, 1732* (1732), the blackmailer Joseph Powis remembered once stealing homosexual love letters beginning 'Dear Miss Sukey Tooke' (p. 28).

92.36. '*B—ry*': buggery, meaning both anal intercourse (with either male or female) and bestiality (sex with animals).

92.45–6. 'Jermain....*late Clerk of St.* Dunstan*'s in the East*': not traced in the trial records. Dunton may be confusing this suicide with an earlier incident from 1701: 'The Parish Clerk of St. Dunstans in the East, being turned out of his Place upon Suspicion of an unnatural Crime &c. Cut his Throat on Wednesday Night almost from Ear to Ear' (*English Post*, 5–7 Mar. 1701).

93.23. 'For Two Pence wet and Two Pence dry': all sexual intercourse at the same price, whether vaginal or anal.

93.40. '*Stal—n Ladies*': A stallion lady is a filly kept by a stallion (a whoremaster); the same line in John Dunton's *Bumography: or, A Touch at the Lady's Tails* (1707) used 'KEEPING-LADYS', i.e. kept women.

94.10. '*Heart Adultery*': 'But I say unto you that every one who looks at a woman lustfully has already committed adultery with her in his heart' (Matthew 5:28).

The Play of Sodom, A Tragedy

101.2–10. '*Names of the Persons in this Tragedy…Three Angels*': The Bible does not give the names of any of the persons involved in the story of Sodom and Gomorrah except for that of Lot. Saphira is the wife of Ananias, both struck dead for telling a lie (Acts 5:1); Pharez is a son of Judah (Genesis 38:29); Jared is a descendant of

Seth (e.g. Genesis 5:15–20); the angel Raphael is mentioned not in the canonical Bible but in the apocryphal Book of Tobit; Balthazar and Melchior are two of the Three Wise Men in the traditional Christmas story, also not in the Bible. I have not identified Mabellah/Mabellagh or Jeminah.

101.22–4. *'the noble Reformation…pious Magistrates'*: the moral reform movement advocated by the Societies for the Reformation of Manners (who were responsible for the arrests of sodomites in 1707), and the subject of several Royal Proclamations, notably King William III's Proclamation for Suppressing Prophaneness and Immorality published at the end of February 1698 (re-proclaimed in spring 1699, and by Queen Anne on several occasions), which encouraged justices of the peace and constables to take an active role in enforcing statutes against swearing, drunkenness, working on the Sabbath, prostitution and other offences against morals.

106.11–12. 'in Conjunction…Substances Ætherial and Divine': Though the story in Genesis 19 simply says that the Sodomites wished to 'know' the angels visiting Lot, the Jewish apocrypha defined the Sodomites' 'unnatural' sins as 'changing the order of nature' and 'going after strange flesh', an interpretation well established in Christian commentary by the end of the first century AD.

A New Ballad. To the Tune of Fair Rosamond

109.2. 'the Tune of *Fair Rosamond*': 'Fair Rosamond' was a popular old English ballad about the extramarital love of King Henry II (1133–89) for Rosamond, by whom he had two sons and for whom he built a bower to protect her from the fury of Queen Eleanor. Maynwaring's direct source was Thomas Deloney's frequently reprinted *Mournefull Dittie on the Death of Faire Rosamond* (1607).

109.I.1. 'Qu---- A----': 'Queen Anne' (reigned 1702–14).

109.II.1. *'Ab----i'*: 'Abigail', i.e. Abigail Hill Masham (d. 1734), Queen Anne's favourite (see headnote).

109.V.3. 'R----': 'Rogue', i.e. Robert Harley, later Earl of Oxford (1661–1724), Secretary of State (1704–8) who worked through Abigail Masham to undermine the influence of Godolphin and Marlborough.

109.VI.4. 'Sl----': 'Slut'.

109.VII.3. 'B----': 'Bitch'.

109.VII.4. 'for the Church entire': Abigail Masham was of the High Church party.

109.VIII.1. *'Machiavel'*: allusion to Robert Harley, nicknamed Robin the Trickster, who was called 'the *Matchiavel* of *Great-Britain*' in Dunton's *The Rival Dutchess* (1708, p. 3). Niccolò Machiavelli (1469–1527), who advocated political hypocrisy in *The Prince* (1532), became a byword for cynical cunning and intrigue.

109.X.3. 'A Dutchess bountiful': Sarah, Duchess of Marlborough (1660–1744), mistress of the robes and keeper of the privy purse under Queen Anne.

110.XVII.2. 'one that bears the Wand': Sidney, 1st Earl of Godolphin (1645–1712), Lord Treasurer, and his staff of office.

110.XXII.3. 'high Divines': Anne appointed two High Churchman to the bishoprics of Exeter and Chester in 1707.

110.XXIV.2–4. 'A General Abroad…The *French*, could well afford': John Churchill, Duke of Marlborough (1650–1722), Commander-in-Chief. The War of the Spanish Succession (1701–14) was called 'Marlborough's War', and he had some notable successes against the French at Blenheim (1704), Ramilles (1706) and Oudenarde (1708).

110.XXVI.3. 'there should be a thorough Change': The Masham/Harley faction was accused of plotting to betray England to James Francis Edward Stuart, the Pretender, a Roman Catholic, who made a botched attempt to invade England in March 1708. The charge is made more explicit in Dunton's *King-Abigail: or, The Secret Reign of the She-Favourite* (1714).

110.XXVII.1. '*J----y M----h*': 'Johnny Marlborough', i.e. John Churchill, Duke of Marlborough.

110.XXVII.3. 'should he unto *Paris* go': After Marlborough defeated the French at the battle of Oudenarde in July 1708, he proposed to invade France, but the government rejected this as being too ambitious.

110.XXVIII. '*S----d*': Charles Spencer, 3rd Earl of Sunderland (1674–1722), the only Whig in the government at the time.

110.XXIX.1. 'the Admiral': unclear, perhaps the Lord High Admiral, i.e. Anne's consort George, Prince of Denmark.

110.XXX.1. 'the Man that kept the Cash': Godolphin, Lord Treasurer.

110.XXX.3. 'an old Acquaintance': Charles Talbot, 1st Duke of Shrewsbury (1660–1718), colleague of Godolphin.

110.XXXI.1. 'but one Eye': Shrewsbury was 'the duke with one eye' according to contemporary satires.

110.XXXI.4. 'Club-Law': rule by force rather than reason.

110.XXXIII.1–3. 'Dr. *B----ss*…slipt his Cloak': Daniel Burgess (1645–1713), celebrated minister who defected from the Established Church because he refused to submit to the Act of Uniformity (1662).

110.XXXV.3–4. 'She *Ab----l* turn'd out of Doors, / And hang'd up *Machiavel*': This is wishful thinking by the author: Abigail Masham continued in power, and Harley was not impeached until 1715, when he was imprisoned (but not hanged) in the Tower of London.

The Second Part, Of the London Clubs

113.Frontispiece: The woodcut illustrates a quack doctor, standing on a platform raised above the crowd, selling his patent medicines with the assistance of his mountebank.

114.1. 'NO-NOSE-CLUB': those bearing the sign of syphilis, which eats away the fleshy part of the nose.

114.5. 'our *English Sodom*': Salisbury Court, leading off Fleet Street, was called 'Sodom' and 'Little Sodom'; Ned Ward in the *London Spy* for May 1699 called the Court a '*Corporation of Whores, Coiners, Highway-men, Pick-pockets*, and *House-breakers*' (2nd edn (1704), p. 156).

114.10–11. 'salivated': having ingested mercury to stimulate the spitting of saliva to throw off venereal disease.

114.33. 'Mumper's Feast': a beggar's feast.

115.25–6. 'flat things always love long Snouts': The female pudenda was characterized as being flat, and the male organ as being long (hopefully).

115.37–8. '*Don John*': Don Juan, famed for his many conquests.

115.41. 'Salivation': See note to 114.10–11.

116.16. 'Finikin': overrefined, fastidious, dainty.

116.22. 'Muckinders': handkerchiefs.

116.34. 'Sir Foplings': Sir Fopling Flutter in George Etherege's play *The Man of Mode* (1676) was the archetypal affected dandy or fop.

116.38. 'Snush-Boxes, with Orangeree, *Brazil*, and plain *Spanish*': snuff-boxes, with different varieties of snuff (powdered tobacco).

117.24. 'B----ch': bitch.

118.4. 'Sarsenet': fine soft silk.

118.4. 'Night-rail': dressing gown.

118.6. 'Groaning Woman': woman in labour.

118.6. 'Jointed-Baby': wooden doll.

118.9–10. 'I am old Beldams Pinner': misprint for '& an old Beldams Pinner', corrected in the 1710 edition to 'and an old Beldams Pinner'. A pinner is an old woman's coif with two flaps pinned on and hanging down either side.

118.22. 'preternatural Polotions': unnatural pollutions, perverse sexual acts (often used to mean masturbation as well as homosexual acts).

118.33. 'Empericks': physicians whose practice was based on experience rather than dogma or method (in ancient discourse, *Empirici*, *Dogmatici*, *Methodici* respectively).

119.2. 'Dr. *Saffold*': Dr Thomas Saffold, an empiric who died in 1691 under his own treatment.

119.10. 'Querpo Formalities': well dressed (with flowing cloaks and so on).

119.13. 'Monutebanks Stage': i.e., mountebank's stage, the raised platform at a fair on which the itinerant quack (mountebank) or his assistant clown performed tricks such as juggling to attract the attention of a crowd, as illustrated in the frontispiece.

119.29. '*Bartholomew*-Fools': the clowns who, at Bartholomew Fair, stirred up the interest of a crowd, persuading them to buy a ticket to go into a theatrical booth to see a show.

119.30. 'Rural *Coridons*': country bumpkins (from Corydon, pastoral name for a shepherd).

119.32. '*Ceslante Tollitur, causa Effectus*': 'When the cause ceases, the effect ceases' (common legal phrase; correct spelling is 'cessante').

119.34. 'Dr. *Kerleus*': Thomas Kirleus (d. 1696?), quack doctor and physician-in-ordinary to Charles II, called 'the great Kirleus' by Samuel Garth in *The Dispensary* (1699), 3.259.

120.25. '*Crepitations*': crackling noise caused by the breaking of wind.

Love-Letters between a Certain Late Nobleman and the Famous Beau Wilson

127.10. '*Pro* Venere *sæpe, pro* Adonide *semper*': 'for Venus often, for Adonis always'.

131.19–20. '*The dead Languages…Pictures of this Kind*': Classical Greek and Roman literature and history have many stories about homosexuals (pederasts).

134.8–9. 'Greenwich-Park, *be behind* Flamstead*'s House*': John Flamsteed (1646–1719), first astronomer royal from 1675, lived at the Royal Observatory in Greenwich Park. The house/observatory is on a high brow of a hill, beneath which, on the side towards Blackheath, is a secluded dell.

136.7. 'my *Willy*': Captain Wilson's name was Edward, not William, but 'Willy' could be an affectionate contraction of his last name 'Wilson'. 'Willy' as an affectionate term for the male organ is not documented before the 20th century.

136.16–17. 'Brussels *Head and* Indian *Atlass*': lace headdress (for the manufacture of which Brussels was noted) and silk-satin gown made in the East.

137.7. 'drowzy *N—k*': perhaps Henry Howard, 7th Duke of Norfolk (1654–1707), lampooned for his divorce and his coarse taste for prostitutes.

137.11. 'Mrs. *V—l—s*': Elizabeth Villiers, Countess of Orkney (1657?–1733), mistress of William III until 1694, married Lord George Hamilton (later created Earl of Orkney) in 1695.

137.17–18. '*nemine Contradicente*': without contradiction.

139.22. 'a certain GREAT LADY': Elizabeth Villiers (see note to 137.11).

143.13–15. '*to Her at Park-Corner; direct mine for Mrs.* Gray': not the modern Hyde Park Corner near Marble Arch, but the southeast corner, at the end of Piccadilly. Sunderland House was next to Burlington House, Piccadilly.

151.5. 'the *Mall*': Pall Mall, parallel to St James's Park, lined with fashionable houses, e.g. that of King Charles II's mistress Nell Gwynne.

156.14. 'G—n': perhaps Sidney Godolphin, 1st Earl of Godolphin (1654–1712), whose chief interests were politics, gaming and racehorses, often lampooned for amorous (heterosexual) intrigue.

159.4–5. 'to make use of my Pillow': to masturbate into a pillow.

159.7. '*Mr. L—*': John Law (1671–1729), financier, killed Beau Wilson in a duel in 1694; he later founded the 'Mississippi scheme' which became the model for the South Sea Bubble (see headnote).

166.21. '*Johnasco*': pet monkey (like 'Jackanapes'), i.e. John Law.

167.3. 'a Spunging-house': small shed-like gaol where disorderly persons and debtors were temporarily imprisoned.

An Epistle from Signora F----a to a Lady

185.7–8. '*They do Let Heav'n…their Husbands*': Othello, III. iii. 206–7.

186.12. 'Quadrille': a newly fashionable card game for four persons using forty cards.

186..18. '*Aretin*': Pietro Aretino (1492–1556), famous for his salacious *Sonetti lussuriosi* (*c.* 1527) written to accompany a series of engravings (*Postures*) by Marcantonio Raimondi, after Giulio Romano (1524), often called *Aretine's Postures*.

187.18. '*Swiss*-like': Swiss men, unable to exercise their arms in a country that maintained political neutrality, enlisted as mercenaries in foreign armies.

187.25. 'tramontane': 'beyond the Alps', specifically Italy.

188.16. '*Durestanti*': the prima donna Margherita Durastanti (born *c.* 1685). See headnote.

Plain Reasons for the Growth of Sodomy, in England

191.12. '*Trolly-Lolly*': contemptuous term for lilting and insipidly pretty discourse.

191.14–15. '*A. Dodd…E. Nutt*': printers of many popular works such as thieves' lives.

197.15. '*Slip Slops*': a wishy-washy drink or gruel, such as curds and whey, sometimes mixed with medicine.

198.3. 'mock Christnings': Though this refers specifically to games played by girls and their dolls, it probably also alludes to the mock christenings and mock births performed by mollies.

198.24. '*Petits Maitres*': effeminate youths (literally 'little masters'), a term perhaps first used in English by Addison in *Spectator* 83 (5 June 1711), referring to the subjects of an imaginary painter named Vanity. Aphra Behn's popular play *The Town Fop: or, Sir Timothy Tawdry* (produced *c.* Sept. 1676; published 1677) was translated into French by Delphine Vallon as *Le petit maître* (1676).

198.29. '*Milksops*': effeminate or unmanly young men.

199.22. '*Cotqueanism*': old-womanism. 'Cotquean' is a contemptuous term for a man who acts like a housewife (queen of the cot or cottage).

199.29. '*Clouts*': worthless rags.

200.11–12. 'those Gentlemen who call themselves pretty Fellows': gallants, stylish and affected youths, fine fellows, fops. This may be an echo of the *Tatler* 26 (9 June 1709), perhaps by Richard Steele, referring to 'an insinuating increasing set of people, who...do assume the name of "Pretty Fellows;" nay, and even to get new names....Some of them I have heard calling to one another as I have sat at White's and St. James's, by the names of Betty, Nelly, and so forth. You see them accost each other with effeminate airs: they have their signs and tokens like freemasons. They rail at woman-kind; receive visits on their beds in gowns, and do a thousand other unintelligible prettinesses that I cannot tell what to make of.'

200.13–14. 'Suit of Pinners': an old woman's coif with two flaps pinned on and hanging down either side.

201.5. 'Running Footmen': footmen ran alongside the coaches of their masters.

201.5–6. 'poising a great Oaken Plant, fitter for a Bailiff's Follower': brandishing a staff or tall walking stick (which symbolized their status), rather like the billy-club carried by officials taking possession of the property of debtors.

201.21. '*Joke Hats*': unidentified as a specific type of hat, but there may be an allusion here to the high-crowned hats that mollies allegedly wore at mock christenings.

203.18–20. 'our *Sessions-Papers*...the *Crimes* of these *Beastly Wretches*': More than twenty trials for sodomy offences were published in the *Proceedings in the Old Bailey* from 1726 through 1728.

206.25. 'Reformation': the moral reform campaign led by the Societies for the Reformation of Manners, now on its last legs (defunct by 1730).

207.15. '*Ganymede*': catamite, derived from the name of the Trojan prince ravished by Zeus.

207.17. '*Pandars*': pimps.

207.21–2. '*Casto* and *Culo*': prick (*cazzo*) and arse.

208..4. '*Foutre*': fuck.

208.23. 'of this the *Philosopher* complains': Plato condemns the Lydian chromatic mode for its softening effect, and praises the nobler Dorian mode (*Republic*, 11).

209.18. 'ADDISON'S *Cato*': tragedy (1713) by Joseph Addison (1672–1719).

209.21. '*Drolls*': burlesques.

209.24. '*Congreve*': William Congreve (1670–1729), playwright.

209.25. '*Booth* and *Oldfield*': Barton Booth (1681–1733), actor, played the hero in Addison's tragedy *Cato*; he retired in 1727. Anne Oldfield (1683–1730) was a popular actress at Drury Lane.

210.22. 'a vagabond *Swiss*': John James Heidegger (1659?–1748), Swiss impresario and manager of the Haymarket Theatre, who introduced 'midnight masquerades' early in the century. Richard Steele went to one such masquerade where a parson called him 'a pretty fellow' and tried to pick him up.

210.24–5. '*Cock-Bawd*': pimp, procurer.

211.4. '*QUADRILLE*': a newly fashionable card game for four persons using forty cards.

213.5–8. 'the *Scandal* of a *Child*…innocent *Babes* perished': Most illegitimate children during this period were either murdered or abandoned. Bastard children were usually murdered by their mothers shortly after birth, by cutting their throats with a penknife or dropping them down the privy or burying them alive in a rubbish heap in the garden. Those maidservants who did not kill their newborn infants were usually dismissed, and after a month of two of poverty let their babies starve to death or gave them to the Foundling Hospital. Parish authorities often farmed out abandoned children to nurses in the country, who accepted the fee and then ignored the infants, most of whom died. Hundreds of cases of newborn child murder are reported in trial records and the newspapers. Infanticide decreased later in the century due to rigorous prosecution. Most newborn child murderers were women, but there was a case in 1727 of a clerk of a Meeting House in Dorset accused of murdering six of his bastards by the same woman, one every nine months or so.

215.6. 'Gentleman Commoner': a privileged undergraduate at either Oxford or Cambridge university.

215.8. 'Hob'dehoy': hobbledehoy, clumsy adolescent.

217.16. '*motly Garb*': parti-coloured clothes.

College-Wit Sharpen'd; or, The Head of a House, with, A Sting in the Tail

221.17. '*S-d-m* and *G-m-rr-h*': Sodom and Gomorrah, the biblical Cities of the Plain, here understood as the universities of Oxford and Cambridge.

221.19. 'Printed for J. WADHAM': false imprint, alluding to Wadham College, Oxford.

223.5. '*Quære*': formal question on which a vote is taken.

224.3. '*Whitefield*': George Whitefield (1714–70), graduate of Pembroke College, Oxford. A popular Calvinist Methodist organizer in rivalry with John Wesley, he went as a missionary to Georgia in 1738–9.

224.8. '*W-rd-ns*, and *C---ll--r*': Wardens and Chancellor (though the dashes do not exactly match the missing letters).

225.8. '*Sw-nt-n*': John Swinton (1703–77), tutor at Wadham College (see headnote).

226.1. 'Not *Pembroke*'s *Warden*; no, 'tis *W-dh-m*': not the Warden of Pembroke College, Oxford, but the Warden of Wadham College, Oxford.

226.7. '*Fr--ch*': Master William French, student of Robert Thistlethwayte, Warden of Wadham College (see headnote).

226.10. '*Manciple*': servant who buys provisions for a college.

226.11. 'Dr. *Th-stle-th-te*': Robert Thistlethwayte (1687–1744), Doctor of Divinity and Warden of Wadham College (see headnote).

227.7. '*Nolens Volens*': willy-nilly.

229.3. '*L--gf--d*, and *H-dg-s*': Robert Langford and William Hodges, respectively the butler and barber of the College, to whom Thistlethwayte made sexual advances (see headnote).

230.2. '*Turk*': The Turks, like the Italians, were believed to be addicted to sodomy.

231.4. '*Wh-re*': whore.

233.8–9. 'should have been *De Wit-ted*': should have been treated as the De Witt brothers. In 1672, Cornelius De Witt was falsely accused of plotting to poison William of Orange and was arrested then tortured; his brother Jan came to prison to join him in his banishment; the mob tore the brothers to pieces.

235.2. '*Fiat*': 'Let it be done.'

241.11. '*Bob*': Robert Trustin, a dim-witted servant boy who described his sexual relations with Swinton (see headnote).

243.5. '*B-k-r*': George Baker, who defended William French and became involved in the affair, who was forced to retract his claims but later defended himself with *A Faithful Narrative of the Proceedings between John Swinton and George Baker* (1739, reprinted in set I of *Eighteenth-Century British Erotica* (London, 2002), vol. v, pp. 357–90).

The Pretty Gentleman: or, Softness of Manners Vindicated

250.28. 'PHILAUTUS': Philautus is the friend of Euphues in John Lyly's *Euphues, the Anatomy of Wit* (1578) and *Euphues and his England* (1580).

252.15–19. '*James* I…LORD *Clarendon*': James I's fondness for handsome young men was widely recognized by his contemporaries as having an erotic expression, and was often commented upon, as by Edward Hyde, Earl of Clarendon, e.g., 'of all wise men living, he [James] was the most delighted and taken with handsome persons and with fine clothes' (*The History of the Rebellion and Civil Wars in England Begun in the Year 1641, by Edward, Earl of Clarendon*, ed. W. Dunn Macray (Oxford, 1888), vol. i, pp. 10–11).

253.3. '*Charles* I': King Charles I (1600–49), a model family man, conspicuously uxorious in marked contrast to his father James VI/I.

253.6. '*Falkland*': Lucius Cary, 2nd Viscount Falkland (1610–43), Secretary of State and the 'hero' of Clarendon's *History of the Rebellion and Civil Wars in England*.

253.7. '*Waller*': Edmund Waller (1606–87), writer of simple but polished verse. Supported Charles I, then Cromwell, then Charles II.

253.21–2. '*Milton, Denham, Dorset, Buckingham* and *Dryden*': John Milton (1608–74), epic poet; Sir John Denham (1615–69), Royalist poet; Charles Sackville, 6th Earl of Dorset (1638–1706), poet and patron of Dryden; George Villiers, 2nd Duke of Buckingham (1628–87), satirist, poet, friend of Dryden and influential courtier under Charles II; John Dryden (1631–1700), poet and dramatist.

254.5–11. 'a Set of malevolent Spirits…set up an *Idol* of their own Fancy': authors of the early periodicals the *Tatler* (e.g. no. 26 for 9 June 1709), the *Spectator* and the *Guardian* attacked 'Pretty Fellows' and 'Beaux' as false gentlemen constructed merely by their hairdressers and tailors, in contrast to the model of the true Gentleman characterized by respectable gentility and good taste.

255.17. '*The sacred* Theban *Band*': Greek elite military company of 150 pairs of male lovers, who died fighting to the last man at the battle of Chaeronea in 338 BC (see Plutarch, *Life of Pelopidas*, 18–19; Plato, *Symposium*, 178e–179b).

256.7. '*Magna est inter* MOLLES *concordia!*': 'male effeminates [i.e. fairies, faggots] agree wondrously well among themselves' (Juvenal, *Satires*, ii. 47). The passage continues: 'never in our sex will you find such loathsome examples of evil'.

257.1. 'Tiring Room': dressing room.

258.24. '*Sippius…Fannius*': genuine Roman names, but probably meant to suggest fastidiousness and effeminacy.

263.15. '*Lepidulus*': 'delightful, charming'.

264.16. '*Tenellus*': 'tender, delicate'.

266.11–12. '*Spinage*': spinach.

266.15. 'Draps': perhaps smelling-salts (drops), or some sort of reviving medicine such as the 'Pepper Mint-water' mentioned in lines 21–2.

266.15–16. '*Molliculo*': 'soft-arse'.

268.10–11. 'Sir *Roley Tenellus*': See note to 264.16.

269.1–2. 'Sir *Thomasin Lepidulus*': See note to 263.15.

269.2–3. '*Narcissus Shadow*': 'lover of his own image'.

270.17. 'Amoriculus': 'arse-lover'.

270.19–20. '*become a Parent by his Criminal Gratifications*': possibly an allusion to molly mock-birth rituals.

271.1. 'Sons of *Momus*': satirists. The classical god Momus was noted for ridiculing the other gods.

271.22–3. 'what *Quintilian* did of *Seneca*'s, *Abundat Dulcibus Vitiis*': David Hume, criticizing the dangerous seductive powers of elegant writing, says 'Seneca abounds with agreeable faults, says Quintilian, *abundat dulcibus vitiis*' ('Of the Standard of Taste', in *Essays, Moral, Political, and Literary* (1758), I. xx. 11; referring to Quintilian, *Institutio Oratoria*, X. i. 129).

272.9. '*Addison*': Joseph Addison (1672–1719), essayist and playwright.

272.18–20. 'those, who…steal Beggars Children, only to cloath them the better': 'Where he [Dryden] was allow'd to have Sentiments superior to all other, they [critics] charged him with Theft: But how did he Steal? no otherwise, than like those, that steal Beggars Children, only to cloath them the better' (Sir Samuel Garth (1661–1719), Preface to *Ovid's Metamorphoses in Fifteen Books* (1717), p. xx).

275.5. '*Delicatulus*': 'fastidious, effeminate'.

275.14. '*vitious*': vicious.

276.12. 'Pigs-petitoes': pigs' trotters, i.e. feet, which are cut off when the pig is dressed and prepared separately.

276.14. 'White-pot': custard, milk pudding.

276.14. 'Tanzeys': egg puddings.

276.14. 'Flommery': sweet dish made of milk, flour, eggs.

276.20. '*Panada*': bread pudding.

276.27. '*Middleton*'s Life of *Cicero*': Conyers Middleton (1683–1750), *The History of the Life of Marcus Tullius Cicero* (1741).

277.9. '*Umbratilis*': 'carried out in darkness'.

277.10. 'Lord *Molly*': alluding to 'soft' ('mollifying') and to mollies, i.e. fairies or effeminate homosexuals.

278.22. 'Concinnity': consistency.

278.24–28. '*Horace's Barine…Publica cura*': Barine is the model of shameless infidelity. 'If any penalty for forsworn vows Had ever done harm to you, Barine, If you might be made more ugly by one Blackened tooth or nail, I might believe. But no sooner have you bound Your faithless word with vows than you gleam more Beautiful, much younger and become a universal Object of desire'; inaccurate quotation from Horace, *Odes*, 2.8.

280.4–5. 'L--ds, K----ts, and B----s, now assembled in P--------t': 'Lords, Knights, and Barons, now assembled in Parliament'.

282.20. '*Mollis & parùm Vir*': soft and insufficiently manly.

A Letter to David Garrick, Esq. from William Kenrick, LL.D. (including Love in the Suds;
A Town Eclogue)

285.7. '*Meo deo irato*. TER. PHOR.': actually 'deo irato meo', 'My guardian angel had a grudge against me' (Terence, *Phormio*, 74).

287.7. '*Roscius*': Garrick was honoured with the name Roscius in memory of the famous Roman comic actor Quintus Roscius Gallus (*c.* 126–62 BC).

287.8. '*Nyky*': Nyky is the diminuitive of Isaac, i.e. Isaac Bickerstaffe; fortuitously it is also the nickname for a simpleton.

287.11–12. '*Qui capit ille facit*': 'he who takes it to himself has done it' (i.e. 'if the shoe fits, wear it').

287.20. '*in utrumque paratus*': 'prepared for either event'.

287.22–3. '*Nil conscire sibi, nulla pallascere culpa*': 'to be conscious of no fault, to turn pale at no accusation' (Horace, *Epistles*, I. i. 61).

287.31. '*genus irritabile vatum*': 'that easily irritated race of poets' (Horace, *Epistles*, II. ii. 102).

288.22. '*nemo me impune lacessit*': 'no-one provokes me with impunity.'

289.1. 'in the SUDS': in trouble, in difficulty.

289.8. '*Dixin' ego vobis, in hôc esse Atticam elegantiam?* TER.': 'I told you he'd got real Attick polish, didn't I?' (penultimate line of Terence, *Eunuchus*).

289.9–11. '*O me infelicem! — / — quæ laudâram quantum luctus habuerint!* PHÆD.': Phaedrus, *Fabularum Æsopiarum*, i. 12, Cervus ad Fontem, 13–15 (*Aesop's Fables*, The Crow and the Serpent, 'O unhappy me! who have found in that which I deemed a happy windfall the source of my destruction').

291.4. 'GEORGE': Garrick's widowed younger brother George acted as his assistant in numerous projects, notably the Stratford Jubilee of 1769.

291.15–19. 'Quo te, Mœri, pedes; an quò via ducit in urbem?…Quid sacerem?': parts of Virgil, *Eclogues*, vii and ix. Kenrick's 'Imitations' quote the classical sources which he has adapted for his own satire; his imitations of the originals are more or less accurate translations, and will not be translated in these notes.

292.2. 'PEGGY': Margaret (Peg) Woffington (1714?–60), very successful actress, who had an affair with Garrick.

292.15–22. 'Sæpe ego longos…Hyla, Hyla, omne sonaret': Virgil, *Eclogues*, ix, a lament for Hylas.

293.2. 'Blest had there never been a grenadier!': referring to the Guardsman whom Bickerstaffe tried to pick up (see headnote).

293.5 and 27–8. 'horse-marine': In the first edition Kenrick's note explained that 'A horse-marine is a kind of *meretricious* HOBBY-HORSE', in other words, a prostitute, in this instance a male prostitute.

293.14–22. 'Quem fugis?…tu nunc in montibus erras!': parts of Virgil, *Eclogues*, ii, vi.

293.28. '*Modò vir modò fœmina*': 'at one time, man; at another, woman'.

294.12. 'look out sharp and frequently behind': a sodomitical joke on guarding one's rear.

294.18–23. 'Nisus ait…custodi et consule longè': Virgil, *Aeneid*, ix.

295.16 and 27. 'Hampton's shore….celebrated villa of Roscius': Garrick bought a country house on the banks of the Thames on the road to Hampton Court in 1754, which he had beautifully decorated and on the grounds of which he built a Temple to Shakespeare.

295.18–25. 'Spreto Ciconum…flumine ripæ!': Virgil, *Georgics*, iv; the story of Orpheus and Eurydice.

296.4. 'Here Catherine Hayes serv'd Goodman Hayes the same': In 1726 Catherine Hayes butchered her husband (with the help of her son and lover), for which she was burned alive at Tyburn in May.

296.22. 'Omnia vincit amor et nos cedamus amori': 'Love conquers all things, let us too yield to love' (Virgil, *Eclogues*, x. 69).

297.20. 'Th' Italian *gusto* and *bon ton* of France': i.e. the sodomitical tastes imported from Italy and France.

298.4. 'Fashionable Lover': *The Fashionable Lover*, a sentimental comedy by Richard Cumberland (1732–1811), was staged by Garrick in January 1772.

299.7–8. 'The gay Petronius…bestow'd on youth their soft regards': Although the word 'gay' is not documented as slang for 'homosexual' until the 20th century, there are occasional much earlier suggestive usages such as this one. Petronius's *Satyricon* was noted for its licentious realism.

299.13. 'Lot': the story of Sodom and Gomorrah (Genesis 19).

299.22. 'Formosum pastor Corydon ardebat Alexin': 'Corydon the shepherd pined with love for the beautiful boy Alexis', the infamous first line of Virgil, *Eclogues*, ii.

299.24. 'The Jesuit Ruæus': Carolus Ruaeus, SJ (Charles de la Rue, 1643–1725), author of a Latin prose summary of and commentary on Virgil's *Aeneid* (Paris, 1675; London, 1722).

299.25. '*Amabat Virgilius puerum*': 'Virgil loved boys'.

300.20–5. 'Deos didici securum agere agere ævum…mea carmina ducite Daphnim': Virgil, *Eclogues*, viii, of which 'Ducite ab urbe…' is the refrain sung by Alphesiboeus: 'Bring Daphnis home, my song, bring him home from town'.

301.1. 'MANSFIELD': Sir James Mansfield (1733–1821), adviser to John Wilkes in 1768 and the Duchess of Kingston in her bigamy trial in 1772 (see headnote to next selection, *Sodom and Onan*); not to be confused with William Murray, 1st Earl of Mansfield (1705–93), Lord Chief Justice from 1756.

301.3. 'Merlin': the wizard or magician in the tales of King Arthur (see note to 301.22).

301.4. 'Grimbald DUNNING': a barrister employed by Garrick. Around 1 July 1772 'Mr. Dunning made a motion in the Court of King's Bench, for a rule to shew cause why an information should not be laid against the author of *Love in the Suds*. When the court was pleased to grant a rule for the first day of next term' (from a newspaper report reprinted in the Appendix to the fourth edition of *Love in the Suds* (1772), p. 30).

301.22. 'King Arthur, lately revived at Drury-lane Theatre': Dryden's play, with music by Purcell, was first performed in 1691, revived in 1735 as *Merlin, or the British Enchanter*, and by Garrick as *King Arthur, or the British Worthy*, which opened at Drury Lane on 13 December 1770.

302.2. 'S—Y': sodomy.

302.12. 'Macaronis': dandified young men who affected the fashions and tastes of Italy.

302.12. 'Cheapside': a major market in the City of London.

302.13. 'petty-jury-men': Whereas the formal Grand Jury sat to determine indictments, just a few justices of the peace could meet informally in a 'petty jury', used mainly for issuing writs for apprehending disorderly persons and prostitutes.

302.16. 'B—TTI': In October 1769 the Italian critic Joseph (Giuseppe) Baretti (1719–89), famous for compiling an Italian–English Dictionary (1760), was approached by a prostitute in the Haymarket. When he refused her advances, she hit him in the genitals. He then struck her, whereupon she called him 'a French Bougre' and 'a woman-hater' and three bullies came up and began shoving him about. He drew a knife and stabbed two of them, one of whom later died of his wound. Baretti was tried for murder. Witnesses who testified to his good character included Sir Joshua Reynolds, Dr Johnson, Edmund Burke and David Garrick, whose words especially affected the jury. The jury considered that Baretti had received sufficient provocation to defend himself and acquitted him after a few minutes' deliberation.

302.18–20. 'Ex illo Corydon...ducite Daphnim': Virgil, *Eclogues*, vii. 70, and the refrain of *Eclogues*, viii.

303.1. 'Stratford Jubilee': the great Shakespearean festival organized by Garrick in September 1769 (during which Kenrick played the Ghost of Hamlet's father).

303.16–21. 'Ut sceptrum hoc...VIRG.': Virgil, *Aeneid*, xii. 206–11: the covenant of King Latinus with Aeneas.

303.22–26. 'Hanc ego magnanimi spolium...VAL. FLAC.': Valerius Flaccus, *Argonautica*, iii. 707–11.

303.27. 'the Sessions-paper': the trial of Baretti reported in the *Proceedings of the Sessions in the Old Bailey* (1769).

304.1 and 11. 'JOHNSON...pompous pseudo-philosopher': Dr Samuel Johnson (1709–84), compiler of the famous *Dictionary* (1755), friend of Oliver Goldsmith, Isaac Bickerstaffe, Hugh Kelly, Garrick, and many others.

304.3. 'Goldsmith': Oliver Goldsmith (1730?–74), poet, dramatist, essayist, fiction-writer and friend of Garrick.

304.22. '*Kelly*': the playwright Hugh Kelly (1739–77), whose comedy *False Delicacy* was staged by Garrick in 1768.

305.5. 'Tho' cheap in French translations MURPHY deals': Arthur Murphy (1727–1805), Irish poet, actor, playwright, whose plays in the 1760s were often based on plays by Voltaire, Molière and Crébillon *père*. Murphy was one of Foote's attorneys at the latter's trial for sodomitical assault (see also the next selection, *Sodom and Onan*).

305.7. 'Tho' modest CRADDOC scorns to sell his play': Joseph Cradock (1742–1826), man of letters, gave private theatricals where Garrick played the Ghost and he played Hamlet; he helped significantly with Garrick's 1769 Stratford Jubilee.

305.9. 'the courtly CUMBERLAND': See note to 298.4.

305.14. 'Ducite ab urbe domum mea carmina ducite Daphnim': See note to 300.20–5.

305.17. '*midnight masquerades*': the masquerade balls first popularized by the Swiss impresario and theatre manager John James Heidegger (1659?–1748).

305.25. '*Kelly*': See note to 304.21.

305.28–9. '*like Sterne…Turn pimp and die cock-bawd at sixty-five*': probably Lawrence Sterne (1713–68), vicar who wrote the famous novel *Tristram Shandy* (1760–7) – regarded by Dr Johnson and others as an immoral book – and other works to earn money. (But Sterne died before the age of sixty-five.)

306.1. 'the author of the New Bath Guide': Christopher Anstey (1724–1805) published his fashionable work *The New Bath Guide* in 1766.

306.3. 'HIFFERNAN': Paul Hiffernan (1719–77), wrote farces for Drury Lane and Covent Garden, and dedicated *Dramatic Genius* (1770) to Garrick and was Bickerstaffe's friend.

306.5. 'Hodmandod': snail.

306.6. 'Turnham-Green': Dr Ralph Griffiths, editor of the *Monthly Review*, lived at Linden House in the genteel West London village of Turnham Green. The rival *Critical Review* was edited by Archibald Hamilton, with Tobias Smollett as its chief contributor.

306.10. 'Mr. A.': Christopher Anstey (see note to 306.1).

306.15. 'Mess. G. and A.': Messrs Griffiths and Anstey (see notes to 306.1 and 306.6).

306.31–2. 'LUSUS NATURÆ TYPOGRAPHUS….ingens cui lumen ademptum. VIRG.': 'a frightful monster, deformed, immense, blinded' (Virgil, *Aeneid*, iii. 658).

306.32–3. 'I thought some of Nature's journeymen…SHAKESPEARE': *Hamlet*, III. ii. 33–5.

307.1. 'HARRY WOODFALL': Henry Sampson Woodfall (1739–1805), printer and journalist, prosecuted in December 1769 for publishing the *Public Advertiser* which contained an attack on the government by 'Junius'.

307.1. 'BALDWIN': Richard Baldwin, bookseller in Paternoster Row, and distributor of quack medicines in the 1760s.

307.1. 'EVANS': Thomas Evans (1739–84), bookseller, publisher of the *Morning Chronicle*, who was told by Kenrick that he did not really believe Garrick was guilty of sodomy.

307.1. 'SAY': Charles Green Say (d. 1775), printer of the *Gazetteer*. His widow Mary Say continued with the *General Evening Post* and the *Craftsman, or Say's Weekly Journal*.

307.15. '*Hodmandod*': snail.

307.26. 'his brother GEORGE': See note to 291.4.

308.1. 'BECKET': Though in the footnote Kenrick claims to be referring to the famous Thomas à Becket, Archbishop of Canterbury (1118?–70), he is also probably alluding to Thomas Becket, the printer and bookseller, friend of Garrick and sometimes employed by him.

308.10. 'kiss'd my br– –': kissed my breech (i.e. my arse).

308.13–14. 'removed by *certiorari* to another court': writ of *certiorari* whereby a case is referred to the judgment of a higher court.

309.5. 'Ledger…Whitehall': the newspapers the *Public Ledger* and *Whitehall Evening Post*.

309.9. 'FOOTE': Samuel Foote (1720–77), dramatist and actor. In 1766, after a fall from a horse, his leg had to be amputated and replaced by a cork leg – which gave rise to 'foot' and 'leg' jokes amongst his detractors. He is the subject of the next selection, *Sodom and Onan*.

309.15. 'STEVENS': George Alexander Stevens (1710–84), who first gave his famous theatrical monologue, 'The Lecture upon Heads' satirizing human behaviour, at the Haymarket Theatre in 1764.

309.18. 'The Fantoccini': term for travelling puppeteers (from Italian *fantoccio*, puppet).

309.21. 'Ducite ab urbe domum mea carmina ducite Daphnim': See note to 300.20–5.

309.25–6. 'not the Macaroni editor of Shakespeare': George Steevens (1736–1800), Shakespearean critic, to whom Garrick lent his famous collection of quarto editions of Shakespeare.

310.32. '*Nor Hughes nor Astley, vaulting in the air*': Charles Hughes (1747–97), equestrian performer and circus manager; Philip Astley (1742–1814), equestrian performer who exhibited his horsemanship at his own circus at Westminster from 1770.

310.35. '*Nor Lun nor Woodward ever gave the spring*': 'Lun' (*tout court*) was the stage name of John Rich (1692–1761), actor and theatre manager, when he played the role of Harlequin in pantomime, which he invented for the English stage in the season of 1716–17 in *Harlequin Executed*. Henry Woodward (1714–77), actor and dancer, was billed as 'Lun, Jr.' when he danced in pantomimes.

310.40. 'French b--gres': French bougres, i.e. buggers.

310.44. '*He sips* aqua-vitæ *and spits* aqua-fortis': he sips medicinal alcoholic drink (usually brandy) and spits nitric acid.

311.10. 'Aut petis aut urges ruiturum, Sysiphe, saxum': Ovid, *Metamorphoses*, 459.

311.16. 'Falstaff's Wedding': a play written by Kenrick, which Garrick had turned down for production in the early 1750s.

313.3. 'galling paper-squibs': lampoons or bad critical reviews.

313.17. 'B—TTI': Joseph Baretti; see note to 302.16.

313.20–2. 'Sordidus ac dives…in arca': Horace, *Satires*, i. 65–7.

313.23–7. 'Ducite ab urbe…quid non speremus amantes?': Virgil, *Eclogues*, viii.

314.8. 'Men call that M—r, this a Catamite!': alluding to Garrick's two friends, i.e. Baretti, accused of being a murderer, and Bickerstaffe, accused of being a sodomite.

314.12. 'Wycherly…Congreve': William Wycherley (1640–1716) and William Congreve (1670–1729), two playwrights considered by some to be licentious and indecent.

314.17–20. 'Jugentur jam *Gryphes* equis...trahit sua quemque voluptas': Virgil, *Eclogues*, ii. 27–8, 63, 65; 'trahit sua quemque voluptas' is a proverb, used in several classical works, meaning 'each man follows his own taste'.

315.4. 'PAPHOS': the city in Cyprus where Venus was worshipped, the *locus classicus* of heterosexuality, in opposition to the homosexual Sodom and Gomorrah.

Sodom and Onan. A Satire

319.1. 'SODOM and ONAN': The title refers to the story of Sodom and Gomorrah (Genesis 19), hence 'sodomy', i.e. homosexuality, and to the story of Onan, who was commanded by the Lord to beget a child upon his brother's childless second wife. Onan, not wishing to beget offspring for his brother, 'spilled his seed upon the ground', an act which so displeased the Lord that he slew him (Genesis 38: 7–10), hence 'onanism', i.e. masturbation, or 'self-pollution'. Homosexuality and masturbation were usually linked in public perception because both were 'anti-venereal', i.e. involving non-procreative sex.

319.5. 'the *DEVIL* upon two Sticks': In 1768 Foote cleared several thousand pounds with his immensely successful play *The Devil upon Two Sticks*.

321.8. 'THALIA': the Muse of comedy.

321.16–18. 'your S— –...Minden Hero': Lord George Sackville-Germain, 1st Viscount Sackville (1716–85), who at the Battle of Minden in 1759 refused to obey orders for his troops to advance, allowing the French to escape from certain defeat, for which he was court-martialled and disgraced. He was nevertheless favoured by George III and later joined Rockingham's ministry as Vice-Treasurer of Ireland in 1765, and then Lord North's ministry from 1770. The author, Reverend William Jackson, suggests that just as the coward turned his back at the Battle of Minden, he now turns his back (i.e. presents his posteriors) to his sodomitical friends, who included Foote. In 1775 Sackville was appointed Lord Commissioner of Trade and Plantations and Secretary of State for the American Colonies. Though twice married, he was called 'the pederastical American Secretary' and lived with his wife and protégé. (The dashes are removed from his name at 343.16.)

322.2. 'POPE': Alexander Pope (1688–1744), whose *Essay on Man* (1732–4) is alluded to, and who was widely believed to be impotent due to an accident in his childhood.

323.4. 'CRIMES, and the Man I sing': a parody of 'Arms, and the man I sing', the famous first line of Pope's translation of Virgil's *Aeneid*.

323.10. 'Churchill': Charles Churchill (1731–64), virulent satirist, noted especially for his attack on actors in *The Rosciad* (1761). His satire *The Times* (1764) has a long section attacking sodomites, including Sackville; Jackson quotes 'To stop the propagation of mankind' from line 554 of that satire.

324.21. 'Mr. *Ap-price*': The character of Cadwallader played by Foote in his farce *The Author* in 1757–8 was a caricature of Mr Apreece, an uncle of Foote's intimate friend Sir Francis Blake Delaval. At first Apreece was amused, but after a dozen performances he demanded that Garrick and Foote withdraw the play or join him in a duel. The play closed, but was advertised for performance later in 1758 'with alterations', upon which Apreece applied to the Lord Chamberlain and had it stopped.

325.18. 'Polluting Onan': See note to 319.1.

326.6. 'like Ganeymede': Ganymede was the beautiful Trojan prince ravished by Zeus and created his cupbearer. However, the reference here is to Samuel Drybutter, known as 'Ganymede': See note to 327.1.

326.10. 'An handsome Boy's a *Jewel* in his Eyes': a pointed allusion to William Jewell, the treasurer of the Haymarket Theatre and Foote's close friend. After Foote's funeral on 27 October 1777, Jewell arranged for his body to be removed to his house in Suffolk Street at the back of the Haymarket Theatre, and that night the body was attended to Westminster Abbey by three mourning coaches, where Foote was secretly buried by torchlight somewhere in the cloisters, without a carved stone or any other mark. Jewell set up a monument to him in St Martin's Church, Cannon Street, Dover, on which he signed himself 'his affectionate friend'.

326.14. 'S-d--y': sodomy.

327.1. '*GANYMEDE*': The tipped-in illustration printed by M. Darly on 1 March 1771 portrays the bookseller Samuel Drybutter, known as 'Ganymede', who was arrested for attempted sodomy on 23 January 1770. It was later re-used by Darly as 'GANYMEDE & JACK-CATCH' (undated but probably after Drybutter's second arrest for attempted sodomy on 6 July 1774, when he fled abroad to escape prosecution), with the figure reversed, leg-irons added to his legs, and with the additional figure of Jack Ketch (the hangman) holding a noose. In this latter illustration, Jack Ketch says 'Dammee Sammy you'r a sweet pretty creature & I long to have you at the end of my string', and Ganymede replies 'You don't love me Jacky'. In both illustrations, the odd disproportion between torso and legs may suggest a composite of two separate illustrations. Note the white handkerchief hanging out of Ganymede's pocket. Just as female prostitutes displayed a white handkerchief to attract attention to themselves, one of the signals which 'madge culls' (i.e. homosexual men) used to discover themselves to one another while they cruised Birdcage Walk in St James's Park was to 'put a white handkerchief thro' the skirts of their coat, and wave it to and fro' (George Parker, *A View of Society and Manners in High and Low Life* (1781), vol. ii, pp. 85–8).

329.13. 'Drybutter': See previous note.

330.13. 'Dunning': John Dunning, 1st Baron Ashburton (1731–83), barrister.

331.2. 'Mansfield': William Murray, 1st Earl of Mansfield (1705–93), Lord Chief Justice from 1756.

331.4. 'Aristophanes': the nickname by which Foote was known.

331.16. 'A-t-n': probably the judge Sir Richard Aston (d. 1778), who sat on King's Bench from 1765.

332.14. 'W-ll-s': probably Sir John Willes (1685–1761), Chief Justice of Common Pleas, noted for his indolence.

333.13. 'Ashurst': William Henry Ashurst (1725–1807), judge, who sat on King's Bench 1770–99.

334.7. 'F—te': Foote.

334.17. 'Dunning': See note to 330.13.

335.2–3. 'B—y...B—'s': buggery, buggers.

335.17. '*Grieve*-ous': perhaps an allusion to James Grieve (d. 1773), appointed to the Charterhouse in 1765, Fellow of the College of Physicians from 1771.

336.1. 'Bearc—t': perhaps Philip Bearcroft (1696–1761), Master of the Charterhouse, antiquary.

336.8. 'Turkish Crimes': The Turks were perceived as being addicted to sodomy.

336.18. 'B—s': buggers.

338.7. 'the fatal Tree': the gallows at Tyburn.

338.13. 'Jones': Robert Jones, called Captain Jones, a Lieutenant in the artillery corps of the army. In July 1772 he was convicted at the Old Bailey for sodomy upon Francis Henry Hay, aged thirteen. The newspapers debated his case, as he was a famous character in 18th-century popular culture. He was sentenced to death, but on the day he was scheduled to be hanged, this was respited to imprisonment; he was granted a pardon by King George III on condition that he go into exile. A newspaper reported in June 1773 that 'The famous Capt. Jones lives now in grandeur with a lovely Ganymede (his footboy) at Lyons, in the South of France.' There are many allusions to the scandal in contemporary satires and poetry; see, e.g. 'Latin Epitaph on Bob Jones', published in a newspaper in July 1773: 'Underneath this stone there lies / A face turn'd downward to the skies; / A captain who employ'd his parts / Upon male b[um]s, not female hearts'.

339.3–4. 'Christ'nings…Caudle-makings': the mock birth pantomimes in which mollies were believed to engage (see Introduction, pp. xiii–xiv, above).

339.13–16. 'in Kingston…Bristol's Countess': referring to Foote's conflict with the Duchess of Kingston; see headnote.

340.2. 'Woman hater': common 18th-century term for a homosexual man.

340.7. 'Friction': sexual intercourse.

341.9. 'George': King George III.

341.18. 'G—e': King George III.

341.19. 'Scotch Insinuation': Lord Chief Justice Mansfield was a Scotsman.

342.1. 'S—e, both Coward, and Catamite': Lord George Sackville; see note to 319.16–18.

342.3–4. 'With lips that oft' in blandishment obscene / Have been employed': perhaps fellatio is alluded to here, though oral sex was very rare in the 18th century.

342.7. 'stradling B-rt--, that Bedchamber Lord': Peregrine Bertie, Duke of Ancaster and Kesteven, Earl of Lindsey, Lord Great Chamberlain and Master of the Horse (d. 1779 aged sixty-four). Bisexuality may be indicated by 'stradling'. The dashes are removed from his name at 343.16.

342.8. 'Gyves': shackles, leg irons.

342.9. 'M—': perhaps William Murray, 1st Earl of Mansfield; or perhaps John Savile, Earl of Mexborough, Foote's sometime patron and friend. It was during a visit to Mexborough that Foote fell from his horse and broke his leg.

342.10. '****': probably 'cunt'.

342.17. 'Chester and Holdernesse': Robert D'Arcy, 4th Earl of Holdernesse (1718–78), a secretary of state 1754–61, dismissed in 1761 for party-political reasons, replaced by John Stuart, 3rd Earl of Bute. Chester is unidentified.

343.15. 'Bute': John Stuart, 3rd Earl of Bute (1713–92), Secretary of State 1761, First Lord of the Treasury 1762, resigned 1763, travelled abroad incognito after 1766; patron of Dr Samuel Johnson.

343.16. 'Sackville and Bertie': See notes to 321.16–18 and 342.7.

343.17. 'Cits': contemptuous diminutive of 'citizen', implying tradesmen rather than gentlemen.

344.9–10. 'the village Love...Isaac Bickerstaff': Isaac Bickerstaffe (*c.*1733–*c.*1808), who fled abroad in 1762 to avoid prosecution for sodomy, and his play *Love in a Village* (1762). See also headnote to *A Letter to David Garrick...Love in the Suds*, above.

344.12. 'kicking 'gainst the *Pricks*': catchphrase meaning to be obstinant or recalicitrant to one's own hurt (literally, striking one's foot against sharp pointed spurs).

344.14. 'Tilney': Many Englishmen fled abroad to escape prosecution for sodomy, including John Tilney (or Tylney), 2nd Earl Tylney of Castlemaine (1712–84), who spent many years in Naples, where he died unmarried. The Earl of Buckinghamshire, commenting on 12 July 1783 to a friend on the nudity of bathers in Weymouth, observed that 'the exhibition of boys is far more numerous. Had Lord Tylney visited Weymouth, he could never have deserted his native country' (quoted in Jeremy Black, *The British Abroad* (1992), p. 201). Jeremy Bentham, in his notes on 'paederasty' written around 1816, identifies Tylney as the aristocrat upon whom Tobias Smollett modelled the homosexual character Lord Strutwell in his novel *Roderick Random* (1748).

344.14. 'B—l': A certain Burrel has been suggested for 'B—l', but with no further explanation. Perhaps it is Frederick Augustus Hervey, 4th Earl of Bristol (1730–1803), Bishop of Derry, the 'mitred earl' who spent much of his life in Italy, whose brother was Elizabeth Chudleigh's first (and only legal) husband.

344.14. 'Jones': Captain Robert Jones (see note to 338.13).

345.10. 'B—'d': buggered.

346.4. 'Maiming her votaries': The suggestion is that practitioners of heterosexual love are infected with venereal disease, from which catamites ironically escape.

346.14. 'B---ers': buggers.

349.11. 'S—s': sodomites.

351.5. 'B--boe': bulboe, a running sore on the bulb of the urethra or, sometimes, rectal membrane.

351.6. 'Corona veneris': syphilitic sores on the forehead.

351.20. 'Drybutter': See note to 327.1.

352.1. 'Bick-----ff, B--t-e, B—l, Bu—rs all, / Jones, S—e, D--v-s': Bickerstaffe (see note to 344.9–10); Bertie (see note to 342.7); Burrel or Bristol (see note to 344.14); 'buggers all'; Jones (see note to 338.13); Sackville (see note to 321.16–18); and perhaps Thomas Davies, a bookseller and former actor who appeared as a witness on behalf of Foote at the latter's trial for sodomitical assault.

352.4. 'Niky': name for a simpleton, and a diminutive for Isaac, i.e. Isaac Bickerstaffe.

352.9. 'Sheldon': John Sheldon (1752–1808), anatomist.

352.10. 'late limping Bayes': On 24 August 1772 at the Theatre Royal, Haymarket, Foote played the conceited playwright and poet Bayes in *The Rehearsal* (1672), written by, among others, George Villiers, 2nd Duke of Buckingham. This one-night benefit was for Foote's friend William Jewell, the theatre's treasurer. 'Limping' refers to Foote's artificial leg.

352.14. 'the Furor Anus': homosexual/sodomitical desire (literally anal madness).

352.17. 'Barowby': William Barrowby (1682–1751), physician and writer on anatomy.

A Sapphick Epistle, from Jack Cavendish to the Honourable and Most Beautiful Mrs.
D★★★★

357.6 'Mrs. D★★★★': Anne Seymour Damer (1749–1828), sculptor (see headnote).

359.7. 'Sappho': the Greek poet Sappho, or Psappha (*c.* 620–*c.* 560 BC), who was born on the island of Lesbos, then went to Mytilene, and later was sent into exile into Sicily before returning to Lesbos where she founded a school for aristocratic girls. She was the first Greek poet to write love lyrics, and the best and most famous female poet of the ancient world, but her works survive only in fragments and in quotations by later authors. She attracted girl pupils from all parts of the Hellenic world, forming a kind of cultic union between herself as headmistress and the circle of girls that surrounded her, performing rites that she celebrated in her one complete poem, *Hymn to Aphrodite*, and was famous even in antiquity for writing lyrics about her passion for girls, or *eros paidagogikos*.

359.10. 'Phaon': Sappho's presumed male lover, who spurned her and for whom she committed suicide by leaping from a cliff into the sea. The story of Phaon was invented by writers several centuries after her death (which was not by suicide).

359.13. 'Mrs. Montague': Elizabeth Montagu (1720–1800), Bluestocking, literary critic and philanthropist (called 'the female Maecenas').

359.13. 'Mrs. Greville': Frances Greville (1726?–89), poet, godmother of Frances Burney, friend of Lady Carlisle and Samuel Foote.

359.13. 'Miss Carter': Elizabeth Carter (1717–1806), scholar and poet, Bluestocking; unmarried, had a thirty-year romantic friendship with Catherine Talbot.

359.13. 'Miss Aikin': Anna Laetitia Aikin, later Mrs Barbauld (1743–1825), poet and friend of Elizabeth Carter, Bluestocking. (See headnote. I am grateful to William McCarthy for pointing out other references to 'Miss Aikin' in the 1780s.)

359.16. 'Tommy': masculine woman, specifically lesbian (see the Introduction, p. xxi, for its first usage).

359.20. 'Pope…Ovid': Alexander Pope (1688–1744) translated Ovid's (43 BC–AD 17) Epistle XV, 'Sappho to Phaon', in 1707. Pope explicitly acknowledged the nature of Sappho's love for her girls: 'No more the Lesbian dames my passion move, / Once the dear object of my guilty love' (17–19, translating 'quas non sine crimine amavi').

361.12. 'Gany-boy': catamite (passive partner in homosexual sex), from Ganymede, the Trojan prince whom Jove ravished and carried to heaven to be his cup-bearer.

3622. 'Jacques Rousseau': Jean Jacques Rousseau (1712–78), French philosopher and writer, famous for his pedagogic novels *Julie, ou la nouvelle Héloïse* (1761) and *Émile* (1762) and other works (though his *Confessions* were not published until 1782 and later). He came to London in 1766 and met the Scottish philosopher David Hume.

363.16–17. 'But ah beware…so lately lost': Pope, 'Sappho to Phaon', 65–6.

364.9. 'pretty C—': to rhyme with 'true', probably Frances Anne Crewe, Lady Crewe (d. 1818), a fashionable beauty, daughter of Frances Greville (see 359.13) and friend of the playwright Richard Brinsley Sheridan.

364.14. 'Swellings, distortions, cramps and strains': physical symptoms attendant upon pregnancy and childbirth.

365.14. 'Charlotte…Russia's Kate': Charlotte Sophia (1744–1818), Queen of Great Britain and Ireland, wife of King George III; Catherine II ('the Great'; 1729–96), Empress of Russia.

366.10. 'Propontis': now called the sea of Marmora, separating Europe and Asia.

366.13. 'author of the Meretriciad': Commodore Edward Thompson (1738–86), author of the licentious satire *The Meretriciad* (1761); he had obtained his captain's commission through Garrick.

369.13. 'Strawberry-hill': The actress Kitty Clive (see following note) lived at Twickenham, often visiting her friend and neighbour Horace Walpole (1717–97) at his 'Gothick' villa Strawberry Hill and participating in private theatricals there.

369.15. 'Kitty *****': to rhyme with 'thrive'; Catherine (Kitty) Clive (1711–85), actress, performed at Drury Lane for Colley Cibber (1728–41) and for Garrick (1746–69). She was pensioned by Horace Walpole after her retirement in 1769.

370.6. 'B****b**ke': probably Henry Saint-John, 1st Viscount Bolingbroke (1678–1751), Tory politician and friend of Pope.

372.10. 'Lady G-------r': In March 1770 Richard Grosvenor, Earl of Grosvenor successfully sued the Duke of Cumberland for 'criminal conversation' with his wife Lady Henrietta Vernon (i.e. Lady Grosvenor), and received damages of £10,000 after a famous adultery trial.

372,11. 'Vernon': the Vernon family (tarnished by the adultery of Lady Henrietta Vernon; see preceding note).

373.1. 'M---, Bird of Paradise': Gertrude Mahon (1752–1809), called 'the Bird of Paradise', one of a group of fashionable courtesans called 'the Avians' and given names of birds in lists of prostitutes such as Harris's *List of Covent-Garden Ladies* and the *Rambler* magazine.

373.6. 'Sir John L---d': The *Rambler* magazine for June 1783 reports on an 'Auction of Cyprians', in which one of the bidders for Gertrude Mahon – the 'Bird of Paradise' – was Sir John Lade.

375.3. 'C--t--n': obviously Clinton, to rhyme with 'hint-on', but otherwise unidentified.

377.7. '"I burn, I burn," like Portsmouth Dock': The rope-house at Portsmouth was set on fire by an incendiary on 7 December 1776, who continued his arson attacks in Bristol in January 1777.

Index to Primary Texts